PENGUIN BOOKS

WINESBURG, OHIO
Text and Criticism

John H. Ferres teaches in the Department of American Thought and Language at Michigan State University, East Lansing, Michigan.

THE VIKING CRITICAL LIBRARY

SHERWOOD ANDERSON

Winesburg, Ohio

TEXT AND CRITICISM

EDITED BY JOHN H. FERRES

PENGUIN BOOKS

Penguin Books Ltd, Harmondsworth,
Middlesex, England
Penguin Books, 625 Madison Avenue,
New York, New York 10022, U.S.A.
Penguin Books Australia Ltd, Ringwood,
Victoria, Australia
Penguin Books Canada Limited, 2801 John Street,
Markham, Ontario, Canada L3R 1B4
Penguin Books (N.Z.) Ltd, 182–190 Wairau Road,
Auckland 10, New Zealand

Winesburg, Ohio first published in the
United States of America by B. W. Huebsch 1919
Revised edition published by The Viking Press 1960
The Viking Critical Library Winesburg, Ohio first published
in the United States of America by The Viking Press 1966
Reprinted 1968, 1969 (twice), 1971, 1973 (twice),
1974, 1975 (twice), 1976
Published in Penguin Books 1977
Reprinted 1977

LIBRARY OF CONGRESS CATALOGING IN PUBLICATION DATA
Anderson, Sherwood, 1876–1941.
Winesburg, Ohio.
(The Viking critical library)
Bibliography: p. 507
I. Title.
[PZ3.A55win14] [PS3501.N4] 813'.5'2 76-30631
ISBN 0 14 015.501 5

Printed in the United States of America
by The Murray Printing Co., Westford, Massachusetts
Set in Linotype Electra, Baskerville and Bank Script

CONTENTS

EDITOR'S PREFACE

In the words of its original subtitle, Sherwood Anderson's *Winesburg, Ohio* is "a group of tales of Ohio small town life" at the close of the last century. It is supposed to be a simple book, but one of its most perceptive critics, Walter B. Rideout, has concluded that its simplicity is quite complicated; and several other critics have written quite complicated essays about it. It is supposed to be a book of peculiar appeal to adolescents, yet the critics interested enough to write on it who are represented in this volume have all left adolescence far behind. And if it is true, as the surveys claim, that adolescents do not read books, then the facts that it has been continuously in print since its first appearance in 1919, that it has been translated into twenty-two languages, and that a new text was established as recently as 1960, might suggest that most of its readers have also left adolescence behind. It once had a reputation for being "shocking," or at least controversial, yet today it carries almost everywhere the PTA's seal of good reading for the young; instead of being immoral or "dirty," it is now viewed as a profoundly moral book.

The paradoxes continue. *Winesburg* was supposed to represent a revolt against the American village; modern readers find its dominant tone to be one of nostalgia. It was supposed to be a landmark in the development of the American short story, which of course it is; yet critics have always discussed it as if it were a novel, and some early reviewers believed it had no form at all. Its author was supposed to have been influenced by writers and thinkers he had never read or heard of. He denied having any interest in religion, yet *Winesburg* is full of biblical accents. Its admirers greeted this "favorite child" of Anderson's as the beginning of a great career, but the author decided that as a serious writer he must turn his back on stories of adolescence and the past, and partly as a result nothing he wrote thereafter equaled his achievement in *Winesburg*.

In *Winesburg*, then, there are a number of puzzles to which a critical edition can address itself. As background to help solve them, this volume includes some relevant statements by Anderson himself from his memoirs and letters, samples of the early reviews of *Winesburg*—all of them reprinted here for the first time—and a selection of critical essays on it. The critical essays deal with significant aspects of *Winesburg*, specific as well as general, and will help to provide answers to some of the questions I have framed in a section for students, "Topics for Discussion and Papers," which follows the critical material. An annotated bibliography of *Winesburg* criticism, as well as some on wider subjects, is designed to facilitate library research.

The twenty critical essays collected in Part II represent a variety of points of view and analytical methods. A number are by professional critics (Malcolm Cowley, Maxwell Geismar, Irving Howe, Alfred Kazin, Lionel Trilling); others are by writers of fiction (William Faulkner, Herbert Gold). All of them date from the period since 1941, when Anderson's death spurred a revival of interest in his work, and in particular of intense critical scrutiny of *Winesburg*. Though I have avoided formal divisions, the essays follow a logical arrangement. An introductory pair, by Phillips and Rideout, deal mainly with the origins and composition of the book. Gregory, Hoffman, and Kazin are concerned with literary and intellectual influences on Anderson; and Thurston, Asselineau, and Cowley with technique. A central group of eight essays (Frank, Geismar, Fussell, Gold, Howe, Anderson, Walcutt, and Sister M. Joselyn) seem to ask the question, what *is Winesburg*? A final group represents a summing up, through a debate on Anderson's merits (Trilling, San Juan) and a discussion of his influence (Flanagan) or, in the case of Faulkner, a testimony to it. I have identified more closely a number of the approaches, arguments, and relationships among the essays in the "Topics for Discussion and Papers," and the student may be expected to discern others.

With this volume, which contains much of the best and most authoritative criticism on the subject, the student could make an intensive study of *Winesburg* without consulting other sources. However, about a third of the topics suggested for class discussion or for formal or informal papers require library research. This critical edition might also be used as illustrative reading in the areas of literature (introductory and advanced courses in American literature, as well as courses in the short story and in literary criticism), American studies, and the social sciences.

A note on editorial procedures: I have in some cases given a new title (indicated by square brackets) to an essay not reproduced in full, and have indicated the original title in the acknowledgment at the foot of the page. Omissions are indicated by ellipses. In certain essays I have, with permission of the authors, omitted both explanatory notes and footnote references, incorporating them where necessary in the body of the text within brackets.

I wish to express my appreciation to the authors of the essays reprinted, as well as to the publishers or magazines who gave their permission for the use of the material. I would like also to extend my thanks to Malcolm Cowley, literary adviser to The Viking Press and General Editor of The Viking Critical Library; to David D. Anderson for professional counsel; to William A. Sutton for advice about the chronology; to Edwin Fussell and Ray L. White for cooperation in various matters; and to Amy Nyholm, curator of the Sherwood Anderson Collection at the Newberry Library. I owe special thanks to Alan D. Williams of The Viking Press for his cheerful forbearance in all things.

J. H. F.

June 1966

SOME DATES
IN ANDERSON'S LIFE

1 8 7 6   Born in Camden, Ohio, September 13, the third of seven children. For the next eight years the family drifts about Ohio while the father, a harnessmaker and "story-teller," searches for work.

1 8 8 4   The family settles in Clyde, Ohio, a town which will later serve as a model for Winesburg. Anderson's schooling is irregular because of his efforts to help support the family as a paper boy and race-track swipe.

1 8 9 5   His mother dies of consumption.

1 8 9 6
(or–'97)   Leaves Clyde to work as a stock handler in a Chicago warehouse.

1 8 9 8   Joins the Army during the Spanish-American War and is sent to Cuba after the Spanish surrender.

1 8 9 9   Attends Wittenberg Academy in Springfield, Ohio, for a year.

1 9 0 0   Returns to Chicago to write and sell advertising copy; writes "booster" articles for an advertising periodical.

1 9 0 4   Marries Cornelia Lane, May 16.

1 9 0 6   Becomes head of the United Factories Company, a Cleveland mail-order firm.

1 9 0 7   Buys and operates a "paint factory" in Elyria, Ohio.

1 9 1 2   Suffers a mental collapse as a result of the pressures of his private and business life, and the added strain of his writing.

1 9 1 3 –   Recovering, he moves to Chicago and advertising work
1 9 1 5   again. With Carl Sandburg, Floyd Dell, Ben Hecht, Eunice Tietjens, Lewis Galantière, Burton Rascoe, and others, he takes part in the "Chicago Renaissance," contributing to Margaret Anderson's *The Little Review*, and writing the first of the *Winesburg* tales in the fall of 1915.

1 9 1 6   Publishes some of the *Winesburg* tales in *The Masses*,

The Little Review, and *Seven Arts.* With help from Theodore Dreiser and Floyd Dell, his first novel, *Windy McPherson's Son,* is published. Divorced from Cornelia, he marries Tennessee Mitchell.

1917   Publishes *Marching Men,* a novel.

1918   Publishes *Mid-American Chants,* poems.

1919   Publishes *Winesburg, Ohio.*

1920   Publishes *Poor White,* a novel.

1921 – Publishes *The Triumph of the Egg,* impressions of
1922   American life in tales and poems. Wins the *Dial* award of two thousand dollars, meets Ernest Hemingway and, in Europe, James Joyce, Gertrude Stein, and Ford Madox Ford.

1923   Publishes *Many Marriages,* a novel, and *Horses and Men,* stories.

1924   Publishes *A Story Teller's Story,* autobiography. Divorced from Tennessee in April, he marries Elizabeth Prall.

1925   Publishes "The Modern Writer," an essay, and *Dark Laughter,* his only commercially successful novel. Lives for several months in New Orleans, becoming the friend and mentor of William Faulkner.

1926   Publishes *Sherwood Anderson's Notebook* and *Tar: A Midwest Childhood.* Makes a lecture tour to help pay for the farm he buys near Marion, Virginia, and the house he builds on it. This is to be his home for the rest of his life.

1927   Publishes *A New Testament,* prose-poems. Travels to Europe again, where he renews his acquaintance with Joyce and Gertrude Stein. Continues lecturing in America. Buys two local Virginia newspapers.

1929   Publishes *Hello Towns,* pieces from his newspapers, "Nearer the Grass Roots," an essay, and *Alice and the Lost Novel,* stories. His third marriage ends in divorce.

1930   Tours Southern mill towns, supports workers' protest movements.

1931   Publishes *Perhaps Women,* essays.

1 9 3 2   Publishes *Beyond Desire*, a novel.

1 9 3 3   Publishes *Death in the Woods and Other Stories*. Marries Eleanor Copenhaver.

1 9 3 4   Publishes "No Swank," an essay. His dramatic version of *Winesburg, Ohio* is presented at the Hedgerow Theatre.

1 9 3 5   Publishes *Puzzled America*, essays.

1 9 3 6   Publishes *Kit Brandon*, a novel.

1 9 3 7   Publishes *Plays: Winesburg and Others*. The others were three one-act plays: *The Triumph of the Egg, Mother,* and *They Married Later.* Elected to The National Institute of Arts and Letters.

1 9 3 9   Publishes *Home Town*, prose sketches.

1 9 4 1   Dies of peritonitis in Colon, Panama Canal Zone, at the beginning of a South American good-will tour encouraged by the State Department.

1 9 4 2   *Sherwood Anderson's Memoirs* is published.

Anderson on

WINESBURG, OHIO

❖◇❖◇❖◇❖◇❖◇❖◇❖◇❖◇❖◇❖◇❖◇❖◇❖◇❖◇❖◇❖◇❖◇❖◇❖

LANGUAGE AND FORM

. . . My own vocabulary was small. I had no Latin and no Greek, no French. When I wanted to arrive at anything like delicate shades of meaning in my writing I had to do it with my own very limited vocabulary.

And even my reading had not much increased my vocabulary. Oh, how many words I knew in books that I could not pronounce.

But should I use in my writing words that were not a part of my own everyday speech, of my own everyday thought?

I did not think so.

"No," I had long been telling myself, "you will have to stay where you have put yourself." There was the language of the streets, of American towns and cities, the language of the factories and warehouses where I had worked, of laborers' rooming houses, the saloons, the farms.

"It is my own language, limited as it is. I will have to learn to work with it. There was a kind of poetry I was seeking in my prose, word to be laid against word in just a certain way, a kind of word color, a march of words and sentences, the color to be squeezed out of simple words, simple sentence construction." Just how much of all this had been thought out, as I have spoken of it here, I do not know. What I do know is the fact of my awareness of the limitations I had to face; my feeling that the writing, the telling of tales had got too far away from the manner in which we men of the time were living our lives. [*Memoirs*][1]

The stories belonged together. I felt that, taken together, they made something like a novel, a complete story. . . . I considered then, as I now consider, that my earliest stories, both *Windy McPherson* and at least in the writing, *Marching Men*, had been the result not so much of my own feeling about life as of reading the novels of others. There had been too much H. G. Wells, that sort of thing. I was being too heroic. I came down off my perch. I have even sometimes thought that the novel form does not fit an American writer, that it is a form which had been brought in. What is wanted is a new looseness; and in *Winesburg* I had made it my own form. There were individual tales but all about lives in some way connected. By this method I did succeed, I think, in giving the feeling of the life of a boy growing into young manhood in a town. Life is a loose, flowing thing. There are no plot stories in life. [*Memoirs*] Our writers, our storytellers, in wrapping life up into neat little packages were only betraying life. [*Letters*][2]

My stories were obviously written by one who did not know the answers. They were simple little tales of happenings, things observed and felt. There were no cowboys or daring wild game hunters. None of the people in the tales got lost in burning deserts or went seeking the North Pole. [*Letters*]

WINESBURG AND ITS PEOPLE

. . . Winesburg of course was no particular town. It was a mythical town. It was people. I had got the characters of the

---

[1] From *Sherwood Anderson's Memoirs* (New York: Harcourt, Brace, 1942), copyright 1942 by Eleanor Anderson. These and following selections reprinted by permission of Harold Ober Associates.

[2] From *Letters of Sherwood Anderson*, eds., Walter B. Rideout and Howard Mumford Jones (New York: Little Brown, 1953).

book everywhere about me, in towns in which I had lived, in the army, in factories and offices. When I gave the book its title I had no idea there really was an Ohio town by that name. I even consulted a list of towns but it must have been a list giving only towns that were situated on railroads. [*Memoirs*]

In my stories I simply stayed at home among my own people. . . . I think I must, very early, have realized that this was my milieu, that is to say, common everyday lives. The ordinary beliefs of the people about me, that love lasted indefinitely, that success meant happiness, simply did not seem true to me. [*Letters*]

There was all of this starved side of American small town life. Perhaps I was even vain enough to think that these stories told would, in the end, have the effect of breaking down a little the curious separateness of so much of life, these walls we build up about us. [*Memoirs*]

If *Winesburg, Ohio* tried to tell the story of the defeated figures of an Old American individualistic small town life, then my later books have been but an attempt to carry these same people forward into the new American life, into the whirl and roar of modern machines. [*Memoirs*]

RECEPTION

. . . [The book was rejected by several] publishers. One of them, on whom I called, handed me a copy of a novel by an Anglo-American author he was then promoting. "Read this and learn how to write," said he.

Then on a Sunday, a cold wintry day, I waited at the corner of Fifty-ninth Street and the Park in New York. I had gotten a letter from Ben Huebsch, now editor-in-chief of the Viking Press, but then doing business under his own name. He wrote asking me to see him when I next came to New York, and, within a few weeks, being in New York, I phoned him. He told me where to meet him, as I understood at the Central Park corner. We were to go to a certain restaurant.

"I will meet you there at the corner at four," he had said over the phone and I think I must have been, at what I understood to be the appointed place, at three.

I stood and waited and he did not come. The hours passed. It was four o'clock, then five, then six. I am sure it will be difficult for me to make the reader understand how I felt.

It is to be borne in mind that, by this time, my stories had been rather kicked around for three or four years. I had been tender about these people of my stories, had wanted understanding and tenderness for them; and it had happened already with men on whom I had counted, that when I had shown them the stories they had rejected them.

I was there, in the city, on the Sunday afternoon, waiting on the street corner and it was cold and my heart was cold. I had got the notion that Mr. Huebsch, like so many other publishers, did not want my stories.

What a shabby trick he had played me! "Why," I asked myself, "did he need to encourage me?"

. . . At least other publishers, to whom my book had been submitted, had been frankly cold. They had not aroused my hopes. I went back to my hotel and threw myself on the bed. It all seems very silly now but on the evening in the hotel room, with the tears flowing from my eyes . . . Occasionally I stopped weeping to curse, consigning all publishers to Hell and reserving a special place in Hell for poor Ben Huebsch . . . on that evening I was really more desperate than I had ever been before in my life.

And then, at last . . . it must have been about nine . . . my telephone rang and there was Mr. Huebsch and I managed to control myself while he told me that, while I had been on one corner waiting for him he had been on the other waiting for me. There had been a simple misunderstanding and, as for the book, he said that he would make no bones about that.

"Yes," he said, over the phone, "I want the book. I only wanted to meet you to talk over details," he said.

"And you do not want to tinker, to change my stories, to tell me how you think they should be written?"

I am quite sure that my voice must have trembled as I asked the question.

"You do not want to tell me that they are not stories?"

"No, of course not," he said. [*Memoirs*]

Well, it was published. And immediately there was a strange reaction, a strange reception. In justice I ought to speak of the fact that criticism had been poured over all my Chicago contemporaries from the start. We had the notion that sex had something to do with people's lives, and it had barely been mentioned in American writing before our time. No one it seemed ever used a profane word. And bringing sex back to take what seemed to us its normal place in the picture of life, we were called sex-obsessed.

Still the reception of *Winesburg* amazed and confounded me. The book was widely condemned, called nasty and dirty by most of its critics. It was more than two years selling its first five thousand. The book had been so personal to me that, when the reviews began to appear and I found that, for the most part, it was being taken as the work of a perverted mind . . . in review after review it was called "a sewer" and the man who had written it taken as a strangely sex-obsessed man . . . a kind of sickness came over me, a sickness that lasted for months.

It is very strange to think, as I sit writing, that this book, now used in many of our colleges as a textbook of the short story, should have been so misinterpreted when published twenty years ago. I had felt peculiarly clean and healthy while I was at work on it.

"What can be the matter with me?" I began asking myself. It is true that nowadays I am constantly meeting men who tell me of the effect had upon them by the book when it first came into their hands and every now and then a man declares that, when the book was published he praised it, but if there was any such praise, at the time, it escaped my notice.

That the book did not sell did not at all bother me. The abuse did. There was the public abuse, condemnation, ugly words used and there was also, at once, a curious kind of private abuse.

My mail became filled with letters, many of them very strange. It went on and on for weeks and months. In many of the letters there were dirty words used. It was as though by these simple tales I had, as one might say, jerked open doors to many obscure and often twisted lives. They did not like it. They wrote me the letters and, often, in the letters there was a spewing forth of something like poison.

And for a time it poisoned me.

Item . . . A letter from a woman, the wife of an acquaintance. Her husband was a banker. I had once sat at her table and she wrote to tell me that, having sat next to me at the table and, having read my book, she felt that she could never, while she lived, be clean again.

Item . . . There was a man friend who was spending some weeks in a New England town. He was leaving the town one morning on an early train and, as he walked to the railroad station, he passed a small park.

In the park, in the early morning, there was a little group of people, two men, he said, and three women, and they were bending over a small bonfire. He said that his curiosity was aroused and that he approached.

"There were three copies of your book," he said. The little group of New Englanders, men and women . . . he thought they must all have been past fifty . . . he spoke of the thin sharp Calvin Coolidge faces . . . "they were the town library board."

They had bought the three copies of my book and were burning them. My friend who saw all of this, thought there must have been compaints made. He said he spoke to the group gathered in the little town square before the town library building . . . and that a woman of their group answered his question.

He said she made a sour mouth.

"Ugh!" she said. "The filthy things, the filthy things."

Item . . . A well-known woman writer of New Orleans. She

spoke to a friend of mine who asked her if she had seen the book.

"I got fire tongs," she said. "I read one of the stories and, after that, I would not touch it with my hands. With the tongs I carried it down into the cellar. I put it in the furnace. I knew that I should feel unclean while it was in my house." [*Memoirs*]

And the people of the actual Winesburg protested. They declared the book immoral and that the actual inhabitants of the real Winesburg were a highly moral people. . . . Certainly the people of my book, who had lived their little fragments of lives in my imagination, were not specially immoral. They were just people, and . . . if the people of [the] real Winesburg were as all around decent as those of my imagined town then the real Winesburg might be indeed a very decent town to live in.

And here is something very curious. The book has become a kind of American classic, and has been said by many critics to have started a kind of revolution in American short-story writing. And the stories themselves which in 1919 were almost universally condemned as immoral, might today almost be published in the *Ladies' Home Journal,* so innocent they seem. All of that new frankness about life while a new born babe is growing to voting age. [*Memoirs*]

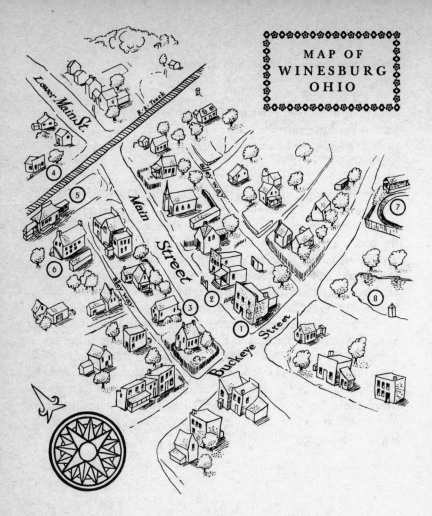

MAP OF
WINESBURG
OHIO

LEGEND

1 Office, *Winesburg Eagle*
2 Hern's Grocery
3 Sinning's Hardware Store
4 Biff Carter's Lunch Room
5 Railroad Station
6 New Willard House
7 Fair Ground
8 Waterworks Pond

I

WINESBURG, OHIO

The Text

TO THE MEMORY OF MY MOTHER,

EMMA SMITH ANDERSON,

whose keen observations on the life about her first awoke
in me the hunger to see beneath the surface of lives,
this book is dedicated.

THE BOOK OF
THE GROTESQUE

THE WRITER, an old man with a white mustache, had some difficulty in getting into bed. The windows of the house in which he lived were high and he wanted to look at the trees when he awoke in the morning. A carpenter came to fix the bed so that it would be on a level with the window.

Quite a fuss was made about the matter. The carpenter, who had been a soldier in the Civil War, came into the writer's room and sat down to talk of building a platform for the purpose of raising the bed. The writer had cigars lying about and the carpenter smoked.

For a time the two men talked of the raising of the bed and then they talked of other things. The soldier got on the subject of the war. The writer, in fact, led him to that subject. The carpenter had once been a prisoner in Andersonville prison and had lost a brother. The brother had died of starvation, and whenever the carpenter got upon that subject he cried. He, like the old writer, had a white mustache, and when he cried he puckered up his lips and the mustache bobbed up and down. The weeping old man with the cigar in his mouth was ludicrous. The plan the writer had for the raising of his bed was forgotten and later the carpenter did it in his own way and the writer, who was past sixty, had to help himself with a chair when he went to bed at night.

In his bed the writer rolled over on his side and lay quite still. For years he had been beset with notions concerning his heart. He was a hard smoker and his heart fluttered. The idea had got into his mind that he would some time die unexpectedly and always when he got into bed he thought of that. It did not alarm him. The effect in fact was quite a special thing and not easily explained. It made him more alive, there in bed, than at any other time. Perfectly still he lay and his body was old and not of much use any more, but something inside him was altogether young. [He was like a pregnant woman, only that the thing inside him was not a baby but a youth. No, it wasn't a youth, it was a woman, young, and wearing a coat of mail like a knight.] It is absurd, you see, to try to tell what was inside the old writer as he lay on his high bed and listened to the fluttering of his heart. The thing to get at is what the writer, or the young thing within the writer, was thinking about.

The old writer, like all of the people in the world, had got, during his long life, a great many notions in his head. He had once been quite handsome and a number of women had been in love with him. And then, of course, he had known people, many people, known them in a peculiarly intimate way that was different from the way in which you and I know people. At least that is what the writer thought and the thought pleased him. Why quarrel with an old man concerning his thoughts?

In the bed the writer had a dream that was not a dream. As he grew somewhat sleepy but was still conscious, figures began to appear before his eyes. He imagined the young indescribable thing within himself was driving a long procession of figures before his eyes.

You see the interest in all this lies in the figures that went before the eyes of the writer. They were all grotesques. All of the men and women the writer had ever known had become grotesques.

The grotesques were not all horrible. Some were amusing, some almost beautiful, and one, a woman all drawn out of shape, hurt the old man by her grotesqueness. When she passed he made a noise like a small dog whimpering. Had you come into the room you might have supposed the old man had unpleasant dreams or perhaps indigestion.

For an hour the procession of grotesques passed before the eyes of the old man, and then, although it was a painful thing to do, he crept out of bed and began to write. Some one of the grotesques had made a deep impression on his mind and he wanted to describe it.

At his desk the writer worked for an hour. In the end he wrote a book which he called "The Book of the Grotesque." It was never published, but I saw it once and it made an indelible impression on my mind. The book had one central thought that is very strange and has always remained with me. By remembering it I have been able to understand many people and things that I was never able to understand before. The thought was involved but a simple statement of it would be something like this:

That in the beginning when the world was young there were a great many thoughts but no such thing as a truth. Man made the truths himself and each truth was a composite of a great many vague thoughts. All about in the world were the truths and they were all beautiful.

The old man had listed hundreds of the truths in his book. I will not try to tell you of all of them. There was the truth of virginity and the truth of passion, the truth of wealth and of poverty, of thrift and of profligacy, of carelessness and abandon. Hundreds and hundreds were the truths and they were all beautiful.

And then the people came along. Each as he appeared snatched up one of the truths and some who were quite strong snatched up a dozen of them.

It was the truths that made the people grotesques. The

old man had quite an elaborate theory concerning the matter. It was his notion that the moment one of people took one of the truths to himself, called it his truth, and tried to live his life by it, he became a grotesque and the truth he embraced became a falsehood.

You can see for yourself how the old man, who had spent all of his life writing and was filled with words, would write hundreds of pages concerning this matter. The subject would become so big in his mind that he himself would be in danger of becoming a grotesque. He didn't, I suppose, for the same reason that he never published the book. It was the young thing inside him that saved the old man.

Concerning the old carpenter who fixed the bed for the writer, I only mentioned him because he, like many of what are called very common people, became the nearest thing to what is understandable and lovable of all the grotesques in the writer's book.

HANDS

UPON THE half decayed veranda of a small frame house
that stood near the edge of a ravine near the town
of Winesburg, Ohio, a fat little old man walked nervously up and down. Across a long field that had been
seeded for clover but that had produced only a dense crop
of yellow mustard weeds, he could see the public highway along which went a wagon filled with berry pickers returning from the fields. The berry pickers, youths and
maidens, laughed and shouted boisterously. A boy clad in
a blue shirt leaped from the wagon and attempted to drag
after him one of the maidens, who screamed and protested
shrilly. The feet of the boy in the road kicked up a cloud
of dust that floated across the face of the departing sun.
Over the long field came a thin girlish voice. "Oh,
you Wing Biddlebaum, comb your hair, it's falling into
your eyes," commanded the voice to the man, who was
bald and whose nervous little hands fiddled about the
bare white forehead as though arranging a mass of tangled
locks.

Wing Biddlebaum, forever frightened and beset by a
ghostly band of doubts, did not think of himself as in any
way a part of the life of the town where he had lived for
twenty years. Among all the people of Winesburg but one
had come close to him. With George Willard, son of Tom
Willard, the proprietor of the New Willard House, he
had formed something like a friendship. George Willard
was the reporter on the *Winesburg Eagle* and sometimes

27

in the evenings he walked out along the highway to Wing Biddlebaum's house. Now as the old man walked up and down on the veranda, his hands moving nervously about, he was hoping that George Willard would come and spend the evening with him. After the wagon containing the berry pickers had passed, he went across the field through the tall mustard weeds and climbing a rail fence peered anxiously along the road to the town. For a moment he stood thus, rubbing his hands together and looking up and down the road, and then, fear overcoming him, ran back to walk again upon the porch on his own house.

In the presence of George Willard, Wing Biddlebaum, who for twenty years had been the town mystery, lost something of his timidity, and his shadowy personality, submerged in a sea of doubts, came forth to look at the world. With the young reporter at his side, he ventured in the light of day into Main Street or strode up and down on the rickety front porch of his own house, talking excitedly. The voice that had been low and trembling became shrill and loud. The bent figure straightened. With a kind of wriggle, like a fish returned to the brook by the fisherman, Biddlebaum the silent began to talk, striving to put into words the ideas that had been accumulated by his mind during long years of silence.

Wing Biddlebaum talked much with his hands. The slender expressive fingers, forever active, forever striving to conceal themselves in his pockets or behind his back, came forth and became the piston rods of his machinery of expression.

The story of Wing Biddlebaum is a story of hands. Their restless activity, like unto the beating of the wings of an imprisoned bird, had given him his name. Some obscure poet of the town had thought of it. The hands alarmed their owner. He wanted to keep them hidden away and looked with amazement at the quiet inexpressive hands of other men who worked beside him in the fields, or passed, driving sleepy teams on country roads.

When he talked to George Willard, Wing Biddlebaum closed his fists and beat with them upon a table or on the walls of his house. The action made him more comfortable. If the desire to talk came to him when the two were walking in the fields, he sought out a stump or the top board of a fence and with his hands pounding busily talked with renewed ease.

The story of Wing Biddlebaum's hands is worth a book in itself. Sympathetically set forth it would tap many strange, beautiful qualities in obscure men. It is a job for a poet. In Winesburg the hands had attracted attention merely because of their activity. With them Wing Biddlebaum had picked as high as a hundred and forty quarts of strawberries in a day. They became his distinguishing feature, the source of his fame. Also they made more grotesque an already grotesque and elusive individuality. Winesburg was proud of the hands of Wing Biddlebaum in the same spirit in which it was proud of Banker White's new stone house and Wesley Moyer's bay stallion, Tony Tip, that had won the two-fifteen trot at the fall races in Cleveland.

As for George Willard, he had many times wanted to ask about the hands. At times an almost overwhelming curiosity had taken hold of him. He felt that there must be a reason for their strange activity and their inclination to keep hidden away and only a growing respect for Wing Biddlebaum kept him from blurting out the questions that were often in his mind.

Once he had been on the point of asking. The two were walking in the fields on a summer afternoon and had stopped to sit upon a grassy bank. All afternoon Wing Biddlebaum had talked as one inspired. By a fence he had stopped and beating like a giant woodpecker upon the top board had shouted at George Willard, condemning his tendency to be too much influenced by the people about him. "You are destroying yourself," he cried. "You have the inclination to be alone and to dream and you are afraid of dreams. You want to be like others in town here. You hear them talk and you try to imitate them."

On the grassy bank Wing Biddlebaum had tried again to drive his point home. His voice became soft and reminiscent, and with a sigh of contentment he launched into a long rambling talk, speaking as one lost in a dream.

Out of the dream Wing Biddlebaum made a picture for George Willard. In the picture men lived again in a kind of pastoral golden age. Across a green open country came clean-limbed young men, some afoot, some mounted upon horses. In crowds the young men came to gather about the feet of an old man who sat beneath a tree in a tiny garden and who talked to them.

Wing Biddlebaum became wholly inspired. For once he forgot the hands. Slowly they stole forth and lay upon George Willard's shoulders. Something new and bold came into the voice that talked. "You must try to forget all you have learned," said the old man. "You must begin to dream. From this time on you must shut your ears to the roaring of the voices."

Pausing in his speech, Wing Biddlebaum looked long and earnestly at George Willard. His eyes glowed. Again he raised the hands to caress the boy and then a look of horror swept over his face.

With a convulsive movement of his body, Wing Biddlebaum sprang to his feet and thrust his hands deep into his trousers pockets. Tears came to his eyes. "I must be getting along home. I can talk no more with you," he said nervously.

Without looking back, the old man had hurried down the hillside and across a meadow, leaving George Willard perplexed and frightened upon the grassy slope. With a shiver of dread the boy arose and went along the road toward town. "I'll not ask him about his hands," he thought, touched by the memory of the terror he had seen in the man's eyes. "There's something wrong, but I don't want to know what it is. His hands have something to do with his fear of me and of everyone."

And George Willard was right. Let us look briefly into the story of the hands. Perhaps our talking of them will arouse the poet who will tell the hidden wonder story of the influence for which the hands were but fluttering pennants of promise.

In his youth Wing Biddlebaum had been a school teacher in a town in Pennsylvania. He was not then known as Wing Biddlebaum, but went by the less euphonic name of Adolph Myers. As Adolph Myers he was much loved by the boys of his school.

Adolph Myers was meant by nature to be a teacher of youth. He was one of those rare, little-understood men who rule by a power so gentle that it passes as a lovable weakness. In their feeling for the boys under their charge such men are not unlike the finer sort of women in their love of men.

And yet that is but crudely stated. It needs the poet there. With the boys of his school, Adolph Myers had walked in the evening or had sat talking until dusk upon the schoolhouse steps lost in a kind of dream. Here and there went his hands, caressing the shoulders of the boys, playing about the tousled heads. As he talked his voice became soft and musical. There was a caress in that also. In a way the voice and the hands, the stroking of the shoulders and the touching of the hair were a part of the schoolmaster's effort to carry a dream into the young minds. By the caress that was in his fingers he expressed himself. He was one of those men in whom the force that creates life is diffused, not centralized. Under the caress of his hands doubt and disbelief went out of the minds of the boys and they began also to dream.

And then the tragedy. A half-witted boy of the school became enamored of the young master. In his bed at night he imagined unspeakable things and in the morning went forth to tell his dreams as facts. Strange, hideous accusations fell from his loose-hung lips. Through the Pennsylvania town went a shiver. Hidden, shadowy doubts that had been in men's minds concerning Adolph Myers were galvanized into beliefs.

The tragedy did not linger. Trembling lads were jerked out of bed and questioned. "He put his arms about me," said one. "His fingers were always playing in my hair," said another.

One afternoon a man of the town, Henry Bradford, who kept a saloon, came to the schoolhouse door. Calling Adolph Myers into the school yard he began to beat him with his fists. As his hard knuckles beat down into the frightened face of the schoolmaster, his wrath became more and more terrible. Screaming with dismay, the children ran here and there like disturbed insects. "I'll teach you to put your hands on my boy, you beast," roared the saloon keeper, who, tired of beating the master, had begun to kick him about the yard.

Adolph Myers was driven from the Pennsylvania town in the night. With lanterns in their hands a dozen men came to the door of the house where he lived alone and commanded that he dress and come forth. It was raining and one of the men had a rope in his hands. They had intended to hang the schoolmaster, but something in his figure, so small, white, and pitiful, touched their hearts and they let him escape. As he ran away into the darkness they repented of their weakness and ran after him, swearing and throwing sticks and great balls of soft mud at the figure that screamed and ran faster and faster into the darkness.

For twenty years Adolph Myers had lived alone in Winesburg. He was but forty but looked sixty-five. The name of Biddlebaum he got from a box of goods seen at a freight station as he hurried through an eastern Ohio town. He had an aunt in Winesburg, a black-toothed old woman who raised chickens, and with her he lived until she died. He had been ill for a year after the experience in Pennsylvania, and after his recovery worked as a day laborer in the fields, going timidly about and striving to conceal his hands. Although he did not understand what had happened he felt that the hands must be to blame. Again and again the fathers of the boys had talked of the hands. "Keep your hands to yourself," the saloon keeper had roared, dancing with fury in the schoolhouse yard.

Upon the veranda of his house by the ravine, Wing Biddlebaum continued to walk up and down until the sun had disappeared and the road beyond the field was lost in the grey shadows. Going into his house he cut slices of bread and spread honey upon them. When the rumble of the evening train that took away the express cars loaded with the day's harvest of berries had passed and restored the silence of the summer night, he went again to walk upon the veranda. In the darkness he could not see the hands and they became quiet. Although he still hungered for the presence of the boy, who was the medium through which he expressed his love of man, the hunger became again a part of his loneliness and his waiting. Lighting a lamp, Wing Biddlebaum washed the few dishes soiled by his simple meal and, setting up a folding cot by the screen door that led to the porch, prepared to undress for the night. A few stray white bread crumbs lay on the cleanly washed floor by the table; putting the lamp upon a low stool he began to pick up the crumbs, carrying them to his mouth one by one with unbelievable rapidity. In the dense blotch of light beneath the table, the kneeling figure looked like a priest engaged in some service of his church. The nervous expressive fingers, flashing in and out of the light, might well have been mistaken for the fingers of the devotee going swiftly through decade after decade of his rosary.

PAPER PILLS

H E W A S an old man with a white beard and huge nose and hands. Long before the time during which we will know him, he was a doctor and drove a jaded white horse from house to house through the streets of Winesburg. Later he married a girl who had money. She had been left a large fertile farm when her father died. The girl was quiet, tall, and dark, and to many people she seemed very beautiful. Everyone in Winesburg wondered why she married the doctor. Within a year after the marriage she died.

The knuckles of the doctor's hands were extraordinarily large. When the hands were closed they looked like clusters of unpainted wooden balls as large as walnuts fastened together by steel rods. He smoked a cob pipe and after his wife's death sat all day in his empty office close by a window that was covered with cobwebs. He never opened the window. Once on a hot day in August he tried but found it stuck fast and after that he forgot all about it.

Winesburg had forgotten the old man, but in Doctor Reefy there were the seeds of something very fine. Alone in his musty office in the Heffner Block above the Paris Dry Goods Company's store, he worked ceaselessly, building up something that he himself destroyed. Little pyramids of truth he erected and after erecting knocked them down again that he might have the truths to erect other pyramids.

Doctor Reefy was a tall man who had worn one suit of

35

clothes for ten years. It was frayed at the sleeves and little holes had appeared at the knees and elbows. In the office he wore also a linen duster with huge pockets into which he continually stuffed scraps of paper. After some weeks the scraps of paper became little hard round balls, and when the pockets were filled he dumped them out upon the floor. For ten years he had but one friend, another old man named John Spaniard who owned a tree nursery. Sometimes, in a playful mood, old Doctor Reefy took from his pockets a handful of the paper balls and threw them at the nursery man. "That is to confound you, you blithering old sentimentalist," he cried, shaking with laughter.

The story of Doctor Reefy and his courtship of the tall dark girl who became his wife and left her money to him is a very curious story. It is delicious, like the twisted little apples that grow in the orchards of Winesburg. In the fall one walks in the orchards and the ground is hard with frost underfoot. The apples have been taken from the trees by the pickers. They have been put in barrels and shipped to the cities where they will be eaten in apartments that are filled with books, magazines, furniture, and people. On the trees are only a few gnarled apples that the pickers have rejected. They look like the knuckles of Doctor Reefy's hands. One nibbles at them and they are delicious. Into a little round place at the side of the apple has been gathered all of its sweetness. One runs from tree to tree over the frosted ground picking the gnarled, twisted apples and filling his pockets with them. Only the few know the sweetness of the twisted apples.

The girl and Doctor Reefy began their courtship on a summer afternoon. He was forty-five then and already he had begun the practice of filling his pockets with the scraps of paper that became hard balls and were thrown away. The habit had been formed as he sat in his buggy behind the jaded white horse and went slowly along country roads. On the papers were written thoughts, ends of thoughts, beginnings of thoughts.

One by one the mind of Doctor Reefy had made the thoughts. Out of many of them he formed a truth that arose gigantic in his mind. The truth clouded the world. It became terrible and then faded away and the little thoughts began again.

The tall dark girl came to see Doctor Reefy because she was in the family way and had become frightened. She was in that condition because of a series of circumstances also curious.

The death of her father and mother and the rich acres of land that had come down to her had set a train of suitors on her heels. For two years she saw suitors almost every evening. Except two they were all alike. They talked to her of passion and there was a strained eager quality in their voices and in their eyes when they looked at her. The two who were different were much unlike each other. One of them, a slender young man with white hands, the son of a jeweler in Winesburg, talked continually of virginity. When he was with her he was never off the subject. The other, a black-haired boy with large ears, said nothing at all but always managed to get her into the darkness, where he began to kiss her.

For a time the tall dark girl thought she would marry the jeweler's son. For hours she sat in silence listening as he talked to her and then she began to be afraid of something. Beneath his talk of virginity she began to think there was a lust greater than in all the others. At times it seemed to her that as he talked he was holding her body in his hands. She imagined him turning it slowly about in the white hands and staring at it. At night she dreamed that he had bitten into her body and that his jaws were dripping. She had the dream three times, then she became in the family way to the one who said nothing at all but who in the moment of his passion actually did bite her shoulder so that for days the marks of his teeth showed.

After the tall dark girl came to know Doctor Reefy it seemed to her that she never wanted to leave him again. She went into his office one morning and without her saying anything he seemed to know what had happened to her.

In the office of the doctor there was a woman, the wife of the man who kept the bookstore in Winesburg. Like all old-fashioned country practitioners, Doctor Reefy pulled teeth, and the woman who waited held a handkerchief to her teeth and groaned. Her husband was with her and when the tooth was taken out they both screamed and blood ran down on the woman's white dress. The tall dark girl did not pay any attention. When the woman and the man had gone the doctor smiled. "I will take you driving into the country with me," he said.

For several weeks the tall dark girl and the doctor were together almost every day. The condition that had brought her to him passed in an illness, but she was like one who has discovered the sweetness of the twisted apples, she could not get her mind fixed again upon the round perfect fruit that is eaten in the city apartments. In the fall after the beginning of her acquaintanceship with him she married Doctor Reefy and in the following spring she died. During the winter he read to her all of the odds and ends of thoughts he had scribbled on the bits of paper. After he had read them he laughed and stuffed them away in his pockets to become round hard balls.

MOTHER

ELIZABETH WILLARD, the mother of George Willard, was tall and gaunt and her face was marked with smallpox scars. Although she was but forty-five, some obscure disease had taken the fire out of her figure. Listlessly she went about the disorderly old hotel looking at the faded wall-paper and the ragged carpets and, when she was able to be about, doing the work of a chambermaid among beds soiled by the slumbers of fat traveling men. Her husband, Tom Willard, a slender, graceful man with square shoulders, a quick military step, and a black mustache trained to turn sharply up at the ends, tried to put the wife out of his mind. The presence of the tall ghostly figure, moving slowly through the halls, he took as a reproach to himself. When he thought of her he grew angry and swore. The hotel was unprofitable and forever on the edge of failure and he wished himself out of it. He thought of the old house and the woman who lived there with him as things defeated and done for. The hotel in which he had begun life so hopefully was now a mere ghost of what a hotel should be. As he went spruce and business-like through the streets of Winesburg, he sometimes stopped and turned quickly about as though fearing that the spirit of the hotel and of the woman would follow him even into the streets. "Damn such a life, damn it!" he sputtered aimlessly.

Tom Willard had a passion for village politics and for years had been the leading Democrat in a strongly Repub-

lican community. Some day, he told himself, the tide of
things political will turn in my favor and the years of ineffectual service count big in the bestowal of rewards. He
dreamed of going to Congress and even of becoming gov-
ernor. Once when a younger member of the party arose at
a political conference and began to boast of his faithful
service, Tom Willard grew white with fury. "Shut up,
you," he roared, glaring about. "What do you know of
service? What are you but a boy? Look at what I've done
here! I was a Democrat here in Winesburg when it was a
crime to be a Democrat. In the old days they fairly hunted
us with guns."

Between Elizabeth and her one son George there was a
deep unexpressed bond of sympathy, based on a girlhood
dream that had long ago died. In the son's presence she
was timid and reserved, but sometimes while he hurried
about town intent upon his duties as a reporter, she went
into his room and closing the door knelt by a little desk,
made of a kitchen table, that sat near a window. In the
room by the desk she went through a ceremony that was
half a prayer, half a demand, addressed to the skies. In
the boyish figure she yearned to see something half forgotten that had once been a part of herself re-created. The
prayer concerned that. "Even though I die, I will in some
way keep defeat from you," she cried, and so deep was her
determination that her whole body shook. Her eyes glowed
and she clenched her fists. "If I am dead and see him becoming a meaningless drab figure like myself, I will come
back," she declared. "I ask God now to give me that privilege. I demand it. I will pay for it. God may beat me with
his fists. I will take any blow that may befall if but this
my boy be allowed to express something for us both."
Pausing uncertainly, the woman stared about the boy's

room. "And do not let him become smart and successful either," she added vaguely.

The communion between George Willard and his mother was outwardly a formal thing without meaning. When she was ill and sat by the window in her room he sometimes went in the evening to make her a visit. They sat by a window that looked over the roof of a small frame building into Main Street. By turning their heads they could see through another window, along an alleyway that ran behind the Main Street stores and into the back door of Abner Groff's bakery. Sometimes as they sat thus a picture of village life presented itself to them. At the back door of his shop appeared Abner Groff with a stick or an empty milk bottle in his hand. For a long time there was a feud between the baker and a grey cat that belonged to Sylvester West, the druggist. The boy and his mother saw the cat creep into the door of the bakery and presently emerge followed by the baker, who swore and waved his arms about. The baker's eyes were small and red and his black hair and beard were filled with flour dust. Sometimes he was so angry that, although the cat had disappeared, he hurled sticks, bits of broken glass, and even some of the tools of his trade about. Once he broke a window at the back of Sinning's Hardware Store. In the alley the grey cat crouched behind barrels filled with torn paper and broken bottles above which flew a black swarm of flies. Once when she was alone, and after watching a prolonged and ineffectual outburst on the part of the baker, Elizabeth Willard put her head down on her long white hands and wept. After that she did not look along the alleyway any more, but tried to forget the contest between the bearded man and the cat. It seemed like a rehearsal of her own life, terrible in its vividness.

In the evening when the son sat in the room with his mother, the silence made them both feel awkward. Darkness came on and the evening train came in at the station. In the street below feet tramped up and down upon a board sidewalk. In the station yard, after the evening train had gone, there was a heavy silence. Perhaps Skinner Leason, the express agent, moved a truck the length of the station platform. Over on Main Street sounded a man's voice, laughing. The door of the express office banged. George Willard arose and crossing the room fumbled for the doorknob. Sometimes he knocked against a chair, making it scrape along the floor. By the window sat the sick woman, perfectly still, listless. Her long hands, white and bloodless, could be seen drooping over the ends of the arms of the chair. "I think you had better be out among the boys. You are too much indoors," she said, striving to relieve the embarrassment of the departure. "I thought I would take a walk," replied George Willard, who felt awkward and confused.

One evening in July, when the transient guests who made the New Willard House their temporary home had become scarce, and the hallways, lighted only by kerosene lamps turned low, were plunged in gloom, Elizabeth Willard had an adventure. She had been ill in bed for several days and her son had not come to visit her. She was alarmed. The feeble blaze of life that remained in her body was blown into a flame by her anxiety and she crept out of bed, dressed and hurried along the hallway toward her son's room, shaking with exaggerated fears. As she went along she steadied herself with her hand, slipped along the papered walls of the hall and breathed with difficulty. The air whistled through her teeth. As she hurried forward she thought how foolish she was. "He is concerned with boyish affairs," she told herself. "Perhaps he has now begun to walk about in the evening with girls."

Elizabeth Willard had a dread of being seen by guests in the hotel that had once belonged to her father and the ownership of which still stood recorded in her name in the county courthouse. The hotel was continually losing patronage because of its shabbiness and she thought of herself as also shabby. Her own room was in an obscure corner and when she felt able to work she voluntarily worked among the beds, preferring the labor that could be done when the guests were abroad seeking trade among the merchants of Winesburg.

By the door of her son's room the mother knelt upon the floor and listened for some sound from within. When she heard the boy moving about and talking in low tones a smile came to her lips. George Willard had a habit of talking aloud to himself and to hear him doing so had always given his mother a peculiar pleasure. The habit in him, she felt, strengthened the secret bond that existed between them. A thousand times she had whispered to herself of the matter. "He is groping about, trying to find himself," she thought. "He is not a dull clod, all words and smartness. Within him there is a secret something that is striving to grow. It is the thing I let be killed in myself."

In the darkness in the hallway by the door the sick woman arose and started again toward her own room. She was afraid that the door would open and the boy come upon her. When she had reached a safe distance and was about to turn a corner into a second hallway she stopped and bracing herself with her hands waited, thinking to shake off a trembling fit of weakness that had come upon her. The presence of the boy in the room had made her happy. In her bed, during the long hours alone, the little fears that had visited her had become giants. Now they were all gone. "When I get back to my room I shall sleep," she murmured gratefully.

But Elizabeth Willard was not to return to her bed and to sleep. As she stood trembling in the darkness the door of her son's room opened and the boy's father, Tom Willard, stepped out. In the light that streamed out at the door he stood with the knob in his hand and talked. What he said infuriated the woman.

Tom Willard was ambitious for his son. He had always thought of himself as a successful man, although nothing he had ever done had turned out successfully. However, when he was out of sight of the New Willard House and had no fear of coming upon his wife, he swaggered and began to dramatize himself as one of the chief men of the town. He wanted his son to succeed. He it was who had secured for the boy the position on the *Winesburg Eagle*. Now, with a ring of earnestness in his voice, he was advising concerning some course of conduct. "I tell you what, George, you've got to wake up," he said sharply. "Will Henderson has spoken to me three times concerning the matter. He says you go along for hours not hearing when you are spoken to and acting like a gawky girl. What ails you?" Tom Willard laughed good-naturedly. "Well, I guess you'll get over it," he said. "I told Will that. You're not a fool and you're not a woman. You're Tom Willard's son and you'll wake up. I'm not afraid. What you say clears things up. If being a newspaper man had put the notion of becoming a writer into your mind that's all right. Only I guess you'll have to wake up to do that too, eh?"

Tom Willard went briskly along the hallway and down a flight of stairs to the office. The woman in the darkness could hear him laughing and talking with a guest who was striving to wear away a dull evening by dozing in a chair by the office door. She returned to the door of her son's room.

The weakness had passed from her body as by a miracle and she stepped boldly along. A thousand ideas raced through her head. When she heard the scraping of a chair and the sound of a pen scratching upon paper, she again turned and went back along the hallway to her own room.

A definite determination had come into the mind of the defeated wife of the Winesburg hotel keeper. The determination was the result of long years of quiet and rather ineffectual thinking. "Now," she told herself, "I will act. There is something threatening my boy and I will ward it off." The fact that the conversation between Tom Willard and his son had been rather quiet and natural, as though an understanding existed between them, maddened her. Although for years she had hated her husband, her hatred had always before been a quite impersonal thing. He had been merely a part of something else that she hated. Now, and by the few words at the door, he had become the thing personified. In the darkness of her own room she clenched her fists and glared about. Going to a cloth bag that hung on a nail by the wall she took out a long pair of sewing scissors and held them in her hand like a dagger. "I will stab him," she said aloud. "He has chosen to be the voice of evil and I will kill him. When I have killed him something will snap within myself and I will die also. It will be a release for all of us."

In her girlhood and before her marriage with Tom Willard, Elizabeth had borne a somewhat shaky reputation in Winesburg. For years she had been what is called "stage-struck" and had paraded through the streets with traveling men guests at her father's hotel, wearing loud clothes and urging them to tell her of life in the cities out of which they had come. Once she startled the town by putting on men's clothes and riding a bicycle down Main Street.

In her own mind the tall dark girl had been in those days much confused. A great restlessness was in her and it expressed itself in two ways. First there was an uneasy desire for change, for some big definite movement to her life. It was this feeling that had turned her mind to the stage. She dreamed of joining some company and wandering over the world, seeing always new faces and giving something out of herself to all people. Sometimes at night she was quite beside herself with the thought, but when she tried to talk of the matter to the members of the theatrical companies that came to Winesburg and stopped at her father's hotel, she got nowhere. They did not seem to know what she meant, or if she did get something of her passion expressed, they only laughed. "It's not like that," they said. "It's as dull and uninteresting as this here. Nothing comes of it."

With the traveling men when she walked about with them, and later with Tom Willard, it was quite different. Always they seemed to understand and sympathize with her. On the side streets of the village, in the darkness under the trees, they took hold of her hand and she thought that something unexpressed in herself came forth and became a part of an unexpressed something in them.

And then there was the second expression of her restlessness. When that came she felt for a time released and happy. She did not blame the men who walked with her and later she did not blame Tom Willard. It was always the same, beginning with kisses and ending, after strange wild emotions, with peace and then sobbing repentance. When she sobbed she put her hand upon the face of the man and had always the same thought. Even though he were large and bearded she thought he had become suddenly a little boy. She wondered why he did not sob also.

In her room, tucked away in a corner of the old Willard

House, Elizabeth Willard lighted a lamp and put it on a dressing table that stood by the door. A thought had come into her mind and she went to a closet and brought out a small square box and set it on the table. The box contained material for make-up and had been left with other things by a theatrical company that had once been stranded in Winesburg. Elizabeth Willard had decided that she would be beautiful. Her hair was still black and there was a great mass of it braided and coiled about her head. The scene that was to take place in the office below began to grow in her mind. No ghostly worn-out figure should confront Tom Willard, but something quite unexpected and startling. Tall and with dusky cheeks and hair that fell in a mass from her shoulders, a figure should come striding down the stairway before the startled loungers in the hotel office. The figure would be silent—it would be swift and terrible. As a tigress whose cub had been threatened would she appear, coming out of the shadows, stealing noiselessly along and holding the long wicked scissors in her hand.

With a little broken sob in her throat, Elizabeth Willard blew out the light that stood upon the table and stood weak and trembling in the darkness. The strength that had been as a miracle in her body left and she half reeled across the floor, clutching at the back of the chair in which she had spent so many long days staring out over the tin roofs into the main street of Winesburg. In the hallway there was the sound of footsteps and George Willard came in at the door. Sitting in a chair beside his mother he began to talk. "I'm going to get out of here," he said. "I don't know where I shall go or what I shall do but I am going away."

The woman in the chair waited and trembled. An impulse came to her. "I suppose you had better wake up," she said. "You think that? You will go to the city and make money, eh? It will be better for you, you think, to be a

business man, to be brisk and smart and alive?" She waited
and trembled.

The son shook his head. "I suppose I can't make you
understand, but oh, I wish I could," he said earnestly. "I
can't even talk to father about it. I don't try. There isn't
any use. I don't know what I shall do. I just want to go
away and look at people and think."

Silence fell upon the room where the boy and woman
sat together. Again, as on the other evenings, they were
embarrassed. After a time the boy tried again to talk. "I
suppose it won't be for a year or two but I've been thinking
about it," he said, rising and going toward the door. "Something father said makes it sure that I shall have to go
away." He fumbled with the door knob. In the room the
silence became unbearable to the woman. She wanted to
cry out with joy because of the words that had come from
the lips of her son, but the expression of joy had become
impossible to her. "I think you had better go out among
the boys. You are too much indoors," she said. "I thought
I would go for a little walk," replied the son stepping
awkwardly out of the room and closing the door.

THE PHILOSOPHER

DOCTOR PARCIVAL was a large man with a drooping mouth covered by a yellow mustache. He always wore a dirty white waistcoat out of the pockets of which protruded a number of the kind of black cigars known as stogies. His teeth were black and irregular and there was something strange about his eyes. The lid of the left eye twitched; it fell down and snapped up; it was exactly as though the lid of the eye were a window shade and someone stood inside the doctor's head playing with the cord.

Doctor Parcival had a liking for the boy, George Willard. It began when George had been working for a year on the *Winesburg Eagle* and the acquaintanceship was entirely a matter of the doctor's own making.

In the late afternoon Will Henderson, owner and editor of the *Eagle*, went over to Tom Willy's saloon. Along an alleyway he went and slipping in at the back door of the saloon began drinking a drink made of a combination of sloe gin and soda water. Will Henderson was a sensualist and had reached the age of forty-five. He imagined the gin renewed the youth in him. Like most sensualists he enjoyed talking of women, and for an hour he lingered about gossiping with Tom Willy. The saloon keeper was a short, broad-shouldered man with peculiarly marked hands. That flaming kind of birthmark that sometimes paints with red the faces of men and women had touched with red Tom Willy's fingers and the backs of his hands. As he stood by the bar talking to Will Henderson he rubbed the

49

hands together. As he grew more and more excited the red of his fingers deepened. It was as though the hands had been dipped in blood that had dried and faded.

As Will Henderson stood at the bar looking at the red hands and talking of women, his assistant, George Willard, sat in the office of the *Winesburg Eagle* and listened to the talk of Doctor Parcival.

Doctor Parcival appeared immediately after Will Henderson had disappeared. One might have supposed that the doctor had been watching from his office window and had seen the editor going along the alleyway. Coming in at the front door and finding himself a chair, he lighted one of the stogies and crossing his legs began to talk. He seemed intent upon convincing the boy of the advisability of adopting a line of conduct that he was himself unable to define.

"If you have your eyes open you will see that although I call myself a doctor I have mighty few patients," he began. "There is a reason for that. It is not an accident and it is not because I do not know as much of medicine as anyone here. I do not want patients. The reason, you see, does not appear on the surface. It lies in fact in my character, which has, if you think about it, many strange turns. Why I want to talk to you of the matter I don't know. I might keep still and get more credit in your eyes. I have a desire to make you admire me, that's a fact. I don't know why. That's why I talk. It's very amusing, eh?"

Sometimes the doctor launched into long tales concerning himself. To the boy the tales were very real and full of meaning. He began to admire the fat unclean-looking man and, in the afternoon when Will Henderson had gone, looked forward with keen interest to the doctor's coming.

Doctor Parcival had been in Winesburg about five years.

He came from Chicago and when he arrived was drunk and got into a fight with Albert Longworth, the baggage-man. The fight concerned a trunk and ended by the doctor's being escorted to the village lockup. When he was released he rented a room above a shoe-repairing shop at the lower end of Main Street and put out the sign that announced himself as a doctor. Although he had but few patients and these of the poorer sort who were unable to pay, he seemed to have plenty of money for his needs. He slept in the office that was unspeakably dirty and dined at Biff Carter's lunch room in a small frame building oppo-site the railroad station. In the summer the lunch room was filled with flies and Biff Carter's white apron was more dirty than his floor. Doctor Parcival did not mind. Into the lunch room he stalked and deposited twenty cents upon the counter. "Feed me what you wish for that," he said laughing. "Use up food that you wouldn't otherwise sell. It makes no difference to me. I am a man of distinction, you see. Why should I concern myself with what I eat."

The tales that Doctor Parcival told George Willard began nowhere and ended nowhere. Sometimes the boy thought they must all be inventions, a pack of lies. And then again he was convinced that they contained the very essence of truth.

"I was a reporter like you here," Doctor Parcival began. "It was in a town in Iowa—or was it in Illinois? I don't remember and anyway it makes no difference. Perhaps I am trying to conceal my identity and don't want to be very definite. Have you ever thought it strange that I have money for my needs although I do nothing? I may have stolen a great sum of money or been involved in a murder before I came here. There is food for thought in that, eh? If you were a really smart newspaper reporter you would look me up. In Chicago there was a Doctor Cronin who was murdered. Have you heard of that? Some men murdered him and put him in a trunk. In the early morning they hauled the trunk across the city. It sat on the back of an express wagon and they were on the seat as unconcerned as anything. Along they went through quiet streets where everyone was asleep. The sun was just coming up over the lake. Funny, eh—just to think of them smoking pipes and chattering as they drove along as unconcerned as I am now. Perhaps I was one of those men. That would be a strange turn of things, now wouldn't it, eh?" Again Doctor Parcival began his tale: "Well, anyway there I was, a reporter on a paper just as you are here, running about and getting little items to print. My mother was poor. She took in washing. Her dream was to make me a Presbyterian minister and I was studying with that end in view.

"My father had been insane for a number of years. He was in an asylum over at Dayton, Ohio. There you see I have let it slip out! All of this took place in Ohio, right here in Ohio. There is a clew if you ever get the notion of looking me up.

"I was going to tell you of my brother. That's the object of all this. That's what I'm getting at. My brother was a railroad painter and had a job on the Big Four. You know that road runs through Ohio here. With other men he lived in a box car and away they went from town to town painting the railroad property—switches, crossing gates, bridges, and stations.

"The Big Four paints its stations a nasty orange color. How I hated that color! My brother was always covered with it. On pay days he used to get drunk and come home wearing his paint-covered clothes and bringing his money with him. He did not give it to mother but laid it in a pile on our kitchen table.

"About the house he went in the clothes covered with the nasty orange colored paint. I can see the picture. My mother, who was small and had red, sad-looking eyes, would come into the house from a little shed at the back. That's where she spent her time over the washtub scrubbing people's dirty clothes. In she would come and stand by the table, rubbing her eyes with her apron that was covered with soap-suds.

" 'Don't touch it! Don't you dare touch that money,' my brother roared, and then he himself took five or ten dollars and went tramping off to the saloons. When he had spent what he had taken he came back for more. He never gave my mother any money at all but stayed about until he had spent it all, a little at a time. Then he went back to his job with the painting crew on the railroad. After he had gone things began to arrive at our house, groceries and such things. Sometimes there would be a dress for mother or a pair of shoes for me.

"Strange, eh? My mother loved my brother much more than she did me, although he never said a kind word to either of us and always raved up and down threatening us if we dared so much as touch the money that sometimes lay on the table three days.

"We got along pretty well. I studied to be a minister and prayed. I was a regular ass about saying prayers. You should have heard me. When my father died I prayed all night, just as I did sometimes when my brother was in town drinking and going about buying the things for us. In the evening after supper I knelt by the table where the money lay and prayed for hours. When no one was looking I stole a dollar or two and put it in my pocket. That makes me laugh now but then it was terrible. It was on my mind all the time. I got six dollars a week from my job on the paper and always took it straight home to mother. The few dollars I stole from my brother's pile I spent on myself, you know, for trifles, candy and cigarettes and such things.

"When my father died at the asylum over at Dayton, I went over there. I borrowed some money from the man for whom I worked and went on the train at night. It was raining. In the asylum they treated me as though I were a king.

"The men who had jobs in the asylum had found out I was a newspaper reporter. That made them afraid. There had been some negligence, some carelessness, you see, when father was ill. They thought perhaps I would write it up in the paper and make a fuss. I never intended to do anything of the kind.

"Anyway, in I went to the room where my father lay dead and blessed the dead body. I wonder what put that notion into my head. Wouldn't my brother, the painter, have laughed, though. There I stood over the dead body and spread out my hands. The superintendent of the asylum and some of his helpers came in and stood about looking sheepish. It was very amusing. I spread out my hands and said, 'Let peace brood over this carcass.' That's what I said."

Jumping to his feet and breaking off the tale, Doctor Parcival began to walk up and down in the office of the *Winesburg Eagle* where George Willard sat listening. He was awkward and, as the office was small, continually knocked against things. "What a fool I am to be talking," he said. "That is not my object in coming here and forcing my acquaintanceship upon you. I have something else in mind. You are a reporter just as I was once and you have attracted my attention. You may end by becoming just such another fool. I want to warn you and keep on warning you. That's why I seek you out."

Doctor Parcival began talking of George Willard's attitude toward men. It seemed to the boy that the man had but one object in view, to make everyone seem despicable. "I want to fill you with hatred and contempt so that you will be a superior being," he declared. "Look at my brother. There was a fellow, eh? He despised everyone, you see. You have no idea with what contempt he looked upon mother and me. And was he not our superior? You know he was. You have not seen him and yet I have made you feel that. I have given you a sense of it. He is dead. Once when he was drunk he lay down on the tracks and the car in which he lived with the other painters ran over him."

❀◇❀

One day in August Doctor Parcival had an adventure in Winesburg. For a month George Willard had been going each morning to spend an hour in the doctor's office. The visits came about through a desire on the part of the doctor to read to the boy from the pages of a book he was in the process of writing. To write the book Doctor Parcival declared was the object of his coming to Winesburg to live.

On the morning in August before the coming of the boy, an incident had happened in the doctor's office. There had been an accident on Main Street. A team of horses had been frightened by a train and had run away. A little girl, the daughter of a farmer, had been thrown from a buggy and killed.

On Main Street everyone had become excited and a cry

for doctors had gone up. All three of the active practitioners of the town had come quickly but had found the child
dead. From the crowd someone had run to the office of
Doctor Parcival who had bluntly refused to go down out
of his office to the dead child. The useless cruelty of his
refusal had passed unnoticed. Indeed, the man who had
come up the stairway to summon him had hurried away
without hearing the refusal.

All of this, Doctor Parcival did not know and when
George Willard came to his office he found the man shaking with terror. "What I have done will arouse the people
of this town," he declared excitedly. "Do I not know human nature? Do I not know what will happen? Word of
my refusal will be whispered about. Presently men will
get together in groups and talk of it. They will come here.
We will quarrel and there will be talk of hanging. Then
they will come again bearing a rope in their hands."

Doctor Parcival shook with fright. "I have a presenti-
ment," he declared emphatically. "It may be that what I
am talking about will not occur this morning. It may be
put off until tonight but I will be hanged. Everyone will
get excited. I will be hanged to a lamp-post on Main
Street."

Going to the door of his dirty office, Doctor Parcival
looked timidly down the stairway leading to the street.
When he returned the fright that had been in his eyes
was beginning to be replaced by doubt. Coming on tiptoe
across the room he tapped George Willard on the shoulder.
"If not now, sometime," he whispered, shaking his head.
"In the end I will be crucified, uselessly crucified."

Doctor Parcival began to plead with George Willard.
"You must pay attention to me," he urged. "If something
happens perhaps you will be able to write the book that
I may never get written. The idea is very simple, so simple

that if you are not careful you will forget it. It is this—that
everyone in the world is Christ and they are all crucified.
That's what I want to say. Don't you forget that. Whatever happens, don't you dare let yourself forget."

NOBODY KNOWS

LOOKING CAUTIOUSLY about, George Willard arose from his desk in the office of the *Winesburg Eagle* and went hurriedly out at the back door. The night was warm and cloudy and although it was not yet eight o'clock, the alleyway back of the *Eagle* office was pitch dark. A team of horses tied to a post somewhere in the darkness stamped on the hard-baked ground. A cat sprang from under George Willard's feet and ran away into the night. The young man was nervous. All day he had gone about his work like one dazed by a blow. In the alleyway he trembled as though with fright.

In the darkness George Willard walked along the alleyway, going carefully and cautiously. The back doors of the Winesburg stores were open and he could see men sitting about under the store lamps. In Myerbaum's Notion Store Mrs. Willy the saloon keeper's wife stood by the counter with a basket on her arm. Sid Green the clerk was waiting on her. He leaned over the counter and talked earnestly.

George Willard crouched and then jumped through the path of light that came out at the door. He began to run forward in the darkness. Behind Ed Griffith's saloon old Jerry Bird the town drunkard lay asleep on the ground. The runner stumbled over the sprawling legs. He laughed brokenly.

George Willard had set forth upon an adventure. All day he had been trying to make up his mind to go through with the adventure and now he was acting. In the office of the *Winesburg Eagle* he had been sitting since six o'clock trying to think.

There had been no decision. He had just jumped to his feet, hurried past Will Henderson who was reading proof in the printshop and started to run along the alleyway.

Through street after street went George Willard, avoiding the people who passed. He crossed and recrossed the road. When he passed a street lamp he pulled his hat down over his face. He did not dare think. In his mind there was a fear but it was a new kind of fear. He was afraid the adventure on which he had set out would be spoiled, that he would lose courage and turn back.

George Willard found Louise Trunnion in the kitchen of her father's house. She was washing dishes by the light of a kerosene lamp. There she stood behind the screen door in the little shedlike kitchen at the back of the house. George Willard stopped by a picket fence and tried to control the shaking of his body. Only a narrow potato patch separated him from the adventure. Five minutes passed before he felt sure enough of himself to call to her. "Louise! Oh, Louise!" he called. The cry stuck in his throat. His voice became a hoarse whisper.

Louise Trunnion came out across the potato patch holding the dish cloth in her hand. "How do you know I want to go out with you," she said sulkily. "What makes you so sure?"

George Willard did not answer. In silence the two stood in the darkness with the fence between them. "You go on along," she said. "Pa's in there. I'll come along. You wait by Williams' barn."

The young newspaper reporter had received a letter from Louise Trunnion. It had come that morning to the office of the *Winesburg Eagle*. The letter was brief. "I'm yours if you want me," it said. He thought it annoying that in the darkness by the fence she had pretended there was nothing between them. "She has a nerve! Well, gracious sakes, she has a nerve," he muttered as he went along the street and passed a row of vacant lots where corn grew. The corn was shoulder high and had been planted right down to the sidewalk.

When Louise Trunnion came out of the front door of her house she still wore the gingham dress in which she had been washing dishes. There was no hat on her head. The boy could see her standing with the doorknob in her hand talking to someone within, no doubt to old Jake Trunnion, her father. Old Jake was half deaf and she shouted. The door closed and everything was dark and silent in the little side street. George Willard trembled more violently than ever.

In the shadows by Williams' barn George and Louise stood, not daring to talk. She was not particularly comely and there was a black smudge on the side of her nose. George thought she must have rubbed her nose with her finger after she had been handling some of the kitchen pots.

The young man began to laugh nervously. "It's warm," he said. He wanted to touch her with his hand. "I'm not very bold," he thought. Just to touch the folds of the soiled gingham dress would, he decided, be an exquisite pleasure. She began to quibble. ["You think you're better than I am. Don't tell me, I guess I know,"] she said drawing closer to him.

[A flood of words] burst from George Willard. He remembered the look that had lurked in the girl's eyes when they had met on the streets and thought of the note she had

written. Doubt left him. The whispered tales concerning
her that had gone about town gave him confidence. He became wholly the male, bold and aggressive. In his heart
there was no sympathy for her. "Ah, come on, it'll be all
right. There won't be anyone know anything. How can
they know?" he urged.

They began to walk along a narrow brick sidewalk between the cracks of which tall weeds grew. Some of the
bricks were missing and the sidewalk was rough and irregular. He took hold of her hand that was also rough and
thought it delightfully small. "I can't go far," she said and
her voice was quiet, unperturbed.

They crossed a bridge that ran over a tiny stream and
passed another vacant lot in which corn grew. The street
ended. In the path at the side of the road they were compelled to walk one behind the other. Will Overton's berry
field lay beside the road and there was a pile of boards.
"Will is going to build a shed to store berry crates here,"
said George and they sat down upon the boards.

❀❖❀

When George Willard got back into Main Street it was
past ten o'clock and had begun to rain. Three times he
walked up and down the length of Main Street. Sylvester
West's Drug Store was still open and he went in and
bought a cigar. When Shorty Crandall the clerk came out
at the door with him he was pleased. For five minutes the
two stood in the shelter of the store awning and talked.
George Willard felt satisfied. He had wanted more than
anything else to talk to some man. Around a corner toward the New Willard House he went whistling softly.

On the sidewalk at the side of Winney's Dry Goods

Store where there was a high board fence covered with circus pictures, he stopped whistling and stood perfectly still in the darkness, attentive, listening as though for a voice calling his name. Then again he laughed nervously. "She hasn't got anything on me. Nobody knows," he muttered doggedly and went on his way.

GODLINESS

A TALE IN FOUR PARTS

Part One

THERE WERE always three or four old people
sitting on the front porch of the house or puttering about
the garden of the Bentley farm. Three of the old people
were women and sisters to Jesse. They were a colorless,
soft-voiced lot. Then there was a silent old man with thin
white hair who was Jesse's uncle.

The farmhouse was built of wood, a board outer-cover-
ing over a framework of logs. It was in reality not one
house but a cluster of houses joined together in a rather
haphazard manner. Inside, the place was full of surprises.
One went up steps from the living room into the dining
room and there were always steps to be ascended or descended in passing from one room to another. At meal
times the place was like a beehive. At one moment all was
quiet, then doors began to open, feet clattered on stairs, a
murmur of soft voices arose and people appeared from a
dozen obscure corners.

Beside the old people, already mentioned, many others
lived in the Bentley house. There were four hired men, a
woman named Aunt Callie Beebe, who was in charge of
the housekeeping, a dull-witted girl named Eliza Stough-

ton, who made beds and helped with the milking, a boy who worked in the stables, and Jesse Bentley himself, the owner and overlord of it all.

By the time the American Civil War had been over for twenty years, that part of Northern Ohio where the Bentley farms lay had begun to emerge from pioneer life. Jesse then owned machinery for harvesting grain. He had built modern barns and most of his land was drained with carefully laid tile drain, but in order to understand the man we will have to go back to an earlier day.

The Bentley family had been in Northern Ohio for several generations before Jesse's time. They came from New York State and took up land when the country was new and land could be had at a low price. For a long time they, in common with all the other Middle Western people, were very poor. The land they had settled upon was heavily wooded and covered with fallen logs and underbrush. After the long hard labor of clearing these away and cutting the timber, there were still the stumps to be reckoned with. Plows run through the fields caught on hidden roots, stones lay all about, on the low places water gathered, and the young corn turned yellow, sickened and died.

When Jesse Bentley's father and brothers had come into their ownership of the place, much of the harder part of the work of clearing had been done, but they clung to old traditions and worked like driven animals. They lived as practically all of the farming people of the time lived. In the spring and through most of the winter the highways leading into the town of Winesburg were a sea of mud. The four young men of the family worked hard all day in the fields, they ate heavily of coarse, greasy food, and at night slept like tired beasts on beds of straw. Into their lives came little that was not coarse and brutal and outwardly they were themselves coarse and brutal. On Saturday afternoons they hitched a team of horses to a three-seated wagon and went off to town. In town they stood about the stoves in the stores talking to other farmers or to the store keepers. They were dressed in overalls and in the winter wore heavy coats that were flecked with mud. Their hands as they stretched them out to the heat of the stoves were cracked and red. It was difficult for them to talk and so they for the most part kept silent. When they had bought meat, flour, sugar, and salt, they went into one of the Winesburg saloons and drank beer. Under the influence of drink the naturally strong lusts of their natures, kept suppressed by the heroic labor of breaking up new ground, were released. A kind of crude and animal-like poetic fervor took possession of them. On the road home they stood up on the wagon seats and shouted at the stars. Sometimes they fought long and bitterly and at other times they broke forth into songs. Once Enoch Bentley, the older one of the boys, struck his father, old Tom Bentley, with the butt of a teamster's whip, and the old man seemed likely to die. For days Enoch lay hid in the straw in the loft of the stable ready to flee if the result of his momentary passion turned out to be murder. He was kept alive with food brought by his mother, who also kept him informed of the injured man's condition. When all turned out well he emerged from his hiding place and went back to the work of clearing land as though nothing had happened.

❀◆❀

The Civil War brought a sharp turn to the fortunes of the Bentleys and was responsible for the rise of the youngest son, Jesse. Enoch, Edward, Harry, and Will Bentley all enlisted and before the long war ended they were all killed. For a time after they went away to the South, old Tom tried to run the place, but he was not successful. When the last of the four had been killed he sent word to Jesse that he would have to come home.

Then the mother, who had not been well for a year, died suddenly, and the father became altogether discouraged. He talked of selling the farm and moving into town. All day he went about shaking his head and muttering. The work in the fields was neglected and weeds grew high in the corn. Old Tom hired men but he did not use them intelligently. When they had gone away to the fields in the morning he wandered into the woods and sat down on a log. Sometimes he forgot to come home at night and one of the daughters had to go in search of him.

When Jesse Bentley came home to the farm and began to take charge of things he was a slight, sensitive-looking man of twenty-two. At eighteen he had left home to go to school to become a scholar and eventually to become a minister of the Presbyterian Church. All through his boyhood he had been what in our country was called an "odd sheep" and had not got on with his brothers. Of all the family only his mother had understood him and she was now dead. When he came home to take charge of the farm, that had at that time grown to more than six hundred acres, everyone on the farms about and in the nearby town of Winesburg smiled at the idea of his trying to handle the work that had been done by his four strong brothers.

There was indeed good cause to smile. By the standards of his day Jesse did not look like a man at all. He was small and very slender and womanish of body and, true to the traditions of young ministers, wore a long black coat and a narrow black string tie. The neighbors were amused when they saw him, after the years away, and they were even more amused when they saw the woman he had married in the city.

As a matter of fact, Jesse's wife did soon go under. That was perhaps Jesse's fault. A farm in Northern Ohio in the hard years after the Civil War was no place for a delicate woman, and Katherine Bentley was delicate. Jesse was hard with her as he was with everybody about him in those days. She tried to do such work as all the neighbor women about her did and he let her go on without interference. She helped to do the milking and did part of the housework; she made the beds for the men and prepared their food. For a year she worked every day from sunrise until late at night and then after giving birth to a child she died.

As for Jesse Bentley—although he was a delicately built man there was something within him that could not easily be killed. He had brown curly hair and grey eyes that were at times hard and direct, at times wavering and uncertain. Not only was he slender but he was also short of stature. His mouth was like the mouth of a sensitive and very determined child. Jesse Bentley was a fanatic. He was a man born out of his time and place and for this he suffered and made others suffer. Never did he succeed in getting what he wanted out of life and he did not know what he wanted. Within a very short time after he came home to the Bentley farm he made everyone there a little afraid of him, and his wife, who should have been close to him as his mother had been, was afraid also. At the end of two weeks after his coming, old Tom Bentley made over to him the entire ownership of the place and retired into the background. Everyone retired into the background. In spite of his youth and inexperience, Jesse had the trick of mastering the souls of his people. He was so in earnest in everything he did and said that no one understood him. He made everyone on the farm work as they had never worked before and yet there was no joy in the work. If things went well they went well for Jesse and never for the people who were his dependents. Like a thousand other strong men who have come into the world here in America in these later times, Jesse was but half strong. He could master others but he could not master himself. The running of the farm as it had never been run before was easy for him. When he came home from Cleveland where he had been in school, he shut himself off from all of his people and began to make plans. He thought about the farm night and day and that made him successful. Other men on the farms about him worked too hard and were too tired to think, but to think of the farm and to be everlastingly making plans for its success was a relief to Jesse. It partially satisfied something in his passionate nature. Immediately after he came home he had a wing built on to the old house and in a large room facing the west he had windows that looked into the barnyard and other windows that looked off across the fields. By the window he sat down to think. Hour after hour and day after day he sat and looked over the land and thought out his new place in life. The passionate burning thing in his nature flamed up and his eyes became hard. He wanted to make the farm produce as no farm in his state had ever produced before and then he wanted something else. It was the indefinable hunger within that made his eyes waver and that kept him always more and more silent before people. He would have given much to achieve peace and in him was a fear that peace was the thing he could not achieve.

All over his body Jesse Bentley was alive. In his small frame was gathered the force of a long line of strong men.

He had always been extraordinarily alive when he was a
small boy on the farm and later when he was a young man
in school. In the school he had studied and thought of
God and the Bible with his whole mind and heart. As time
passed and he grew to know people better, he began to
think of himself as an extraordinary man, one set apart
from his fellows. He wanted terribly to make his life
a thing of great importance, and as he looked about at his
fellow men and saw how like clods they lived it seemed to
him that he could not bear to become also such a clod. Although in his absorption in himself and in his own destiny
he was blind to the fact that his young wife was doing a
strong woman's work even after she had become large
with child and that she was killing herself in his service,
he did not intend to be unkind to her. When his father,
who was old and twisted with toil, made over to him the
ownership of the farm and seemed content to creep away
to a corner and wait for death, he shrugged his shoulders
and dismissed the old man from his mind.

In the room by the window overlooking the land that
had come down to him sat Jesse thinking of his own affairs.
In the stables he could hear the tramping of his horses
and the restless movement of his cattle. Away in the fields
he could see other cattle wandering over green hills. The
voices of men, his men who worked for him, came in to
him through the window. From the milkhouse there was
the steady thump, thump of a churn being manipulated
by the half-witted girl, Eliza Stoughton. Jesse's mind went
back to the men of Old Testament days who had
also owned lands and herds. He remembered how God
had come down out of the skies and talked to these men
and he wanted God to notice and to talk to him also. A
kind of feverish boyish eagerness to in some way achieve
in his own life the flavor of significance that had hung

over these men took possession of him. Being a prayerful man he spoke of the matter aloud to God and the sound of his own words strengthened and fed his eagerness.

"I am a new kind of man come into possession of these fields," he declared. "Look upon me, O God, and look Thou also upon my neighbors and all the men who have gone before me here! O God, create in me another Jesse, like that one of old, to rule over men and to be the father of sons who shall be rulers!" Jesse grew excited as he talked aloud and jumping to his feet walked up and down in the room. In fancy he saw himself living in old times and among old peoples. The land that lay stretched out before him became of vast significance, a place peopled by his fancy with a new race of men sprung from himself. It seemed to him that in his day as in those other and older days, kingdoms might be created and new impulses given to the lives of men by the power of God speaking through a chosen servant. He longed to be such a servant. "It is God's work I have come to the land to do," he declared in a loud voice and his short figure straightened and he thought that something like a halo of Godly approval hung over him.

❧◆❧

It will perhaps be somewhat difficult for the men and women of a later day to understand Jesse Bentley. In the last fifty years a vast change has taken place in the lives of our people. A revolution has in fact taken place. The coming of industrialism, attended by all the roar and rattle of affairs, the shrill cries of millions of new voices that have come among us from overseas, the going and coming of trains, the growth of cities, the building of the interurban car lines that weave in and out of towns and past farm-

houses, and now in these later days the coming of the auto-
mobiles has worked a tremendous change in the lives
and in the habits of thought of our people of Mid-
America. Books, badly imagined and written though they
may be in the hurry of our times, are in every household,
magazines circulate by the millions of copies, newspapers
are everywhere. In our day a farmer standing by the stove
in the store in his village has his mind filled to overflowing
with the words of other men. The newspapers and the
magazines have pumped him full. [Much of the old brutal
ignorance that had in it also a kind of beautiful childlike
innocence is gone forever. The farmer by the stove is
brother to the men of the cities, and if you listen you will
find him talking as glibly and as senselessly as the best city
man of us all.]

In Jesse Bentley's time and in the country districts of
the whole Middle West in the years after the Civil War it
was not so. Men labored too hard and were too tired to
read. In them was no desire for words printed upon paper. As they worked in the fields, vague, half-formed
thoughts took possession of them. They believed in God
and in God's power to control their lives. In the little Protestant churches they gathered on Sunday to hear of God
and his works. The churches were the center of the social
and intellectual life of the times. The figure of God was
big in the hearts of men.

And so, having been born an imaginative child and having within him a great intellectual eagerness, Jesse
Bentley had turned wholeheartedly toward God. When
the war took his brothers away, he saw the hand of God in
that. When his father became ill and could no longer attend to the running of the farm, he took that also as a sign
from God. In the city, when the word came to him, he
walked about at night through the streets thinking of the

matter and when he had come home and had got the work
on the farm well under way, he went again at night to
walk through the forests and over the low hills and to
think of God.

As he walked the importance of his own figure in some
divine plan grew in his mind. He grew avaricious and was
impatient that the farm contained only six hundred acres.
Kneeling in a fence corner at the edge of some meadow,
he sent his voice abroad into the silence and looking up
he saw the stars shining down at him.

One evening, some months after his father's death, and
when his wife Katherine was expecting at any moment to
be laid abed of childbirth, Jesse left his house and went
for a long walk. The Bentley farm was situated in a tiny
valley watered by Wine Creek, and Jesse walked along
the banks of the stream to the end of his own land and on
through the fields of his neighbors. As he walked the valley broadened and then narrowed again. Great open
stretches of field and wood lay before him. The moon
came out from behind clouds, and, climbing a low hill, he
sat down to think.

Jesse thought that as the true servant of God the entire
stretch of country through which he had walked should
have come into his possession. He thought of his dead
brothers and blamed them that they had not worked
harder and achieved more. Before him in the moonlight
the tiny stream ran down over stones, and he began to
think of the men of old times who like himself had owned
flocks and lands.

A fantastic impulse, half fear, half greediness, took possession of Jesse Bentley. He remembered how in the old
Bible story the Lord had appeared to that other Jesse and
told him to send his son David to where Saul and the men
of Israel were fighting the Philistines in the Valley

of Elah. Into Jesse's mind came the conviction that all of the Ohio farmers who owned land in the valley of Wine Creek were Philistines and enemies of God. "Suppose," he whispered to himself, "there should come from among them one who, like Goliath the Philistine of Gath, could defeat me and take from me my possessions." In fancy he felt the sickening dread that he thought must have lain heavy on the heart of Saul before the coming of David. Jumping to his feet, he began to run through the night. As he ran he called to God. His voice carried far over the low hills. "Jehovah of Hosts," he cried, "send to me this night out of the womb of Katherine, a son. Let Thy grace alight upon me. Send me a son to be called David who shall help me to pluck at last all of these lands out of the hands of the Philistines and turn them to Thy service and to the building of Thy kingdom on earth."

Part Two

DAVID HARDY of Winesburg, Ohio, was the grandson of Jesse Bentley, the owner of Bentley farms. When he was twelve years old he went to the old Bentley place to live. His mother, Louise Bentley, the girl who came into the world on that night when Jesse ran through the fields crying to God that he be given a son, had grown to womanhood on the farm and had married young John Hardy of Winesburg, who became a banker. Louise and her husband did not live happily together and everyone agreed that she was to blame. She was a small woman with sharp grey eyes and black hair. From childhood she had been inclined to fits of temper and when not angry she was often morose and silent. In Winesburg it was said that she drank. Her husband, the banker, who was a careful, shrewd man, tried hard to make her happy. When he began to make money he bought for her a large brick house on Elm Street in Winesburg and he was the first man in that town to keep a manservant to drive his wife's carriage.

But Louise could not be made happy. She flew into half insane fits of temper during which she was sometimes silent, sometimes noisy and quarrelsome. She swore and cried out in her anger. She got a knife from the kitchen and threatened her husband's life. Once she deliberately set fire to the house, and often she hid herself away for days in her own room and would see no one. Her life, lived as a half recluse, gave rise to all sorts of stories concerning her. It was said that she took drugs and that she hid herself away from people because she was often so under the influence of drink that her condition could not be concealed. Sometimes on summer afternoons she came out of the house and got into her carriage. Dismissing the driver she took the reins in her own hands and drove off at top speed through the streets. If a pedestrian got in her way she drove straight ahead and the frightened citizen had to escape as best he could. To the people of the town it seemed as though she wanted to run them down. When she had driven through several streets, tearing around corners and beating the horses with the whip, she drove off into the country. On the country roads after she had gotten out of sight of the houses she let the horses slow down to a walk and her wild, reckless mood passed She became thoughtful and muttered words. Sometimes tears came into her eyes. And then when she came back into town she again drove furiously through the quiet streets. But for the influence of her husband and the respect he inspired in people's minds she would have been arrested more than once by the town marshal.

Young David Hardy grew up in the house with this woman and as can well be imagined there was not much joy in his childhood. He was too young then to have opinions of his own about people, but at times it was difficult for him not to have very definite opinions about the woman who was his mother. David was always a quiet, orderly boy and for a long time was thought by the people of Winesburg to be something of a dullard. His eyes were brown and as a child he had a habit of looking at things and people a long time without appearing to see what he was looking at. When he heard his mother spoken of harshly or when he overheard her berating his father, he was frightened and ran away to hide. Sometimes he could not find a hiding place and that confused him. Turning his face toward a tree or if he was indoors toward the wall, he closed his eyes and tried not to think of anything. He had a habit of talking aloud to himself, and early in life a spirit of quiet sadness often took possession of him.

On the occasions when David went to visit his grandfather on the Bentley farm, he was altogether contented and happy. Often he wished that he would never have to go back to town and once when he had come home from the farm after a long visit, something happened that had a lasting effect on his mind.

David had come back into town with one of the hired men. The man was in a hurry to go about his own affairs and left the boy at the head of the street in which the Hardy house stood. It was early dusk of a fall evening and the sky was overcast with clouds. Something happened to David. He could not bear to go into the house where his mother and father lived, and on an impulse he decided to run away from home. He intended to go back to the farm and to his grandfather, but lost his way and for hours he wandered weeping and frightened on country roads. It started to rain and lightning flashed in the sky. The boy's imagination was excited and he fancied that he could see and hear strange things in the darkness. Into his mind came the conviction that he was walking and running in some terrible void where no one had ever been before. The darkness about him seemed limitless. The sound of the wind blowing in trees was terrifying. When a team of horses approached along the road in which he walked he was frightened and climbed a fence. Through a field he ran until he came into another road and getting upon his knees felt of the soft ground with his fingers. But for the figure of his grandfather, whom he was afraid he would never find in the darkness, he thought the world must be altogether empty. When his cries were heard by a farmer who was walking home from town and he was brought back to his father's house, he was so tired and excited that he did not know what was happening to him.

By chance David's father knew that he had disappeared. On the street he had met the farm hand from the Bentley place and knew of his son's return to town. When the boy did not come home an alarm was set up and John Hardy with several men of the town went to search the country. The report that David had been kidnapped ran about through the streets of Winesburg. When he came home there were no lights in the house, but his mother appeared and clutched him eagerly in her arms. David thought she had suddenly become another woman. He could not believe that so delightful a thing had happened. With her own hands Louise Hardy bathed his tired young body and cooked him food. She would not let him go to bed but, when he had put on his nightgown, blew out the lights and sat down in a chair to hold him in her arms. For an hour the woman sat in the darkness and held her boy. All the time she kept talking in a low voice. David could not understand what had so changed her. Her habitually dissatisfied face had become, he thought, the most peaceful and lovely thing he had ever seen. When he began to weep she held him more and more tightly. On and on went her voice. It was not harsh or shrill as when she talked to her husband, but was like rain falling on trees. Presently men began coming to the door to report that he had not been found, but she made him hide and be silent until she had sent them away. He thought it must be a game his mother and the men of the town were playing with him and laughed joyously. Into his mind came the thought that his having been lost and frightened in the darkness was an altogether unimportant matter. He thought that he would have been willing to go through the frightful experience a thousand times to be sure of finding at the end of the long black road a thing so lovely as his mother had suddenly become.

❀❖❀

During the last years of young David's boyhood he saw his mother but seldom and she became for him just a woman with whom he had once lived. Still he could not get her figure out of his mind and as he grew older it became more definite. When he was twelve years old he went to the Bentley farm to live. Old Jesse came into town and fairly demanded that he be given charge of the boy. The old man was excited and determined on having his own way. He talked to John Hardy in the office of the Winesburg Savings Bank and then the two men went to the house on Elm Street to talk with Louise. They both expected her to make trouble but were mistaken. She was very quiet and when Jesse had explained his mission and had gone on at some length about the advantages to come through having the boy out of doors and in the quiet atmosphere of the old farmhouse, she nodded her head in approval. "It is an atmosphere not corrupted by my presence," she said sharply. Her shoulders shook and she seemed about to fly into a fit of temper. "It is a place for a man child, although it was never a place for me," she went on. "You never wanted me there and of course the air of your house did me no good. It was like poison in my blood but it will be different with him."

Louise turned and went out of the room, leaving the

two men to sit in embarrassed silence. As very often happened she later stayed in her room for days. Even when the boy's clothes were packed and he was taken away she did not appear. The loss of her son made a sharp break in her life and she seemed less inclined to quarrel with her husband. John Hardy thought it had all turned out very well indeed.

And so young David went to live in the Bentley farmhouse with Jesse. Two of the old farmer's sisters were alive and still lived in the house. They were afraid of Jesse and rarely spoke when he was about. One of the women who had been noted for her flaming red hair when she was younger was a born mother and became the boy's caretaker. Every night when he had gone to bed she went into his room and sat on the floor until he fell asleep. When he became drowsy she became bold and whispered things that he later thought he must have dreamed.

Her soft low voice called him endearing names and he dreamed that his mother had come to him and that she had changed so that she was always as she had been that time after he ran away. He also grew bold and reaching out his hand stroked the face of the woman on the floor so that she was ecstatically happy. Everyone in the old house became happy after the boy went there. The hard insistent thing in Jesse Bentley that had kept the people in the house silent and timid and that had never been dispelled by the presence of the girl Louise was apparently swept away by the coming of the boy. It was as though God had relented and sent a son to the man.

The man who had proclaimed himself the only true servant of God in all the valley of Wine Creek, and who had wanted God to send him a sign of approval by way of a son out of the womb of Katherine, began to think that at last his prayers had been answered. Although he was at that time only fifty-five years old he looked seventy and was worn out with much thinking and scheming. The effort he had made to extend his land holdings had been successful and there were few farms in the valley that did not belong to him, but until David came he was a bitterly disappointed man.

There were two influences at work in Jesse Bentley and all his life his mind had been a battleground for these influences. First there was the old thing in him. He wanted to be a man of God and a leader among men of God. His walking in the fields and through the forests at night had brought him close to nature and there were forces in the passionately religious man that ran out to the forces in nature. The disappointment that had come to him when a daughter and not a son had been born to Katherine had fallen upon him like a blow struck by some unseen hand and the blow had somewhat softened his egotism. He still believed that God might at any moment make himself manifest out of the winds or the clouds, but he no longer demanded such recognition. Instead he prayed for it. Sometimes he was altogether doubtful and thought God had deserted the world. He regretted the fate that had not let him live in a simpler and sweeter time when at the beckoning of some strange cloud in the sky men left their lands and houses and went forth into the wilderness to create new races. While he worked night and day to make his farms more productive and to extend his holdings of land, he regretted that he could not use his own restless energy in the building of temples, the slaying of unbelievers and in general in the work of glorifying God's name on earth.

That is what Jesse hungered for and then also he hungered for something else. He had grown into maturity in America in the years after the Civil War and he, like all

men of his time, had been touched by the deep influences
that were at work in the country during those years when
modern industrialism was being born. He began to buy
machines that would permit him to do the work of the
farms while employing fewer men and he sometimes
thought that if he were a younger man he would give up
farming altogether and start a factory in Winesburg for
the making of machinery. Jesse formed the habit of reading newspapers and magazines. He invented a machine
for the making of fence out of wire. Faintly he realized
that the atmosphere of old times and places that he had
always cultivated in his own mind was strange and foreign
to the thing that was growing up in the minds of others.
The beginning of the most materialistic age in the history of the world, when wars would be fought without
patriotism, when men would forget God and only pay attention to moral standards, when the will to power would
replace the will to serve and beauty would be well-nigh
forgotten in the terrible headlong rush of mankind toward
the acquiring of possessions, was telling its story to Jesse
the man of God as it was to the men about him.
The greedy thing in him wanted to make money faster
than it could be made by tilling the land. More than once
he went into Winesburg to talk with his son-in-law John
Hardy about it. "You are a banker and you will have
chances I never had," he said and his eyes shone. "I am
thinking about it all the time. Big things are going to be
done in the country and there will be more money to be
made than I ever dreamed of. You get into it. I wish I
were younger and had your chance." Jesse Bentley walked
up and down in the bank office and grew more and more
excited as he talked. At one time in his life he had been
threatened with paralysis and his left side remained somewhat weakened. As he talked his left eyelid twitched. La-

ter when he drove back home and when night came on and the stars came out it was harder to get back the old feeling of a close and personal God who lived in the sky overhead and who might at any moment reach out his hand, touch him on the shoulder, and appoint for him some heroic task to be done. Jesse's mind was fixed upon the things read in newspapers and magazines, on fortunes to be made almost without effort by shrewd men who bought and sold. For him the coming of the boy David did much to bring back with renewed force the old faith and it seemed to him that God had at last looked with favor upon him.

As for the boy on the farm, life began to reveal itself to him in a thousand new and delightful ways. The kindly attitude of all about him expanded his quiet nature and he lost the half timid, hesitating manner he had always had with his people. At night when he went to bed after a long day of adventures in the stables, in the fields, or driving about from farm to farm with his grandfather, he wanted to embrace everyone in the house If Sherley Bentley, the woman who came each night to sit on the floor by his bedside, did not appear at once, he went to the head of the stairs and shouted, his young voice ringing through the narrow halls where for so long there had been a tradition of silence. In the morning when he awoke and lay still in bed, the sounds that came in to him through the windows filled him with delight. He thought with a shudder of the life in the house in Winesburg and of his mother's angry voice that had always made him tremble. There in the country all sounds were pleasant sounds. When he awoke at dawn the barnyard back of the house also awoke. In the house people stirred about. Eliza Stoughton the half-witted girl was poked in the ribs by a farm hand and giggled noisily, in some distant field a cow bawled and was answered by the cattle in the stables, and one of the farm hands spoke sharply to the horse he was grooming by the stable door. David leaped out of bed and ran to a window. All of the people stirring about excited his mind, and he wondered what his mother was doing in the house in town.

From the windows of his own room he could not see directly into the barnyard where the farm hands had now all assembled to do the morning chores, but he could hear the voices of the men and the neighing of the horses. When one of the men laughed, he laughed also. Leaning out at the open window, he looked into an orchard where a fat sow wandered about with a litter of tiny pigs at her heels. Every morning he counted the pigs. "Four, five, six, seven," he said slowly, wetting his finger and making straight up and down marks on the window ledge. David ran to put on his trousers and shirt. A feverish desire to get out of doors took possession of him. Every morning he made such a noise coming down stairs that Aunt Callie, the housekeeper, declared he was trying to tear the house down. When he had run through the long old house, shutting doors behind him with a bang, he came into the barnyard and looked about with an amazed air of expectancy. It seemed to him that in such a place tremendous things might have happened during the night. The farm hands looked at him and laughed. Henry Strader, an old man who had been on the farm since Jesse came into possession and who before David's time had never been known to make a joke, made the same joke every morning. It amused David so that he laughed and clapped his hands. "See, come here and look," cried the old man. "Grandfather Jesse's white mare has torn the black stocking she wears on her foot."

Day after day through the long summer, Jesse Bentley

drove from farm to farm up and down the valley of Wine
Creek, and his grandson went with him. They rode in a
comfortable old phaeton drawn by the white horse. The
old man scratched his thin white beard and talked to himself of his plans for increasing the productiveness of the
fields they visited and of God's part in the plans all men
made. Sometimes he looked at David and smiled happily
and then for a long time he appeared to forget the boy's
existence. More and more every day now his mind turned
back again to the dreams that had filled his mind when
he had first come out of the city to live on the land. One
afternoon he startled David by letting his dreams take
entire possession of him. With the boy as a witness, he
went through a ceremony and brought about an accident
that nearly destroyed the companionship that was growing up between them.

Jesse and his grandson were driving in a distant part of
the valley some miles from home. A forest came down to
the road and through the forest Wine Creek wriggled its
way over stones toward a distant river. All the afternoon
Jesse had been in a meditative mood and now he began
to talk. His mind went back to the night when he had
been frightened by thoughts of a giant that might come
to rob and plunder him of his possessions, and again as on
that night when he had run through the fields crying for a
son, he became excited to the edge of insanity. Stopping
the horse he got out of the buggy and asked David to get
out also. The two climbed over a fence and walked along
the bank of the stream. The boy paid no attention to the
muttering of his grandfather, but ran along beside him
and wondered what was going to happen. When a rabbit
jumped up and ran away through the woods, he clapped
his hands and danced with delight. He looked at the tall
trees and was sorry that he was not a little animal to climb

high in the air without being frightened. Stooping, he picked up a small stone and threw it over the head of his grandfather into a clump of bushes. "Wake up, little animal. Go and climb to the top of the trees," he shouted in a shrill voice.

Jesse Bentley went along under the trees with his head bowed and with his mind in a ferment. His earnestness affected the boy, who presently became silent and a little alarmed. Into the old man's mind had come the notion that now he could bring from God a word or a sign out of the sky, that the presence of the boy and man on their knees in some lonely spot in the forest would make the miracle he had been waiting for almost inevitable. "It was in just such a place as this that other David tended the sheep when his father came and told him to go down unto Saul," he muttered.

Taking the boy rather roughly by the shoulder, he climbed over a fallen log and when he had come to an open place among the trees he dropped upon his knees and began to pray in a loud voice.

A kind of terror he had never known before took possession of David. Crouching beneath a tree he watched the man on the ground before him and his own knees began to tremble. It seemed to him that he was in the presence not only of his grandfather but of someone else, someone who might hurt him, someone who was not kindly but dangerous and brutal. He began to cry and reaching down picked up a small stick, which he held tightly gripped in his fingers. When Jesse Bentley, absorbed in his own idea, suddenly arose and advanced toward him, his terror grew until his whole body shook. In the woods an intense silence seemed to lie over everything and suddenly out of the silence came the old man's harsh and insistent voice. Gripping the boy's shoulders, Jesse turned his face to the

sky and shouted. The whole left side of his face twitched
and his hand on the boy's shoulder twitched also. "Make
a sign to me, God," he cried. "Here I stand with the boy
David. Come down to me out of the sky and make Thy
presence known to me."

With a cry of fear, David turned and, shaking himself
loose from the hands that held him, ran away through the
forest. He did not believe that the man who turned up his
face and in a harsh voice shouted at the sky was his grandfather at all. The man did not look like his grandfather.
The conviction that something strange and terrible had
happened, that by some miracle a new and dangerous person had come into the body of the kindly old man, took
possession of him. On and on he ran down the hillside,
sobbing as he ran. When he fell over the roots of a tree and
in falling struck his head, he arose and tried to run on
again. His head hurt so that presently he fell down and lay
still, but it was only after Jesse had carried him to
the buggy and he awoke to find the old man's hand stroking his head tenderly that the terror left him. "Take me
away. There is a terrible man back there in the woods,"
he declared firmly, while Jesse looked away over the tops
of the trees and again his lips cried out to God. "What
have I done that Thou dost not approve of me," he whispered softly, saying the words over and over as he drove
rapidly along the road with the boy's cut and bleeding
head held tenderly against his shoulder.

Part Three

SURRENDER

THE STORY of Louise Bentley, who became Mrs. John Hardy and lived with her husband in a brick house on Elm Street in Winesburg, is a story of misunderstanding.

Before such women as Louise can be understood and their lives made livable, much will have to be done. Thoughtful books will have to be written and thoughtful lives lived by people about them.

Born of a delicate and overworked mother, and an impulsive, hard, imaginative father, who did not look with favor upon her coming into the world, Louise was from childhood a neurotic, one of the race of over-sensitive women that in later days industrialism was to bring in such great numbers into the world.

During her early years she lived on the Bentley farm, a silent, moody child, wanting love more than anything else in the world and not getting it. When she was fifteen she went to live in Winesburg with the family of Albert Hardy, who had a store for the sale of buggies and wagons, and who was a member of the town board of education.

Louise went into town to be a student in the Winesburg High School and she went to live at the Hardys' because Albert Hardy and her father were friends.

Hardy, the vehicle merchant of Winesburg, like thousands of other men of his times, was an enthusiast on the subject of education. He had made his own way in the world without learning got from books, but he was convinced that had he but known books things would have gone better with him. To everyone who came into his shop he talked of the matter, and in his own household he drove his family distracted by his constant harping on the subject.

He had two daughters and one son, John Hardy, and more than once the daughters threatened to leave school altogether. As a matter of principle they did just enough work in their classes to avoid punishment. "I hate books and I hate anyone who likes books," Harriet, the younger of the two girls, declared passionately.

In Winesburg as on the farm Louise was not happy. For years she had dreamed of the time when she could go forth into the world, and she looked upon the move into the Hardy household as a great step in the direction of freedom. Always when she had thought of the matter, it had seemed to her that in town all must be gaiety and life, that there men and women must live happily and freely, giving and taking friendship and affection as one takes the feel of a wind on the cheek. After the silence and the cheerlessness of life in the Bentley house, she dreamed of stepping forth into an atmosphere that was warm and pulsating with life and reality. And in the Hardy household Louise might have got something of the thing for which she so hungered but for a mistake she made when she had just come to town.

Louise won the disfavor of the two Hardy girls, Mary and Harriet, by her application to her studies in school. She did not come to the house until the day when school was to begin and knew nothing of the feeling they had in the matter. She was timid and during the first month made no acquaintances. Every Friday afternoon one of the hired men from the farm drove into Winesburg and took her home for the week-end, so that she did not spend the Saturday holiday with the town people. Because she was embarrassed and lonely she worked constantly at her studies. To Mary and Harriet, it seemed as though she tried to make trouble for them by her proficiency. In her eagerness to appear well Louise wanted to answer every question put to the class by the teacher. She jumped up and down and her eyes flashed. Then when she had answered some question the others in the class had been unable to answer, she smiled happily. "See, I have done it for you," her eyes seemed to say. "You need not bother about the matter. I will answer all questions. For the whole class it will be easy while I am here."

In the evening after supper in the Hardy house, Albert Hardy began to praise Louise. One of the teachers had spoken highly of her and he was delighted. "Well, again I have heard of it," he began, looking hard at his daughters and then turning to smile at Louise. "Another of the teachers has told me of the good work Louise is doing. Everyone in Winesburg is telling me how smart she is. I am ashamed that they do not speak so of my own girls." Arising, the merchant marched about the room and lighted his evening cigar.

The two girls looked at each other and shook their heads wearily. Seeing their indifference the father became angry. "I tell you it is something for you two to be thinking about," he cried, glaring at them. "There is a big change coming here in America and in learning is the only hope of the coming generations. Louise is the daughter of a rich man but she is not ashamed to study. It should make you ashamed to see what she does."

The merchant took his hat from a rack by the door and

prepared to depart for the evening. At the door he stopped and glared back. So fierce was his manner that Louise was frightened and ran upstairs to her own room. The daughters began to speak of their own affairs. "Pay attention to me," roared the merchant. "Your minds are lazy. Your indifference to education is affecting your characters. You will amount to nothing. Now mark what I say —Louise will be so far ahead of you that you will never catch up."

The distracted man went out of the house and into the street shaking with wrath. He went along muttering words and swearing, but when he got into Main Street his anger passed. He stopped to talk of the weather or the crops with some other merchant or with a farmer who had come into town and forgot his daughters altogether or, if he thought of them, only shrugged his shoulders. "Oh, well, girls will be girls," he muttered philosophically.

In the house when Louise came down into the room where the two girls sat, they would have nothing to do with her. One evening after she had been there for more than six weeks and was heartbroken because of the continued air of coldness with which she was always greeted, she burst into tears. "Shut up your crying and go back to your own room and to your books," Mary Hardy said sharply.

❀◇❀

The room occupied by Louise was on the second floor of the Hardy house, and her window looked out upon an orchard. There was a stove in the room and every evening young John Hardy carried up an armful of wood and put it in a box that stood by the wall. During the second month after she came to the house, Louise gave up all hope of getting on a friendly footing with the Hardy girls and went to her own room as soon as the evening meal was at an end.

Her mind began to play with thoughts of making friends with John Hardy. When he came into the room with the wood in his arms, she pretended to be busy with her studies but watched him eagerly. When he had put the wood in the box and turned to go out, she put down her head and blushed. She tried to make talk but could say nothing, and after he had gone she was angry at herself for her stupidity.

The mind of the country girl became filled with the idea of drawing close to the young man. She thought that in him might be found the quality she had all her life been seeking in people. It seemed to her that between herself and all the other people in the world, a wall had been built up and that she was living just on the edge of some warm inner circle of life that must be quite open and understandable to others. She became obsessed with the thought that it wanted but a courageous act on her part to make all of her association with people something quite different, and that it was possible by such an act to pass into a new life as one opens a door and goes into a room. Day and night she thought of the matter, but although the thing she wanted so earnestly was something very warm and close it had as yet no conscious connection with sex. It had not become that definite, and her mind had only alighted upon the person of John Hardy because he was at hand and unlike his sisters had not been unfriendly to her.

The Hardy sisters, Mary and Harriet, were both older than Louise. In a certain kind of knowledge of the world they were years older. They lived as all of the young women of Middle Western towns lived. In those days young women did not go out of our towns to Eastern colleges and ideas in regard to social classes had hardly begun to exist. A daughter of a laborer was in much the same social position as a daughter of a farmer or a merchant, and there were no leisure classes. A girl was "nice" or she was "not nice." If a nice girl, she had a young man who came to her house to see her on Sunday and on Wednesday evenings. Sometimes she went with her young man to a dance or a church social. At other times she received him at the house and was given the use of the parlor for that purpose. No one intruded upon her. For hours the two sat behind closed doors. Sometimes the lights were turned low and the young man and woman embraced. Cheeks became hot and hair disarranged. After a year or two, if the impulse within them became strong and insistent enough, they married.

One evening during her first winter in Winesburg, Louise had an adventure that gave a new impulse to her desire to break down the wall that she thought stood between her and John Hardy. It was Wednesday and immediately after the evening meal Albert Hardy put on his hat and went away. Young John brought the wood and put it in the box in Louise's room. "You do work hard, don't you?" he said awkwardly, and then before she could answer he also went away.

Louise heard him go out of the house and had a mad desire to run after him. Opening her window she leaned out and called softly. "John, dear John, come back, don't go away." The night was cloudy and she could not see far into the darkness, but as she waited she fancied she could hear a soft little noise as of someone going on tiptoes through the trees in the orchard. She was frightened and closed the window quickly. For an hour she moved about the room trembling with excitement and when she could not longer bear the waiting, she crept into the hall and down the stairs into a closet-like room that opened off the parlor.

Louise had decided that she would perform the courageous act that had for weeks been in her mind. She was convinced that John Hardy had concealed himself in the orchard beneath her window and she was determined to find him and tell him that she wanted him to come close to her, to hold her in his arms, to tell her of his thoughts and dreams and to listen while she told him her thoughts and dreams. "In the darkness it will be easier to say things," she whispered to herself, as she stood in the little room groping for the door.

And then suddenly Louise realized that she was not alone in the house. In the parlor on the other side of the door a man's voice spoke softly and the door opened. Louise just had time to conceal herself in a little opening beneath the stairway when Mary Hardy, accompanied by her young man, came into the little dark room.

For an hour Louise sat on the floor in the darkness and listened. Without words Mary Hardy, with the aid of the man who had come to spend the evening with her, brought to the country girl a knowledge of men and women. Putting her head down until she was curled into a little ball she lay perfectly still. It seemed to her that by some strange impulse of the gods, a great gift had been brought to Mary Hardy and she could not understand the older woman's determined protest.

The young man took Mary Hardy into his arms and kissed her. When she struggled and laughed, he but held her the more tightly. For an hour the contest between them went on and then they went back into the parlor and Louise escaped up the stairs. "I hope you were quiet out there. You must not disturb the little mouse at her studies," she heard Harriet saying to her sister as she stood by her own door in the hallway above.

Louise wrote a note to John Hardy and late that night, when all in the house were asleep, she crept downstairs and slipped it under his door. She was afraid that if she did not do the thing at once her courage would fail. In the note she tried to be quite definite about what she wanted. "I want someone to love me and I want to love someone," she wrote. "If you are the one for me I want you to come into the orchard at night and make a noise under my window. It will be easy for me to crawl down over the shed and come to you. I am thinking about it all the time, so if you are to come at all you must come soon."

For a long time Louise did not know what would be the outcome of her bold attempt to secure for herself a lover. In a way she still did not know whether or not she wanted him to come. Sometimes it seemed to her that to be held tightly and kissed was the whole secret of life, and then a new impulse came and she was terribly afraid. The age-old woman's desire to be possessed had taken possession of her, but so vague was her notion of life that it seemed to her just the touch of John Hardy's hand upon her own hand would satisfy. She wondered if he would understand that. At the table next day while Albert Hardy talked and the two girls whispered and laughed, she did not look at John but at the table and as soon as possible escaped. In the evening she went out of the house until she was sure he had taken the wood to her room and gone away. When after several evenings of intense listening she heard no call from the darkness in the orchard, she was half beside herself with grief and decided that for her there was no way to break through the wall that had shut her off from the joy of life.

And then on a Monday evening two or three weeks after

the writing of the note, John Hardy came for her. Louise had so entirely given up the thought of his coming that for a long time she did not hear the call that came up from the orchard. On the Friday evening before, as she was being driven back to the farm for the week-end by one of the hired men, she had on an impulse done a thing that had startled her, and as John Hardy stood in the darkness below and called her name softly and insistently, she walked about in her room and wondered what new impulse had led her to commit so ridiculous an act.

The farm hand, a young fellow with black curly hair, had come for her somewhat late on that Friday evening and they drove home in the darkness. Louise, whose mind was filled with thoughts of John Hardy, tried to make talk but the country boy was embarrassed and would say nothing. Her mind began to review the loneliness of her childhood and she remembered with a pang the sharp new loneliness that had just come to her. "I hate everyone," she cried suddenly, and then broke forth into a tirade that frightened her escort. "I hate father and old man Hardy, too," she declared vehemently. "I get my lessons there in the school in town but I hate that also."

Louise frightened the farm hand still more by turning and putting her cheek down upon his shoulder. Vaguely she hoped that he like that young man who had stood in the darkness with Mary would put his arms about her and kiss her, but the country boy was only alarmed. He struck the horse with the whip and began to whistle. "The road is rough, eh?" he said loudly. Louise was so angry that reaching up she snatched his hat from his head and threw it into the road. When he jumped out of the buggy and went to get it, she drove off and left him to walk the rest of the way back to the farm.

Louise Bentley took John Hardy to be her lover. That

was not what she wanted but it was so the young man had
interpreted her approach to him, and so anxious was she
to achieve something else that she made no resistance.
When after a few months they were both afraid that she
was about to become a mother, they went one evening to
the county seat and were married. For a few months they
lived in the Hardy house and then took a house of their
own. All during the first year Louise tried to make her
husband understand the vague and intangible hunger
that had led to the writing of the note and that was still
unsatisfied. Again and again she crept into his arms and
tried to talk of it, but always without success. Filled with
his own notions of love between men and women, he did
not listen but began to kiss her upon the lips. That confused her so that in the end she did not want to be kissed.
She did not know what she wanted.

When the alarm that had tricked them into marriage
proved to be groundless, she was angry and said bitter,
hurtful things. Later when her son David was born, she
could not nurse him and did not know whether she
wanted him or not. Sometimes she stayed in the room
with him all day, walking about and occasionally creeping
close to touch him tenderly with her hands, and then other
days came when she did not want to see or be near the
tiny bit of humanity that had come into the house. When
John Hardy reproached her for her cruelty, she laughed.
"It is a man child and will get what it wants anyway," she
said sharply. "Had it been a woman child there is nothing
in the world I would not have done for it."

Part Four

TERROR

WHEN DAVID HARDY was a tall boy of fifteen, he, like his mother, had an adventure that changed the whole current of his life and sent him out of his quiet corner into the world. The shell of the circumstances of his life was broken and he was compelled to start forth. He left Winesburg and no one there ever saw him again. After his disappearance, his mother and grandfather both died and his father became very rich. He spent much money in trying to locate his son, but that is no part of this story.

It was in the late fall of an unusual year on the Bentley farms. Everywhere the crops had been heavy. That spring, Jesse had bought part of a long strip of black swamp land that lay in the valley of Wine Creek. He got the land at a low price but had spent a large sum of money to improve it. Great ditches had to be dug and thousands of tile laid. Neighboring farmers shook their heads over the expense. Some of them laughed and hoped that Jesse would lose heavily by the venture, but the old man went silently on with the work and said nothing.

When the land was drained he planted it to cabbages and onions, and again the neighbors laughed. The crop was, however, enormous and brought high prices. In the one year Jesse made enough money to pay for all the cost of preparing the land and had a surplus that enabled him

97

to buy two more farms. He was exultant and could not conceal his delight. For the first time in all the history of his ownership of the farms, he went among his men with a smiling face.

Jesse bought a great many new machines for cutting down the cost of labor and all of the remaining acres in the strip of black fertile swamp land. One day he went into Winesburg and bought a bicycle and a new suit of clothes for David and he gave his two sisters money with which to go to a religious convention at Cleveland, Ohio.

In the fall of that year when the frost came and the trees in the forests along Wine Creek were golden brown, David spent every moment when he did not have to attend school, out in the open. Alone or with other boys he went every afternoon into the woods to gather nuts. The other boys of the countryside, most of them sons of laborers on the Bentley farms, had guns with which they went hunting rabbits and squirrels, but David did not go with them. He made himself a sling with rubber bands and a forked stick and went off by himself to gather nuts. As he went about thoughts came to him. He realized that he was almost a man and wondered what he would do in life, but before they came to anything, the thoughts passed and he was a boy again. One day he killed a squirrel that sat on one of the lower branches of a tree and chattered at him. Home he ran with the squirrel in his hand. One of the Bentley sisters cooked the little animal and he ate it with great gusto. The skin he tacked on a board and suspended the board by a string from his bedroom window.

That gave his mind a new turn. After that he never went into the woods without carrying the sling in his pocket and he spent hours shooting at imaginary animals concealed among the brown leaves in the trees. Thoughts of his coming manhood passed and he was content to be a boy with a boy's impulses.

One Saturday morning when he was about to set off for the woods with the sling in his pocket and a bag for nuts on his shoulder, his grandfather stopped him. In the eyes of the old man was the strained serious look that always a little frightened David. At such times Jesse Bentley's eyes did not look straight ahead but wavered and seemed to be looking at nothing. Something like an invisible curtain appeared to have come between the man and all the rest of the world. "I want you to come with me," he said briefly, and his eyes looked over the boy's head into the sky. "We have something important to do today. You may bring the bag for nuts if you wish. It does not matter and anyway we will be going into the woods."

Jesse and David set out from the Bentley farmhouse in the old phaeton that was drawn by the white horse. When they had gone along in silence for a long way they stopped at the edge of a field where a flock of sheep were grazing. Among the sheep was a lamb that had been born out of season, and this David and his grandfather caught and tied so tightly that it looked like a little white ball. When they drove on again Jesse let David hold the lamb in his arms. "I saw it yesterday and it put me in mind of what I have long wanted to do," he said, and again he looked away over the head of the boy with the wavering, uncertain stare in his eyes.

After the feeling of exaltation that had come to the farmer as a result of his successful year, another mood had taken possession of him. For a long time he had been going about feeling very humble and prayerful. Again he walked alone at night thinking of God and as he walked he again connected his own figure with the figures of old days. Under the stars he knelt on the wet grass and raised up his voice in prayer. Now he had decided that like the men whose stories filled the pages of the Bible, he would make a sacrifice to God. "I have been given these abundant crops and God has also sent me a boy who is called David," he whispered to himself. "Perhaps I should have done this thing long ago." He was sorry the idea had not come into his mind in the days before his daughter Louise had been born and thought that surely now when he had erected a pile of burning sticks in some lonely place in the woods and had offered the body of a lamb as a burnt offering, God would appear to him and give him a message.

More and more as he thought of the matter, he thought also of David and his passionate self-love was partially forgotten. "It is time for the boy to begin thinking of going out into the world and the message will be one concerning him," he decided. "God will make a pathway for him. He will tell me what place David is to take in life and when he shall set out on his journey. It is right that the boy should be there. If I am fortunate and an angel of God should appear, David will see the beauty and glory of God made manifest to man. It will make a true man of God of him also."

In silence Jesse and David drove along the road until they came to that place where Jesse had once before appealed to God and had frightened his grandson. The morning had been bright and cheerful, but a cold wind now began to blow and clouds hid the sun. When David saw the place to which they had come he began to tremble with fright, and when they stopped by the bridge where the creek came down from among the trees, he wanted to spring out of the phaeton and run away.

A dozen plans for escape ran through David's head, but when Jesse stopped the horse and climbed over the fence into the wood, he followed. "It is foolish to be afraid. Nothing will happen," he told himself as he went along with the lamb in his arms. There was something in the helplessness of the little animal held so tightly in his arms that gave him courage. He could feel the rapid beating of the beast's heart and that made his own heart beat less rapidly. As he walked swiftly along behind his grandfather, he untied the string with which the four legs of the lamb were fastened together. "If anything happens we will run away together," he thought.

In the woods, after they had gone a long way from the road, Jesse stopped in an opening among the trees where a clearing, overgrown with small bushes, ran up from the creek. He was still silent but began at once to erect a heap of dry sticks which he presently set afire. The boy sat on the ground with the lamb in his arms. His imagination began to invest every movement of the old man with significance and he became every moment more afraid. "I must put the blood of the lamb on the head of the boy," Jesse muttered when the sticks had begun to blaze greedily, and taking a long knife from his pocket he turned and walked rapidly across the clearing toward David.

Terror seized upon the soul of the boy. He was sick with it. For a moment he sat perfectly still and then his body stiffened and he sprang to his feet. His face became as white as the fleece of the lamb that, now finding itself suddenly released, ran down the hill. David ran also. Fear made his feet fly. Over the low bushes and logs he leaped frantically. As he ran he put his hand into his pocket and took out the branched stick from which the sling for shooting squirrels was suspended. When he came to the creek that was shallow and splashed down over the stones, he dashed into the water and turned to look back, and when he saw his grandfather still running toward him with the long knife held tightly in his hand he did not hesitate, but reaching down, selected a stone and put it in the sling. With all his strength he drew back the heavy rubber bands and the stone whistled through the air. It hit Jesse, who had entirely forgotten the boy and was pursuing the lamb, squarely in the head. With a groan he pitched forward and fell almost at the boy's feet. When David saw that he lay still and that he was apparently dead, his fright increased immeasurably. It became an insane panic.

With a cry he turned and ran off through the woods weeping convulsively. "I don't care—I killed him, but I don't care," he sobbed. As he ran on and on he decided suddenly that he would never go back again to the Bentley farms or to the town of Winesburg. "I have killed the man of God and now I will myself be a man and go into the world," he said stoutly as he stopped running and walked rapidly down a road that followed the windings of Wine Creek as it ran through fields and forests into the west.

On the ground by the creek Jesse Bentley moved uneasily about. He groaned and opened his eyes. For a long time he lay perfectly still and looked at the sky. When at last he got to his feet, his mind was confused and he was not surprised by the boy's disappearance. By the roadside he sat down on a log and began to talk about God. That is all they ever got out of him. Whenever David's name was mentioned he looked vaguely at the sky and said that a messenger from God had taken the boy. "It happened because I was too greedy for glory," he declared, and would have no more to say in the matter.

A MAN OF IDEAS

HE LIVED with his mother, a grey, silent woman with a peculiar ashy complexion. The house in which they lived stood in a little grove of trees beyond where the main street of Winesburg crossed Wine Creek. His name was Joe Welling, and his father had been a man of some dignity in the community, a lawyer and a member of the state legislature at Columbus. Joe himself was small of body and in his character unlike anyone else in town. He was like a tiny little volcano that lies silent for days and then suddenly spouts fire. No, he wasn't like that—he was like a man who is subject to fits, one who walks among his fellow men inspiring fear because a fit may come upon him suddenly and blow him away into a strange uncanny physical state in which his eyes roll and his legs and arms jerk. He was like that, only that the visitation that descended upon Joe Welling was a mental and not a physical thing. He was beset by ideas and in the throes of one of his ideas was uncontrollable. Words rolled and tumbled from his mouth. A peculiar smile came upon his lips. The edges of his teeth that were tipped with gold glistened in the light. Pouncing upon a bystander he began to talk. For the bystander there was no escape. The excited man breathed into his face, peered into his eyes, pounded upon his chest with a shaking forefinger, demanded, compelled attention.

In those days the Standard Oil Company did not deliver oil to the consumer in big wagons and motor trucks as it does now, but delivered instead to retail grocers, hardware stores, and the like. Joe was the Standard Oil agent in Winesburg and in several towns up and down the railroad that went through Winesburg. He collected bills, booked orders, and did other things. His father, the legislator, had secured the job for him.

In and out of the stores of Winesburg went Joe Welling —silent, excessively polite, intent upon his business. Men watched him with eyes in which lurked amusement tempered by alarm. They were waiting for him to break forth, preparing to flee. Although the seizures that came upon him were harmless enough, they could not be laughed away. They were overwhelming. Astride an idea, Joe was overmastering. His personality became gigantic. It overrode the man to whom he talked, swept him away, swept all away, all who stood within sound of his voice.

In Sylvester West's Drug Store stood four men who were talking of horse racing. Wesley Moyer's stallion, Tony Tip, was to race at the June meeting at Tiffin, Ohio, and there was a rumor that he would meet the stiffest competition of his career. It was said that Pop Geers, the great racing driver, would himself be there. A doubt of the success of Tony Tip hung heavy in the air of Winesburg.

Into the drug store came Joe Welling, brushing the screen door violently aside. With a strange absorbed light in his eyes he pounced upon Ed Thomas, he who knew Pop Geers and whose opinion of Tony Tip's chances was worth considering.

"The water is up in Wine Creek," cried Joe Welling with the air of Pheidippides bringing news of the victory of the Greeks in the struggle at Marathon. His finger beat a tattoo upon Ed Thomas's broad chest. "By Trunion bridge it is within eleven and a half inches of the flooring," he went on, the words coming quickly and with a little whistling noise from between his teeth. An expression of helpless annoyance crept over the faces of the four.

"I have my facts correct. Depend upon that. I went to Sinnings' Hardware Store and got a rule. Then I went back and measured. I could hardly believe my own eyes. It hasn't rained you see for ten days. At first I didn't know what to think. Thoughts rushed through my head. I thought of subterranean passages and springs. Down under the ground went my mind, delving about. I sat on the floor of the bridge and rubbed my head. There wasn't a cloud in the sky, not one. Come out into the street and you'll see. There wasn't a cloud. There isn't a cloud now. Yes, there was a cloud. I don't want to keep back any facts. There was a cloud in the west down near the horizon, a cloud no bigger than a man's hand.

"Not that I think that has anything to do with it. There it is, you see. You understand how puzzled I was.

"Then an idea came to me. I laughed. You'll laugh, too. Of course it rained over in Medina County. That's interesting, eh? If we had no trains, no mails, no telegraph, we would know that it rained over in Medina County. That's where Wine Creek comes from. Everyone knows that. Little old Wine Creek brought us the news. That's interesting. I laughed. I thought I'd tell you—it's interesting, eh?"

Joe Welling turned and went out at the door. Taking a book from his pocket, he stopped and ran a finger down one of the pages. Again he was absorbed in his duties as agent of the Standard Oil Company. "Hern's Grocery will be getting low on coal oil. I'll see them," he muttered, hurrying along the street, and bowing politely to the right and left at the people walking past.

When George Willard went to work for the *Winesburg Eagle* he was besieged by Joe Welling. Joe envied the boy.

It seemed to him that he was meant by Nature to be a reporter on a newspaper. "It is what I should be doing, there is no doubt of that," he declared, stopping George Willard on the sidewalk before Daugherty's Feed Store. His eyes began to glisten and his forefinger to tremble. "Of course I make more money with the Standard Oil Company and I'm only telling you," he added. "I've got nothing against you but I should have your place. I could do the work at odd moments. Here and there I would run finding out things you'll never see."

Becoming more excited Joe Welling crowded the young reporter against the front of the feed store. He appeared to be lost in thought, rolling his eyes about and running a thin nervous hand through his hair. A smile spread over his face and his gold teeth glittered. "You get out your note book," he commanded. "You carry a little pad of paper in your pocket, don't you? I knew you did. Well, you set this down. I thought of it the other day. Let's take decay. Now what is decay? It's fire. It burns up wood and other things. You never thought of that? Of course not. This sidewalk here and this feed store, the trees down the street there—they're all on fire. They're burning up. Decay you see is always going on. It don't stop. Water and paint can't stop it. If a thing is iron, then what? It rusts, you see. That's fire, too. The world is on fire. Start your pieces in the paper that way. Just say in big letters 'The World Is On Fire.' That will make 'em look up. They'll say you're a smart one. I don't care. I don't envy you. I just snatched that idea out of the air. I would make a newspaper hum. You got to admit that."

Turning quickly, Joe Welling walked rapidly away. When he had taken several steps he stopped and looked back. "I'm going to stick to you," he said. "I'm going to make you a regular hummer. I should start a newspaper

myself, that's what I should do. I'd be a marvel. Everybody knows that."

When George Willard had been for a year on the
Winesburg Eagle, four things happened to Joe Welling.
His mother died, he came to live at the New Willard
House, he became involved in a love affair, and he organ-
ized the Winesburg Baseball Club.

Joe organized the baseball club because he wanted to
be a coach and in that position he began to win the respect
of his townsmen. "He is a wonder," they declared after
Joe's team had whipped the team from Medina County.
"He gets everybody working together. You just watch
him."

Upon the baseball field Joe Welling stood by first base,
his whole body quivering with excitement. In spite of
themselves all of the players watched him closely. The opposing pitcher became confused.

"Now! Now! Now! Now!" shouted the excited man.
"Watch me! Watch me! Watch my fingers! Watch my
hands! Watch my feet! Watch my eyes! Let's work together here! Watch me! In me you see all the movements
of the game! Work with me! Work with me! Watch me!
Watch me! Watch me!"

With runners of the Winesburg team on bases, Joe
Welling became as one inspired. Before they knew what
had come over them, the base runners were watching the
man, edging off the bases, advancing, retreating, held as
by an invisible cord. The players of the opposing team
also watched Joe. They were fascinated. For a moment
they watched and then, as though to break a spell that
hung over them, they began hurling the ball wildly about,
and amid a series of fierce animal-like cries from the coach,
the runners of the Winesburg team scampered home.

Joe Welling's love affair set the town of Winesburg on

edge. When it began everyone whispered and shook his head. When people tried to laugh, the laughter was forced and unnatural. Joe fell in love with Sarah King, a lean, sad-looking woman who lived with her father and brother in a brick house that stood opposite the gate leading to the Winesburg Cemetery.

The two Kings, Edward the father, and Tom the son, were not popular in Winesburg. They were called proud and dangerous. They had come to Winesburg from some place in the South and ran a cider mill on the Trunion Pike. Tom King was reported to have killed a man before he came to Winesburg. He was twenty-seven years old and rode about town on a grey pony. Also he had a long yellow mustache that dropped down over his teeth, and always carried a heavy, wicked-looking walking stick in his hand. Once he killed a dog with the stick. The dog belonged to Win Pawsey, the shoe merchant, and stood on the sidewalk wagging its tail. Tom King killed it with one blow. He was arrested and paid a fine of ten dollars.

Old Edward King was small of stature and when he passed people in the street laughed a queer unmirthful laugh. When he laughed he scratched his left elbow with his right hand. The sleeve of his coat was almost worn through from the habit. As he walked along the street, looking nervously about and laughing, he seemed more dangerous than his silent, fierce-looking son.

When Sarah King began walking out in the evening with Joe Welling, people shook their heads in alarm. She was tall and pale and had dark rings under her eyes. The couple looked ridiculous together. Under the trees they walked and Joe talked. His passionate eager protestations of love, heard coming out of the darkness by the cemetery wall, or from the deep shadows of the trees on the hill that ran up to the Fair Grounds from Waterworks Pond, were repeated in the stores. Men stood by the bar in the New Willard House laughing and talking of Joe's courtship. After the laughter came silence. The Winesburg baseball team, under his management, was winning game after game, and the town had begun to respect him. Sensing a tragedy, they waited, laughing nervously.

Late on a Saturday afternoon the meeting between Joe Welling and the two Kings, the anticipation of which had set the town on edge, took place in Joe Welling's room in the New Willard House. George Willard was a witness to the meeting. It came about in this way:

When the young reporter went to his room after the evening meal he saw Tom King and his father sitting in the half darkness in Joe's room. The son had the heavy walking stick in his hand and sat near the door. Old Edward King walked nervously about, scratching his left elbow with his right hand. The hallways were empty and silent.

George Willard went to his own room and sat down at his desk. He tried to write but his hand trembled so that he could not hold the pen. He also walked nervously up and down. Like the rest of the town of Winesburg he was perplexed and knew not what to do.

It was seven-thirty and fast growing dark when Joe Welling came along the station platform toward the New Willard House. In his arms he held a bundle of weeds and grasses. In spite of the terror that made his body shake, George Willard was amused at the sight of the small spry figure holding the grasses and half running along the platform.

Shaking with fright and anxiety, the young reporter lurked in the hallway outside the door of the room in which Joe Welling talked to the two Kings. There had been an oath, the nervous giggle of old Edward King, and then silence. Now the voice of Joe Welling, sharp and clear, broke forth. George Willard began to laugh. He understood. As he had swept all men before him, so now Joe Welling was carrying the two men in the room off their feet with a tidal wave of words. The listener in the hall walked up and down, lost in amazement.

Inside the room Joe Welling had paid no attention to the grumbled threat of Tom King. Absorbed in an idea he closed the door and, lighting a lamp, spread the handful of weeds and grasses upon the floor. "I've got something here," he announced solemnly. "I was going to tell George Willard about it, let him make a piece out of it for the paper. I'm glad you're here. I wish Sarah were here also. I've been going to come to your house and tell you of some of my ideas. They're interesting. Sarah wouldn't let me. She said we'd quarrel. That's foolish."

Running up and down before the two perplexed men, Joe Welling began to explain. "Don't you make a mistake now," he cried. "This is something big." His voice was shrill with excitement. "You just follow me, you'll be interested. I know you will. Suppose this—suppose all of the wheat, the corn, the oats, the peas, the potatoes, were all by some miracle swept away. Now here we are, you see, in this county. There is a high fence built all around us. We'll suppose that. No one can get over the fence and all the fruits of the earth are destroyed, nothing left but these wild things, these grasses. Would we be done for? I ask you that. Would we be done for?" Again Tom King growled and for a moment there was silence in the room. Then again Joe plunged into the exposition of his idea. "Things would go hard for a time. I admit that. I've got to admit that. No getting around it. We'd be hard put to it. More than one fat stomach would cave in. But they couldn't down us. I should say not."

Tom King laughed good naturedly and the shivery, nervous laugh of Edward King rang through the house. Joe Welling hurried on. "We'd begin, you see, to breed up new vegetables and fruits. Soon we'd regain all we had lost. Mind, I don't say the new things would be the same as the old. They wouldn't. Maybe they'd be better, maybe not so good. That's interesting, eh? You can think about that. It starts your mind working, now don't it?"

In the room there was silence and then again old Edward King laughed nervously. "Say, I wish Sarah was here," cried Joe Welling. "Let's go up to your house. I want to tell her of this."

There was a scraping of chairs in the room. It was then that George Willard retreated to his own room. Leaning out at the window he saw Joe Welling going along the street with the two Kings. Tom King was forced to take extraordinary long strides to keep pace with the little man. As he strode along, he leaned over, listening—absorbed, fascinated. Joe Welling again talked excitedly. "Take milkweed now," he cried. "A lot might be done with milkweed, eh? It's almost unbelievable. I want you to think about it. I want you two to think about it. There would be a new vegetable kingdom you see. It's interesting, eh? It's an idea. Wait till you see Sarah, she'll get the idea. She'll be interested. Sarah is always interested in ideas. You can't be too smart for Sarah, now can you? Of course you can't. You know that."

ADVENTURE

ALICE HINDMAN, a woman of twenty-seven
when George Willard was a mere boy, had lived in Winesburg all her life. She clerked in Winney's Dry Goods Store
and lived with her mother, who had married a second husband.

Alice's step-father was a carriage painter, and given to
drink. His story is an odd one. It will be worth telling some day.

At twenty-seven Alice was tall and somewhat slight. Her
head was large and overshadowed her body. Her shoulders were a little stooped and her hair and eyes brown.
She was very quiet but beneath a placid exterior a con-
tinual ferment went on.

When she was a girl of sixteen and before she began to
work in the store, Alice had an affair with a young man.
The young man, named Ned Currie, was older than Alice.
He, like George Willard, was employed on the *Winesburg
Eagle* and for a long time he went to see Alice almost every
evening. Together the two walked under the trees
through the streets of the town and talked of what they
would do with their lives. Alice was then a very pretty
girl and Ned Currie took her into his arms and kissed her.
[He became excited and said things he did not intend to
say and Alice, betrayed by her desire to have something
beautiful come into her rather narrow life, also grew excited. She also talked.] The outer crust of her life, all of her
natural diffidence and reserve, was torn away and she gave

112

herself over to the emotions of love. When, late in the fall of her sixteenth year, Ned Currie went away to Cleveland where he hoped to get a place on a city newspaper and rise in the world, she wanted to go with him. With a trembling voice she told him what was in her mind. "I will work and you can work," she said. "I do not want to harness you to a needless expense that will prevent your making progress. Don't marry me now. We will get along without that and we can be together. Even though we live in the same house no one will say anything. In the city we will be unknown and people will pay no attention to us."

Ned Currie was puzzled by the determination and abandon of his sweetheart and was also deeply touched. He had wanted the girl to become his mistress but changed his mind. He wanted to protect and care for her. "You don't know what you're talking about," he said sharply; "you may be sure I'll let you do no such thing. As soon as I get a good job I'll come back. For the present you'll have to stay here. It's the only thing we can do."

On the evening before he left Winesburg to take up his new life in the city, Ned Currie went to call on Alice. They walked about through the streets for an hour and then got a rig from Wesley Moyer's livery and went for a drive in the country. The moon came up and they found themselves unable to talk. In his sadness the young man forgot the resolutions he had made regarding his conduct with the girl.

They got out of the buggy at a place where a long meadow ran down to the bank of Wine Creek and there in the dim light became lovers. When at midnight they returned to town they were both glad. It did not seem to them that anything that could happen in the future could blot out the wonder and beauty of the thing that had happened. "Now we will have to stick to each other, whatever happens we will have to do that," Ned Currie said as he left the girl at her father's door.

The young newspaper man did not succeed in getting a place on a Cleveland paper and went west to Chicago. For a time he was lonely and wrote to Alice almost every day. Then he was caught up by the life of the city; he began to make friends and found new interests in life. In Chicago he boarded at a house where there were several women. One of them attracted his attention and he forgot Alice in Winesburg. At the end of a year he had stopped writing letters, and only once in a long time, when he was lonely or when he went into one of the city parks and saw the moon shining on the grass as it had shone that night on the meadow by Wine Creek, did he think of her at all.

In Winesburg the girl who had been loved grew to be a woman. When she was twenty-two years old her father, who owned a harness repair shop, died suddenly. The harness maker was an old soldier, and after a few months his wife received a widow's pension. She used the first money she got to buy a loom and became a weaver of carpets, and Alice got a place in Winney's store. For a number of years nothing could have induced her to believe that Ned Currie would not in the end return to her.

She was glad to be employed because the daily round of toil in the store made the time of waiting seem less long and uninteresting. She began to save money, thinking that when she had saved two or three hundred dollars she would follow her lover to the city and try if her presence would not win back his affections.

Alice did not blame Ned Currie for what had happened in the moonlight in the field, but felt that she could never marry another man. To her the thought of giving to another what she still felt could belong only to Ned seemed his mouth, was not given to conversation, and sometimes, on rainy days and in the winter when a storm raged in Main Street, long hours passed when no customers came in. Alice arranged and rearranged the stock. She stood near the front window where she could look down the deserted street and thought of the evenings when she had walked with Ned Currie and of what he had said. "We will have to stick to each other now." The words echoed and re-echoed through the mind of the maturing woman. Tears came into her eyes. Sometimes when her employer had gone out and she was alone in the store she put her head on the counter and wept. "Oh, Ned, I am waiting," she whispered over and over, and all the time the creeping fear that he would never come back grew stronger within her.

In the spring when the rains have passed and before the long hot days of summer have come, the country about Winesburg is delightful. The town lies in the midst of open fields, but beyond the fields are pleasant patches of woodlands. In the wooded places are many little cloistered nooks, quiet places where lovers go to sit on Sunday afternoons. Through the trees they look out across the fields and see farmers at work about the barns or people driving up and down on the roads. In the town bells ring and occasionally a train passes, looking like a toy thing in the distance.

For several years after Ned Currie went away Alice did not go into the wood with other young people on Sunday, but one day after he had been gone for two or three years and when her loneliness seemed unbearable, she put on her best dress and set out. Finding a little sheltered place from which she could see the town and a long stretch of the fields, she sat down. Fear of age and ineffectuality took possession of her. She could not sit still, and arose. As she

monstrous. When other young men tried to attract her
tention she would have nothing to do with them. "I
his wife and shall remain his wife whether he comes ba
or not," she whispered to herself, and for all of her willin
ness to support herself could not have understood tl
growing modern idea of a woman's owning herself an
giving and taking for her own ends in life.

Alice worked in the dry goods store from eight in th
morning until six at night and on three evenings a wee
went back to the store to stay from seven until nine. A
time passed and she became more and more lonely shu
began to practice the devices common to lonely people.
When at night she went upstairs into her own room she
knelt on the floor to pray and in her prayers whispered
things she wanted to say to her lover. She became attached
to inanimate objects, and because it was her own, could
not bear to have anyone touch the furniture of her room.
The trick of saving money, begun for a purpose, was carried on after the scheme of going to the city to find Ned
Currie had been given up. It became a fixed habit, and
when she needed new clothes she did not get them. Sometimes on rainy afternoons in the store she got out her bank
book and, letting it lie open before her, spent hours
dreaming impossible dreams of saving money enough so
that the interest would support both herself and her future husband.

"Ned always liked to travel about," she thought. "I'll
give him the chance. Some day when we are married and
I can save both his money and my own, we will be rich.
Then we can travel together all over the world."

In the dry goods store weeks ran into months and
months into years as Alice waited and dreamed of her
lover's return. Her employer, a grey old man with false
teeth and a thin grey mustache that drooped down over

stood looking out over the land something, perhaps the thought of never ceasing life as it expresses itself in the flow of the seasons, fixed her mind on the passing years. [With a shiver of dread, she realized that for her the beauty and freshness of youth had passed. For the first time she felt that she had been cheated. She did not blame Ned Currie and did not know what to blame. Sadness swept over her. Dropping to her knees, she tried to pray, but instead of prayers words of protest came to her lips. "It is not going to come to me. I will never find happiness. Why do I tell myself lies?" she cried, and an odd sense of relief came with this, her first bold attempt to face the fear that had become a part of her everyday life.]

In the year when Alice Hindman became twenty-five two things happened to disturb the dull uneventfulness of her days. Her mother married Bush Milton, the carriage painter of Winesburg, and she herself became a member of the Winesburg Methodist Church. Alice joined the church because she had become frightened by the loneliness of her position in life. Her mother's second marriage had emphasized her isolation. "I am becoming old and queer. If Ned comes he will not want me. In the city where he is living men are perpetually young. There is so much going on that they do not have time to grow old," she told herself with a grim little smile, and went resolutely about the business of becoming acquainted with people. Every Thursday evening when the store had closed she went to a prayer meeting in the basement of the church and on Sunday evening attended a meeting of an organization called The Epworth League.

When Will Hurley, a middle-aged man who clerked in a drug store and who also belonged to the church, offered to walk home with her she did not protest. "Of course I will not let him make a practice of being with me, but if he comes to see me once in a long time there can be no harm in that," she told herself, still determined in her loyalty to Ned Currie.

Without realizing what was happening, Alice was trying feebly at first, but with growing determination, to get a new hold upon life. Beside the drug clerk she walked in silence, but sometimes in the darkness as they went stolidly along she put out her hand and touched softly the folds of his coat. When he left her at the gate before her mother's house she did not go indoors, but stood for a moment by the door. She wanted to call to the drug clerk, to ask him to sit with her in the darkness on the porch before the house, but was afraid he would not understand. "It is not him that I want," she told herself; "I want to avoid being so much alone. If I am not careful I will grow unaccustomed to being with people."

❀❖❀

During the early fall of her twenty-seventh year a passionate restlessness took possession of Alice. She could not bear to be in the company of the drug clerk, and when, in the evening, he came to walk with her she sent him away. Her mind became intensely active and when, weary from the long hours of standing behind the counter in the store, she went home and crawled into bed, she could not sleep. With staring eyes she looked into the darkness. Her imagination, like a child awakened from long sleep, played about the room. Deep within her there was something that would not be cheated by phantasies and that demanded some definite answer from life.

Alice took a pillow into her arms and held it tightly against her breasts. Getting out of bed, she arranged a blanket so that in the darkness it looked like a form lying between the sheets and, kneeling beside the bed, she caressed it, whispering words over and over, like a refrain. "Why doesn't something happen? Why am I left here alone?" she muttered. Although she sometimes thought of Ned Currie, she no longer depended on him. [Her desire had grown vague. She did not want Ned Currie or any other man. She wanted to be loved, to have something answer the call that was growing louder and louder within her.]

And then one night when it rained Alice had an adventure. It frightened and confused her. She had come home from the store at nine and found the house empty. Bush Milton had gone off to town and her mother to the house of a neighbor. Alice went upstairs to her room and undressed in the darkness. For a moment she stood by the window hearing the rain beat against the glass and then a strange desire took possession of her. Without stopping to think of what she intended to do, she ran downstairs through the dark house and out into the rain. As she stood on the little grass plot before the house and felt the cold rain on her body a mad desire to run naked through the streets took possession of her.

She thought that the rain would have some creative and wonderful effect on her body. Not for years had she felt so full of youth and courage. She wanted to leap and run, to cry out, to find some other lonely human and embrace him. On the brick sidewalk before the house a man stumbled homeward. Alice started to run. A wild, desperate mood took possession of her. "What do I care who it is. He is alone, and I will go to him," she thought; and then without stopping to consider the possible result of her madness, called softly. "Wait!" she cried. "Don't go away. Whoever you are, you must wait."

The man on the sidewalk stopped and stood listening.

He was an old man and somewhat deaf. Putting his hand to his mouth, he shouted. "What? What say?" he called.

Alice dropped to the ground and lay trembling. She was so frightened at the thought of what she had done that when the man had gone on his way she did not dare get to her feet, but crawled on hands and knees through the grass to the house. When she got to her own room she bolted the door and drew her dressing table across the doorway. Her body shook as with a chill and her hands trembled so that she had difficulty getting into her night-dress. When she got into bed she buried her face in the pillow and wept brokenheartedly. ["What is the matter with me? I will do something dreadful if I am not careful," she thought, and turning her face to the wall, began trying to force herself to face bravely the fact that many people must live and die alone, even in Winesburg.]

RESPECTABILITY

I F Y O U have lived in cities and have walked in the park on a summer afternoon, you have perhaps seen, blinking in a corner of his iron cage, a huge, grotesque kind of monkey, a creature with ugly, sagging, hairless skin below his eyes and a bright purple underbody. This monkey is a true monster. In the completeness of his ugliness he achieved a kind of perverted beauty. Children stopping before the cage are fascinated, men turn away with an air of disgust, and women linger for a moment, trying perhaps to remember which one of their male acquaintances the thing in some faint way resembles.

Had you been in the earlier years of your life a citizen of the village of Winesburg, Ohio, there would have been for you no mystery in regard to the beast in his cage. "It is like Wash Williams," you would have said. "As he sits in the corner there, the beast is exactly like old Wash sitting on the grass in the station yard on a summer evening after he has closed his office for the night."

Wash Williams, the telegraph operator of Winesburg, was the ugliest thing in town. His girth was immense, his neck thin, his legs feeble. He was dirty. Everything about him was unclean. Even the whites of his eyes looked soiled.

I go too fast. Not everything about Wash was unclean. He took care of his hands. His fingers were fat, but there was something sensitive and shapely in the hand that lay on the table by the instrument in the telegraph office. In

his youth Wash Williams had been called the best telegraph operator in the state, and in spite of his degrade-
ment to the obscure office at Winesburg, he was still proud
of his ability.

Wash Williams did not associate with the men of the
town in which he lived. "I'll have nothing to do with
them," he said, looking with bleary eyes at the men who
walked along the station platform past the telegraph
office. Up along Main Street he went in the evening to
Ed Griffith's saloon, and after drinking unbelievable quan-
tities of beer staggered off to his room in the New Willard
House and to his bed for the night.

Wash Williams was a man of courage. A thing had happened to him that made him hate life, and he hated it
whole-heartedly, with the abandon of a poet. First of all,
he hated women. "Bitches," he called them. His feeling
toward men was somewhat different. He pitied them.
"Does not every man let his life be managed for him by
some bitch or another?" he asked.

In Winesburg no attention was paid to Wash Williams
and his hatred of his fellows. Once Mrs. White, the
banker's wife, complained to the telegraph company, saying that the office in Winesburg was dirty and smelled
abominably, but nothing came of her complaint. Here and
there a man respected the operator. Instinctively the man
felt in him a glowing resentment of something he had not
the courage to resent. When Wash walked through the
streets such a one had an instinct to pay him homage, to
raise his hat or to bow before him. The superintendent
who had supervision over the telegraph operators on the
railroad that went through Winesburg felt that way. He
had put Wash into the obscure office at Winesburg to
avoid discharging him, and he meant to keep him there.
When he received the letter of complaint from the

banker's wife, he tore it up and laughed unpleasantly. For some reason he thought of his own wife as he tore up the letter.

Wash Williams once had a wife. When he was still a young man he married a woman at Dayton, Ohio. The woman was tall and slender and had blue eyes and yellow hair. Wash was himself a comely youth. He loved the woman with a love as absorbing as the hatred he later felt for all women.

In all of Winesburg there was but one person who knew the story of the thing that had made ugly the person and the character of Wash Williams. He once told the story to George Willard and the telling of the tale came about in this way:

George Willard went one evening to walk with Belle Carpenter, a trimmer of women's hats who worked in a millinery shop kept by Mrs. Kate McHugh. The young man was not in love with the woman, who, in fact, had a suitor who worked as bartender in Ed Griffith's saloon, but as they walked about under the trees they occasionally embraced. The night and their own thoughts had aroused something in them. As they were returning to Main Street they passed the little lawn beside the railroad station and saw Wash Williams apparently asleep on the grass beneath a tree. On the next evening the operator and George Willard walked out together. Down the railroad they went and sat on a pile of decaying railroad ties beside the tracks. It was then that the operator told the young reporter his story of hate.

Perhaps a dozen times George Willard and the strange, shapeless man who lived at his father's hotel had been on the point of talking. The young man looked at the hideous, leering face staring about the hotel dining room and was consumed with curiosity. Something he saw lurking in the staring eyes told him that the man who had nothing to say to others had nevertheless something to say to him. On the pile of railroad ties on the summer evening, he waited expectantly. When the operator remained silent and seemed to have changed his mind about talking, he tried to make conversation. "Were you ever married, Mr. Williams?" he began. "I suppose you were and your wife is dead, is that it?"

Wash Williams spat forth a succession of vile oaths. "Yes, she is dead," he agreed. "She is dead as all women are dead. She is a living-dead thing, walking in the sight of men and making the earth foul by her presence." Staring into the boy's eyes, the man became purple with rage. "Don't have fool notions in your head," he commanded. "My wife, she is dead; yes, surely. I tell you, all women are dead, my mother, your mother, that tall dark woman who works in the millinery store and with whom I saw you walking about yesterday—all of them, they are all dead. I tell you there is something rotten about them. I was married, sure. My wife was dead before she married me, she was a foul thing come out of a woman more foul. She was a thing sent to make life unbearable to me. I was a fool, do you see, as you are now, and so I married this woman. I would like to see men a little begin to understand women. They are sent to prevent men making the world worth while. It is a trick in Nature. Ugh! They are creeping, crawling, squirming things, they with their soft hands and their blue eyes. The sight of a woman sickens me. Why I don't kill every woman I see I don't know."

Half frightened and yet fascinated by the light burning in the eyes of the hideous old man, George Willard listened, afire with curiosity. Darkness came on and he leaned forward trying to see the face of the man who talked. When, in the gathering darkness, he could no longer see the purple, bloated face and the burning eyes, a curious fancy came to him. Wash Williams talked in low even tones that made his words seem the more terrible. In the darkness the young reporter found himself imagining that he sat on the railroad ties beside a comely young man with black hair and black shining eyes. There was something almost beautiful in the voice of Wash Williams, the hideous, telling his story of hate.

The telegraph operator of Winesburg, sitting in the darkness on the railroad ties, had become a poet. Hatred had raised him to that elevation. "It is because I saw you kissing the lips of that Belle Carpenter that I tell you my story," he said. "What happened to me may next happen to you. I want to put you on your guard. Already you may be having dreams in your head. I want to destroy them."

Wash Williams began telling the story of his married life with the tall blonde girl with blue eyes whom he had met when he was a young operator at Dayton, Ohio. Here and there his story was touched with moments of beauty intermingled with strings of vile curses. The operator had married the daughter of a dentist who was the youngest of three sisters. On his marriage day, because of his ability, he was promoted to a position as dispatcher at an increased salary and sent to an office at Columbus, Ohio. There he settled down with his young wife and began buying a house on the installment plan.

The young telegraph operator was madly in love. With a kind of religious fervor he had managed to go through the pitfalls of his youth and to remain virginal until after his marriage. He made for George Willard a picture of his life in the house at Columbus, Ohio, with the young wife. "In the garden back of our house we planted vegetables," he said, "you know, peas and corn and such things. We went to Columbus in early March and as soon as the days became warm I went to work in the garden. With a spade I turned up the black ground while she ran about laughing and pretending to be afraid of the worms I uncovered. Late in April came the planting. In the little paths among the seed beds she stood holding a paper bag in her hand. The bag was filled with seeds. A few at a time she handed me the seeds that I might thrust them into the warm, soft ground."

For a moment there was a catch in the voice of the man talking in the darkness. "I loved her," he said. "I don't claim not to be a fool. I love her yet. There in the dusk in the spring evening I crawled along the black ground to her feet and groveled before her. I kissed her shoes and the ankles above her shoes. When the hem of her garment touched my face I trembled. When after two years of that life I found she had managed to acquire three other lovers who came regularly to our house when I was away at work, I didn't want to touch them or her. I just sent her home to her mother and said nothing. There was nothing to say. I had four hundred dollars in the bank and I gave her that. I didn't ask her reasons. I didn't say anything. When she had gone I cried like a silly boy. Pretty soon I had a chance to sell the house and I sent that money to her."

Wash Williams and George Willard arose from the pile of railroad ties and walked along the tracks toward town. The operator finished his tale quickly, breathlessly.

"Her mother sent for me," he said. "She wrote me a letter and asked me to come to their house at Dayton. When I got there it was evening about this time."

Wash Williams' voice rose to a half scream. "I sat in the parlor of that house two hours. Her mother took me in there and left me. Their house was stylish. They were what is called respectable people. There were plush chairs and a couch in the room. I was trembling all over. I hated the men I thought had wronged her. I was sick of living alone and wanted her back. The longer I waited the more raw and tender I became. I thought that if she came in and just touched me with her hand I would perhaps faint away. I ached to forgive and forget."

Wash Williams stopped and stood staring at George Willard. The boy's body shook as from a chill. Again the man's voice became soft and low. "She came into the room naked," he went on. "Her mother did that. While I sat there she was taking the girl's clothes off, perhaps coaxing her to do it. First I heard voices at the door that led into a little hallway and then it opened softly. The girl was ashamed and stood perfectly still staring at the floor. The mother didn't come into the room. When she had pushed the girl in through the door she stood in the hallway waiting, hoping we would—well, you see—waiting."

George Willard and the telegraph operator came into the main street of Winesburg. The lights from the store windows lay bright and shining on the sidewalks. People moved about laughing and talking. The young reporter felt ill and weak. In imagination, he also became old and shapeless. "I didn't get the mother killed," said Wash Williams, staring up and down the street. "I struck her once with a chair and then the neighbors came in and took it away. She screamed so loud you see. I won't ever have a chance to kill her now. She died of a fever a month after that happened."

THE THINKER

THE HOUSE in which Seth Richmond of Winesburg lived with his mother had been at one time the show place of the town, but when young Seth lived there its glory had become somewhat dimmed. The huge brick house which Banker White had built on Buckeye Street had overshadowed it. The Richmond place was in a little valley far out at the end of Main Street. Farmers coming into town by a dusty road from the south passed by a grove of walnut trees, skirted the Fair Ground with its high board fence covered with advertisements, and trotted their horses down through the valley past the Richmond place into town. As much of the country north and south of Winesburg was devoted to fruit and berry raising, Seth saw wagon-loads of berry pickers—boys, girls, and women —going to the fields in the morning and returning covered with dust in the evening. The chattering crowd, with their rude jokes cried out from wagon to wagon, sometimes irritated him sharply. He regretted that he also could not laugh boisterously, shout meaningless jokes and make of himself a figure in the endless stream of moving, giggling activity that went up and down the road.

The Richmond house was built of limestone, and, although it was said in the village to have become run down, had in reality grown more beautiful with every passing year. Already time had begun a little to color the stone, lending a golden richness to its surface and in the evening or on dark days touching the shaded places beneath the eaves with wavering patches of browns and blacks.

The house had been built by Seth's grandfather, a stone quarryman, and it, together with the stone quarries on Lake Erie eighteen miles to the north, had been left to his son, Clarence Richmond, Seth's father. Clarence Richmond, a quiet passionate man extraordinarily admired by his neighbors, had been killed in a street fight with the editor of a newspaper in Toledo, Ohio. The fight concerned the publication of Clarence Richmond's name coupled with that of a woman school teacher, and as the dead man had begun the row by firing upon the editor, the effort to punish the slayer was unsuccessful. After the quarryman's death it was found that much of the money left to him had been squandered in speculation and in insecure investments made through the influence of friends.

Left with but a small income, Virginia Richmond had settled down to a retired life in the village and to the raising of her son. Although she had been deeply moved by the death of the husband and father, she did not at all believe the stories concerning him that ran about after his death. To her mind, the sensitive, boyish man whom all had instinctively loved, was but an unfortunate, a being too fine for everyday life. "You'll be hearing all sorts of stories, but you are not to believe what you hear," she said to her son. "He was a good man, full of tenderness for everyone, and should not have tried to be a man of affairs. No matter how much I were to plan and dream of your future, I could not imagine anything better for you than that you turn out as good a man as your father."

Several years after the death of her husband, Virginia Richmond had become alarmed at the growing demands upon her income and had set herself to the task of increasing it. She had learned stenography and through the influence of her husband's friends got the position of court stenographer at the county seat. There she went by train each morning during the sessions of the court, and when no court sat, spent her days working among the rosebushes in her garden. She was a tall, straight figure of a woman with a plain face and a great mass of brown hair.

In the relationship between Seth Richmond and his mother, there was a quality that even at eighteen had begun to color all of his traffic with men. An almost unhealthy respect for the youth kept the mother for the most part silent in his presence. When she did speak sharply to him he had only to look steadily into her eyes to see dawning there the puzzled look he had already noticed in the eyes of others when he looked at them.

The truth was that the son thought with remarkable clearness and the mother did not. She expected from all people certain conventional reactions to life. A boy was your son, you scolded him and he trembled and looked at the floor. When you had scolded enough he wept and all was forgiven. After the weeping and when he had gone to bed, you crept into his room and kissed him.

Virginia Richmond could not understand why her son did not do these things. After the severest reprimand, he did not tremble and look at the floor but instead looked steadily at her, causing uneasy doubts to invade her mind. As for creeping into his room—after Seth had passed his fifteenth year, she would have been half afraid to do anything of the kind.

Once when he was a boy of sixteen, Seth in company with two other boys ran away from home. The three boys climbed into the open door of an empty freight car and rode some forty miles to a town where a fair was being held. One of the boys had a bottle filled with a combination of whiskey and blackberry wine, and the three sat with legs dangling out of the car door drinking from the bottle. Seth's two companions sang and waved their hands to idlers about the stations of the towns through which the train passed. They planned raids upon the baskets of farmers who had come with their families to the fair. "We will live like kings and won't have to spend a penny to see the fair and horse races," they declared boastfully.

After the disappearance of Seth, Virginia Richmond walked up and down the floor of her home filled with vague alarms. Although on the next day she discovered, through an inquiry made by the town marshal, on what adventure the boys had gone, she could not quiet herself. All through the night she lay awake hearing the clock tick and telling herself that Seth, like his father, would come to a sudden and violent end. So determined was she that the boy should this time feel the weight of her wrath that, although she would not allow the marshal to interfere with his adventure, she got out pencil and paper and wrote down a series of sharp, stinging reproofs she intended to pour out upon him. The reproofs she committed to memory, going about the garden and saying them aloud like an actor memorizing his part.

And when, at the end of the week, Seth returned, a little weary and with coal soot in his ears and about his eyes, she again found herself unable to reprove him. Walking into the house he hung his cap on a nail by the kitchen door and stood looking steadily at her. "I wanted to turn back within an hour after we had started," he explained. "I didn't know what to do. I knew you would be bothered, but I knew also that if I didn't go on I would be ashamed of myself. I went through with the thing for my own good. It was uncomfortable, sleeping on wet straw, and two drunken Negroes came and slept with us. When I stole a

lunch basket out of a farmer's wagon I couldn't help thinking of his children going all day without food. I was sick
of the whole affair, but I was determined to stick it out
until the other boys were ready to come back."

"I'm glad you did stick it out," replied the mother, half
resentfully, and kissing him upon the forehead pretended
to busy herself with the work about the house.

On a summer evening Seth Richmond went to the New
Willard House to visit his friend, George Willard. It had
rained during the afternoon, but as he walked through
Main Street, the sky had partially cleared and a golden
glow lit up the west. Going around a corner, he turned in
at the door of the hotel and began to climb the stairway
leading up to his friend's room. In the hotel office the proprietor and two traveling men were engaged in a discussion
of politics.

On the stairway Seth stopped and listened to the voices
of the men below. They were excited and talked rapidly.
Tom Willard was berating the traveling men. "I am a
Democrat but your talk makes me sick," he said. "You
don't understand McKinley. McKinley and Mark Hanna
are friends. It is impossible perhaps for your mind to grasp
that. If anyone tells you that a friendship can be deeper and
bigger and more worth while than dollars and cents, or
even more worth while than state politics, you snicker and
laugh."

The landlord was interrupted by one of the guests, a
tall, grey-mustached man who worked for a wholesale
grocery house. "Do you think that I've lived in Cleveland
all these years without knowing Mark Hanna?" he demanded. "Your talk is piffle. Hanna is after money and
nothing else. This McKinley is his tool. He has McKinley
bluffed and don't you forget it."

The young man on the stairs did not linger to hear the

rest of the discussion, but went on up the stairway and into a little dark hall. Something in the voices of the men talking in the hotel office started a chain of thoughts in his mind. [He was lonely and had begun to think that loneliness was a part of his character, something that would always stay with him.] Stepping into a side hall he stood by a window that looked into an alleyway. At the back of his shop stood Abner Groff, the town baker. His tiny bloodshot eyes looked up and down the alleyway. In his shop someone called the baker, who pretended not to hear. The baker had an empty milk bottle in his hand and an angry sullen look in his eyes.

In Winesburg, Seth Richmond was called the "deep one." "He's like his father," men said as he went through the streets. "He'll break out some of these days. You wait and see."

The talk of the town and the respect with which men and boys instinctively greeted him, as all men greet silent people, had affected Seth Richmond's outlook on life and on himself. He, like most boys, was deeper than boys are given credit for being, but he was not what the men of the town, and even his mother, thought him to be. [No great underlying purpose lay back of his habitual silence, and he had no definite plan for his life.] When the boys with whom he associated were noisy and quarrelsome, he stood quietly at one side. With calm eyes he watched the gesticulating lively figures of his companions. He wasn't particularly interested in what was going on, and sometimes wondered if he would ever be particularly interested in anything. Now, as he stood in the half-darkness by the window watching the baker, he wished that he himself might become thoroughly stirred by something, even by the fits of sullen anger for which Baker Groff was noted. "It would be better for me if I could become excited and wrangle about politics like windy old Tom Willard," he thought, as he left the window and went again along the hallway to the room occupied by his friend, George Willard.

George Willard was older than Seth Richmond, but in the rather odd friendship between the two, it was he who was forever courting and the younger boy who was being courted. The paper on which George worked had one policy. It strove to mention by name in each issue, as many as possible of the inhabitants of the village. Like an excited dog, George Willard ran here and there, noting on his pad of paper who had gone on business to the county seat or had returned from a visit to a neighboring village. All day he wrote little facts upon the pad. "A. P. Wringlet had received a shipment of straw hats. Ed Byerbaum and Tom Marshall were in Cleveland Friday. Uncle Tom Sinnings is building a new barn on his place on the Valley Road."

The idea that George Willard would some day become a writer had given him a place of distinction in Winesburg, and to Seth Richmond he talked continually of the matter. "It's the easiest of all lives to live," he declared, becoming excited and boastful. "Here and there you go and there is no one to boss you. Though you are in India or in the South Seas in a boat, you have but to write and there you are. Wait till I get my name up and then see what fun I shall have."

In George Willard's room, which had a window looking down into an alleyway and one that looked across railroad tracks to Biff Carter's Lunch Room facing the railroad station, Seth Richmond sat in a chair and looked at the floor. George Willard, who had been sitting for an hour idly playing with a lead pencil, greeted him effusively. "I've been trying to write a love story," he explained, laughing nervously. Lighting a pipe he began walking up and down the room. "I know what I'm going to do. I'm going to fall in love. I've been sitting here and thinking it over and I'm going to do it."

As though embarrassed by his declaration, George went to a window and turning his back to his friend leaned out. "I know who I'm going to fall in love with," he said sharply. "It's Helen White. She is the only girl in town with any 'get-up' to her."

Struck with a new idea, young Willard turned and walked toward his visitor. "Look here," he said. "You know Helen White better than I do. I want you to tell her what I said. You just get to talking to her and say that I'm in love with her. See what she says to that. See how she takes it, and then you come and tell me."

Seth Richmond arose and went toward the door. The words of his comrade irritated him unbearably. "Well, good-bye," he said briefly.

George was amazed. Running forward he stood in the darkness trying to look into Seth's face. "What's the matter? What are you going to do? You stay here and let's talk," he urged.

A wave of resentment directed against his friend, the men of the town who were, he thought, perpetually talking of nothing, and most of all, against his own habit of silence, made Seth half desperate. "Aw, speak to her yourself," he burst forth and then, going quickly through the door, slammed it sharply in his friend's face. "I'm going to find Helen White and talk to her, but not about him," he muttered.

Seth went down the stairway and out at the front door of the hotel muttering with wrath. Crossing a little dusty street and climbing a low iron railing, he went to sit upon the grass in the station yard. George Willard he thought a profound fool, and he wished that he had said so more vigorously. Although his acquaintanceship with Helen White, the banker's daughter, was outwardly but casual, she was often the subject of his thoughts and he felt that she was something private and personal to himself. "The busy fool with his love stories," he muttered, staring back over his shoulder at George Willard's room, "why does he never tire of his eternal talking."

It was berry harvest time in Winesburg and upon the station platform men and boys loaded the boxes of red, fragrant berries into two express cars that stood upon the siding. A June moon was in the sky, although in the west a storm threatened, and no street lamps were lighted. In the dim light the figures of the men standing upon the express truck and pitching the boxes in at the doors of the cars were but dimly discernible. Upon the iron railing that protected the station lawn sat other men. Pipes were lighted. Village jokes went back and forth. Away in the distance a train whistled and the men loading the boxes into the cars worked with renewed activity.

Seth arose from his place on the grass and went silently past the men perched upon the railing and into Main Street. He had come to a resolution. "I'll get out of here," he told himself. "What good am I here? I'm going to some city and go to work. I'll tell mother about it tomorrow."

Seth Richmond went slowly along Main Street, past Wacker's Cigar Store and the Town Hall, and into Buckeye Street. He was depressed by the thought that he was not a part of the life in his own town, but the depression did not cut deeply as he did not think of himself as at fault. In the heavy shadows of a big tree before Doctor Welling's house, he stopped and stood watching half-witted Turk Smollet, who was pushing a wheelbarrow in the road. The old man with his absurdly boyish mind had a dozen long boards on the wheelbarrow, and, as he hurried along the road, balanced the load with extreme nicety. "Easy there, Turk! Steady now, old boy!" the old man shouted to himself, and laughed so that the load of boards rocked dangerously.

Seth knew Turk Smollet, the half dangerous old wood chopper whose peculiarities added so much of color to the life of the village. He knew that when Turk got into Main Street he would become the center of a whirlwind of cries and comments, that in truth the old man was going far out of his way in order to pass through Main Street and exhibit his skill in wheeling the boards. "If George Willard were here, he'd have something to say," thought Seth. "George belongs to this town. He'd shout at Turk and Turk would shout at him. They'd both be secretly pleased by what they had said. It's different with me. I don't belong. I'll not make a fuss about it, but I'm going to get out of here."

Seth stumbled forward through the half-darkness, feeling himself an outcast in his own town. He began to pity himself, but a sense of the absurdity of his thoughts made him smile. In the end he decided that he was simply old beyond his years and not at all a subject for self-pity. "I'm made to go to work. I may be able to make a place for myself by steady working, and I might as well be at it," he decided.

Seth went to the house of Banker White and stood in the darkness by the front door. On the door hung a heavy brass knocker, an innovation introduced into the village by Helen White's mother, who had also organized a women's club for the study of poetry. Seth raised the knocker and let it fall. Its heavy clatter sounded like a report from distant guns. "How awkward and foolish I am," he thought. "If Mrs. White comes to the door, I won't know what to say."

It was Helen White who came to the door and found Seth standing at the edge of the porch. Blushing with pleasure, she stepped forward, closing the door softly. "I'm going to get out of town. I don't know what I'll do, but I'm going to get out of here and go to work. I think I'll go to Columbus," he said. "Perhaps I'll get into the State University down there. Anyway, I'm going. I'll tell mother tonight." He hesitated and looked doubtfully about. "Perhaps you wouldn't mind coming to walk with me?"

Seth and Helen walked through the streets beneath the trees. Heavy clouds had drifted across the face of the moon, and before them in the deep twilight went a man with a short ladder upon his shoulder. Hurrying forward, the man stopped at the street crossing and, putting the ladder against the wooden lamp-post, lighted the village lights so that their way was half lighted, half darkened, by the lamps and by the deepening shadows cast by the low-branched trees. In the tops of the trees the wind began to play, disturbing the sleeping birds so that they flew about calling plaintively. In the lighted space before one of the lamps, two bats wheeled and circled, pursuing the gathering swarm of night flies.

Since Seth had been a boy in knee trousers there had been a half expressed intimacy between him and the maiden who now for the first time walked beside him. For a time she had been beset with a madness for writing notes which she addressed to Seth. He had found them concealed in his books at school and one had been given him by a child met in the street, while several had been delivered through the village post office.

The notes had been written in a round, boyish hand and had reflected a mind inflamed by novel reading. Seth had not answered them, although he had been moved and flattered by some of the sentences scrawled in pencil upon the stationery of the banker's wife. Putting them into the pocket of his coat, he went through the street or stood by the fence in the school yard with something burning at his side. He thought it fine that he should be thus selected as the favorite of the richest and most attractive girl in town.

Helen and Seth stopped by a fence near where a low dark building faced the street. The building had once been a factory for the making of barrel staves but was now vacant. Across the street upon the porch of a house a man and woman talked of their childhood, their voices coming clearly across to the half-embarrassed youth and maiden. There was the sound of scraping chairs and the man and woman came down the gravel path to a wooden gate. Standing outside the gate, the man leaned over and kissed the woman. "For old times' sake," he said and, turning, walked rapidly away along the sidewalk.

"That's Belle Turner," whispered Helen, and put her hand boldly into Seth's hand. "I didn't know she had a fellow. I thought she was too old for that." Seth laughed uneasily. The hand of the girl was warm and a strange, dizzy feeling crept over him. Into his mind came a desire to tell her something he had been determined not to tell. "George Willard's in love with you," he said, and in spite of his agitation his voice was low and quiet. "He's writing a story, and he wants to be in love. He wants to know how it feels. He wanted me to tell you and see what you said."

Again Helen and Seth walked in silence. They came to the garden surrounding the old Richmond place and going through a gap in the hedge sat on a wooden bench beneath a bush.

On the street as he walked beside the girl new and daring thoughts had come into Seth Richmond's mind. He began to regret his decision to get out of town. "It would be something new and altogether delightful to remain and walk often through the streets with Helen White," he thought. In imagination he saw himself putting his arm about her waist and feeling her arms clasped tightly about his neck. One of those odd combinations of events and places made him connect the idea of love-making with this girl and a spot he had visited some days before. He had gone on an errand to the house of a farmer who lived on a hillside beyond the Fair Ground and had returned by a path through a field. At the foot of the hill below the farmer's house Seth had stopped beneath a sycamore tree and looked about him. A soft humming noise had greeted his ears. For a moment he had thought the tree must be the home of a swarm of bees.

And then, looking down, Seth had seen the bees everywhere all about him in the long grass. He stood in a mass of weeds that grew waist-high in the field that ran away from the hillside. The weeds were abloom with tiny purple blossoms and gave forth an overpowering fragrance. Upon the weeds the bees were gathered in armies, singing as they worked.

Seth imagined himself lying on a summer evening, buried deep among the weeds beneath the tree. Beside him, in the scene built in his fancy, lay Helen White, her hand lying in his hand. A peculiar reluctance kept him from kissing her lips, but he felt he might have done that if he wished. Instead, he lay perfectly still, looking at her and listening to the army of bees that sang the sustained masterful song of labor above his head.

On the bench in the garden Seth stirred uneasily. Releasing the hand of the girl, he thrust his hands into his trouser pockers. A desire to impress the mind of his companion with the importance of the resolution he had made came over him and he nodded his head toward the house. "Mother'll make a fuss, I suppose," he whispered. "She hasn't thought at all about what I'm going to do in life. She thinks I'm going to stay on here forever just being a boy."

Seth's voice became charged with boyish earnestness. "You see, I've got to strike out. I've got to get to work. It's what I'm good for."

Helen White was impressed. She nodded her head and a feeling of admiration swept over her. "This is as it should be," she thought. "This boy is not a boy at all, but a strong, purposeful man." Certain vague desires that had been invading her body were swept away and she sat up very straight on the bench. The thunder continued to rumble and flashes of heat lightning lit up the eastern sky. The garden that had been so mysterious and vast, a place that with Seth beside her might have become the background for strange and wonderful adventures, now seemed no more than an ordinary Winesburg back yard, quite definite and limited in its outlines.

"What will you do up there?" she whispered.

Seth turned half around on the bench, striving to see her face in the darkness. He thought her infinitely more sensible and straightforward than George Willard, and was glad he had come away from his friend. A feeling of impatience with the town that had been in his mind returned, and he tried to tell her of it. "Everyone talks and talks," he began. "I'm sick of it. I'll do something, get into some kind of work where talk don't count. Maybe I'll just be a mechanic in a shop. I don't know. I guess I don't care much. I just want to work and keep quiet. That's all I've got in my mind."

Seth arose from the bench and put out his hand. He

did not want to bring the meeting to an end but could not think of anything more to say. "It's the last time we'll see each other," he whispered.

A wave of sentiment swept over Helen. Putting her hand upon Seth's shoulder, she started to draw his face down toward her own upturned face. The act was one of pure affection and cutting regret that some vague adventure that had been present in the spirit of the night would now never be realized. "I think I'd better be going along," she said, letting her hand fall heavily to her side. A thought came to her. "Don't you go with me; I want to be alone," she said. "You go and talk with your mother. You'd better do that now."

Seth hesitated and, as he stood waiting, the girl turned and ran away through the hedge. A desire to run after her came to him, but he only stood staring, perplexed and puzzled by her action as he had been perplexed and puzzled by all of the life of the town out of which she had come. Walking slowly toward the house, he stopped in the shadow of a large tree and looked at his mother sitting by a lighted window busily sewing. The feeling of loneliness that had visited him earlier in the evening returned and colored his thoughts of the adventure through which he had just passed. "Huh!" he exclaimed, turning and staring in the direction taken by Helen White. "That's how things'll turn out. She'll be like the rest. I suppose she'll begin now to look at me in a funny way." He looked at the ground and pondered this thought. "She'll be embarrassed and feel strange when I'm around," he whispered to himself. "That's how it'll be. That's how everything'll turn out. When it comes to loving someone, it won't never be me. It'll be someone else—some fool—someone who talks a lot—someone like that George Willard."

TANDY

U NTIL SHE was seven years old she lived in
an old unpainted house on an unused road that led off
Trunion Pike. Her father gave her but little attention and
her mother was dead. The father spent his time talking
and thinking of religion. He proclaimed himself an
agnostic and was so absorbed in destroying the ideas of
God that had crept into the minds of his neighbors that
he never saw God manifesting himself in the little child
that, half forgotten, lived here and there on the bounty of
her dead mother's relatives.

A stranger came to Winesburg and saw in the child
what the father did not see. He was a tall, red-haired young
man who was almost always drunk. Sometimes he sat in a
chair before the New Willard House with Tom Hard,
the father. As Tom talked, declaring there could be no
God, the stranger smiled and winked at the bystanders.
He and Tom became friends and were much together.

The stranger was the son of a rich merchant of Cleveland
and had come to Winesburg on a mission. He wanted to
cure himself of the habit of drink, and thought that by
escaping from his city associates and living in a rural community he would have a better chance in the struggle with
the appetite that was destroying him.

His sojourn in Winesburg was not a success. The dullness of the passing hours led to his drinking harder than
ever. But he did succeed in doing something. He gave a
name rich with meaning to Tom Hard's daughter.

One evening when he was recovering from a long debauch the stranger came reeling along the main street of the town. Tom Hard sat in a chair before the New Willard House with his daughter, then a child of five, on his knees. Beside him on the board sidewalk sat young George Willard. The stranger dropped into a chair beside them. His body shook and when he tried to talk his voice trembled.

It was late evening and darkness lay over the town and over the railroad that ran along the foot of a little incline before the hotel. Somewhere in the distance, off to the west, there was a prolonged blast from the whistle of a passenger engine. A dog that had been sleeping in the roadway arose and barked. The stranger began to babble and made a prophecy concerning the child that lay in the arms of the agnostic.

"I came here to quit drinking," he said, and tears began to run down his cheeks. He did not look at Tom Hard, but leaned forward and stared into the darkness as though seeing a vision. "I ran away to the country to be cured, but I am not cured. There is a reason." He turned to look at the child who sat up very straight on her father's knee and returned the look.

The stranger touched Tom Hard on the arm. "Drink is not the only thing to which I am addicted," he said. "There is something else. I am a lover and have not found my thing to love. That is a big point if you know enough to realize what I mean. It makes my destruction inevitable, you see. There are few who understand that."

The stranger became silent and seemed overcome with sadness, but another blast from the whistle of the passenger engine aroused him. "I have not lost faith. I proclaim that. I have only been brought to the place where I know my faith will not be realized," he declared hoarsely.

He looked hard at the child and began to address her, pay-no more attention to the father. "There is a woman com-ing," he said, and his voice was now sharp and earnest. "I have missed her, you see. She did not come in my time. You may be the woman. It would be like fate to let me stand in her presence once, on such an evening as this, when I have destroyed myself with drink and she is as yet only a child."

The shoulders of the stranger shook violently, and when he tried to roll a cigarette the paper fell from his trembling fingers. He grew angry and scolded. "They think it's easy to be a woman, to be loved, but I know better," he de-clared. Again he turned to the child. "I understand," he cried. "Perhaps of all men I alone understand."

His glance again wandered away to the darkened street. "I know about her, although she has never crossed my path," he said softly. "I know about her struggles and her defeats. It is because of her defeats that she is to me the lovely one. Out of her defeats has been born a new quality in woman. I have a name for it. I call it Tandy. I made up the name when I was a true dreamer and before my body became vile. It is the quality of being strong to be loved. It is something men need from women and that they do not get."

The stranger arose and stood before Tom Hard. His body rocked back and forth and he seemed about to fall, but instead he dropped to his knees on the sidewalk and raised the hands of the little girl to his drunken lips. He kissed them ecstatically. "Be Tandy, little one," he pleaded. "Dare to be strong and courageous. That is the road. Venture anything. Be brave enough to dare to be loved. Be something more than man or woman. Be Tandy."

The stranger arose and staggered off down the street. A day or two later he got aboard a train and returned to his home in Cleveland. On the summer evening, after the talk before the hotel, Tom Hard took the girl child to the house of a relative where she had been invited to spend the night. As he went along in the darkness under the trees he forgot the babbling voice of the stranger and his mind returned to the making of arguments by which he might destroy men's faith in God. He spoke his daughter's name and she began to weep.

"I don't want to be called that," she declared. "I want to be called Tandy—Tandy Hard." The child wept so bitterly that Tom Hard was touched and tried to comfort her. He stopped beneath a tree and, taking her into his arms, began to caress her. "Be good, now," he said sharply; but she would not be quieted. With childish abandon she gave herself over to grief, her voice breaking the evening stillness of the street. "I want to be Tandy. I want to be Tandy. I want to be Tandy Hard," she cried, shaking her head and sobbing as though her young strength were not enough to bear the vision the words of the drunkard had brought to her.

THE STRENGTH OF GOD

THE REVEREND CURTIS HARTMAN was pastor of the Presbyterian Church of Winesburg, and had been in that position ten years. He was forty years old, and by his nature very silent and reticent. To preach, standing in the pulpit before the people, was always a hardship for him and from Wednesday morning until Saturday evening he thought of nothing but the two sermons that must be preached on Sunday. Early on Sunday morning he went into a little room called a study in the bell tower of the church and prayed. In his prayers there was one note that always predominated. "Give me strength and courage for Thy work, O Lord!" he pleaded, kneeling on the bare floor and bowing his head in the presence of the task that lay before him.

The Reverend Hartman was a tall man with a brown beard. His wife, a stout, nervous woman, was the daughter of a manufacturer of underwear at Cleveland, Ohio. The minister himself was rather a favorite in the town. The elders of the church liked him because he was quiet and unpretentious and Mrs. White, the banker's wife, thought him scholarly and refined.

The Presbyterian Church held itself somewhat aloof from the other churches of Winesburg. It was larger and more imposing and its minister was better paid. He even had a carriage of his own and on summer evenings sometimes drove about town with his wife. Through Main Street and up and down Buckeye Street he went, bowing gravely to the people, while his wife, afire with secret pride, looked at him out of the corners of her eyes and worried lest the horse become frightened and run away.

For a good many years after he came to Winesburg things went well with Curtis Hartman. He was not one to arouse keen enthusiasm among the worshippers in his church but on the other hand he made no enemies. In reality he was much in earnest and sometimes suffered prolonged periods of remorse because he could not go crying the word of God in the highways and byways of the town. He wondered if the flame of the spirit really burned in him and dreamed of a day when a strong sweet new current of power would come like a great wind into his voice and his soul and the people would tremble before the spirit of God made manifest in him. "I am a poor stick and that will never really happen to me," he mused dejectedly, and then a patient smile lit up his features. "Oh well, I suppose I'm doing well enough," he added philosophically.

The room in the bell tower of the church, where on Sunday mornings the minister prayed for an increase in him of the power of God, had but one window. It was long and narrow and swung outward on a hinge like a door. On the window, made of little leaded panes, was a design showing the Christ laying his hand upon the head of a child. One Sunday morning in the summer as he sat by his desk in the room with a large Bible opened before him, and the sheets of his sermon scattered about, the minister was shocked to see, in the upper room of the house next door, a woman lying in her bed and smoking a cigarette while she read a book. Curtis Hartman went on tiptoe to the window and closed it softly. He was horror stricken at the thought of a woman smoking and trembled also to think that his eyes, just raised from the pages of the book of God, had looked upon the bare shoulders and white throat of a woman. With his brain in a whirl he went down into the pulpit and preached a long sermon without once thinking of his gestures or his voice. The sermon attracted unusual attention because of its power and clearness. "I wonder if she is listening, if my voice is carrying a message into her soul," he thought and began to hope that on future Sunday mornings he might be able to say words that would touch and awaken the woman apparently far gone in secret sin.

The house next door to the Presbyterian Church, through the windows of which the minister had seen the sight that had so upset him, was occupied by two women. Aunt Elizabeth Swift, a grey competent-looking widow with money in the Winesburg National Bank, lived there with her daughter Kate Swift, a school teacher. The school teacher was thirty years old and had a neat trim-looking figure. She had few friends and bore a reputation of having a sharp tongue. When he began to think about her, Curtis Hartman remembered that she had been to Europe and had lived for two years in New York City. "Perhaps after all her smoking means nothing," he thought. He began to remember that when he was a student in college and occasionally read novels, good although somewhat worldly women, had smoked through the pages of a book that had once fallen into his hands. With a rush of new determination he worked on his sermons all through the week and forgot, in his zeal to reach the ears and the soul of this new listener, both his embarrassment in the pulpit and the necessity of prayer in the study on Sunday mornings.

Reverend Hartman's experience with women had been somewhat limited. He was the son of a wagon maker from Muncie, Indiana, and had worked his way through college. The daughter of the underwear manufacturer had boarded in a house where he lived during his school days and he had married her after a formal and prolonged courtship, carried on for the most part by the girl herself. On his marriage day the underwear manufacturer had given his daughter five thousand dollars and he promised to leave her at least twice that amount in his will. The minister had thought himself fortunate in marriage and had never permitted himself to think of other women. He did not want to think of other women. What he wanted was to do the work of God quietly and earnestly.

In the soul of the minister a struggle awoke. From wanting to reach the ears of Kate Swift, and through his sermons to delve into her soul, he began to want also to look again at the figure lying white and quiet in the bed. On a Sunday morning when he could not sleep because of his thoughts he arose and went to walk in the streets. When he had gone along Main Street almost to the old Richmond place he stopped and picking up a stone rushed off to the room in the bell tower. With the stone he broke out a corner of the window and then locked the door and sat down at the desk before the open Bible to wait. When the shade of the window to Kate Swift's room was raised he could see, through the hole, directly into her bed, but she was not there. She also had arisen and had gone for a walk and the hand that raised the shade was the hand of Aunt Elizabeth Swift.

The minister almost wept with joy at this deliverance from the carnal desire to "peep" and went back to his own house praising God. In an ill moment he forgot, however, to stop the hole in the window. The piece of glass broken out at the corner of the window just nipped off the bare heel of the boy standing motionless and looking with rapt eyes into the face of the Christ.

Curtis Hartman forgot his sermon on that Sunday morning. He talked to his congregation and in his talk said that it was a mistake for people to think of their minister as a man set aside and intended by nature to lead a blameless life. "Out of my own experience I know that we, who are the ministers of God's word, are beset by the same temptations that assail you," he declared. "I have been tempted and have surrendered to temptation. It is only the hand of God, placed beneath my head, that has raised me up. As he has raised me so also will he raise you. Do not despair. In your hour of sin raise your eyes to the skies and you will be again and again saved."

Resolutely the minister put the thoughts of the woman in the bed out of his mind and began to be something like a lover in the presence of his wife. One evening when they drove out together he turned the horse out of Buckeye Street and in the darkness on Gospel Hill, above Waterworks Pond, put his arm about Sarah Hartman's waist. When he had eaten breakfast in the morning and was ready to retire to his study at the back of his house he went around the table and kissed his wife on the cheek. When thoughts of Kate Swift came into his head, he smiled and raised his eyes to the skies. "Intercede for me, Master," he muttered, "keep me in the narrow path intent on Thy work."

And now began the real struggle in the soul of the brown-bearded minister. By chance he discovered that Kate Swift was in the habit of lying in her bed in the evenings and reading a book. A lamp stood on a table by the side of the bed and the light streamed down upon her white shoulders and bare throat. On the evening when he made the discovery the minister sat at the desk in the study from nine until after eleven and when her light was put out stumbled out of the church to spend two more hours walking and praying in the streets. He did not want to kiss the shoulders and the throat of Kate Swift and had not allowed his mind to dwell on such thoughts. He did not know what he wanted. "I am God's child and he must save me from myself," he cried, in the darkness under the trees as he wandered in the streets. By a tree he stood and looked at the sky that was covered with hurrying clouds. He began to talk to God intimately and closely. "Please, Father, do not forget me. Give me power to go tomorrow and repair the hole in the window. Lift my eyes again to the skies. Stay with me, Thy servant, in his hour of need."

Up and down through the silent streets walked the minister and for days and weeks his soul was troubled. He could not understand the temptation that had come to him nor could he fathom the reason for its coming. In a way he began to blame God, saying to himself that he had tried to keep his feet in the true path and had not run about seeking sin. "Through my days as a young man and all through my life here I have gone quietly about my work," he declared. "Why now should I be tempted? What have I done that this burden should be laid on me?"

Three times during the early fall and winter of that year Curtis Hartman crept out of his house to the room in the bell tower to sit in the darkness looking at the figure of Kate Swift lying in her bed and later went to walk and pray in the streets. He could not understand himself. For weeks he would go along scarcely thinking of the school teacher and telling himself that he had conquered the carnal desire to look at her body. And then something would happen. As he sat in the study of his own house, hard at work on a sermon, he would become nervous and begin to walk up and down the room. "I will go out into the streets," he told himself and even as he let himself in at the church door he persistently denied to himself the cause of his being there. "I will not repair the hole in the window and I will train myself to come here at night and sit in the presence of this woman without raising my eyes. I will not be defeated in this thing. The Lord has devised this temptation as a test of my soul and I will grope my way out of darkness into the light of righteousness."

One night in January when it was bitter cold and snow lay deep on the streets of Winesburg Curtis Hartman paid his last visit to the room in the bell tower of the church. It was past nine o'clock when he left his own house and he set out so hurriedly that he forgot to put on his overshoes. In Main Street no one was abroad but Hop Higgins the night watchman and in the whole town no one was awake but the watchman and young George Willard, who sat in the office of the *Winesburg Eagle* trying to write a story. Along the street to the church went the minister, plowing through the drifts and thinking that this time he would utterly give way to sin. "I want to look at the woman and to think of kissing her shoulders and I am going to let myself think what I choose," he declared bitterly and tears came into his eyes. He began to think that he would get out of the ministry and try some other way of life. "I shall go to some city and get into business," he declared. "If my nature is such that I cannot resist sin, I shall give myself over to sin. At least I shall not be a hypocrite, preaching the word of God with my mind thinking of the shoulders and neck of a woman who does not belong to me."

It was cold in the room of the bell tower of the church on that January night and almost as soon as he came into the room Curtis Hartman knew that if he stayed he would be ill. His feet were wet from tramping in the snow and there was no fire. In the room in the house next door Kate Swift had not yet appeared. With grim determination the man sat down to wait. Sitting in the chair and gripping the edge of the desk on which lay the Bible he stared into the darkness thinking the blackest thoughts of his life. He thought of his wife and for the moment almost hated her. "She has always been ashamed of passion and has cheated me," he thought. "Man has a right to expect living passion and beauty in a woman. He has no right to forget that he is an animal and in me there is something that is Greek. I will throw off the woman of my bosom and seek other women. I will besiege this school teacher. I will fly in the face of all men and if I am a creature of carnal lusts I will live then for my lusts."

The distracted man trembled from head to foot, partly from cold, partly from the struggle in which he was engaged. Hours passed and a fever assailed his body. His throat began to hurt and his teeth chattered. His feet on the study floor felt like two cakes of ice. Still he would not give up. "I will see this woman and will think the thoughts I have never dared to think," he told himself, gripping the edge of the desk and waiting.

Curtis Hartman came near dying from the effects of that night of waiting in the church, and also he found in the thing that happened what he took to be the way of life for him. On other evenings when he had waited he had not been able to see, through the little hole in the glass, any part of the school teacher's room except that occupied by her bed. In the darkness he had waited until the woman suddenly appeared sitting in the bed in her white night-robe. When the light was turned up she propped herself up among the pillows and read a book. Sometimes she smoked one of the cigarettes. Only her bare shoulders and throat were visible.

On the January night, after he had come near dying with cold and after his mind had two or three times ac-

tually slipped away into an odd land of fantasy so that he
had by an exercise of will power to force himself back into
consciousness, Kate Swift appeared. In the room next door
a lamp was lighted and the waiting man stared into an
empty bed. Then upon the bed before his eyes a naked
woman threw herself. Lying face downward she wept
and beat with her fists upon the pillow. With a final outburst of weeping she half arose, and in the presence of the
man who had waited to look and to think thoughts the
woman of sin began to pray. In the lamplight her figure,
slim and strong, looked like the figure of the boy in the
presence of the Christ on the leaded window.

Curtis Hartman never remembered how he got out of
the church. With a cry he arose, dragging the heavy desk
along the floor. The Bible fell, making a great clatter in
the silence. When the light in the house next door went
out he stumbled down the stairway and into the street.
Along the street he went and ran in at the door of
the *Winesburg Eagle*. To George Willard, who was
tramping up and down in the office undergoing a struggle
of his own, he began to talk half incoherently. "The ways
of God are beyond human understanding," he cried, running in quickly and closing the door. He began to advance
upon the young man, his eyes glowing and his voice ringing with fervor. "I have found the light," he cried. "After
ten years in this town, God has manifested himself to me
in the body of a woman." His voice dropped and he began
to whisper. "I did not understand," he said. "What I took
to be a trial of my soul was only a preparation for a new
and more beautiful fervor of the spirit. God has appeared
to me in the person of Kate Swift, the school teacher,
kneeling naked on a bed. Do you know Kate Swift? Although she may not be aware of it, she is an instrument of
God, bearing the message of truth."

Reverend Curtis Hartman turned and ran out of the office. At the door he stopped, and after looking up and down the deserted street, turned again to George Willard. "I am delivered. Have no fear." He held up a bleeding fist for the young man to see. "I smashed the glass of the window," he cried. "Now it will have to be wholly replaced. The strength of God was in me and I broke it with my fist."

THE TEACHER

Snow lay deep in the streets of Winesburg. It had begun to snow about ten o'clock in the morning and a wind sprang up and blew the snow in clouds along Main Street. The frozen mud roads that led into town were fairly smooth and in places ice covered the mud. "There will be good sleighing," said Will Henderson, standing by the bar in Ed Griffith's saloon. Out of the saloon he went and met Sylvester West the druggist stumbling along in the kind of heavy overshoes called arctics. "Snow will bring the people into town on Saturday," said the druggist. The two men stopped and discussed their affairs. Will Henderson, who had on a light overcoat and no overshoes, kicked the heel of his left foot with the toe of the right. "Snow will be good for the wheat," observed the druggist sagely.

Young George Willard, who had nothing to do, was glad because he did not feel like working that day. The weekly paper had been printed and taken to the post office Wednesday evening and the snow began to fall on Thursday. At eight o'clock, after the morning train had passed, he put a pair of skates in his pocket and went up to Waterworks Pond but did not go skating. Past the pond and along a path that followed Wine Creek he went until he came to a grove of beech trees. There he built a fire against the side of a log and sat down at the end of the log to think. When the snow began to fall and the wind to blow he hurried about getting fuel for the fire.

The young reporter was thinking of Kate Swift, who had once been his school teacher. On the evening before he had gone to her house to get a book she wanted him to read and had been alone with her for an hour. For the fourth or fifth time the woman had talked to him with great earnestness and he could not make out what she meant by her talk. He began to believe she might be in love with him and the thought was both pleasing and annoying.

Up from the log he sprang and began to pile sticks on the fire. Looking about to be sure he was alone he talked aloud pretending he was in the presence of the woman. "Oh, you're just letting on, you know you are," he declared. "I am going to find out about you. You wait and see."

The young man got up and went back along the path toward town leaving the fire blazing in the wood. As he went through the streets the skates clanked in his pocket. In his own room in the New Willard House he built a fire in the stove and lay down on top of the bed. He began to have lustful thoughts and pulling down the shade of the window closed his eyes and turned his face to the wall. He took a pillow into his arms and embraced it thinking first of the school teacher, who by her words had stirred something within him, and later of Helen White, the slim daughter of the town banker, with whom he had been for a long time half in love.

By nine o'clock of that evening snow lay deep in the streets and the weather had become bitter cold. It was difficult to walk about. The stores were dark and the people had crawled away to their houses. The evening train from Cleveland was very late but nobody was interested in its arrival. By ten o'clock all but four of the eighteen hundred citizens of the town were in bed.

Hop Higgins, the night watchman, was partially awake. He was lame and carried a heavy stick. On dark nights he carried a lantern. Between nine and ten o'clock he went his rounds. Up and down Main Street he stumbled through the drifts trying the doors of the stores. Then he went into alleyways and tried the back doors. Finding all tight he hurried around the corner to the New Willard House and beat on the door. Through the rest of the night he intended to stay by the stove. "You go to bed. I'll keep the stove going," he said to the boy who slept on a cot in the hotel office.

Hop Higgins sat down by the stove and took off his shoes. When the boy had gone to sleep he began to think of his own affairs. He intended to paint his house in the spring and sat by the stove calculating the cost of paint and labor. That led him into other calculations. The night watchman was sixty years old and wanted to retire. He had been a soldier in the Civil War and drew a small pension. He hoped to find some new method of making a living and aspired to become a professional breeder of ferrets. Already he had four of the strangely shaped savage little creatures, that are used by sportsmen in the pursuit of rabbits, in the cellar of his house. "Now I have one male and three females," he mused. "If I am lucky by spring I shall have twelve or fifteen. In another year I shall be able to begin advertising ferrets for sale in the sporting papers."

The night watchman settled into his chair and his mind became a blank. He did not sleep. By years of practice he had trained himself to sit for hours through the long nights neither asleep nor awake. In the morning he was almost as refreshed as though he had slept.

With Hop Higgins safely stowed away in the chair behind the stove only three people were awake in Wines-

burg. George Willard was in the office of the *Eagle* pretending to be at work on the writing of a story but in reality continuing the mood of the morning by the fire in the
wood. In the bell tower of the Presbyterian Church the
Reverend Curtis Hartman was sitting in the darkness preparing himself for a revelation from God, and Kate Swift,
the school teacher, was leaving her house for a walk in the
storm.

It was past ten o'clock when Kate Swift set out and the
walk was unpremeditated. It was as though the man and
the boy, by thinking of her, had driven her forth into the
wintry streets. Aunt Elizabeth Swift had gone to the
county seat concerning some business in connection with
mortgages in which she had money invested and would
not be back until the next day. By a huge stove, called a
base burner, in the living room of the house sat the daughter reading a book. Suddenly she sprang to her feet and,
snatching a cloak from a rack by the front door, ran out of
the house.

At the age of thirty Kate Swift was not known in Winesburg as a pretty woman. Her complexion was not good
and her face was covered with blotches that indicated ill
health. Alone in the night in the winter streets she was
lovely. Her back was straight, her shoulders square, and
her features were as the features of a tiny goddess on a
pedestal in a garden in the dim light of a summer evening.

During the afternoon the school teacher had been to
see Doctor Welling concerning her health. The doctor had
scolded her and had declared she was in danger of losing
her hearing. It was foolish for Kate Swift to be abroad in
the storm, foolish and perhaps dangerous.

The woman in the streets did not remember the words
of the doctor and would not have turned back had she re-

membered. She was very cold but after walking for five minutes no longer minded the cold. First she went to the end of her own street and then across a pair of hay scales set in the ground before a feed barn and into Trunion Pike. Along Trunion Pike she went to Ned Winters' barn and turning east followed a street of low frame houses that led over Gospel Hill and into Sucker Road that ran down a shallow valley past Ike Smead's chicken farm to Water-works Pond. As she went along, the bold, excited mood that had driven her out of doors passed and then returned again.

There was something biting and forbidding in the character of Kate Swift. Everyone felt it. In the school-room she was silent, cold, and stern, and yet in an odd way very close to her pupils. Once in a long while something seemed to have come over her and she was happy. All of the children in the schoolroom felt the effect of her happi-ness. For a time they did not work but sat back in their chairs and looked at her.

With hands clasped behind her back the school teacher walked up and down in the schoolroom and talked very rapidly. It did not seem to matter what subject came into her mind. Once she talked to the children of Charles Lamb and made up strange, intimate little stories con-cerning the life of the dead writer. The stories were told with the air of one who had lived in a house with Charles Lamb and knew all the secrets of his private life. The children were somewhat confused, thinking Charles Lamb must be someone who had once lived in Winesburg.

On another occasion the teacher talked to the children of Benvenuto Cellini. That time they laughed. What a bragging, blustering, brave, lovable fellow she made of the old artist! Concerning him also she invented anec-dotes. There was one of a German music teacher who had a room above Cellini's lodgings in the city of Milan that made the boys guffaw. Sugars McNutts, a fat boy with red cheeks, laughed so hard that he became dizzy and fell off his seat and Kate Swift laughed with him. Then suddenly she became again cold and stern.

On the winter night when she walked through the deserted snow-covered streets, a crisis had come into the life of the school teacher. Although no one in Winesburg would have suspected it, her life had been very adventurous. It was still adventurous. Day by day as she worked in the schoolroom or walked in the streets, grief, hope, and desire fought within her. Behind a cold exterior the most extraordinary events transpired in her mind. The people of the town thought of her as a confirmed old maid and because she spoke sharply and went her own way thought her lacking in all the human feeling that did so much to make and mar their own lives. In reality she was the most eagerly passionate soul among them, and more than once, in the five years since she had come back from her travels to settle in Winesburg and become a school teacher, had been compelled to go out of the house and walk half through the night fighting out some battle raging within. Once on a night when it rained she had stayed out six hours and when she came home had a quarrel with Aunt Elizabeth Swift. "I am glad you're not a man," said the mother sharply. "More than once I've waited for your father to come home, not knowing what new mess he had got into. I've had my share of uncertainty and you cannot blame me if I do not want to see the worst side of him reproduced in you."

❀◆❀

Kate Swift's mind was ablaze with thoughts of George Willard. In something he had written as a school boy she thought she had recognized the spark of genius and wanted to blow on the spark. One day in the summer she had gone to the *Eagle* office and finding the boy unoccupied had taken him out Main Street to the Fair Ground, where the two sat on a grassy bank and talked. The school teacher tried to bring home to the mind of the boy some conception of the difficulties he would have to face as a writer. "You will have to know life," she declared, and her voice trembled with earnestness. She took hold of George Willard's shoulders and turned him about so that she could look into his eyes. A passer-by might have thought them about to embrace. "If you are to become a writer you'll have to stop fooling with words," she explained. "It would be better to give up the notion of writing until you are better prepared. Now it's time to be living. I don't want to frighten you, but I would like to make you understand the import of what you think of attempting. You must not become a mere peddler of words. The thing to learn is to know what people are thinking about, not what they say."

On the evening before that stormy Thursday night when the Reverend Curtis Hartman sat in the bell tower of the church waiting to look at her body, young Willard had gone to visit the teacher and to borrow a book. It was then the thing happened that confused and puzzled the boy. He had the book under his arm and was preparing to depart. Again Kate Swift talked with great earnestness. Night was coming on and the light in the room grew dim. As he turned to go she spoke his name softly and with an impulsive movement took hold of his hand. Because the reporter was rapidly becoming a man something of his man's appeal, combined with the winsomeness of the boy, stirred the heart of the lonely woman. A passionate desire to have him understand the import of life, to learn to interpret it truly and honestly, swept over her. Leaning forward, her lips brushed his cheek. At the same moment he for the first time became aware of the marked beauty of her features. They were both embarrassed, and to relieve her feeling she became harsh and domineering. "What's the use? It will be ten years before you begin to understand what I mean when I talk to you," she cried passionately.

❦◆❦

On the night of the storm and while the minister sat in the church waiting for her, Kate Swift went to the office of the *Winesburg Eagle,* intending to have another talk with the boy. After the long walk in the snow she was cold, lonely, and tired. As she came through Main Street she saw the light from the printshop window shining on the snow and on an impulse opened the door and went in. For an hour she sat by the stove in the office talking of life. She talked with passionate earnestness. The impulse that had driven her out into the snow poured itself out into talk. She became inspired as she sometimes did in the presence of the children in school. A great eagerness to open the door of life to the boy, who had been her pupil and who she thought might possess a talent for the understanding of life, had possession of her. So strong was her passion that it became something physical. Again her hands took hold of his shoulders and she turned him about. In the dim light her eyes blazed. She arose and laughed, not sharply as was customary with her, but in a queer, hesitating way. "I must be going," she said. "In a moment, if I stay, I'll be wanting to kiss you."

In the newspaper office a confusion arose. Kate Swift turned and walked to the door. She was a teacher but she was also a woman. As she looked at George Willard, the passionate desire to be loved by a man, that had a thousand times before swept like a storm over her body, took possession of her. In the lamplight George Willard looked no longer a boy, but a man ready to play the part of a man.

The school teacher let George Willard take her into his arms. In the warm little office the air became suddenly heavy and the strength went out of her body. Leaning against a low counter by the door she waited. When he came and put a hand on her shoulder she turned and let her body fall heavily against him. For George Willard the confusion was immediately increased. For a moment he held the body of the woman tightly against his body and then it stiffened. Two sharp little fists began to beat on his face. When the school teacher had run away and left him alone, he walked up and down in the office swearing furiously.

It was into this confusion that the Reverend Curtis Hartman protruded himself. When he came in George Willard thought the town had gone mad. Shaking a bleeding fist in the air, the minister proclaimed the woman George had only a moment before held in his arms an instrument of God bearing a message of truth.

❄◇❄

George blew out the lamp by the window and locking the door of the printshop went home. Through the hotel office, past Hop Higgins lost in his dream of the raising of ferrets, he went and up into his own room. The fire in the stove had gone out and he undressed in the cold. When he got into bed the sheets were like blankets of dry snow.

George Willard rolled about in the bed on which he

had lain in the afternoon hugging the pillow and thinking thoughts of Kate Swift. The words of the minister, who he thought had gone suddenly insane, rang in his ears. His eyes stared about the room. The resentment, natural to the baffled male, passed and he tried to understand what had happened. He could not make it out. Over and over he turned the matter in his mind. Hours passed and he began to think it must be time for another day to come. At four o'clock he pulled the covers up about his neck and tried to sleep. When he became drowsy and closed his eyes, he raised a hand and with it groped about in the darkness. "I have missed something. I have missed something Kate Swift was trying to tell me," he muttered sleepily. Then he slept and in all Winesburg he was the last soul on that winter night to go to sleep.

LONELINESS

HE WAS the son of Mrs. Al Robinson who once owned a farm on a side road leading off Trunion Pike, east of Winesburg and two miles beyond the town limits. The farmhouse was painted brown and the blinds to all of the windows facing the road were kept closed. In the road before the house a flock of chickens, accompanied by two guinea hens, lay in the deep dust. Enoch lived in the house with his mother in those days and when he was a young boy went to school at the Winesburg High School. Old citizens remembered him as a quiet, smiling youth inclined to silence. He walked in the middle of the road when he came into town and sometimes read a book. Drivers of teams had to shout and swear to make him realize where he was so that he would turn out of the beaten track and let them pass.

When he was twenty-one years old Enoch went to New York City and was a city man for fifteen years. He studied French and went to an art school, hoping to develop a faculty he had for drawing. In his own mind he planned to go to Paris and to finish his art education among the masters there, but that never turned out.

Nothing ever turned out for Enoch Robinson. He could draw well enough and he had many odd delicate thoughts hidden away in his brain that might have expressed themselves through the brush of a painter, but he was always a child and that was a handicap to his worldly development. He never grew up and of course he couldn't

understand people and he couldn't make people understand him. The child in him kept bumping against things,
against actualities like money and sex and opinions. Once
he was hit by a street car and thrown against an iron post.
That made him lame. It was one of the many things that
kept things from turning out for Enoch Robinson.

In New York City, when he first went there to live and
before he became confused and disconcerted by the facts
of life, Enoch went about a good deal with young men. He
got into a group of other young artists, both men and
women, and in the evenings they sometimes came to visit
him in his room. Once he got drunk and was taken to a
police station where a police magistrate frightened him
horribly, and once he tried to have an affair with a woman
of the town met on the sidewalk before his lodging house.
The woman and Enoch walked together three blocks and
then the young man grew afraid and ran away. The
woman had been drinking and the incident amused her.
She leaned against the wall of a building and laughed so
heartily that another man stopped and laughed with her.
The two went away together, still laughing, and Enoch
crept off to his room trembling and vexed.

The room in which young Robinson lived in New York
faced Washington Square and was long and narrow like a
hallway. It is important to get that fixed in your mind.
The story of Enoch is in fact the story of a room almost
more than it is the story of a man.

And so into the room in the evening came young
Enoch's friends. There was nothing particularly striking
about them except that they were artists of the kind that
talk. Everyone knows of the talking artists. Throughout
all of the known history of the world they have gathered
in rooms and talked. They talk of art and are passionately,

almost feverishly, in earnest about it. They think it matters much more than it does.

And so these people gathered and smoked cigarettes and talked and Enoch Robinson, the boy from the farm near Winesburg, was there. He stayed in a corner and for the most part said nothing. How his big blue childlike eyes stared about! On the walls were pictures he had made, crude things, half finished. His friends talked of these. Leaning back in their chairs, they talked and talked with their heads rocking from side to side. Words were said about line and values and composition, lots of words, such as are always being said.

Enoch wanted to talk too but he didn't know how. He was too excited to talk coherently. When he tried he sputtered and stammered and his voice sounded strange and squeaky to him. That made him stop talking. He knew what he wanted to say, but he knew also that he could never by any possibility say it. When a picture he had painted was under discussion, he wanted to burst out with something like this: "You don't get the point," he wanted to explain; "the picture you see doesn't consist of the things you see and say words about. There is something else, something you don't see at all, something you aren't intended to see. Look at this one over here, by the door here, where the light from the window falls on it. The dark spot by the road that you might not notice at all is, you see, the beginning of everything. There is a clump of elders there such as used to grow beside the road before our house back in Winesburg, Ohio, and in among the elders there is something hidden. It is a woman, that's what it is. She has been thrown from a horse and the horse has run away out of sight. Do you not see how the old man who drives a cart looks anxiously about? That

is Thad Grayback who has a farm up the road. He is taking corn to Winesburg to be ground into meal at Com-
stock's mill. He knows there is something in the elders,
something hidden away, and yet he doesn't quite know.

"It's a woman you see, that's what it is! It's a woman
and, oh, she is lovely! She is hurt and is suffering but she
makes no sound. Don't you see how it is? She lies quite
still, white and still, and the beauty comes out from her
and spreads over everything. It is in the sky back there
and all around everywhere. I didn't try to paint the
woman, of course. She is too beautiful to be painted. How
dull to talk of composition and such things! Why do you
not look at the sky and then run away as I used to do when
I was a boy back there in Winesburg, Ohio?"

That is the kind of thing young Enoch Robinson
trembled to say to the guests who came into his room when
he was a young fellow in New York City, but he always
ended by saying nothing. Then he began to doubt his
own mind. He was afraid the things he felt were not getting expressed in the pictures he painted. In a half indignant mood he stopped inviting people into his room
and presently got into the habit of locking the door. He
began to think that enough people had visited him, that
he did not need people any more. With quick imagination he began to invent his own people to whom he could
really talk and to whom he explained the things he had
been unable to explain to living people. His room began
to be inhabited by the spirits of men and women among
whom he went, in his turn saying words. It was as though
everyone Enoch Robinson had ever seen had left with
him some essence of himself, something he could mould
and change to suit his own fancy, something that understood all about such things as the wounded woman behind
the elders in the pictures.

The mild, blue-eyed young Ohio boy was a complete egotist, as all children are egotists. He did not want friends for the quite simple reason that no child wants friends. He wanted most of all the people of his own mind, people with whom he could really talk, people he could harangue and scold by the hour, servants, you see, to his fancy. Among these people he was always self-confident and bold. They might talk, to be sure, and even have opinions of their own, but always he talked last and best. He was like a writer busy among the figures of his brain, a kind of tiny blue-eyed king he was, in a six-dollar room facing Washington Square in the city of New York.

Then Enoch Robinson got married. He began to get lonely and to want to touch actual flesh-and-bone people with his hands. Days passed when his room seemed empty. Lust visited his body and desire grew in his mind. At night strange fevers, burning within, kept him awake. He married a girl who sat in a chair next to his own in the art school and went to live in an apartment house in Brooklyn. Two children were born to the woman he married, and Enoch got a job in a place where illustrations are made for advertisements.

That began another phase of Enoch's life. He began to play at a new game. For a while he was very proud of himself in the role of producing citizen of the world. He dismissed the essence of things and played with realities. In the fall he voted at an election and he had a newspaper thrown on his porch each morning. When in the evening he came home from work he got off a streetcar and walked sedately along behind some business man, striving to look very substantial and important. As a payer of taxes he thought he should post himself on how things are run. "I'm getting to be of some moment, a real part of things, of the state and the city and all that," he told himself with an amusing miniature air of dignity. Once, coming home from Philadelphia, he had a discussion with a man met on a train. Enoch talked about the advisability of the government's owning and operating the railroads and the man gave him a cigar. It was Enoch's notion that such a move on the part of the government would be a good thing, and he grew quite excited as he talked. Later he remembered his own words with pleasure. "I gave him something to think about, that fellow," he muttered to himself as he climbed the stairs to his Brooklyn apartment.

To be sure, Enoch's marriage did not turn out. He himself brought it to an end. He began to feel choked and walled in by the life in the apartment, and to feel toward his wife and even toward his children as he had felt concerning the friends who once came to visit him. He began to tell little lies about business engagements that would give him freedom to walk alone in the street at night and, the chance offering, he secretly re-rented the room facing Washington Square. Then Mrs. Al Robinson died on the farm near Winesburg, and he got eight thousand dollars from the bank that acted as trustee of her estate. That took Enoch out of the world of men altogether. He gave the money to his wife and told her he could not live in the apartment any more. She cried and was angry and threatened, but he only stared at her and went his own way. In reality the wife did not care much. She thought Enoch slightly insane and was a little afraid of him. When it was quite sure that he would never come back, she took the two children and went to a village in Connecticut where she had lived as a girl. In the end she married a man who bought and sold real estate and was contented enough.

And so Enoch Robinson stayed in the New York room among the people of his fancy, playing with them, talking

to them, happy as a child is happy. They were an odd lot,
Enoch's people. They were made, I suppose, out of real
people he had seen and who had for some obscure reason
made an appeal to him. [There was a woman with a sword
in her hand, an old man with a long white beard who
went about followed by a dog, a young girl whose stockings were always coming down and hanging over her shoe
tops. There must have been two dozen of the shadow
people, invented by the child-mind of Enoch Robinson,
who lived in the room with him.]

And Enoch was happy. Into the room he went
and locked the door. With an absurd air of importance
he talked aloud, giving instructions, making comments
on life. He was happy and satisfied to go on making his
living in the advertising place until something happened.
Of course something did happen. That is why he went
back to live in Winesburg and why we know about him.
The thing that happened was a woman. It would be that
way. He was too happy. Something had to come into his
world. Something had to drive him out of the New York
room to live out his life an obscure, jerky little figure,
bobbing up and down on the streets of an Ohio town at
evening when the sun was going down behind the roof of
Wesley Moyer's livery barn.

About the thing that happened. Enoch told George Willard about it one night. He wanted to talk to someone,
and he chose the young newspaper reporter because the
two happened to be thrown together at a time when the
younger man was in a mood to understand.

Youthful sadness, young man's sadness, the sadness of
a growing boy in a village at the year's end, opened the lips
of the old man. The sadness was in the heart of George
Willard and was without meaning, but it appealed to
Enoch Robinson.

It rained on the evening when the two met and talked, a drizzly wet October rain. The fruition of the year had come and the night should have been fine with a moon in the sky and the crisp sharp promise of frost in the air, but it wasn't that way. It rained and little puddles of water shone under the street lamps on Main Street. In the woods in the darkness beyond the Fair Ground water dripped from the black trees. Beneath the trees wet leaves were pasted against tree roots that protruded from the ground. In gardens back of houses in Winesburg dry shriveled potato vines lay sprawling on the ground. Men who had finished the evening meal and who had planned to go uptown to talk the evening away with other men at the back of some store changed their minds. George Willard tramped about in the rain and was glad that it rained. He felt that way. He was like Enoch Robinson on the evenings when the old man came down out of his room and wandered alone in the streets. He was like that only that George Willard had become a tall young man and did not think it manly to weep and carry on. For a month his mother had been very ill and that had something to do with his sadness, but not much. He thought about himself and to the young that always brings sadness.

Enoch Robinson and George Willard met beneath a wooden awning that extended out over the sidewalk before Voight's wagon shop on Maumee Street just off the main street of Winesburg. They went together from there through the rain-washed streets to the older man's room on the third floor of the Heffner Block. The young reporter went willingly enough. Enoch Robinson asked him to go after the two had talked for ten minutes. The boy was a little afraid but had never been more curious in his life. A hundred times he had heard the old man spoken of as a little off his head and he thought himself rather brave and manly to go at all. From the very beginning, in the street in the rain, the old man talked in a queer way, trying to tell the story of the room in Washington Square and of his life in the room. "You'll understand if you try hard enough," he said conclusively. "I have looked at you when you went past me on the street and I think you can understand. It isn't hard. All you have to do is to believe what I say, just listen and believe, that's all there is to it."

It was past eleven o'clock that evening when old Enoch, talking to George Willard in the room in the Heffner Block, came to the vital thing, the story of the woman and of what drove him out of the city to live out his life alone and defeated in Winesburg. He sat on a cot by the window with his head in his hand and George Willard was in a chair by a table. A kerosene lamp sat on the table and the room, although almost bare of furniture, was scrupulously clean. As the man talked George Willard began to feel that he would like to get out of the chair and sit on the cot also. He wanted to put his arms about the little old man. In the half darkness the man talked and the boy listened, filled with sadness.

"She got to coming in there after there hadn't been anyone in the room for years," said Enoch Robinson. "She saw me in the hallway of the house and we got acquainted. I don't know just what she did in her own room. I never went there. I think she was a musician and played a violin. Every now and then she came and knocked at the door and I opened it. In she came and sat down beside me, just sat and looked about and said nothing. Anyway, she said nothing that mattered."

The old man arose from the cot and moved about the room. The overcoat he wore was wet from the rain and drops of water kept falling with a soft thump on the floor. When he again sat upon the cot George Willard got out of the chair and sat beside him.

"I had a feeling about her. She sat there in the room with me and she was too big for the room. I felt that she was driving everything else away. We just talked of little things, but I couldn't sit still. I wanted to touch her with my fingers and to kiss her. Her hands were so strong and her face was so good and she looked at me all the time."

The trembling voice of the old man became silent and his body shook as from a chill. "I was afraid," he whispered. "I was terribly afraid. I didn't want to let her come in when she knocked at the door but I couldn't sit still. 'No, no,' I said to myself, but I got up and opened the door just the same. She was so grown up, you see. She was a woman. I thought she would be bigger than I was there in that room."

Enoch Robinson stared at George Willard, his childlike blue eyes shining in the lamplight. Again he shivered. "I wanted her and all the time I didn't want her," he explained. "Then I began to tell her about my people, about everything that meant anything to me. I tried to keep quiet, to keep myself to myself, but I couldn't. I felt just as I did about opening the door. Sometimes I ached to have her go away and never come back any more."

The old man sprang to his feet and his voice shook with excitement. "One night something happened. I became mad to make her understand me and to know what a big thing I was in that room. I wanted her to see how important I was. I told her over and over. When she tried to go away, I ran and locked the door. I followed her about. I talked and talked and then all of a sudden things went to smash. A look came into her eyes and I knew she did un-

derstand. Maybe she had understood all the time. I was
furious. I couldn't stand it. I wanted her to understand
but, don't you see, I couldn't let her understand. I felt
that then she would know everything, that I would be submerged, drowned out, you see. That's how it is. I don't
know why."

The old man dropped into a chair by the lamp and the
boy listened, filled with awe. "Go away, boy," said the
man. "Don't stay here with me any more. I thought it
might be a good thing to tell you but it isn't. I don't want
to talk any more. Go away."

George Willard shook his head and a note of command
came into his voice. "Don't stop now. Tell me the rest of
it," he commanded sharply. "What happened? Tell me
the rest of the story."

Enoch Robinson sprang to his feet and ran to the window that looked down into the deserted main street of
Winesburg. George Willard followed. By the window the
two stood, the tall awkward boy-man and the little
wrinkled man-boy. The childish, eager voice carried forward the tale. "I swore at her," he explained. "I said vile
words. I ordered her to go away and not to come back. Oh,
I said terrible things. At first she pretended not to understand but I kept at it. I screamed and stamped on the floor.
I made the house ring with my curses. I didn't want ever
to see her again and I knew, after some of the things I
said, that I never would see her again."

The old man's voice broke and he shook his head.
"Things went to smash," he said quietly and sadly. "Out
she went through the door and all the life there had been
in the room followed her out. She took all of my people
away. They all went out through the door after her. That's
the way it was."

THEY LEFT BECAUSE HE TOLD THE WOMAN

George Willard turned and went out of Enoch Robinson's room. In the darkness by the window, as he went through the door, he could hear the thin old voice whimpering and complaining. "I'm alone, all alone here," said the voice. "It was warm and friendly in my room but now I'm all alone."

AN AWAKENING

BELLE CARPENTER had a dark skin, grey eyes, and thick lips. She was tall and strong. When black thoughts visited her she grew angry and wished she were a man and could fight someone with her fists. She worked in the millinery shop kept by Mrs. Kate McHugh and during the day sat trimming hats by a window at the rear of the store. She was the daughter of Henry Carpenter, book-keeper in the First National Bank of Winesburg, and lived with him in a gloomy old house far out at the end of Buck-eye Street. The house was surrounded by pine trees and there was no grass beneath the trees. A rusty tin eaves-trough had slipped from its fastenings at the back of the house and when the wind blew it beat against the roof of a small shed, making a dismal drumming noise that some-times persisted all through the night.

When she was a young girl Henry Carpenter made life almost unbearable for Belle, but as she emerged from girl-hood into womanhood he lost his power over her. The bookkeeper's life was made up of innumerable little pet-tinesses. When he went to the bank in the morning he stepped into a closet and put on a black alpaca coat that had become shabby with age. At night when he returned to his home he donned another black alpaca coat. Every evening he pressed the clothes worn in the streets. He had invented an arrangement of boards for the pur-pose. The trousers to his street suit were placed between the boards and the boards were clamped together with heavy screws. In the morning he wiped the boards with a damp cloth and stood them upright behind the dining room door. If they were moved during the day he was speechless with anger and did not recover his equilibrium for a week.

The bank cashier was a little bully and was afraid of his daughter. She, he realized, knew the story of his brutal treatment of her mother and hated him for it. One day she went home at noon and carried a handful of soft mud, taken from the road, into the house. With the mud she smeared the face of the boards used for the pressing of trousers and then went back to her work feeling relieved and happy.

Belle Carpenter occasionally walked out in the evening with George Willard. Secretly she loved another man, but her love affair, about which no one knew, caused her much anxiety. She was in love with Ed Handby, bartender in Ed Griffith's Saloon, and went about with the young reporter as a kind of relief to her feelings. She did not think that her station in life would permit her to be seen in the company of the bartender and walked about under the trees with George Willard and let him kiss her to relieve a longing that was very insistent in her nature. She felt that she could keep the younger man within bounds. About Ed Handby she was somewhat uncertain.

Handby, the bartender, was a tall, broad-shouldered man of thirty who lived in a room upstairs above Griffith's saloon. His fists were large and his eyes unusually small, but his voice, as though striving to conceal the power back of his fists, was soft and quiet.

At twenty-five the bartender had inherited a large farm from an uncle in Indiana. When sold, the farm brought in eight thousand dollars, which Ed spent in six months. Going to Sandusky, on Lake Erie, he began an orgy of dissipation, the story of which afterward filled his home town with awe. Here and there he went throwing the money about, driving carriages through the streets, giving wine parties to crowds of men and women, playing cards for high stakes and keeping mistresses whose wardrobes cost him hundreds of dollars. One night at a resort called Cedar Point, he got into a fight and ran amuck like a wild thing. With his fist he broke a large mirror in the wash room of a hotel and later went about smashing windows and breaking chairs in dance halls for the joy of hearing the glass rattle on the floor and seeing the terror in the eyes of clerks who had come from Sandusky to spend the evening at the resort with their sweethearts.

The affair between Ed Handby and Belle Carpenter on the surface amounted to nothing. He had succeeded in spending but one evening in her company. On that evening he hired a horse and buggy at Wesley Moyer's livery barn and took her for a drive. The conviction that she was the woman his nature demanded and that he must get her settled upon him and he told her of his desires. The bartender was ready to marry and to begin trying to earn money for the support of his wife, but so simple was his nature that he found it difficult to explain his intentions. His body ached with physical longing and with his body he expressed himself. Taking the milliner into his arms and holding her tightly in spite of her struggles, he kissed her until she became helpless. Then he brought her back to town and let her out of the buggy. "When I get hold of you again I'll not let you go. You can't play with me," he declared as he turned to drive away. Then, jumping out of the buggy, he gripped her shoulders with his strong hands. "I'll keep you for good the next time," he said. "You might as well make up your mind to that. It's you and me for it and I'm going to have you before I get through."

One night in January when there was a new moon George Willard, who was in Ed Handby's mind the only obstacle to his getting Belle Carpenter, went for a walk. Early that evening George went into Ransom Surbeck's pool room with Seth Richmond and Art Wilson, son of the town butcher. Seth Richmond stood with his back against the wall and remained silent, but George Willard talked. The pool room was filled with Winesburg boys and they talked of women. The young reporter got into that vein. He said that women should look out for themselves, that the fellow who went out with a girl was not responsible for what happened. As he talked he looked about, eager for attention. He held the floor for five minutes and then Art Wilson began to talk. Art was learning the barber's trade in Cal Prouse's shop and already began to consider himself an authority in such matters as baseball, horse racing, drinking, and going about with women. He began to tell of a night when he with two men from Winesburg went into a house of prostitution at the county seat. The butcher's son held a cigar in the side of his mouth and as he talked spat on the floor. "The women in the place couldn't embarrass me although they tried hard enough," he boasted. "One of the girls in the house tried to get fresh, but I fooled her. As soon as she began to talk I went and sat in her lap. Everyone in the room laughed when I kissed her. I taught her to let me alone."

George Willard went out of the pool room and into Main Street. For days the weather had been bitter cold with a high wind blowing down on the town from Lake Erie, eighteen miles to the north, but on that night the wind had died away and a new moon made the night unusually lovely. Without thinking where he was going or what he wanted to do, George went out of Main Street and began walking in dimly lighted streets filled with frame houses.

Out of doors under the black sky filled with stars he forgot his companions of the pool room. Because it was dark and he was alone he began to talk aloud. In a spirit of play he reeled along the street imitating a drunken man and then imagined himself a soldier clad in shining boots that reached to the knees and wearing a sword that jingled as he walked. As a soldier he pictured himself as an inspector, passing before a long line of men who stood at attention. He began to examine the accoutrements of the men. Before a tree he stopped and began to scold. "Your pack is not in order," he said sharply. "How many times will I have to speak of this matter? Everything must be in order here. We have a difficult task before us and no difficult task can be done without order."

Hypnotized by his own words, the young man stumbled along the board sidewalk saying more words. "There is a law for armies and for men too," he muttered, lost in reflection. "The law begins with little things and spreads out until it covers everything. In every little thing there must be order, in the place where men work, in their clothes, in their thoughts. I myself must be orderly. I must learn that law. I must get myself into touch with something orderly and big that swings through the night like a star. In my little way I must begin to learn something, to give and swing and work with life, with the law."

George Willard stopped by a picket fence near a street lamp and his body began to tremble. He had never before thought such thoughts as had just come into his head and he wondered where they had come from. For the moment it seemed to him that some voice outside of himself had been talking as he walked. He was amazed and delighted with his own mind and when he walked on again spoke of the matter with fervor. "To come out of Ransom Surbeck's pool room and think things like that," he whispered. "It is better to be alone. If I talked like Art Wilson the boys would understand me but they wouldn't understand what I've been thinking down here."

In Winesburg, as in all Ohio towns of twenty years ago, there was a section in which lived day laborers. As the time of factories had not yet come, the laborers worked in the fields or were section hands on the railroads. They worked twelve hours a day and received one dollar for the long day of toil. The houses in which they lived were small cheaply constructed wooden affairs with a garden at the back. The more comfortable among them kept cows and perhaps a pig, housed in a little shed at the rear of the garden.

With his head filled with resounding thoughts, George Willard walked into such a street on the clear January night. The street was dimly lighted and in places there was no sidewalk. In the scene that lay about him there was something that excited his already aroused fancy. For a year he had been devoting all of his odd moments to the reading of books and now some tale he had read concerning life in old world towns of the middle ages came sharply back to his mind so that he stumbled forward with the curious feeling of one revisiting a place that had been a part of some former existence. On an impulse he turned out of the street and went into a little dark alleyway behind the sheds in which lived the cows and pigs.

For a half hour he stayed in the alleyway, smelling the strong smell of animals too closely housed and letting his mind play with the strange new thoughts that came to him. The very rankness of the smell of manure in the clear sweet air awoke something heady in his brain. The poor little houses lighted by kerosene lamps, the smoke from the chimneys mounting straight up into the clear air, the grunting of pigs, the women clad in cheap calico dresses and washing dishes in the kitchens, the footsteps of men coming out of the houses and going off to the stores and saloons of Main Street, the dogs barking and the children crying—all of these things made him seem, as he lurked in the darkness, oddly detached and apart from all life.

The excited young man, unable to bear the weight of his own thoughts, began to move cautiously along the alleyway. A dog attacked him and had to be driven away with stones, and a man appeared at the door of one of the houses and swore at the dog. George went into a vacant lot and throwing back his head looked up at the sky. He felt unutterably big and remade by the simple experience through which he had been passing and in a kind of fervor of emotion put up his hands, thrusting them into the darkness above his head and muttering words. The desire to say words overcame him and he said words without meaning, rolling them over on his tongue and saying them because they were brave words, full of meaning. "Death," he muttered, "night, the sea, fear, loveliness."

George Willard came out of the vacant lot and stood again on the sidewalk facing the houses. He felt that all of the people in the little street must be brothers and sisters to him and he wished he had the courage to call them out of their houses and to shake their hands. "If there were only a woman here I would take hold of her hand and we would run until we were both tired out," he thought. "That would make me feel better." With the thought of a woman in his mind he walked out of the street and went toward the house where Belle Carpenter lived. He thought she would understand his mood and that he could achieve in her presence a position he had long been wanting to

achieve. In the past when he had been with her and had
kissed her lips he had come away filled with anger at himself. He had felt like one being used for some obscure
purpose and had not enjoyed the feeling. Now he thought
he had suddenly become too big to be used.

When George got to Belle Carpenter's house there had
already been a visitor there before him. Ed Handby had
come to the door and calling Belle out of the house had
tried to talk to her. He had wanted to ask the woman to
come away with him and to be his wife, but when she came
and stood by the door he lost his self-assurance and became
sullen. "You stay away from that kid," he growled, thinking of George Willard, and then, not knowing what else
to say, turned to go away. "If I catch you together I will
break your bones and his too," he added. The bartender
had come to woo, not to threaten, and was angry with himself because of his failure.

When her lover had departed Belle went indoors and
ran hurriedly upstairs. From a window at the upper part
of the house she saw Ed Handby cross the street and sit
down on a horse block before the house of a neighbor. In
the dim light the man sat motionless holding his head in
his hands. She was made happy by the sight, and when
George Willard came to the door she greeted him effusively and hurriedly put on her hat. She thought that, as
she walked through the streets with young Willard, Ed
Handby would follow and she wanted to make him suffer.

For an hour Belle Carpenter and the young reporter
walked about under the trees in the sweet night air. George
Willard was full of big words. The sense of power that had
come to him during the hour in the darkness in the alleyway remained with him and he talked boldly, swaggering
along and swinging his arms about. He wanted to make

Belle Carpenter realize that he was aware of his former weakness and that he had changed. "You'll find me different," he declared, thrusting his hands into his pockets and looking boldly into her eyes. "I don't know why but it is so. You've got to take me for a man or let me alone. That's how it is."

Up and down the quiet streets under the new moon went the woman and the boy. When George had finished talking they turned down a side street and went across a bridge into a path that ran up the side of a hill. The hill began at Waterworks Pond and climbed upward to the Winesburg Fair Grounds. On the hillside grew dense bushes and small trees and among the bushes were little open spaces carpeted with long grass, now stiff and frozen.

As he walked behind the woman up the hill George Willard's heart began to beat rapidly and his shoulders straightened. Suddenly he decided that Belle Carpenter was about to surrender herself to him. The new force that had manifested itself in him had, he felt, been at work upon her and had led to her conquest. The thought made him half drunk with the sense of masculine power. Although he had been annoyed that as they walked about she had not seemed to be listening to his words, the fact that she had accompanied him to this place took all his doubts away. "It is different. Everything has become different," he thought and taking hold of her shoulder turned her about and stood looking at her, his eyes shining with pride.

Belle Carpenter did not resist. When he kissed her upon the lips she leaned heavily against him and looked over his shoulder into the darkness. In her whole attitude there was a suggestion of waiting. Again, as in the alley-way, George Willard's mind ran off into words and, holding the woman tightly he whispered the words into the still night. "Lust," he whispered, "lust and night and women."

George Willard did not understand what happened to him that night on the hillside. Later, when he got to his own room, he wanted to weep and then grew half insane with anger and hate. He hated Belle Carpenter and was sure that all his life he would continue to hate her. On the hillside he had led the woman to one of the little open spaces among the bushes and had dropped to his knees beside her. As in the vacant lot, by the laborers' houses, he had put up his hands in gratitude for the new power in himself and was waiting for the woman to speak when Ed Handby appeared.

The bartender did not want to beat the boy, who he thought had tried to take his woman away. He knew that beating was unnecessary, that he had power within himself to accomplish his purpose without using his fists. Gripping George by the shoulder and pulling him to his feet, he held him with one hand while he looked at Belle Carpenter seated on the grass. Then with a quick wide movement of his arm he sent the younger man sprawling away into the bushes and began to bully the woman, who had risen to her feet. "You're no good," he said roughly. "I've half a mind not to bother with you. I'd let you alone if I didn't want you so much."

On his hands and knees in the bushes George Willard stared at the scene before him and tried hard to think. He prepared to spring at the man who had humiliated him. To be beaten seemed to be infinitely better than to be thus hurled ignominiously aside.

Three times the young reporter sprang at Ed Handby and each time the bartender, catching him by the shoulder, hurled him back into the bushes. The older man seemed prepared to keep the exercise going indefinitely but George Willard's head struck the root of a tree and he lay still. Then Ed Handby took Belle Carpenter by the arm and marched her away.

George heard the man and woman making their way through the bushes. As he crept down the hillside his heart was sick within him. He hated himself and he hated the fate that had brought about his humiliation. When his mind went back to the hour alone in the alleyway he was puzzled and stopping in the darkness listened, hoping to hear again the voice outside himself that had so short a time before put new courage into his heart. When his way homeward led him again into the street of frame houses he could not bear the sight and began to run, wanting to get quickly out of the neighborhood that now seemed to him utterly squalid and commonplace.

"QUEER"

FROM HIS SEAT on a box in the rough board shed that stuck like a burr on the rear of Cowley & Son's store in Winesburg, Elmer Cowley, the junior member of the firm, could see through a dirty window into the print-shop of the *Winesburg Eagle*. Elmer was putting new shoe-laces in his shoes. They did not go in readily and he had to take the shoes off. With the shoes in his hand he sat looking at a large hole in the heel of one of his stockings. Then looking quickly up he saw George Willard, the only news-paper reporter in Winesburg, standing at the back door of the *Eagle* printshop and staring absent-mindedly about. "Well, well, what next!" exclaimed the young man with the shoes in his hand, jumping to his feet and creeping away from the window.

A flush crept into Elmer Cowley's face and his hands began to tremble. In Cowley & Son's store a Jewish travel-ing salesman stood by the counter talking to his father. He imagined the reporter could hear what was being said and the thought made him furious. With one of the shoes still held in his hand he stood in a corner of the shed and stamped with a stockinged foot upon the board floor.

Cowley & Son's store did not face the main street of Winesburg. The front was on Maumee Street and beyond it was Voight's wagon shop and a shed for the sheltering of farmers' horses. Beside the store an alleyway ran be-hind the main street stores and all day drays and delivery wagons, intent on bringing in and taking out goods, passed

up and down. The store itself was indescribable. Will
Henderson once said of it that it sold everything and nothing. In the window facing Maumee Street stood a chunk of
coal as large as an apple barrel, to indicate that orders for
coal were taken, and beside the black mass of the coal
stood three combs of honey grown brown and dirty in
their wooden frames.

The honey had stood in the store window for six months.
It was for sale as were also the coat hangers, patent sus-
pender buttons, cans of roof paint, bottles of rheumatism
cure, and a substitute for coffee that companioned the
honey in its patient willingness to serve the public.

Ebenezer Cowley, the man who stood in the store listening to the eager patter of words that fell from the lips of
the traveling man, was tall and lean and looked unwashed.
On his scrawny neck was a large wen partially covered by
a grey beard. He wore a long Prince Albert coat. The
coat had been purchased to serve as a wedding garment.
Before he became a merchant Ebenezer was a farmer and
after his marriage he wore the Prince Albert coat to church
on Sundays and on Saturday afternoons when he came into
town to trade. When he sold the farm to become a merchant he wore the coat constantly. It had become brown
with age and was covered with grease spots, but in it
Ebenezer always felt dressed up and ready for the day in
town.

As a merchant Ebenezer was not happily placed in life
and he had not been happily placed as a farmer. Still he
existed. His family, consisting of a daughter named Mabel
and the son, lived with him in rooms above the store and
it did not cost them much to live. His troubles were not
financial. His unhappiness as a merchant lay in the fact
that when a traveling man with wares to be sold came in
at the front door he was afraid. Behind the counter he

stood shaking his head. He was afraid, first that he would stubbornly refuse to buy and thus lose the opportunity to sell again; second that he would not be stubborn enough and would in a moment of weakness buy what could not be sold.

In the store on the morning when Elmer Cowley saw George Willard standing and apparently listening at the back door of the *Eagle* printshop, a situation had arisen that always stirred the son's wrath. The traveling man talked and Ebenezer listened, his whole figure expressing uncertainty. "You see how quickly it is done," said the traveling man, who had for sale a small flat metal substitute for collar buttons. With one hand he quickly unfastened a collar from his shirt and then fastened it on again. He assumed a flattering wheedling tone. "I tell you what, men have come to the end of all this fooling with collar buttons and you are the man to make money out of the change that is coming. I am offering you the exclusive agency for this town. Take twenty dozen of these fasteners and I'll not visit any other store. I'll leave the field to you."

The traveling man leaned over the counter and tapped with his finger on Ebenezer's breast. "It's an opportunity and I want you to take it," he urged. "A friend of mine told me about you. 'See that man Cowley,' he said. 'He's a live one.'"

The traveling man paused and waited. Taking a book from his pocket he began writing out the order. Still holding the shoe in his hand Elmer Cowley went through the store, past the two absorbed men, to a glass showcase near the front door. He took a cheap revolver from the case and began to wave it about. "You get out of here!" he shrieked. "We don't want any collar fasteners here." An idea came to him. "Mind, I'm not making any threat," he added.

"I don't say I'll shoot. Maybe I just took this gun out of the case to look at it. But you better get out. Yes sir, I'll say that. You better grab up your things and get out."

The young storekeeper's voice rose to a scream and going behind the counter he began to advance upon the two men. "We're through being fools here!" he cried. "We ain't going to buy any more stuff until we begin to sell. We ain't going to keep on being queer and have folks staring and listening. You get out of here!"

The traveling man left. Raking the samples of collar fasteners off the counter into a black leather bag, he ran. He was a small man and very bow-legged and he ran awkwardly. The black bag caught against the door and he stumbled and fell. "Crazy, that's what he is—crazy!" he sputtered as he arose from the sidewalk and hurried away.

In the store Elmer Cowley and his father stared at each other. Now that the immediate object of his wrath had fled, the younger man was embarrassed. "Well, I meant it. I think we've been queer long enough," he declared, going to the showcase and replacing the revolver. Sitting on a barrel he pulled on and fastened the shoe he had been holding in his hand. He was waiting for some word of understanding from his father but when Ebenezer spoke his words only served to reawaken the wrath in the son and the young man ran out of the store without replying. Scratching his grey beard with his long dirty fingers, the merchant looked at his son with the same wavering uncertain stare with which he had confronted the traveling man. "I'll be starched," he said softly. "Well, well, I'll be washed and ironed and starched!"

Elmer Cowley went out of Winesburg and along a country road that paralleled the railroad track. He did not know where he was going or what he was going to do. In the shelter of a deep cut where the road, after turning

sharply to the right, dipped under the tracks he stopped
and the passion that had been the cause of his outburst in
the store began to again find expression. "I will not be
queer—one to be looked at and listened to," he declared
aloud. "I'll be like other people. I'll show that George
Willard. He'll find out. I'll show him!"

The distraught young man stood in the middle of the
road and glared back at the town. He did not know the
reporter George Willard and had no special feeling concerning the tall boy who ran about town gathering the
town news. The reporter had merely come, by his presence in the office and in the printshop of the *Winesburg
Eagle,* to stand for something in the young merchant's
mind. He thought the boy who passed and repassed Cowley
& Son's store and who stopped to talk to people in the street
must be thinking of him and perhaps laughing at him.
George Willard, he felt, belonged to the town, typified
the town, represented in his person the spirit of the town.
Elmer Cowley could not have believed that George
Willard had also his days of unhappiness, that vague hun-
gers and secret unnamable desires visited also his mind.
Did he not represent public opinion and had not the public
opinion of Winesburg condemned the Cowleys to queerness? Did he not walk whistling and laughing through
Main Street? Might not one by striking his person strike
also the greater enemy—the thing that smiled and went
its own way—the judgment of Winesburg?

Elmer Cowley was extraordinarily tall and his arms were
long and powerful. His hair, his eyebrows, and the downy
beard that had begun to grow upon his chin, were pale
almost to whiteness. His teeth protruded from between his
lips and his eyes were blue with the colorless blueness of
the marbles called "aggies" that the boys of Winesburg
carried in their pockets. Elmer had lived in Winesburg

for a year and had made no friends. He was, he felt, one condemned to go through life without friends and he hated the thought.

Sullenly the tall young man tramped along the road with his hands stuffed into his trouser pockets. The day was cold with a raw wind, but presently the sun began to shine and the road became soft and muddy. The tops of the ridges of frozen mud that formed the road began to melt and the mud clung to Elmer's shoes. His feet became cold. When he had gone several miles he turned off the road, crossed a field and entered a wood. In the wood he gathered sticks to build a fire, by which he sat trying to warm himself, miserable in body and in mind.

For two hours he sat on the log by the fire and then, arising and creeping cautiously through a mass of under-brush, he went to a fence and looked across fields to a small farmhouse surrounded by low sheds. A smile came to his lips and he began making motions with his long arms to a man who was husking corn in one of the fields.

In his hour of misery the young merchant had re-turned to the farm where he had lived through boyhood and where there was another human being to whom he felt he could explain himself. The man on the farm was a half-witted old fellow named Mook. He had once been employed by Ebenezer Cowley and had stayed on the farm when it was sold. The old man lived in one of the un-painted sheds back of the farmhouse and puttered about all day in the fields.

Mook the half-wit lived happily. With childlike faith he believed in the intelligence of the animals that lived in the sheds with him, and when he was lonely held long con-versations with the cows, the pigs, and even with the chick-ens that ran about the barnyard. He it was who had put the expression regarding being "laundered" into the mouth of his former employer. When excited or surprised by anything he smiled vaguely and muttered: "I'll be washed and ironed. Well, well, I'll be washed and ironed and starched."

When the half-witted old man left his husking of corn and came into the wood to meet Elmer Cowley, he was neither surprised nor especially interested in the sudden appearance of the young man. His feet also were cold and he sat on the log by the fire, grateful for the warmth and apparently indifferent to what Elmer had to say.

Elmer talked earnestly and with great freedom, walking up and down and waving his arms about. "You don't understand what's the matter with me so of course you don't care," he declared. "With me it's different. Look how it has always been with me. Father is queer and mother was queer, too. Even the clothes mother used to wear were not like other people's clothes, and look at that coat in which father goes about there in town, thinking he's dressed up, too. Why don't he get a new one? It wouldn't cost much. I'll tell you why. Father doesn't know and when mother was alive she didn't know either. Mabel is different. She knows but she won't say anything. I will, though. I'm not going to be stared at any longer. Why look here, Mook, father doesn't know that his store there in town is just a queer jumble, that he'll never sell the stuff he buys. He knows nothing about it. Sometimes he's a little worried that trade doesn't come and then he goes and buys something else. In the evenings he sits by the fire upstairs and says trade will come after a while. He isn't worried. He's queer. He doesn't know enough to be worried."

The excited young man became more excited. "He don't know but I know," he shouted, stopping to gaze down into the dumb, unresponsive face of the half-wit. "I know too well. I can't stand it. When we lived out here it was different. I worked and at night I went to bed and slept. I wasn't always seeing people and thinking as I am now. In the evening, there in town, I go to the post office or to the depot to see the train come in, and no one says anything to me. Everyone stands around and laughs and they talk but they say nothing to me. Then I feel so queer that I can't talk either. I go away. I don't say anything. I can't."

The fury of the young man became uncontrollable. "I won't stand it," he yelled, looking up at the bare branches of the trees. "I'm not made to stand it."

Maddened by the dull face of the man on the log by the fire, Elmer turned and glared at him as he had glared back along the road at the town of Winesburg. "Go on back to work," he screamed. "What good does it do me to talk to you?" A thought came to him and his voice dropped. "I'm a coward too, eh?" he muttered. "Do you know why I came clear out here afoot? I had to tell someone and you were the only one I could tell. I hunted out another queer one, you see. I ran away, that's what I did. I couldn't stand up to someone like that George Willard. I had to come to you. I ought to tell him and I will."

Again his voice arose to a shout and his arms flew about. "I will tell him. I won't be queer. I don't care what they think. I won't stand it."

Elmer Cowley ran out of the woods leaving the half-wit sitting on the log before the fire. Presently the old man arose and climbing over the fence went back to his work in the corn. "I'll be washed and ironed and starched," he declared. "Well, well, I'll be washed and ironed." Mook was interested. He went along a lane to a field where two cows stood nibbling at a straw stack. "Elmer was here," he said to the cows. "Elmer is crazy. You better get behind the stack where he don't see you. He'll hurt someone yet, Elmer will."

At eight o'clock that evening Elmer Cowley put his head in at the front door of the office of the *Winesburg Eagle* where George Willard sat writing. His cap was pulled down over his eyes and a sullen determined look was on his face. "You come on outside with me," he said, stepping in and closing the door. He kept his hand on the knob as though prepared to resist anyone else coming in. "You just come along outside. I want to see you."

George Willard and Elmer Cowley walked through the main street of Winesburg. The night was cold and George Willard had on a new overcoat and looked very spruce and dressed up. He thrust his hands into the overcoat pockets and looked inquiringly at his companion. He had long been wanting to make friends with the young merchant and find out what was in his mind. Now he thought he saw a chance and was delighted. "I wonder what he's up to? Perhaps he thinks he has a piece of news for the paper. It can't be a fire because I haven't heard the fire bell and there isn't anyone running," he thought.

In the main street of Winesburg, on the cold November evening, but few citizens appeared and these hurried along bent on getting to the stove at the back of some store. The windows of the stores were frosted and the wind rattled the tin sign that hung over the entrance to the stairway leading to Doctor Welling's office. Before Hern's Grocery a basket of apples and a rack filled with new brooms stood on the sidewalk. Elmer Cowley stopped and stood facing George Willard. He tried to talk and his arms began to pump up and down. His face worked spasmodically. He seemed about to shout. "Oh, you go on back," he cried. "Don't stay out here with me. I ain't got anything to tell you. I don't want to see you at all."

For three hours the distracted young merchant wandered through the resident streets of Winesburg blind with anger, brought on by his failure to declare his determination not to be queer. Bitterly the sense of defeat settled upon him and he wanted to weep. After the hours of futile sputtering at nothingness that had occupied the afternoon and his failure in the presence of the young reporter, he thought he could see no hope of a future for himself.

And then a new idea dawned for him. In the darkness that surrounded him he began to see a light. Going to the now darkened store, where Cowley & Son had for over a year waited vainly for trade to come, he crept stealthily in and felt about in a barrel that stood by the stove at the rear. In the barrel beneath shavings lay a tin box containing Cowley & Son's cash. Every evening Ebenezer Cowley put the box in the barrel when he closed the store and went upstairs to bed. "They wouldn't never think of a careless place like that," he told himself, thinking of robbers.

Elmer took twenty dollars, two ten-dollar bills, from the little roll containing perhaps four hundred dollars, the cash left from the sale of the farm. Then replacing the box beneath the shavings he went quietly out at the front door and walked again in the streets.

The idea that he thought might put an end to all of his unhappiness was very simple. "I will get out of here, run away from home," he told himself. He knew that a local freight train passed through Winesburg at midnight and went on to Cleveland, where it arrived at dawn. He would steal a ride on the local and when he got to Cleveland would lose himself in the crowds there. He would get work in some shop and become friends with the other workmen and would be indistinguishable. Then he could talk and laugh. He would no longer be queer and would make friends. Life would begin to have warmth and meaning for him as it had for others.

The tall awkward young man, striding through the streets, laughed at himself because he had been angry and had been half afraid of George Willard. He decided he would have his talk with the young reporter before he left town, that he would tell him about things, perhaps challenge him, challenge all of Winesburg through him.

Aglow with new confidence Elmer went to the office of the New Willard House and pounded on the door. A sleep-eyed boy slept on a cot in the office. He received no salary but was fed at the hotel table and bore with pride the title of "night clerk." Before the boy Elmer was bold, insistent. "You wake him up," he commanded. "You tell him to come down by the depot. I got to see him and I'm going away on the local. Tell him to dress and come on down. I ain't got much time."

The midnight local had finished its work in Winesburg and the trainsmen were coupling cars, swinging lanterns and preparing to resume their flight east. George Willard, rubbing his eyes and again wearing the new overcoat, ran down to the station platform afire with curiosity. "Well, here I am. What do you want? You've got something to tell me, eh?" he said.

Elmer tried to explain. He wet his lips with his tongue and looked at the train that had begun to groan and get under way. "Well, you see," he began, and then lost control of his tongue. "I'll be washed and ironed. I'll be washed and ironed and starched," he muttered half incoherently.

Elmer Cowley danced with fury beside the groaning train in the darkness on the station platform. Lights leaped into the air and bobbed up and down before his eyes. Taking the two ten-dollar bills from his pocket he thrust them into George Willard's hand. "Take them," he cried. "I don't want them. Give them to father. I stole them."

With a snarl of rage he turned and his long arms began to flay the air. Like one struggling for release from hands that held him he struck out, hitting George Willard blow after blow on the breast, the neck, the mouth. The young reporter rolled over on the platform half unconscious, stunned by the terrific force of the blows. Springing aboard the passing train and running over the tops of cars, Elmer sprang down to a flat car and lying on his face looked back, trying to see the fallen man in the darkness. Pride surged up in him. "I showed him," he cried. "I guess I showed him. I ain't so queer. I guess I showed him I ain't so queer."

THE UNTOLD LIE

RAY PEARSON and Hal Winters were farm hands employed on a farm three miles north of Winesburg. On Saturday afternoons they came into town and wandered about through the streets with other fellows from the country.

Ray was a quiet, rather nervous man of perhaps fifty with a brown beard and shoulders rounded by too much and too hard labor. In his nature he was as unlike Hal Winters as two men can be unlike.

Ray was an altogether serious man and had a little sharp-featured wife who had also a sharp voice. The two, with half a dozen thin-legged children, lived in a tumble-down frame house beside a creek at the back end of the Wills farm where Ray was employed.

Hal Winters, his fellow employee, was a young fellow. He was not of the Ned Winters family, who were very respectable people in Winesburg, but was one of the three sons of the old man called Windpeter Winters who had a sawmill near Unionville, six miles away, and who was looked upon by everyone in Winesburg as a confirmed old reprobate.

People from the part of Northern Ohio in which Winesburg lies will remember old Windpeter by his unusual and tragic death. He got drunk one evening in town and started to drive home to Unionville along the railroad tracks. Henry Brattenburg, the butcher, who lived out that way, stopped him at the edge of the town and told him he

was sure to meet the down train but Windpeter slashed at
him with his whip and drove on. When the train struck and
killed him and his two horses a farmer and his wife who
were driving home along a nearby road saw the accident.
They said that old Windpeter stood up on the seat of his
wagon, raving and swearing at the onrushing locomotive,
and that he fairly screamed with delight when the team,
maddened by his incessant slashing at them, rushed straight
ahead to certain death. Boys like young George Willard
and Seth Richmond will remember the incident quite
vividly because, although everyone in our town said that
the old man would go straight to hell and that the community was better off without him, they had a secret conviction that he knew what he was doing and admired his
foolish courage. Most boys have seasons of wishing they
could die gloriously instead of just being grocery clerks and
going on with their humdrum lives.

But this is not the story of Windpeter Winters nor yet of
his son Hal who worked on the Wills farm with Ray
Pearson. It is Ray's story. It will, however, be necessary to
talk a little of young Hal so that you will get into the spirit
of it.

Hal was a bad one. Everyone said that. There were three
of the Winters boys in that family, John, Hal, and Edward,
all broad-shouldered big fellows like old Windpeter himself and all fighters and woman-chasers and generally all-
around bad ones.

Hal was the worst of the lot and always up to some devilment. He once stole a load of boards from his father's
mill and sold them in Winesburg. With the money he
bought himself a suit of cheap, flashy clothes. Then he got
drunk and when his father came raving into town to find
him, they met and fought with their fists on Main Street
and were arrested and put into jail together.

Hal went to work on the Wills farm because there was a country school teacher out that way who had taken his fancy. He was only twenty-two then but had already been in two or three of what were spoken of in Winesburg as "women scrapes." Everyone who heard of his infatuation for the school teacher was sure it would turn out badly. "He'll only get her into trouble, you'll see," was the word that went around.

And so these two men, Ray and Hal, were at work in a field on a day in the late October. They were husking corn and occasionally something was said and they laughed. Then came silence. Ray, who was the more sensitive and always minded things more, had chapped hands and they hurt. He put them into his coat pockets and looked away across the fields. He was in a sad, distracted mood and was affected by the beauty of the country. If you knew the Winesburg country in the fall and how the low hills are all splashed with yellows and reds you would understand his feeling. He began to think of the time, long ago when he was a young fellow living with his father, then a baker in Winesburg, and how on such days he had wandered away to the woods to gather nuts, hunt rabbits, or just to loaf about and smoke his pipe. His marriage had come about through one of his days of wandering. He had induced a girl who waited on trade in his father's shop to go with him and something had happened. He was thinking of that afternoon and how it had affected his whole life when a spirit of protest awoke in him. He had forgotten about Hal and muttered words. "Tricked by Gad, that's what I was, tricked by life and made a fool of," he said in a low voice.

As though understanding his thoughts, Hal Winters spoke up. "Well, has it been worth while? What about it, eh? What about marriage and all that?" he asked and then laughed. Hal tried to keep on laughing but he too was in an earnest mood. He began to talk earnestly. "Has a fellow got to do it?" he asked. "Has he got to be harnessed up and driven through life like a horse?"

Hal didn't wait for an answer but sprang to his feet and began to walk back and forth between the corn shocks. He was getting more and more excited. Bending down suddenly he picked up an ear of the yellow corn and threw it at the fence. "I've got Nell Gunther in trouble," he said. "I'm telling you, but you keep your mouth shut."

Ray Pearson arose and stood staring. He was almost a foot shorter than Hal, and when the younger man came and put his two hands on the older man's shoulders they made a picture. There they stood in the big empty field with the quiet corn shocks standing in rows behind them and the red and yellow hills in the distance, and from being just two indifferent workmen they had become all alive to each other. Hal sensed it and because that was his way he laughed. "Well, old daddy," he said awkwardly, "come on, advise me. I've got Nell in trouble. Perhaps you've been in the same fix yourself. I know what everyone would say is the right thing to do, but what do you say? Shall I marry and settle down? Shall I put myself into the harness to be worn out like an old horse? You know me, Ray. There can't anyone break me but I can break myself. Shall I do it or shall I tell Nell to go to the devil? Come on, you tell me. Whatever you say, Ray, I'll do."

Ray couldn't answer. He shook Hal's hands loose and turning walked straight away toward the barn. He was a sensitive man and there were tears in his eyes. He knew there was only one thing to say to Hal Winters, son of old Windpeter Winters, only one thing that all his own training and all the beliefs of the people he knew would approve, but for his life he couldn't say what he knew he should say.

At half-past four that afternoon Ray was puttering about the barnyard when his wife came up the lane along the creek and called him. After the talk with Hal he hadn't returned to the cornfield but worked about the barn. He had already done the evening chores and had seen Hal, dressed and ready for a roistering night in town, come out of the farmhouse and go into the road. Along the path to his own house he trudged behind his wife, looking at the ground and thinking. He couldn't make out what was wrong. Every time he raised his eyes and saw the beauty of the country in the failing light he wanted to do something he had never done before, shout or scream or hit his wife with his fists or something equally unexpected and terrifying. Along the path he went scratching his head and trying to make it out. He looked hard at his wife's back but she seemed all right.

She only wanted him to go into town for groceries and as soon as she had told him what she wanted began to scold. "You're always puttering," she said. "Now I want you to hustle. There isn't anything in the house for supper and you've got to get to town and back in a hurry."

Ray went into his own house and took an overcoat from a hook back of the door. It was torn about the pockets and the collar was shiny. His wife went into the bedroom and presently came out with a soiled cloth in one hand and three silver dollars in the other. Somewhere in the house a child wept bitterly and a dog that had been sleeping by the stove arose and yawned. Again the wife scolded. "The children will cry and cry. Why are you always puttering?" she asked.

Ray went out of the house and climbed the fence into a

field. It was just growing dark and the scene that lay before him was lovely. All the low hills were washed with color and even the little clusters of bushes in the corners by the fences were alive with beauty. The whole world seemed to Ray Pearson to have become alive with something just as he and Hal had suddenly become alive when they stood in the corn field staring into each other's eyes.

The beauty of the country about Winesburg was too much for Ray on that fall evening. That is all there was to it. He could not stand it. Of a sudden he forgot all about being a quiet old farm hand and throwing off the torn overcoat began to run across the field. As he ran he shouted a protest against his life, against all life, against everything that makes life ugly. ["There was no promise made,"] he cried into the empty spaces that lay about him. "I didn't promise my Minnie anything and Hal hasn't made any promise to Nell. I know he hasn't. She went into the woods with him because she wanted to go. What he wanted she wanted. Why should I pay? Why should Hal pay? Why should anyone pay? I don't want Hal to become old and worn out. I'll tell him. I won't let it go on. I'll catch Hal before he gets to town and I'll tell him."

Ray ran clumsily and once he stumbled and fell down. "I must catch Hal and tell him," he kept thinking, and although his breath came in gasps he kept running harder and harder. As he ran he thought of things that hadn't come into his mind for years—how at the time he married he had planned to go west to his uncle in Portland, Oregon—how he hadn't wanted to be a farm hand, but had thought when he got out West he would go to sea and be a sailor or get a job on a ranch and ride a horse into Western towns, shouting and laughing and waking the people in the houses with his wild cries. Then as he ran he remembered his children and in fancy felt their hands clutching at him. All of his thoughts of himself were involved with the thoughts of Hal and he thought the children were clutching at the younger man also. "They are the accidents of life, Hal," he cried. "They are not mine or yours. I had nothing to do with them."

Darkness began to spread over the fields as Ray Pearson ran on and on. His breath came in little sobs. When he came to the fence at the edge of the road and confronted Hal Winters, all dressed up and smoking a pipe as he walked jauntily along, he could not have told what he thought or what he wanted.

Ray Pearson lost his nerve and this is really the end of the story of what happened to him. It was almost dark when he got to the fence and he put his hands on the top bar and stood staring. Hal Winters jumped a ditch and coming up close to Ray put his hands into his pockets and laughed. He seemed to have lost his own sense of what had happened in the corn field and when he put up a strong hand and took hold of the lapel of Ray's coat he shook the old man as he might have shaken a dog that had misbehaved.

"You came to tell me, eh?" he said. "Well, never mind telling me anything. I'm not a coward and I've already made up my mind." He laughed again and jumped back across the ditch. "Nell ain't no fool," he said. "She didn't ask me to marry her. I want to marry her. I want to settle down and have kids."

Ray Pearson also laughed. He felt like laughing at himself and all the world.

As the form of Hal Winters disappeared in the dusk that lay over the road that led to Winesburg, he turned and walked slowly back across the fields to where he had left his torn overcoat. As he went some memory of pleasant evenings spent with the thin-legged children in the tumble-down house by the creek must have come into his mind, for he muttered words. "It's just as well. Whatever I told him would have been a lie," he said softly, and then his form also disappeared into the darkness of the fields.

DRINK

T OM   F OSTER   came   to   Winesburg   from   Cincin-
nati   when   he   was   still   young   and   could   get   many   new   impressions.   His   grandmother   had   been   raised   on   a   farm
near   the   town   and   as   a   young   girl   had   gone   to   school   there
when   Winesburg   was   a   village   of   twelve   or   fifteen   houses
clustered   about   a   general   store   on   the   Trunion   Pike.

What   a   life   the   old   woman   had   led   since   she   went   away
from   the   frontier   settlement   and   what   a   strong,   capable
little   old   thing   she   was!   She   had   been   in   Kansas,   in
Canada,   and   in   New   York   City,   traveling   about   with   her
husband,   a   mechanic,   before   he   died.   Later   she   went   to
stay   with   her   daughter,   who   had   also   married   a   mechanic
and   lived   in   Covington,   Kentucky,   across   the   river   from
Cincinnati.

Then   began   the   hard   years   for   Tom   Foster's   grandmother.   First   her   son-in-law   was   killed   by   a   policeman
during   a   strike   and   then   Tom's   mother   became   an   invalid
and   died   also.   The   grandmother   had   saved   a   little   money,
but   it   was   swept   away   by   the   illness   of   the   daughter   and
by   the   cost   of   the   two   funerals.   She   became   a   half   worn-
out   old   woman   worker   and   lived   with   the   grandson   above
a   junk   shop   on   a   side   street   in   Cincinnati.   For   five   years
she   scrubbed   the   floors   in   an   office   building   and   then   got
a   place   as   dish   washer   in   a   restaurant.   Her   hands   were
all   twisted   out   of   shape.   When   she   took   hold   of   a   mop   or
a   broom   handle   the   hands   looked   like   the   dried   stems   of
an   old   creeping   vine   clinging   to   a   tree.

The old woman came back to Winesburg as soon as she got the chance. One evening as she was coming home from work she found a pocket-book containing thirty-seven dollars, and that opened the way. The trip was a great adventure for the boy. It was past seven o'clock at night when the grandmother came home with the pocket-book held tightly in her old hands and she was so excited she could scarcely speak. She insisted on leaving Cincinnati that night, saying that if they stayed until morning the owner of the money would be sure to find them out and make trouble. Tom, who was then sixteen years old, had to go trudging off to the station with the old woman, bearing all of their earthly belongings done up in a worn-out blanket and slung across his back. By his side walked the grandmother urging him forward. Her toothless old mouth twitched nervously, and when Tom grew weary and wanted to put the pack down at a street crossing, she snatched it up and if he had not prevented would have slung it across her own back. When they got into the train and it had run out of the city she was as delighted as a girl and talked as the boy had never heard her talk before.

All through the night as the train rattled along, the grandmother told Tom tales of Winesburg and of how he would enjoy his life working in the fields and shooting wild things in the woods there. She could not believe that the tiny village of fifty years before had grown into a thriving town in her absence, and in the morning when the train came to Winesburg did not want to get off. "It isn't what I thought. It may be hard for you here," she said, and then the train went on its way and the two stood confused, not knowing where to turn, in the presence of Albert Longworth, the Winesburg baggage master.

But Tom Foster did get along all right. He was one to get along anywhere. Mrs. White, the banker's wife, employed his grandmother to work in the kitchen and he got a place as stable boy in the banker's new brick barn.

In Winesburg servants were hard to get. The woman who wanted help in her housework employed a "hired girl" who insisted on sitting at the table with the family. Mrs. White was sick of hired girls and snatched at the chance to get hold of the old city woman. She furnished a room for the boy Tom upstairs in the barn. "He can mow the lawn and run errands when the horses do not need attention," she explained to her husband.

Tom Foster was rather small for his age and had a large head covered with stiff black hair that stood straight up. The hair emphasized the bigness of his head. His voice was the softest thing imaginable, and he was himself so gentle and quiet that he slipped into the life of the town without attracting the least bit of attention.

One could not help wondering where Tom Foster got his gentleness. In Cincinnati he had lived in a neighborhood where gangs of tough boys prowled through the streets, and all through his early formative years he ran about with tough boys. For a while he was messenger for a telegraph company and delivered messages in a neighborhood sprinkled with houses of prostitution. The women in the houses knew and loved Tom Foster and the tough boys in the gangs loved him also.

He never asserted himself. That was one thing that helped him escape. In an odd way he stood in the shadow of the wall of life, was meant to stand in the shadow. He saw the men and women in the houses of lust, sensed their casual and horrible love affairs, saw boys fighting and listened to their tales of thieving and drunkenness, unmoved and strangely unaffected.

Once Tom did steal. That was while he still lived in the city. The grandmother was ill at the time and he himself was out of work. There was nothing to eat in the house, and so he went into a harness shop on a side street and stole a dollar and seventy-five cents out of the cash drawer.

The harness shop was run by an old man with a long mustache. He saw the boy lurking about and thought nothing of it. When he went out into the street to talk to a teamster Tom opened the cash drawer and taking the money walked away. Later he was caught and his grandmother settled the matter by offering to come twice a week for a month and scrub the shop. The boy was ashamed, but he was rather glad, too. "It is all right to be ashamed and makes me understand new things," he said to the grandmother, who didn't know what the boy was talking about but loved him so much that it didn't matter whether she understood or not.

For a year Tom Foster lived in the banker's stable and then lost his place there. He didn't take very good care of the horses and he was a constant source of irritation to the banker's wife. She told him to mow the lawn and he forgot. Then she sent him to the store or to the post office and he did not come back but joined a group of men and boys and spent the whole afternoon with them, standing about, listening and occasionally, when addressed, saying a few words. As in the city in the houses of prostitution and with the rowdy boys running through the streets at night, so in Winesburg among its citizens he had always the power to be a part of and yet distinctly apart from the life about him.

After Tom lost his place at Banker White's he did not live with his grandmother, although often in the evening she came to visit him. He rented a room at the rear of a little frame building belonging to old Rufus Whiting. The building was on Duane Street, just off Main Street, and had been used for years as a law office by the old man, who had become too feeble and forgetful for the practice of his profession but did not realize his inefficiency. He liked Tom and let him have the room for a dollar a month. In the late afternoon when the lawyer had gone home the boy had the place to himself and spent hours lying on the floor by the stove and thinking of things. In the evening the grandmother came and sat in the lawyer's chair to smoke a pipe while Tom remained silent, as he always did in the presence of everyone.

Often the old woman talked with great vigor. Sometimes she was angry about some happening at the banker's house and scolded away for hours. Out of her own earnings she bought a mop and regularly scrubbed the lawyer's office. Then when the place was spotlessly clean and smelled clean she lighted her clay pipe and she and Tom had a smoke together. "When you get ready to die then I will die also," she said to the boy lying on the floor beside her chair.

Tom Foster enjoyed life in Winesburg. He did odd jobs, such as cutting wood for kitchen stoves and mowing the grass before houses. In late May and early June he picked strawberries in the fields. He had time to loaf and he enjoyed loafing. Banker White had given him a cast-off coat which was too large for him, but his grandmother cut it down, and he had also an overcoat, got at the same place, that was lined with fur. The fur was worn away in spots, but the coat was warm and in the winter Tom slept in it. He thought his method of getting along good enough and was happy and satisfied with the way life in Winesburg had turned out for him.

The most absurd little things made Tom Foster happy. That, I suppose, was why people loved him. In Hern's Grocery they would be roasting coffee on Friday afternoon, preparatory to the Saturday rush of trade, and the rich

odor invaded lower Main Street. Tom Foster appeared
and sat on a box at the rear of the store. For an hour he
did not move but sat perfectly still, filling his being with
the spicy odor that made him half drunk with happiness.
"I like it," he said gently. "It makes me think of things
far away, places and things like that."

One night Tom Foster got drunk. That came about in a
curious way. He never had been drunk before, and indeed
in all his life had never taken a drink of anything intoxi-
cating, but he felt he needed to be drunk that one time
and so went and did it.

In Cincinnati, when he lived there, Tom had found out
many things, things about ugliness and crime and lust.
Indeed, he knew more of these things than anyone else in
Winesburg. The matter of sex in particular had presented
itself to him in a quite horrible way and had made a deep
impression on his mind. He thought, after what he had
seen of the women standing before the squalid houses on
cold nights and the look he had seen in the eyes of the men
who stopped to talk to them, that he would put sex altogether out of his own life. One of the women of the neighborhood tempted him once and he went into a room with
her. He never forgot the smell of the room nor the greedy
look that came into the eyes of the woman. It sickened him
and in a very terrible way left a scar on his soul. He had
always before thought of women as quite innocent things,
much like his grandmother, but after that one experience
in the room he dismissed women from his mind. So gentle
was his nature that he could not hate anything and not being able to understand he decided to forget.

And Tom did forget until he came to Winesburg. After
he had lived there for two years something began to stir
in him. On all sides he saw youth making love and he was
himself a youth. Before he knew what had happened he

was in love also. He fell in love with Helen White, daughter of the man for whom he had worked, and found himself thinking of her at night.

That was a problem for Tom and he settled it in his own way. He let himself think of Helen White whenever her figure came into his mind and only concerned himself with the manner of his thoughts. He had a fight, a quiet determined little fight of his own, to keep his desires in the channel where he thought they belonged, but on the whole he was victorious.

And then came the spring night when he got drunk. Tom was wild on that night. He was like an innocent young buck of the forest that has eaten of some maddening weed. The thing began, ran its course, and was ended in one night, and you may be sure that no one in Winesburg was any the worse for Tom's outbreak.

In the first place, the night was one to make a sensitive nature drunk. The trees along the residence streets of the town were all newly clothed in soft green leaves, in the gardens behind the houses men were puttering about in vegetable gardens, and in the air there was a hush, a waiting kind of silence very stirring to the blood.

Tom left his room on Duane Street just as the young night began to make itself felt. First he walked through the streets, going softly and quietly along, thinking thoughts that he tried to put into words. He said that Helen White was a flame dancing in the air and that he was a little tree without leaves standing out sharply against the sky. Then he said that she was a wind, a strong terrible wind, coming out of the darkness of a stormy sea and that he was a boat left on the shore of the sea by a fisherman.

That idea pleased the boy and he sauntered along playing with it. He went into Main Street and sat on the curb-

ing before Wacker's tobacco store. For an hour he
lingered about listening to the talk of men, but it did not
interest him much and he slipped away. Then he decided
to get drunk and went into Willy's saloon and bought a
bottle of whiskey. Putting the bottle into his pocket, he
walked out of town, wanting to be alone to think more
thoughts and to drink the whiskey.

Tom got drunk sitting on a bank of new grass beside
the road about a mile north of town. Before him was a
white road and at his back an apple orchard in full bloom.
He took a drink out of the bottle and then lay down on
the grass. He thought of mornings in Winesburg and of
how the stones in the graveled driveway by Banker
White's house were wet with dew and glistened in the
morning light. He thought of the nights in the barn when
it rained and he lay awake hearing the drumming of the
raindrops and smelling the warm smell of horses and of
hay. Then he thought of a storm that had gone roaring
through Winesburg several days before and, his mind going back, he relived the night he had spent on the train
with his grandmother when the two were coming from
Cincinnati. Sharply he remembered how strange it had
seemed to sit quietly in the coach and to feel the power of
the engine hurling the train along through the night.

Tom got drunk in a very short time. He kept taking
drinks from the bottle as the thoughts visited him and
when his head began to reel got up and walked along the
road going away from Winesburg. There was a bridge on
the road that ran out of Winesburg north to Lake Erie
and the drunken boy made his way along the road to the
bridge. There he sat down. He tried to drink again, but
when he had taken the cork out of the bottle he became
ill and put it quickly back. His head was rocking back
and forth and so he sat on the stone approach to the bridge

and sighed. His head seemed to be flying about like a pinwheel and then projecting itself off into space and his arms and legs flopped helplessly about.

At eleven o'clock Tom got back into town. George Willard found him wandering about and took him into the *Eagle* printshop. Then he became afraid that the drunken boy would make a mess on the floor and helped him into the alleyway.

The reporter was confused by Tom Foster. The drunken boy talked of Helen White and said he had been with her on the shore of a sea and had made love to her. George had seen Helen White walking in the street with her father during the evening and decided that Tom was out of his head. A sentiment concerning Helen White that lurked in his own heart flamed up and he became angry. "Now you quit that," he said. "I won't let Helen White's name be dragged into this. I won't let that happen." He began shaking Tom's shoulder, trying to make him understand. "You quit it," he said again.

For three hours the two young men, thus strangely thrown together, stayed in the printshop. When he had a little recovered George took Tom for a walk. They went into the country and sat on a log near the edge of a wood. Something in the still night drew them together and when the drunken boy's head began to clear they talked.

"It was good to be drunk," Tom Foster said. "It taught me something. I won't have to do it again. I will think more clearly after this. You see how it is."

George Willard did not see, but his anger concerning Helen White passed and he felt drawn toward the pale, shaken boy as he had never before been drawn toward anyone. With motherly solicitude, he insisted that Tom get to his feet and walk about. Again they went back to the printshop and sat in silence in the darkness.

The reporter could not get the purpose of Tom Foster's action straightened out in his mind. When Tom spoke again of Helen White he again grew angry and began to scold. "You quit that," he said sharply. "You haven't been with her. What makes you say you have? What makes you keep saying such things? Now you quit it, do you hear?"

Tom was hurt. He couldn't quarrel with George Willard because he was incapable of quarreling, so he got up to go away. When George Willard was insistent he put out his hand, laying it on the older boy's arm, and tried to explain.

"Well," he said softly, "I don't know how it was. I was happy. You see how that was. Helen White made me happy and the night did too. I wanted to suffer, to be hurt somehow. I thought that was what I should do. I wanted to suffer, you see, because everyone suffers and does wrong. I thought of a lot of things to do, but they wouldn't work. They all hurt someone else."

Tom Foster's voice arose, and for once in his life he became almost excited. "It was like making love, that's what I mean," he explained. "Don't you see how it is? It hurt me to do what I did and made everything strange. That's why I did it. I'm glad, too. It taught me something, that's it, that's what I wanted. Don't you understand? I wanted to learn things, you see. That's why I did it."

DEATH

THE STAIRWAY leading up to Doctor Reefy's office, in the Heffner Block above the Paris Dry Goods store, was but dimly lighted. At the head of the stairway hung a lamp with a dirty chimney that was fastened by a bracket to the wall. The lamp had a tin reflector, brown with rust and covered with dust. The people who went up the stairway followed with their feet the feet of many who had gone before. The soft boards of the stairs had yielded under the pressure of feet and deep hollows marked the way.

At the top of the stairway a turn to the right brought you to the doctor's door. To the left was a dark hallway filled with rubbish. Old chairs, carpenter's horses, step ladders and empty boxes lay in the darkness waiting for shins to be barked. The pile of rubbish belonged to the Paris Dry Goods Company. When a counter or a row of shelves in the store became useless, clerks carried it up the stairway and threw it on the pile.

Doctor Reefy's office was as large as a barn. A stove with a round paunch sat in the middle of the room. Around its base was piled sawdust, held in place by heavy planks nailed to the floor. By the door stood a huge table that had once been a part of the furniture of Herrick's Clothing Store and that had been used for displaying custom-made clothes. It was covered with books, bottles, and surgical instruments. Near the edge of the table lay three or four apples left by John Spaniard, a tree nurseryman who was Doctor Reefy's friend, and who had slipped the apples out of his pocket as he came in at the door.

At middle age Doctor Reefy was tall and awkward. The grey beard he later wore had not yet appeared, but on the upper lip grew a brown mustache. He was not a graceful man, as when he grew older, and was much occupied with the problem of disposing of his hands and feet.

On summer afternoons, when she had been married many years and when her son George was a boy of twelve or fourteen, Elizabeth Willard sometimes went up the worn steps to Doctor Reefy's office. Already the woman's naturally tall figure had begun to droop and to drag itself listlessly about. Ostensibly she went to see the doctor because of her health, but on the half dozen occasions when she had been to see him the outcome of the visits did not primarily concern her health. She and the doctor talked of that but they talked most of her life, of their two lives and of the ideas that had come to them as they lived their lives in Winesburg.

In the big empty office the man and the woman sat looking at each other and they were a good deal alike. Their bodies were different, as were also the color of their eyes, the length of their noses, and the circumstances of their existence, but something inside them meant the same thing, wanted the same release, would have left the same impression on the memory of an onlooker. Later, and when he grew older and married a young wife, the doctor often talked to her of the hours spent with the sick woman and expressed a good many things he had been unable to express to Elizabeth. He was almost a poet in his old age and his notion of what happened took a poetic turn. "I had come to the time in my life when prayer became necessary and so I invented gods and prayed to them," he said. "I did not say my prayers in words nor did I kneel down but sat perfectly still in my chair. In the late afternoon when it was hot and quiet on Main Street or in the winter when the days were gloomy, the gods came into the office and I thought no one knew about them. Then I found that this woman Elizabeth knew, that she worshipped also the same gods. I have a notion that she came to the office because she thought the gods would be there but she was happy to find herself not alone just the same. It was an experience that cannot be explained, although I suppose it is always happening to men and women in all sorts of places."

❦◆❦

On the summer afternoons when Elizabeth and the doctor sat in the office and talked of their two lives they talked of other lives also. Sometimes the doctor made philosophic epigrams. Then he chuckled with amusement. Now and then after a period of silence, a word was said or a hint given that strangely illuminated the life of the speaker, a wish became a desire, or a dream, half dead, flared suddenly into life. For the most part the words came from the woman and she said them without looking at the man.

Each time she came to see the doctor the hotel keeper's wife talked a little more freely and after an hour or two in his presence went down the stairway into Main Street feeling renewed and strengthened against the dullness of her days. With something approaching a girlhood swing to her body she walked along, but when she had got back to her chair by the window of her room and when darkness had come on and a girl from the hotel dining room brought her dinner on a tray, she let it grow cold. Her thoughts ran away to her girlhood with its passionate

longing for adventure and she remembered the arms of
men that had held her when adventure was a possible
thing for her. Particularly she remembered one who had
for a time been her lover and who in the moment of his
passion had cried out to her more than a hundred times,
saying the same words madly over and over: "You dear!
You dear! You lovely dear!" The words, she thought, expressed something she would have liked to have achieved
in life.

In her room in the shabby old hotel the sick wife of the
hotel keeper began to weep and, putting her hands to her
face, rocked back and forth. The words of her one friend,
Doctor Reefy, rang in her ears. ["Love is like a wind stirring the grass beneath trees on a black night," he had said.
"You must not try to make love definite. It is the divine
accident of life. If you try to be definite and sure about it
and to live beneath the trees, where soft night winds blow,
the long hot day of disappointment comes swiftly and the
gritty dust from passing wagons gathers upon lips inflamed and made tender by kisses."]

Elizabeth Willard could not remember her mother who
had died when she was but five years old. Her girlhood
had been lived in the most haphazard manner imaginable.
Her father was a man who had wanted to be let alone and
the affairs of the hotel would not let him alone. He also
had lived and died a sick man. Every day he arose with
a cheerful face, but by ten o'clock in the morning all the
joy had gone out of his heart. When a guest complained of
the fare in the hotel dining room or one of the girls who
made up the beds got married and went away, he stamped
on the floor and swore. At night when he went to bed he
thought of his daughter growing up among the stream of
people that drifted in and out of the hotel and was overcome with sadness. As the girl grew older and began to

walk out in the evening with men he wanted to talk to her, but when he tried was not successful. He always forgot what he wanted to say and spent the time complaining of his own affairs.

In her girlhood and young womanhood Elizabeth had tried to be a real adventurer in life. At eighteen life had so gripped her that she was no longer a virgin but, although she had a half dozen lovers before she married Tom Willard, she had never entered upon an adventure prompted by desire alone. Like all the women in the world, she wanted a real lover. Always there was something she sought blindly, passionately, some hidden wonder in life. The tall beautiful girl with the swinging stride who had walked under the trees with men was forever putting out her hand into the darkness and trying to get hold of some other hand. [In all the babble of words that fell from the lips of the men with whom she adventured she was trying to find what would be for her the true word.]

Elizabeth had married Tom Willard, a clerk in her father's hotel, because he was at hand and wanted to marry at the time when the determination to marry came to her. For a while, like most young girls, she thought marriage would change the face of life. If there was in her mind a doubt of the outcome of the marriage with Tom she brushed it aside. Her father was ill and near death at the time and she was perplexed because of the meaningless outcome of an affair in which she had just been involved. Other girls of her age in Winesburg were marrying men she had always known, grocery clerks or young farmers. In the evening they walked in Main Street with their husbands and when she passed they smiled happily. She began to think that the fact of marriage might be full of some hidden significance. Young wives with whom she talked spoke softly and shyly. "It changes things to have a man of your own," they said.

On the evening before her marriage the perplexed girl had a talk with her father. Later she wondered if the hours alone with the sick man had not led to her decision to marry. The father talked of his life and advised the daughter to avoid being led into another such muddle. He abused Tom Willard, and that led Elizabeth to come to the clerk's defense. The sick man became excited and tried to get out of bed. When she would not let him walk about he began to complain. "I've never been let alone," he said. "Although I've worked hard I've not made the hotel pay. Even now I owe money at the bank. You'll find that out when I'm gone."

The voice of the sick man became tense with earnestness. Being unable to arise, he put out his hand and pulled the girl's head down beside his own. "There's a way out," he whispered. "Don't marry Tom Willard or anyone else here in Winesburg. There is eight hundred dollars in a tin box in my trunk. Take it and go away."

Again the sick man's voice became querulous. "You've got to promise," he declared. "If you won't promise not to marry, give me your word that you'll never tell Tom about the money. It is mine and if I give it to you I've the right to make that demand. Hide it away. It is to make up to you for my failure as a father. Some time it may prove to be a door, a great open door to you. Come now, I tell you I'm about to die, give me your promise."

❀◆❀

In Doctor Reefy's office, Elizabeth, a tired gaunt old woman at forty-one, sat in a chair near the stove and looked at the floor. By a small desk near the window sat the doctor. His hands played with a lead pencil that lay on the desk. Elizabeth talked of her life as a married woman. She became impersonal and forgot her husband, only using him as a lay figure to give point to her tale. "And then I was married and it did not turn out at all," she said bitterly. "As soon as I had gone into it I began to be afraid. Perhaps I knew too much before and then perhaps I found out too much during my first night with him. I don't remember.

"What a fool I was. When father gave me the money and tried to talk me out of the thought of marriage, I would not listen. I thought of what the girls who were married had said of it and I wanted marriage also. [It wasn't Tom I wanted, it was marriage.] When father went to sleep I leaned out of the window and thought of the life I had led. I didn't want to be a bad woman. The town was full of stories about me. I even began to be afraid Tom would change his mind."

The woman's voice began to quiver with excitement. To Doctor Reefy, who without realizing what was happening had begun to love her, there came an odd illusion. He thought that as she talked the woman's body was changing, that she was becoming younger, straighter, stronger. When he could not shake off the illusion his mind gave it a professional twist. "It is good for both her body and her mind, this talking," he muttered.

The woman began telling of an incident that had happened one afternoon a few months after her marriage. Her voice became steadier. "In the late afternoon I went for a drive alone," she said. "I had a buggy and a little grey pony I kept in Moyer's Livery. Tom was painting and repapering rooms in the hotel. He wanted money and I was trying to make up my mind to tell him about the

eight hundred dollars father had given to me. I couldn't
decide to do it. I didn't like him well enough. There was
always paint on his hands and face during those days and
he smelled of paint. He was trying to fix up the old hotel,
make it new and smart."

The excited woman sat up very straight in her chair
and made a quick girlish movement with her hand as she
told of the drive alone on the spring afternoon. "It was
cloudy and a storm threatened," she said. "Black clouds
made the green of the trees and the grass stand out so that
the colors hurt my eyes. I went out Trunion Pike a mile
or more and then turned into a side road. The little horse
went quickly along up hill and down. I was impatient.
Thoughts came and I wanted to get away from my
thoughts. I began to beat the horse. The black clouds settled down and it began to rain. I wanted to go at a terrible
speed, to drive on and on forever. I wanted to get out of
town, out of my clothes, out of my marriage, out of my
body, out of everything. I almost killed the horse, making
him run, and when he could not run any more I got out
of the buggy and ran afoot into the darkness until I fell
and hurt my side. I wanted to run away from everything
but I wanted to run towards something too. Don't you see,
dear, how it was?"

Elizabeth sprang out of the chair and began to walk
about in the office. She walked as Doctor Reefy thought
he had never seen anyone walk before. To her whole body
there was a swing, a rhythm that intoxicated him. When
she came and knelt on the floor beside his chair he took
her into his arms and began to kiss her passionately. "I
cried all the way home," she said, as she tried to continue
the story of her wild ride, but he did not listen. "You dear!
You lovely dear! Oh you lovely dear!" he muttered and
thought he held in his arms not the tired-out woman of

forty-one but a lovely and innocent girl who had been able by some miracle to project herself out of the husk of the body of the tired-out woman.

Doctor Reefy did not see the woman he had held in his arms again until after her death. On the summer afternoon in the office when he was on the point of becoming her lover a half grotesque little incident brought his love-making quickly to an end. As the man and woman held each other tightly heavy feet came tramping up the office stairs. The two sprang to their feet and stood listening and trembling. The noise on the stairs was made by a clerk from the Paris Dry Goods Company. With a loud bang he threw an empty box on the pile of rubbish in the hallway and then went heavily down the stairs. Elizabeth followed him almost immediately. The thing that had come to life in her as she talked to her one friend died suddenly. She was hysterical, as was also Doctor Reefy, and did not want to continue the talk. Along the street she went with the blood still singing in her body, but when she turned out of Main Street and saw ahead the lights of the New Willard House, she began to tremble and her knees shook so that for a moment she thought she would fail in the street.

The sick woman spent the last few months of her life hungering for death. Along the road of death she went, seeking, hungering. She personified the figure of death and made him now a strong black-haired youth running over hills, now a stern quiet man marked and scarred by the business of living. In the darkness of her room she put out her hand, thrusting it from under the covers of her bed, and she thought that death like a living thing put out his hand to her. "Be patient, lover," she whispered. "Keep yourself young and beautiful and be patient."

On the evening when disease laid its heavy hand upon her and defeated her plans for telling her son George of the eight hundred dollars hidden away, she got out of bed and crept half across the room pleading with death for another hour of life. "Wait, dear! The boy! The boy! The boy!" she pleaded as she tried with all of her strength to fight off the arms of the lover she had wanted so earnestly.

❀◇❀

Elizabeth died one day in March in the year when her son George became eighteen, and the young man had but little sense of the meaning of her death. Only time could give him that. For a month he had seen her lying white and still and speechless in her bed, and then one afternoon the doctor stopped him in the hallway and said a few words.

The young man went into his own room and closed the door. He had a queer empty feeling in the region of his stomach. For a moment he sat staring at the floor and then jumping up went for a walk. Along the station platform he went, and around through residence streets past the high-school building, thinking almost entirely of his own affairs. The notion of death could not get hold of him and he was in fact a little annoyed that his mother had died on that day. He had just received a note from Helen White, the daughter of the town banker, in answer to one from him. "Tonight I could have gone to see her and now it will have to be put off," he thought half angrily.

Elizabeth died on a Friday afternoon at three o'clock. It had been cold and rainy in the morning but in the afternoon the sun came out. Before she died she lay paralyzed for six days unable to speak or move and with only her mind and her eyes alive. For three of the six days she struggled, thinking of her boy, trying to say some few words in regard to his future, and in her eyes there was an appeal so touching that all who saw it kept the memory of the dying woman in their minds for years. Even Tom Willard, who had always half resented his wife, forgot his resentment and the tears ran out of his eyes and lodged in his mustache. The mustache had begun to turn grey and Tom colored it with dye. There was oil in the preparation he used for the purpose and the tears, catching in the mustache and being brushed away by his hand, formed a fine mist-like vapor. In his grief Tom Willard's face looked like the face of a little dog that has been out a long time in bitter weather.

George came home along Main Street at dark on the day of his mother's death and, after going to his own room to brush his hair and clothes, went along the hallway and into the room where the body lay. There was a candle on the dressing table by the door and Doctor Reefy sat in a chair by the bed. The doctor arose and started to go out. He put out his hand as though to greet the younger man and then awkwardly drew it back again. The air of the room was heavy with the presence of the two self-conscious human beings, and the man hurried away.

The dead woman's son sat down in a chair and looked at the floor. He again thought of his own affairs and definitely decided he would make a change in his life, that he would leave Winesburg. "I will go to some city. Perhaps I can get a job on some newspaper," he thought, and then his mind turned to the girl with whom he was to have spent this evening and again he was half angry at the turn of events that had prevented his going to her.

In the dimly lighted room with the dead woman the young man began to have thoughts. His mind played with thoughts of life as his mother's mind had played with the thought of death. He closed his eyes and imagined that the red young lips of Helen White touched his own lips. His body trembled and his hands shook. And then something happened. The boy sprang to his feet and stood stiffly. He looked at the figure of the dead woman under the sheets and shame for his thoughts swept over him so that he began to weep. A new notion came into his mind and he turned and looked guiltily about as though afraid he would be observed.

George Willard became possessed of a madness to lift the sheet from the body of his mother and look at her face. The thought that had come into his mind gripped him terribly. He became convinced that not his mother but someone else lay in the bed before him. The conviction was so real that it was almost unbearable. The body under the sheets was long and in death looked young and graceful. To the boy, held by some strange fancy, it was unspeakably lovely. The feeling that the body before him was alive, that in another moment a lovely woman would spring out of the bed and confront him, became so overpowering that he could not bear the suspense. Again and again he put out his hand. Once he touched and half lifted the white sheet that covered her, but his courage failed and he, like Doctor Reefy, turned and went out of the room. In the hallway outside the door he stopped and trembled so that he had to put a hand against the wall to support himself. "That's not my mother. That's not my mother in there," he whispered to himself and again his body shook with fright and uncertainty. When Aunt Elizabeth Swift, who had come to watch over the body, came out of an adjoining room he put his hand into hers and began to sob, shaking his head from side to side, half blind with grief. "My mother is dead," he said, and then forgetting the woman he turned and stared at the door through which he had just come. "The dear, the dear, oh the lovely dear," the boy, urged by some impulse outside himself, muttered aloud.

❀◆❀

As for the eight hundred dollars the dead woman had kept hidden so long and that was to give George Willard his start in the city, it lay in the tin box behind the plaster by the foot of his mother's bed. Elizabeth had put it there a week after her marriage, breaking the plaster away with a stick. Then she got one of the workmen her husband was at that time employing about the hotel to mend the wall. "I jammed the corner of the bed against it," she had explained to her husband, unable at the moment to give up her dream of release, the release that after all came to her but twice in her life, in the moments when her lovers Death and Doctor Reefy held her in their arms.

SOPHISTICATION

I T W A S early evening of a day in the late fall
and the Winesburg County Fair had brought crowds of
country people into town. The day had been clear and
the night came on warm and pleasant. On the Trunion
Pike, where the road after it left town stretched away between berry fields now covered with dry brown leaves, the
dust from passing wagons arose in clouds. Children, curled
into little balls, slept on the straw scattered on wagon beds.
Their hair was full of dust and their fingers black and
sticky. The dust rolled away over the fields and the departing sun set it ablaze with colors.

In the main street of Winesburg crowds filled the stores
and the sidewalks. Night came on, horses whinnied, the
clerks in the stores ran madly about, children became
lost and cried lustily, an American town worked terribly
at the task of amusing itself.

Pushing his way through the crowds in Main Street,
young George Willard concealed himself in the stairway
leading to Doctor Reefy's office and looked at the people.
With feverish eyes he watched the faces drifting past under the store lights. Thoughts kept coming into his head
and he did not want to think. He stamped impatiently on
the wooden steps and looked sharply about. "Well, is she
going to stay with him all day? Have I done all this waiting for nothing?" he muttered.

George Willard, the Ohio village boy, was fast growing
into manhood and new thoughts had been coming into his

mind. All that day, amid the jam of people at the Fair, he had gone about feeling lonely. He was about to leave Winesburg to go away to some city where he hoped to get work on a city newspaper and he felt grown up. The mood that had taken possession of him was a thing known to men and unknown to boys. He felt old and a little tired. Memories awoke in him. To his mind his new sense of maturity set him apart, made of him a half-tragic figure. He wanted someone to understand the feeling that had taken possession of him after his mother's death.

There is a time in the life of every boy when he for the first time takes the backward view of life. Perhaps that is the moment when he crosses the line into manhood. The boy is walking through the street of his town. He is thinking of the future and of the figure he will cut in the world. Ambitions and regrets awake within him. Suddenly something happens; he stops under a tree and waits as for a voice calling his name. Ghosts of old things creep into his consciousness; the voices outside of himself whisper a message concerning the limitations of life. From being quite sure of himself and his future he becomes not at all sure. If he be an imaginative boy a door is torn open and for the first time he looks out upon the world, seeing, as though they marched in procession before him, the countless figures of men who before his time have come out of nothingness into the world, lived their lives and again disappeared into nothingness. The sadness of sophistication has come to the boy. With a little gasp he sees himself as merely a leaf blown by the wind through the streets of his village. He knows that in spite of all the stout talk of his fellows he must live and die in uncertainty, a thing blown by the winds, a thing destined like corn to wilt in the sun. He shivers and looks eagerly about. The eighteen years he has lived seem but a moment, a breathing space in the long march of humanity. Already he hears death calling. With all his heart he wants to come close to some other human, touch someone with his hands, be touched by the hand of another. If he prefers that the other be a woman, that is because he believes that a woman will be gentle, that she will understand. [He wants, most of all, understanding.]

When the moment of sophistication came to George Willard his mind turned to Helen White, the Winesburg banker's daughter. Always he had been conscious of the girl growing into womanhood as he grew into manhood. Once on a summer night when he was eighteen, he had walked with her on a country road and in her presence had given way to an impulse to boast, to make himself appear big and significant in her eyes. Now he wanted to see her for another purpose. He wanted to tell her of the new impulses that had come to him. He had tried to make her think of him as a man when he knew nothing of manhood and now he wanted to be with her and to try to make her feel the change he believed had taken place in his nature.

As for Helen White, she also had come to a period of change. What George felt, she in her young woman's way felt also. She was no longer a girl and hungered to reach into the grace and beauty of womanhood. She had come home from Cleveland, where she was attending college, to spend a day at the Fair. She also had begun to have memories. During the day she sat in the grand-stand with a young man, one of the instructors from the college, who was a guest of her mother's. The young man was of a pedantic turn of mind and she felt at once he would not do for her purpose. At the Fair she was glad to be seen in his company as he was well dressed and a stranger. She knew that the fact of his presence would create an impression. During the day she was happy, but when night came on she began to grow restless. She wanted to drive the instructor away, to get out of his presence. While they sat together in the grand-stand and while the eyes of former schoolmates were upon them, she paid so much attention to her escort that he grew interested. "A scholar needs money. I should marry a woman with money," he mused.

Helen White was thinking of George Willard even as he wandered gloomily through the crowds thinking of her. She remembered the summer evening when they had walked together and wanted to walk with him again. She thought that the months she had spent in the city, the going to theaters and the seeing of great crowds wandering in lighted thoroughfares, had changed her profoundly. She wanted him to feel and be conscious of the change in her nature.

The summer evening together that had left its mark on the memory of both the young man and woman had, when looked at quite sensibly, been rather stupidly spent. They had walked out of town along a country road. Then they had stopped by a fence near a field of young corn and George had taken off his coat and let it hang on his arm. "Well, I've stayed here in Winesburg—yes—I've not yet gone away but I'm growing up," he had said. "I've been reading books and I've been thinking. I'm going to try to amount to something in life.

"Well," he explained, "that isn't the point. Perhaps I'd better quit talking."

The confused boy put his hand on the girl's arm. His voice trembled. The two started to walk back along the road toward town. In his desperation George boasted, "I'm going to be a big man, the biggest that ever lived here in Winesburg," he declared. "I want you to do something, I don't know what. Perhaps it is none of my business. I want you to try to be different from other women. You see the point. It's none of my business I tell you. I want you to be a beautiful woman. You see what I want."

The boy's voice failed and in silence the two came back into town and went along the street to Helen White's house. At the gate he tried to say something impressive. Speeches he had thought out came into his head, but they seemed utterly pointless. "I thought—I used to think— I had it in my mind you would marry Seth Richmond. Now I know you won't," was all he could find to say as she went through the gate and toward the door of her house.

On the warm fall evening as he stood in the stairway and looked at the crowd drifting through Main Street, George thought of the talk beside the field of young corn and was ashamed of the figure he had made of himself. In the street the people surged up and down like cattle confined in a pen. Buggies and wagons almost filled the narrow thoroughfare. A band played and small boys raced along the sidewalk, diving between the legs of men. Young men with shining red faces walked awkwardly about with girls on their arms. In a room above one of the stores, where a dance was to be held, the fiddlers tuned their instruments. The broken sounds floated down through an open window and out across the murmur of voices and the loud blare of the horns of the band. The medley of sounds got on young Willard's nerves. Everywhere, on all sides, the sense of crowding, moving life closed in about him. He wanted to run away by himself and think. "If she wants to stay with that fellow she may. Why should I care? What difference does it make to me?" he growled and went along Main Street and through Hern's Grocery into a side street.

George felt so utterly lonely and dejected that he

wanted to weep but pride made him walk rapidly along, swinging his arms. He came to Wesley Moyer's livery barn and stopped in the shadows to listen to a group of men who talked of a race Wesley's stallion, Tony Tip, had won at the Fair during the afternoon. A crowd had gathered in front of the barn and before the crowd walked Wesley, prancing up and down and boasting. He held a whip in his hand and kept tapping the ground. Little puffs of dust arose in the lamplight. "Hell, quit your talking," Wesley exclaimed. "I wasn't afraid, I knew I had 'em beat all the time. I wasn't afraid."

Ordinarily George Willard would have been intensely interested in the boasting of Moyer, the horseman. Now it made him angry. He turned and hurried away along the street. "Old windbag," he sputtered. "Why does he want to be bragging? Why don't he shut up?"

George went into a vacant lot and, as he hurried along, fell over a pile of rubbish. A nail protruding from an empty barrel tore his trousers. He sat down on the ground and swore. With a pin he mended the torn place and then arose and went on. "I'll go to Helen White's house, that's what I'll do. I'll walk right in. I'll say that I want to see her. I'll walk right in and sit down, that's what I'll do," he declared, climbing over a fence and beginning to run.

❀◆❀

On the veranda of Banker White's house Helen was restless and distraught. The instructor sat between the mother and daughter. His talk wearied the girl. Although he had also been raised in an Ohio town, the instructor began to put on the airs of the city. He wanted to appear cosmopolitan. "I like the chance you have given me to study the background out of which most of our girls come," he declared. "It was good of you, Mrs. White, to have me down for the day." He turned to Helen and laughed. "Your life is still bound up with the life of this town?" he asked. "There are people here in whom you are interested?" To the girl his voice sounded pompous and heavy.

Helen arose and went into the house. At the door leading to a garden at the back she stopped and stood listening. Her mother began to talk. ["There is no one here fit to associate with a girl of Helen's breeding,"] she said.

Helen ran down a flight of stairs at the back of the house and into the garden. In the darkness she stopped and stood trembling. [It seemed to her that the world was full of meaningless people saying words.] Afire with eagerness she ran through a garden gate and, turning a corner by the banker's barn, went into a little side street. "George! Where are you, George?" she cried, filled with nervous excitement. She stopped running, and leaned against a tree to laugh hysterically. Along the dark little street came George Willard, still saying words. "I'm going to walk right into her house. I'll go right in and sit down," he declared as he came up to her. He stopped and stared stupidly. "Come on," he said and took hold of her hand. With hanging heads they walked away along the street under the trees. Dry leaves rustled under foot. Now that he had found her George wondered what he had better do and say.

❀❀❀

At the upper end of the Fair Ground, in Winesburg, there is a half decayed old grand-stand. It has never been painted and the boards are all warped out of shape. The Fair Ground stands on top of a low hill rising out of the valley of Wine Creek and from the grand-stand one can see at night, over a cornfield, the lights of the town reflected against the sky.

George and Helen climbed the hill to the Fair Ground, coming by the path past Waterworks Pond. The feeling of loneliness and isolation that had come to the young man in the crowded streets of his town was both broken and intensified by the presence of Helen. What he felt was reflected in her.

In youth there are always two forces fighting in people. The warm unthinking little animal struggles against the thing that reflects and remembers, and the older, the more sophisticated thing had possession of George Willard. Sensing his mood, Helen walked beside him filled with respect. When they got to the grand-stand they climbed up under the roof and sat down on one of the long bench-like seats.

There is something memorable in the experience to be had by going into a fair ground that stands at the edge of a Middle Western town on a night after the annual fair has been held. The sensation is one never to be forgotten. On all sides are ghosts, not of the dead, but of living people. Here, during the day just passed, have come the people pouring in from the town and the country around. Farmers with their wives and children and all the people from the hundreds of little frame houses have gathered within these board walls. Young girls have laughed and men with beards have talked of the affairs of their lives. The place has been filled to overflowing with life. It has itched and squirmed with life and now it is night and the life has all gone away. The silence is almost terrifying. One conceals oneself standing silently beside the trunk of a tree and what there is of a reflective tendency in his nature is intensified. One shudders at the thought of the meaninglessness of life while at the same instant, and if the people of the town are his people, one loves life so intensely that tears come into the eyes.

In the darkness under the roof of the grand-stand, George Willard sat beside Helen White and felt very keenly his own insignificance in the scheme of existence. Now that he had come out of town where the presence of the people stirring about, busy with a multitude of affairs, had been so irritating, the irritation was all gone. The presence of Helen renewed and refreshed him. It was as though her woman's hand was assisting him to make some minute readjustment of the machinery of his life. [He began to think of the people in the town where he had always lived with something like reverence. He had reverence for Helen.] He wanted to love and to be loved by her, but he did not want at the moment to be confused by her womanhood.] In the darkness he took hold of her hand and when she crept close put a hand on her shoulder. A wind began to blow and he shivered. With all his strength he tried to hold and to understand the mood that had come upon him. In that high place in the darkness the two oddly sensitive human atoms held each other tightly and waited. In the mind of each was the same thought. "I have come to this lonely place and here is this other," was the substance of the thing felt.

In Winesburg the crowded day had run itself out into the long night of the late fall. Farm horses jogged away along lonely country roads pulling their portion of weary people. Clerks began to bring samples of goods in off the sidewalks and lock the doors of stores. In the Opera House a crowd had gathered to see a show and further down Main Street the fiddlers, their instruments tuned, sweated and worked to keep the feet of youth flying over a dance floor.

THE WASH WILLIAMS TRUE LOVE

In the darkness in the grand-stand Helen White and
George Willard remained silent. Now and then the spell
that held them was broken and they turned and tried in
the dim light to see into each other's eyes. They kissed
but that impulse did not last. At the upper end of the Fair
Ground a half dozen men worked over horses that had
raced during the afternoon. The men had built a fire and
were heating kettles of water. Only their legs could be
seen as they passed back and forth in the light. When the
wind blew the little flames of the fire danced crazily about.

George and Helen arose and walked away into the darkness. They went along a path past a field of corn that had
not yet been cut. The wind whispered among the dry corn
blades. For a moment during the walk back into town the
spell that held them was broken. When they had come
to the crest of Waterworks Hill they stopped by a tree
and George again put his hands on the girl's shoulders.
She embraced him eagerly and then again they drew
quickly back from that impulse. They stopped kissing
and stood a little apart. Mutual respect grew big in them.
They were both embarrassed and to relieve their embarrassment dropped into the animalism of youth. They
laughed and began to pull and haul at each other. In
some way chastened and purified by the mood they had
been in, they became, not man and woman, not boy and
girl, but excited little animals.

It was so they went down the hill. In the darkness they
played like two splendid young things in a young world.
Once, running swiftly forward, Helen tripped George
and he fell. He squirmed and shouted. Shaking with
laughter, he rolled down the hill. Helen ran after him.
For just a moment she stopped in the darkness. There
is no way of knowing what woman's thoughts went
through her mind but, when the bottom of the hill was

reached and she came up to the boy, she took his arm and
walked beside him in dignified silence. [For some reason
they could not have explained they had both got from
their silent evening together the thing needed. Man or
boy, woman or girl, they had for a moment taken hold of
the thing that makes the mature life of men and women
in the modern world possible.]

MATURENESS = UNDERSTANDING
NOT WORDS

DEPARTURE

Young George Willard got out of bed at four in the morning. It was April and the young tree leaves were just coming out of their buds. The trees along the residence streets in Winesburg are maple and the seeds are winged. When the wind blows they whirl crazily about, filling the air and making a carpet underfoot.

George came downstairs into the hotel office carrying a brown leather bag. His trunk was packed for departure. Since two o'clock he had been awake thinking of the journey he was about to take and wondering what he would find at the end of his journey. The boy who slept in the hotel office lay on a cot by the door. His mouth was open and he snored lustily. George crept past the cot and went out into the silent deserted main street. The east was pink with the dawn and long streaks of light climbed into the sky where a few stars still shone.

Beyond the last house on Trunion Pike in Winesburg there is a great stretch of open fields. The fields are owned by farmers who live in town and drive homeward at evening along Trunion Pike in light creaking wagons. In the fields are planted berries and small fruits. In the late afternoon in the hot summers when the road and the fields are covered with dust, a smoky haze lies over the great flat basin of land. To look across it is like looking out across the sea. In the spring when the land is green the effect is somewhat different. The land becomes a wide green billiard table on which tiny human insects toil up and down.

All through his boyhood and young manhood George Willard had been in the habit of walking on Trunion Pike. He had been in the midst of the great open place on winter nights when it was covered with snow and only the moon looked down at him; he had been there in the fall when bleak winds blew and on summer evenings when the air vibrated with the song of insects. On the April morning he wanted to go there again, to walk again in the silence. He did walk to where the road dipped down by a little stream two miles from town and then turned and walked silently back again. When he got to Main Street clerks were sweeping the sidewalks before the stores. "Hey, you George. How does it feel to be going away?" they asked.

The westbound train leaves Winesburg at seven forty-five in the morning. Tom Little is conductor. His train runs from Cleveland to where it connects with a great trunk line railroad with terminals in Chicago and New York. Tom has what in railroad circles is called an "easy run." Every evening he returns to his family. In the fall and spring he spends his Sundays fishing in Lake Erie. He has a round red face and small blue eyes. He knows the people in the towns along his railroad better than a city man knows the people who live in his apartment building.

George came down the little incline from the New Willard House at seven o'clock. Tom Willard carried his bag. The son had become taller than the father.

On the station platform everyone shook the young man's hand. More than a dozen people waited about. Then they talked of their own affairs. Even Will Henderson, who was lazy and often slept until nine, had got out of bed. George was embarrassed. Gertrude Wilmot, a tall thin woman of fifty who worked in the Winesburg post office, came along the station platform. She had never before paid any attention to George. Now she stopped and put out her hand. In two words she voiced what everyone felt. "Good luck," she said sharply and then turning went on her way.

When the train came into the station George felt relieved. He scampered hurriedly aboard. Helen White came running along Main Street hoping to have a parting word with him, but he had found a seat and did not see her. When the train started Tom Little punched his ticket, grinned and, although he knew George well and knew on what adventure he was just setting out, made no comment. Tom had seen a thousand George Willards go out of their towns to the city. It was a commonplace enough incident with him. In the smoking car there was a man who had just invited Tom to go on a fishing trip to Sandusky Bay. He wanted to accept the invitation and talk over details.

George glanced up and down the car to be sure no one was looking, then took out his pocketbook and counted his money. His mind was occupied with a desire not to appear green. Almost the last words his father had said to him concerned the matter of his behavior when he got to the city. "Be a sharp one," Tom Willard had said. "Keep your eyes on your money. Be awake. That's the ticket. Don't let anyone think you're a greenhorn."

After George counted his money he looked out of the window and was surprised to see that the train was still in Winesburg.

The young man, going out of his town to meet the adventure of life, began to think but he did not think of anything very big or dramatic. Things like his mother's death, his departure from Winesburg, the uncertainty of his future life in the city, the serious and larger aspects of his life did not come into his mind.

He thought of little things—Turk Smollet wheeling boards through the main street of his town in the morning, a tall woman, beautifully gowned, who had once stayed overnight at his father's hotel, Butch Wheeler the lamp lighter of Winesburg hurrying through the streets on a summer evening and holding a torch in his hand, Helen White standing by a window in the Winesburg post office and putting a stamp on an envelope.

The young man's mind was carried away by his growing passion for dreams. One looking at him would not have thought him particularly sharp. With the recollection of little things occupying his mind he closed his eyes and leaned back in the car seat. He stayed that way for a long time and when he aroused himself and again looked out of the car window the town of Winesburg had disappeared and his life there had become but a background on which to paint the dreams of his manhood.

A NOTE ON THE TEXT

This text of *Winesburg, Ohio* is reproduced from the 1960 Viking Press edition, for which it was completely redesigned and reset. Pagination is unchanged except for "The Book of the Grotesque," originally pages 21–25, which has been reset for the Critical Library edition as pages 23–26. The 1960 text was prepared by Malcolm Cowley, who supplied the following "Footnote for Bibliographers":

This is the first new edition of *Winesburg* for trade distribution since the book appeared in 1919, all the others having been reproduced page by page from the original plates. There was one change in the second printing; on page 86, line 5, the verb "lay" was corrected to "lie," but in subsequent printings there were, so far as could be learned, no changes whatever in the text. Nobody seemed to notice discrepancies in the spelling of proper names, as when Aunt Callie the housekeeper, in Part I of "Godliness," became Aunt Sallie in Part II. Even the typographical errors—of which I found fourteen, not counting scores of broken letters—were preserved for forty years in copper. This new edition has been copyread and proofread by me and by the publisher's staff in an effort to establish the standard text of an American classic.

The first printing appeared under the imprint of a courageous publisher, B. W. Huebsch, after the book had been rejected by John Lane, who published Anderson's first two novels. It was Mr. Huebsch who called it *Winesburg, Ohio*, with the author's consent; Anderson's original title had been *The Book of the Grotesque*. Ten of the stories had been printed in three magazines, which paid the author, so he said, a total of eighty-five dollars. I found inconsistencies of punctuation between some of these stories and the fifteen that had remained in manuscript; of course I let them stand. I did, however, insert a number of commas—thirty-seven, to be accurate—at points where they were needed to make Anderson's meaning clear. I changed the tense of two verbs, the mood or number of two others, and the case of one pronoun: ". . . the boy, who had been her pupil and who [not whom] she thought might possess a talent. . . ." Knowing that bibliographers worry about such matters, I have made a list of all the corrections, which will be furnished on application to any qualified student of Anderson's work.

II

❀❁❀❁❀❁❀❁❀❁❀❁❀❁❀❁❀❁❀❁❀❁❀❁❀❁❀❁❀❁❀❁❀❁❀❁❀

WINESBURG, OHIO

Criticism

The Reviewers

The New Republic, June 25, 1919

A COUNTRY TOWN

Every Middle Westerner will recognize Winesburg, Ohio, as the town in which he grew up. Devon, Iowa, would have furnished forth just such a book as this had an incisive historian made the community his own; so would Minnewaukan, North Dakota, or Wolf Point, Montana, or any one of ten thousand others. The story of a small town anywhere is the story of the revolt of youth against custom-morality; with youth winning only occasionally and in secret, losing often and publicly. In the middle west the dominant morality of the crossroads is a puritan inheritance. Puritanism went over to Ohio from New England with the settlers, and has taken a firmer hold on the minds and the lives of the inhabitants of the Mississippi valley than it ever had in the east. Hell-fire begins to look a trifle comical in Massachusetts. There is widespread recognition of other inconveniences more direct and immediate. But in Kansas and Nebraska the most potent terror is still the anger of a deity.

The Winesburg of twenty years ago was like the Kansas of today, at least in philosophy. The known and accepted standards were those laid down some thousands of years ago by the leader of one of the nomadic tribes of Asia Minor, crudely adjusted to fit a more complex situation. In many ways the ancient laws could not be adjusted at all; they seem to have confused and darkened more often than they shed light. The wonder is that so few shins were broken on the ten tables of stone. Five hundred sensitive individuals isolated in a haphazard spot on the prairie and seeking to express themselves through the forms of a religion ill-understood, the methods of a business system inherently unjust, and the social customs of a more brutal and bitter era were fated to come upon tragic and pathetic difficulties. For that matter there never has been any truth in the notion of pensive hamlets and quiet little villages. Cranford may have dozed. There were no men in Cranford. But the dwellers in -villes and -bergs and -towns from Jamestown in Maine to Jamestown in California can tell you the truths about their neighbors that will shatter forever what remains of the assumption that life seethes most treacherously in cities and that there are sylvan retreats where the days pass from harvest to harvest like an idyll of Theocritus. There is outward repose over Winesburg, a garment of respectable repose covering alike the infinite pain, the grief, the agony of futile groping, the momentary flare of beauty or passion of which the citizens are ashamed. . . .

As a challenge to the snappy short story form, with its planned proportions of flippant philosophy, epigrammatic conversation and sex danger, nothing better has come out of America than *Winesburg, Ohio*. Because we have so little in the field it is probably easy to over-estimate its excellence. In Chekhov's sketches simplicity is an artistic achievement. With Sherwood Anderson simplicity is both an art and a limitation. But the present book is well within his powers, and he has put into it the observation, the brooding "odds and ends of thoughts," of many years. It was set down by a patient and loving craftsman; it is in a new mood, and one not easily forgotten.

—M. A.[1]

---

[1] A reviewer on the editorial staff of *The New Republic*, probably Maxwell Anderson—*Ed*.

The Chicago Evening Post, June 20, 1919

THE UNROOFING OF WINESBURG:
TALES OF LIFE THAT SEEM
OVERHEARD RATHER THAN WRITTEN

. . . Anderson is not a short story writer in so far as that implies a man who can handle the form of the short story. His metier is rather the—to qualify what alone would sound like a trifle—significant episode. Here, for example, are a number of episodes in the lives of the dwellers in a small Ohio town, in a country where farming and berry growing and merchandising occupy the people. They have no form in the sense of artifice—a bad sense in which to use the word, however. To be more accurate they have no pattern. Artistic form they have in that each episode in its outer garb reflects and presents some emotional reality.

It was in one of Barrie's early books that I first read the remark, which other people have also made, that genius is the ability to prolong one's childhood. Sherwood Anderson has in these pages given remarkable proof of his power to hold in a realm of the mind more intimate than memory the very feel of what his own youth must have been and the inner aspects of all the youth, the age, the whole psychic atmosphere of this Ohio town. He has not merely remembered the peculiarities of his townsfolk and made stories of them, he has in a manner altogether peculiar to himself managed to stay in the center of each little town tragedy or comedy—and he tells you about it. He does not write these stories—the writing seems an accident. A writer would have patterned and transformed the tales. Sherwood Anderson lets you overhear him telling the tales— telling them to himself or to the moon, very often. What writer would tell you a story with this content? A drunkard comes to

Winesburg and, sitting before the hotel, bestows a name—Tandy—a symbolical name which he has made up to represent an ideal for a woman—upon a little seven-year-old girl who is sitting on her father's knee. He has missed love, and he tells the child that he sees implicit in her the woman that he might have loved. Then he goes away, but the child, taken by the name he has bestowed upon her, insists upon its possession.

How slight and fugitive and unimportant that is as prose. And yet what a significant poem Mr. Anderson has made out of his telling of it. And most of the tales in this book have that strange air of seeming inconsequence that only life has, that conscious art strives so hard to avoid. More than once, for instance, Mr. Anderson shows us an "affair" brewing between some village man and maiden, and then a tremor of the soul or an almost imperceptible zephyr of circumstance intervenes. And the story as the reader tried to imagine it fades away. Nothing is left but the revelation of some living soul's thoughts and feelings for a brief time. . . .

—LLEWELLYN JONES

. . . This Anderson is a man of whom a great deal will be heard hereafter. Along with Willa Cather, James Branch Cabell and a few others, he belongs to a small group that has somehow emancipated itself from the prevailing imitativeness and banality of the national letters and is moving steadily toward work that will do honor to the country. His first novel, *Windy McPherson's Son*, printed in 1916, had plenty of faults, but there were so many compensating merits that it stood out clearly above the general run of the fiction of its year. Then came *Marching Men*, another defective but extremely interesting novel, and then a book of dithyrambs, *Mid American Chants*. But these things, for all their brilliant moments, did not adequately represent Anderson. The national vice of ethical purpose corrupted them; they were burdened with *Tendenz*. Now, in *Winesburg, Ohio*, he throws off that handicap. What remains is pure representation—and it is representation so vivid, so full of insight, so shiningly life-like and glowing, that the book is lifted into a category all its own. Nothing quite like it has ever been done in America. It is a book that, at one stroke, turns depression into enthusiasm.

In form, it is a collection of short stories, with common characters welding them into a continued picture of life in a small inland town. But what short stories! Compare them to the popular trade goods of the Gouverneur Morrises and Julian Streets, or even to the more pretentious work of the Alice Browns and Katherine Fullerton Geroulds. It is the difference between music by a Chaminade and music by a Brahms. Into his brief pages Anderson not only gets brilliant images of men and women who walk in all the colors of reality; he also gets a profound sense of the obscure, inner drama of their lives. Consider, for example, the four part story called "Godliness." It is fiction for half a page, but after that it seems indubitable fact—fact that is searching and ferret-like—fact infinitely stealthy and persuasive—the sort of fact that suddenly changes a stolid, inscrutable Captain MacWhirr into a moving symbol of man in his struggle with the fates. And then turn to "respectability," and to "The Strength of God," and to "Adventure," and to "The Teacher." Here one gets all the joy that goes with the discovery of something quite new under the sun—a new order of short story, half tale and half psychological anatomizing, and vastly better than all the kinds that have gone before. Here is the goal that *The Spoon River Anthology* aimed at, and missed by half a mile. Allow everything to the imperfection of the form and everything to the author's occasional failure to rise to it: what remains is a truly extraordinary book, by a man of such palpably unusual talent that it seems almost an impertinence to welcome him.

—H. L. MENCKEN

The Bookman, August 1919

ALL OVER THE LOT

. . . A comparison between [*Winesburg, Ohio*] and the *Spoon River Anthology* is inevitable. Here, as there, the inner individual life of a typical American small town is laid bare, or let us say illuminated from within, so that we perceive its reality shining through the dull masks of convention and humdrum. It is a life of vivid feeling and ardent impulse doomed, for the most part, to be suppressed or misdirected, but still existent and potent as nothing is potent in the life of the community as a community. We must meet the fact at the outset that with this writer sex is well-nigh the mainspring of human action. At worst he seems in this book like a man who has too freely imbibed the doctrine of the psychoanalysts, and fares thereafter with eyes slightly "set" along the path of fiction. At best he seems without consciousness of self or of theory to be getting at the root of the matter—one root, at least—for all of us. His style is plain, staccato, perhaps a little deliberately unliterary:

Wash Williams once had a wife. When he was still a young man he married a woman in Dayton, Ohio. The woman was tall and slender and had blue eyes and yellow hair. Wash was himself a comely youth. He loved the woman with a love as absorbing as the hatred he later felt for all women.

Wash Williams is the telegraph operator in Winesburg, the ugliest man in town. Our business with him is to hear how he became a woman-hater; and it is an unpleasant business, out of which shines the redeeming light of the man's battered yet not defeated idealism. And so it is with all these stories. Frank and momentarily disconcerting as their detail often is, we feel

in them none of the spiritual grossness of the Russian natural-
ists and their imitators. Mr. Anderson is of the race of Steven-
son; he also is "something of the shorter catechist." Always he
seems to be after the true morality that so often governs men
and women when they are at odds with, or merely conforming
to, conventional morality. I do not know where in prose a
tenser moral action is concentrated than in the dozen pages of
"The Strength of God," that amazing tale of the conversion
of the Reverend Curtis Hartman, to whom, Peeping Tom that
he is, God for the first time "manifests himself in the body of
a woman." There are youth and hope and honest love in
Winesburg, Ohio. Yet young George Willard, whose slim figure threads these pages, must go elsewhere to fulfill himself.
He bids farewell to his sweetheart, and we see our last of
Winesburg with him, from the train window:

After George counted his money he looked out of the window
and was surprised to see that the train was still in Winesburg.

The young man, going out of his town to meet the adventure of
life, began to think but he did not think of anything very big or
dramatic. Things like his mother's death, his departure from Winesburg, the uncertainty of his future life in the city, the serious and
larger aspects of his life—did not come into his mind.

He thought of little things—Turk Smollet wheeling boards
through the main street of his town in the morning; a tall woman,
beautifully gowned, who had once stayed overnight at his father's
hotel; Butch Wheeler, the lamplighter of Winesburg, hurrying
through the streets on a summer evening and holding the torch
in his hand; Helen White standing by a window in the Winesburg
post-office and putting a stamp on an envelope.

It may be suspected that most American readers will find themselves so busy recognizing Winesburg that they will have to
be reminded to exercise their inherited prerogative of moral
judgment upon it.

—H. W. Boynton

The Springfield (Mass.) Republican,
July 20, 1919

The step from real merit to worthlessness in writing is so imperceptible that many times the average reader misses it, unless he be the intelligent sort of person who searches his reading matter paragraph by paragraph for new ideas and bits of beauty. And this last is the only sort of reading by which a person may gain any profit from reading Sherwood Anderson's *Winesburg, Ohio,* tales of Ohio small-town life. Mr. Anderson has striven to create stories according to his own conception of the new realism. Some of his sketches, which are all impressionistic, have an underlying significance and real beauty of feeling, but more of them are descriptions, somewhat boldly naked, without a spark of life or creative feeling.

—ANONYMOUS

The New Statesman, July 22, 1922

. . . Mr. Sherwood Anderson's *Winesburg, Ohio* is not such a distinguished book as *The Triumph of the Egg*; but as that contains two of the half dozen most remarkable short stories written in this century that is not surprising. But it is an extraordinarily good book. Yet if one takes it as fiction, particularly if one has read and admired the class of fiction to which to judge from outward appearances it might be trying to belong—Booth Tarkington's provincial novels, Miss Jewett's and Miss Wilkins' and Miss Deland's short stories—one may be disappointed. But it is not fiction. It is poetry. It is unreasonable; it delights in places where those who are not poets could never find delight; it will not follow logic and find connections and trace "plots," but stands in front of things that are of no importance, infatuated with their quality, and hymns them with obstinate ecstasy; it seems persuaded there is beauty in anything, in absolutely anything. In such a spirit Mr. Anderson moves about his ugly little town and watches his dull ugly people. It lives, it glows, they exist as immortal souls. If we have listened truly to the sanctified old tunes we must know that this difficult new tune also is music.

—REBECCA WEST

The Critics

❖❖❖❖❖❖❖❖❖❖❖❖❖❖❖❖❖❖❖❖❖❖❖❖❖❖❖❖❖❖❖❖❖❖❖❖❖

WILLIAM L. PHILLIPS

William L. Phillips is Associate Professor of English and Associate Dean of the College of Arts and Sciences at the University of Washington. His Ph.D. dissertation is entitled *Sherwood Anderson's Winesburg, Ohio: Its Origins, Composition, Technique and Reception.*

HOW SHERWOOD ANDERSON WROTE
WINESBURG, OHIO

Probably the most illuminating of the Sherwood Anderson papers recently made available for study [by the Newberry Library in Chicago] is the manuscript of *Winesburg, Ohio.* There on several pounds of yellowed paper lie the answers to questions which have been only hazily answered by critics content to draw their discussions of Anderson's literary habits from his own highly emotionalized accounts. The manuscript reveals Anderson's methods of work and, as a consequence, the limited extent to which his writing may be called "artless." With particular reference to *Winesburg* itself, moreover, it indicates that the book was conceived as a unit, knit together, however loosely, by the idea of the first tale, "The Book of the Grotesque," and consisting of individual sketches which derived additional power from each other, not, as anthologists of Anderson repeatedly suggest, a collection of short stories which can be separated from each other without loss of effect.

From *American Literature* XXIII (March 1951). Reprinted by permission of William L. Phillips and Duke University Press.

The manuscript, first of all, makes possible a rather accurate dating of the writing itself, a matter not unimportant in the discussion of influences upon Anderson's fiction. In this connection, Anderson's own accounts in his *Memoirs* of the writing of the tales need to be examined as to accuracy. There he said:

I had been published. Books, with my name on their backs standing on a shelf over my desk. And yet, something eating at me.

"No. I have not yet written."

. . . upon the particular occasion I am speaking of . . . it was a late fall night and raining and I had not bothered to put on my pajamas.

I was there naked in the bed and I sprang up. I went to my typewriter and began to write. It was there, under those circumstances, myself sitting near an open window, the rain occasionally blowing in and wetting my bare back, that I did my first writing.

I wrote the first of the stories, afterwards to be known as the Winesburg stories. I wrote it, as I wrote them all, complete in the one sitting. I do not think I afterwards changed a word of it. I wrote it off, so, sitting at my desk, in that room, the rain blowing in on me and wetting my back and when I had written it I got up from my desk.

The rest of the stories in the book came out of me on succeeding evenings, and sometimes during the day while I worked in the advertising office. At intervals there would be a blank space of a week, and then there would be two or three written during a week. I was like a woman having my babies, one after another but without pain. . . . [*Memoirs*].

I had been working so long, so long. Oh, how many thousands, hundreds of thousands of words put down. . . .

And then, on a day, late in the afternoon of a day, I had come home to that room. I sat at a table in a corner of the room. I wrote.

There was the story of another human, quite outside myself, truly told.

The story was one called "Hands." It was about a poor little man, beaten, pounded, frightened by the world in which he lived into something oddly beautiful.

The story was written that night in one sitting. No word of it ever changed. I wrote the story and got up. I walked up and down in that little narrow room. Tears flowed from my eyes.

"It is solid," I said to myself. "It is like a rock. It is there. It is put down. . . ."

In those words, scrawled on the sheets of paper, it is accomplished [*Memoirs*].

The romantic subjectivity of these two accounts indicates the importance of the *Winesburg* stories as a turning point in Anderson's writing career, at least as he saw it; but the same subjectivity suggests that the facts surrounding the composition of the stories should be studied in the light of other evidence. Indeed the mention of the typewritten story in the first account and of the "words, scrawled on the sheets of paper" in the second should warn Anderson's biographers of his lack of interest in fact when invention would make a better story.

If we assume that in the first account when Anderson speaks of "the first of the stories, afterwards to be known as the Winesburg stories" he is referring to "The Book of the Grotesque," the time indicated by the first paragraph is incorrect. This story, actually the first of the *Winesburg* tales to be written and the first to be published, appeared in the *Masses* in February 1916, and thus must have been written at least as early as November 1915. In November 1915 Anderson could not have had "books with [his] name on their backs" on his shelf, since his first book, *Windy McPherson's Son*, was not published until September 1916, and since his second book, *Marching Men*, was not published until the autumn of 1917. If, on the other hand, Anderson in the first account is speaking of the story "Hands," specifically mentioned in the second account, the paragraph still is inaccurate, since "Hands" was published in the *Masses* in March 1916, six months before the publication of his first novel and a year and a half before that of his second.

Furthermore, although Anderson insisted that after writing the story "Hands," "no word of it ever changed," the manuscript shows that the tale underwent extensive revisions of words and phrases after it had been written. And in addition to the manuscript revisions, the first five paragraphs of the *Masses* version of "Hands" are a rearrangement of the corresponding first two paragraphs of the manuscript version, indicating that Anderson reworked the first part of the story before submitting it to the *Masses*.

Two more accounts of the writing appear in Anderson's unpublished papers. On April 21, 1938, he wrote to his friend Roger Sergel that he had recently found a complete manuscript of *Winesburg, Ohio* in an old box of papers; and, explaining the fact that the manuscript was on cheap newsprint paper, he said:

When I wrote the book I was employed in the copy department of an advertising agency and used to cop print paper. The mms [*sic*] is partly on the back of earlier attempts at novels and is mostly in long hand . . . pen, partly pencil.

Anderson's statements in the letter to Sergel agree with the note which Anderson attached to the manuscript which he had found. There he said:

At the time these stories were written, the author was employed as a copy writer in a Chicago advertising agency and the paper is no doubt that used for roughing up advertisements. It is likely the stories were written two or three times, in the writer's room, in a rooming house in Cass Street in Chicago, or in hotels as he traveled about, visiting clients of his employers. It is the author's notion that the manuscript which only showed up after many years in a box of old manuscripts, is the one prepared for the making of a fair copy by a stenographer. At the time these stories were written the author had already published two novels and had made beginnings and sketches for others and some of this manuscript is on the back of sheets covered with these abandoned efforts.

This last account again raises the problem as to when the stories were written. But, as we have shown earlier, Anderson had not "already published two novels" at the time of the writing of the first two stories, and there is good evidence that, as Anderson has indicated in the *Memoirs* passage quoted earlier, many of the stories were written in a short space of time.

The surviving manuscript consists of drafts of each of the *Winesburg* stories, seven of which are written on the cheap, now yellowed print paper used in blocking out advertisements. The other eighteen tales (counting the four parts of "Godliness" as individual tales) are written on the backs of twenty-one separate fragments of early writing, which are, in the main, parts of a novel concerning a character named Talbot Whittingham and variously called "The Golden Circle," "Talbot the Actor," and "Talbot Whittingham."

Since most of the stories are written on the backs of these earlier attempts, and since several *Winesburg* narratives may appear on the back of one fragment, it is possible to set up a chain of the composition of this draft of the tales. The supposition is that if a pile of scrap manuscripts were to be used for writing, the entire pile would be turned over, and what was the last page of the abandoned fragment would appear as the first page of the new story. Thus, for example, when pages 2 to 12 of the manuscript "The Book of the Grotesque" appear on the backs of pages 15 to 5 of an earlier penciled story about a boy named Paul Warden, and the first four pages of the manuscript "Hands" continue down through the pile of the Paul Warden story to complete pages 4 to 1 of the fragment, it seems clear that Anderson wrote the two stories without a delay which would disturb the order of the pile of abandoned attempts.

By the use of such a chain of manuscripts, the order of

composition for three groups of tales may be established. In the first group the following stories appear on the backs of manuscripts the pages of which interlock:

1 "The Book of the Grotesque"   7 "Surrender (Part Three)"
2 "Hands"   8 "Nobody Knows"
3 "Paper Pills"   9 "Respectability"
4 "Tandy"   10 "The Thinker"
5 "Drink"   11 "Terror (Part Four)"
6 "Mother"

The second group begins a second chain of manuscripts, beginning with pages removed from the fragment on which "Mother" (Number 6 above) was written, and continuing on the back of another manuscript:

1 "Godliness (Part One)"
2 "Godliness (Part Two)"

The third group consists of five tales written on the backs of nine fragments, the pages of which do not follow an exact chain but which indicate that the tales were all written on the same small pile of abandoned manuscript. The probable order of these tales is:

1 "Adventure"   4 "Loneliness"
2 "The Strength of God"   5 "An Awakening"
3 "The Teacher"

This third group has connections to the pages of manuscripts on the backs of "The Thinker," "Surrender," and "Terror" in the first group.

Since the first three of the *Winesburg* tales ("The Book of the Grotesque," "Hands," and "Paper Pills" in Group 1) were published in magazines in February, March, and June of 1916 in that order, it seems reasonable to assume that the drafts of all the stories written on the backs of abandoned manuscripts were written in the fall of 1915 and the winter of 1916. It seems proper to assume that over anything but a short period of time, the pile of manuscripts would have been disturbed to such an extent that a grouping like that above would not have been possible, and thus it seems clear that Anderson has correctly indicated that "the rest of the stories came out of me on successive evenings, and sometimes during the day while I worked in the advertising office. At intervals there would be a blank space of a week and then there would be two or three written during a week."

The remaining seven stories, written on the print paper, may well be the stories composed "in the advertising office" or "in hotels as he traveled about visiting clients of his employers." These are "The Philosopher," "A Man of Ideas," "Queer," "The Untold Lie," "Death," "Sophistication," and "Departure." Since two of the seven were published in magazines in December 1916 and January 1917, at least those two may be placed with the stories jotted on the backs of manuscripts; some of the other five, as we shall see, were written later.

Anderson's statement that the manuscript represents "one prepared for the making of a fair copy by a stenographer" suggests that he felt that the manuscript was a late one, prepared just before the collection of the tales into a volume. This, however, is not the case. The preparation of a fair copy for a stenographer would probably have followed the order of the tales in the volume, whereas the order of the manuscripts suggests rather the order of *composition* of the tales. Furthermore, each manuscript contains evidence of extensive revision on the manuscript itself, the results of which revision appear in the magazine version of the tale. A manuscript prepared for the gathering of the tales into a volume might contain revisions from the magazine version to a final version, but could hardly contain revisions from an earlier writing to a magazine version.

Finally, Anderson's statement that "it is likely that the stories were written two or three times" needs to be examined. The revisions on the manuscripts indicate that Anderson was thinking his way through the stories as he wrote them, and that if there were earlier versions, they were mere outlines. Unless this kind of writing were considered a first draft and the revisions made on the manuscripts themselves considered a third draft, Anderson's *Memoirs* statement that "I wrote it, as I wrote them all, complete in one sitting," is closer to the actual manner of composition, although not wholly accurate, as we shall see when we come to consider the revisions themselves. Thus, from Anderson's varying accounts and from the evidence of the manuscripts we may conclude that the *Winesburg* stories were written during a relatively short period of time, one leading to another, and that this period of time was late 1915 and early 1916.

The first *Winesburg* story, as we can see from Anderson's own accounts of its composition, was a starting-point for a career in short-story writing which was to lead Anderson to international fame in the genre. One is naturally curious about the conception of the first tale, how its basic idea and the details of its rendering came about. Such a scene as this can be reconstructed: on a late fall day in 1915 Anderson had come home from his desk at the advertising office of the Critchfield Company to the third floor of a rooming house at 735 Cass Street in Chicago, just a few blocks away from the offices of Harriet Monroe's *Poetry* and Margaret Anderson's *Little Review*. He had perhaps stopped on a bridge over the Chicago River to try to fathom the expression on a face he had passed in the street, and then he had gone up to his room to write at a long table with a bare electric light over it. For nights before, figures had been passing before his eyes as he lay on the bed which he had had built up for him so that he could look out over the Loop. Concerned for his own future as a writer, feeling himself one who "had known people, many people, known them in a peculiarly intimate way," he searched himself by throwing himself into the imagined life of another. That other, an old man with a white mustache, lay on *his* raised bed and watched in a half-dream the procession of figures before his eyes. They were all grotesques, and the old man wrote a book which he called "The Book of the Grotesque."

Whether the conception of Anderson's own book of grotesques came before or immediately after he wrote this first *Winesburg* story, "The Book of the Grotesque," his own gallery of imaginary figures offered him more than enough characters for his book. For the past several years he had been writing novels about a Talbot Whittingham who had lived in a town called Winesburg, Ohio, so far as Anderson knew not a real Ohio town, but one which had the characteristics of Clyde, Ohio, where he had spent his boyhood. The name of the town had perhaps been suggested by Whittenberg, the academy which he had attended, or perhaps there had remained in the back of his mind, lost to consciousness, the real town of Winesburg, to which he may have sent "Roof-fix" from his Elyria paint factory. The name of George Willard was similar in sound to the names of George Bollinger, Joe Welliver, and Trigant Williams which appeared on the pages of the rejected manuscript on which he wrote the *Winesburg* stories. Now he could tell how Tandy Hard got her name; he had told his friends in the rooming house that he was writing a trilogy about a woman named Tandy Hard; and Max Wald, the musician, had said that the name reminded him of nothing but hard candy.

The first figure to be clothed was that of the frightened little man who seemed to be afraid of his hands. Anderson once suggested that the impulse to write about Wing Biddlebaum came from his jokingly calling a friend "Mabel" in a bar and watching the knowing looks of the other men at the bar, but the idea of writing about a man "in whom the force that creates life is diffused, not centralized" must have occurred to him earlier when he questioned a group at the Floyd Dells' parties about Freud's views on homosexuality, two years before. After he had lifted Wing Biddlebaum of Winesburg from the life of imagination into the life of reality, the other "figures on the doorstep of his mind" stood "waiting to be clothed." There was the figure of Dr. Reefy, who, like the father of Talbot Whittingham in the pile of rejected attempts at novels, was a small-town doctor with radical ideas; there was Tandy Hard, the girl whose strange name needed explanation; there were the friends of George Willard, his mother, his father. All of these people were grotesques, suffering from the universal illness of isolation and frustration, and they all belonged in "The Book of the Grotesque."

Here was an opportunity for the novel writer who had not been published; the manuscripts of *Windy McPherson's Son* and *Marching Men*, almost wholly written before he had left his Elyria paint factory in late 1912, were still being peddled from publisher to publisher by Floyd Dell. Perhaps already Anderson was aware of the faults of these books, difficulties which he had not been able to overcome. In a gallery of portraits, a book of grotesques, there would be an opportunity to search back into his boyhood to exploit the material which had provided the most appealing parts of his two early novels. Here was an opportunity to allow the center of the stage to the characters in episodes who had kept intruding into the plots of his earlier novels; here he could build a series of incidents like the tale of Windy McPherson's attempt to blow a bugle in the Fourth of July parade, an episode much more appealing as a portrait of Windy than as a contribution to the growth of Windy's son, the chief character of the novel. Windy really belonged in a "book of the grotesque."

One other factor helped to crystallize Anderson's conception of a "book of the grotesque"—Edgar Lee Masters's *Spoon River Anthology*. When the reviewers of *Winesburg, Ohio* in 1919 made the obvious comparison between the two books, Anderson's publishers replied with an announcement that "Mr. Anderson's 'Winesburg' stories appeared in magazines before Mr. Masters's work appeared," clearly a misstatement of the facts. But Anderson himself, despite the critics' suggestions of influence, kept silent on the matter, while he strongly denied the influence of "the Russians" and Theodore Dreiser. Fortunately, some new evidence has appeared which helps to determine the facts of the matter. Mr. Max Wald, one of the "Little Children of the Arts" who lived with Anderson in the Cass Street rooming house, recently recalled in an interview that shortly after *Spoon River Anthology* appeared in book form (April 1915), he bought a copy, read it, and spoke admiringly of it to Anderson. Anderson, after remarking that Tennessee Mitchell (soon to become his wife) knew Masters, took the book to his room and returned it in the morning, saying that he had stayed up all night reading the poems and that he was much impressed by them. Very probably this reading of Masters's book just six months before the writing of the first *Winesburg* story helped shape the "book of the grotesque" into a collection of sketches in which the characters would be related in their environment and treated as a cross section of village life. It may be suggested furthermore that Anderson's reticence to discuss Masters's work in print may have resulted from his awareness of the past relationship of Tennessee Mitchell (his wife by the time of the book publication of *Winesburg*) and Edgar Lee Masters. Tennessee Mitchell was the "Deirdre" of Masters's *Across Spoon River*, scathingly denounced by him in that work; she had, apparently, been his mistress for eighteen months in 1909 and 1910, and, according to Masters, had been responsible for widening the breach between Masters and his first wife. If Anderson had been aware of the extent of Tennessee Mitchell's alleged involvement with Masters, he could hardly have failed to identify the original of "Georgine Sand Miner" and "Tennessee Claflin Shope" in *Spoon River Anthology* and "Deirdre" in the later *Across Spoon River*, and he may very well have preferred not to open the subject of his relations with Masters. In any event, it seems extremely likely that Anderson's admiration for Masters's portraits and his knowledge of their enthusiastic reception by the

Chicago critics may have hastened his development from *Windy McPherson's Son* to "The Book of the Grotesque," later to be called *Winesburg, Ohio*.

The manuscript shows that from the first the *Winesburg* stories were conceived as complementary parts of a whole, centered in the background of a single community. In the first individual story, "Hands," Anderson had called his town "Winesburg, Ohio"; in "Paper Pills," the next tale to be written, only "Winesburg" appears on the manuscript as the name of the town. In the second story he introduced "the Heffner Block," an actual group of buildings in the Clyde, Ohio, of his boyhood, and "John Spaniard," the disguised nurseryman French of Clyde. In the first story he had mentioned that George Willard was the son of the proprietor of the New Willard House; the third story to be written, "Tandy," might well take place on the steps of the New Willard House. Tandy lives on a road leading off Trunion Pike, a new geographical detail added to the growing conception of the town of Winesburg; in the fourth story to be written, "Drink," the opening paragraph contains a reference to Trunion Pike, and added in this story to the physical picture of the town are Duane Street, the name of a Clyde street, and "Hern's Grocery," the disguised name of Hurd's grocery where Anderson worked as a boy in Clyde. Much of the action of this story takes place in the office of the *Winesburg Eagle*, which had been mentioned earlier in "Hands." One can see how each scrap of description tended to fill in the environment of Winesburg—its stores and its streets—and how after Winesburg was furnished with a Main Street, it would be easy to have a Duane Street, a Buckeye Street, and a Maumee Street branching from it.

As the streets led to each other, and all branched from Main Street, so one scrap of action led to another, and each had some reference to George Willard. In "Drink" it was mentioned in passing that George Willard, like Tom Foster, had a "sentiment concerning Helen White" in his heart. From this brief casual reference must have grown the conception of

George Willard's love affair with Helen White which furnishes part of the interest in "The Thinker" and the entire
interest in "Sophistication," both later stories, and which in
turn suggested George Willard's adventures with the two other
girls of the town, Louise Trunnion and Belle Carpenter, in
"Nobody Knows" and "An Awakening." George's walk with
Belle Carpenter in "An Awakening" provided a beginning for
Wash Williams's lecture on women to George in "Respectability." The outbreak of George's schoolteacher in "The
Teacher" led Anderson to wonder what effect she had on others
of the town, and in "The Strength of God" he described her
impact upon the Presbyterian minister. Kate Swift's naked
form at prayer beside her bed suggested to him another sexu-
ally frustrated spinster, Alice Hindman, who runs naked into
the street in "Adventure." Reading the stories in the order of
their composition, one can watch Anderson follow the excur-
sions of his own imagination, while the town of Winesburg
becomes completed in its physical setting and the people of
Winesburg become tangled in their relations to each other, in
either their awareness of each other or their significant una-
wareness of each other.

A study of the manuscript furthermore reveals something of
the way in which the individual *Winesburg* tales were written.
No outlines or early half-formed versions of the stories exist,
although there may have been some for a few of the tales. On
the backs of the Newberry manuscripts of "Mother" and
"Drink," however, is an earlier story which has been preserved
in an early draft. The manuscript begins with eighteen words
and phrases scrawled in a column down a page, forming a brief
outline, one which might have been jotted down in a few
seconds in an attempt to catch the characteristics of a figure
in Anderson's fancy. Following this outline are thirty pages of
a story, never completed, about a George Bollinger and his
love affair with an Alice Hassinger.

Such brief outlines may or may not have been used for the *Winesburg* tales; with such a story as "Hands" it is likely that the story was written in one frenzied rush of the pencil. Anderson once said:

I am not one who can peck away at a story. It writes itself, as though it used me merely as a medium, or it is n.g. . . . The short story is the result of a sudden passion. It is an idea grasped whole as one would pick an apple in an orchard. All of my own short stories have been written at one sitting [*Memoirs*].

Let us examine for evidence of his working habits the manuscript of "Hands," which Anderson most admired and which he singled out for mention as one that had never been changed in a word.

The manuscript of this story consists of twenty-seven pages written in a penciled scrawl on the backs of three fragments of earlier stories. The handwriting is legible only with difficulty, and it becomes less legible toward the end of the story and in several sections in which the ideas apparently flowed more rapidly than the hand could put them down. Nowhere in the manuscript is there a rearrangement of the parts of the story, the deletion or addition of a paragraph, or even the deletion or addition of a complete sentence, indicating that Anderson followed the order of narration which came most natural to him, in some instances an order which violated the usual chronology of a short story. There are no revisions so far as major changes in the story are concerned, and in this respect Anderson's comment that "no word of it ever changed" is correct; the story was "grasped whole."

There are, however, almost two hundred instances in which earlier words and phrases are deleted, changed, or added to, to provide the readings of the final published version of the story. The larger part of these revisions were apparently made after the story had been written through once, since they are made over the lines and in the margins. But about one-tenth of the revisions were made during the first writing, since they appear on the line of writing before it continues.

Such revisions as were made during the first writing provide an interesting picture of Anderson's habits, his manner of working through a story. He can be seen taking great care in the selection of the exact word for the idea to be expressed, sometimes rejecting one word for another only to reinsert the first one before the rest of the sentence was finished. Occasionally the creative process was stopped while Anderson, always a bad speller, corrected his misspelling of a simple word. One can observe the consolidation of ideas, and in some instances the dawning of new ideas which were then incorporated into the story and developed. Indeed, the entire idea regarding the need for a poet to tell the story of Wing Biddlebaum's hands may have come from Anderson's dissatisfaction with a word used in the first writing and immediately changed. In the first passage mentioning the need for a poet, the story of Biddlebaum's hands originally was called merely "strange"; then for "strange" (a word much used by Anderson and often deleted) was substituted "worth a book in itself." The sentence about the need for a poet then followed: "The story of Wing Biddlebaum's hands is ~~strange.~~ worth a book in itself. Sympathetically set forth it would tap many strange, beautiful qualities in obscure men. It is a job for a poet." It is not too fanciful to suggest that in searching for a better word than "strange" Anderson hit upon the idea of the need for a poet to write the story, a motif repeated later which adds to the frequent intrusion of the author into this tale.

The revisions which Anderson made *during* the first writing, however, are greatly in the minority; about nine-tenths of the changes were made after a first draft had been completed. And it seems clear that the story, although first drafted in a "sudden passion," was reworked several times, since occasionally words which were added above the line of writing of the first draft were later themselves deleted. Most of the revisions of words and phrases were made only once, however. Of these it is significant that while there were 99 *substitutions* of words and phrases for earlier expressions and 58 *additions* of expressions, there were only 21 instances in which expressions were deleted and not replaced by others. Anderson's first writing of the story must have seemed to him sufficiently economical in its treatment, so that instead of paring the story further he was concerned with filling it out.

In the main his deletions simply removed overworked or awkwardly used words, although in one instance he added to the universality of the story by deleting the single word "his": "The story of Wing Biddlebaum is a story of ~~his~~ hands." But the substitutions and additions which he made to the story show more clearly his attempts to give an accurate rendering of the fanciful figure of Wing Biddlebaum and his hands. Anderson was first of all aware that he would have to avoid any details about Wing's case that would disgust the "normal" reader if he were to treat the homosexually inclined character with sympathy. He must avoid the suggestion that Biddlebaum's attraction to George Willard is wholly erotic in nature. Thus he added the qualifying "something like" in "With George Willard . . . he had formed something like a friendship"; instead of "he still hungered for the boy" he wrote "he still hungered for the presence of the boy"; and he replaced "[Biddlebaum's hands] stole to George Willard's shoulders" with "[Biddlebaum's hands] stole forth and lay upon George Willard's shoulders."

Often his revisions increased the suggestiveness of the tale with symbolic details. Instead of an ordinary veranda, Wing's porch was made a "half-decayed veranda," suggesting the state not only of the veranda but of the man who walked upon it; and the field which stood near Biddlebaum's house, originally a corn field grown with "weeds," was changed to "a field that [had] been seeded for clover but that had produced only a dense crop of yellow mustard weeds." Wing Biddlebaum's hands were described as beating like "the wings of an *imprisoned* bird," and were made to appear as something outside

himself, uncontrollable, unattached to himself by the change
of *"his* hands" to *"the* hands."

 the
Again he raised ~~his~~ hands to caress the boy. . . . Again and again
the fathers of the boys had talked of ~~his~~ the hands.

Some of the stylistic traits that have been noticed in Anderson's prose—colloquialisms, repetitive patterns, and frequent
auctorial intrusions—can be seen to have arisen in the revisions.
He can be seen changing a more formal, Latinate expression to
a colloquial, Anglo-Saxon one: "At times an almost overwhelming curiosity had taken ~~possession~~ hold of him." He added
the last name of Wing Biddlebaum three times and of George
Willard twice in the story, so that neither of the men is ever
called by a single name. This repetitive trick, probably learned
from Gertrude Stein's "Melanctha," achieves the simple, casual effect of language comparatively free of pronominal ante-
cedents. Although in "Hands" there are no passages with
marked patterns of repetition of the kind to be found elsewhere in the tales, the revisions of the story indicate that Anderson tended to select a descriptive detail for a character or
place which he repeated whenever the character or place was
again mentioned. For example, in the opening sentence of the
story Wing Biddlebaum is pictured walking upon the "veranda
of a small frame house that stood near the edge of a ravine";
near the end of the story when Wing continues to walk "upon
the veranda of his house," Anderson added "by the ravine,"
and a few lines later he changed the original "he went again
to walk upon the porch" to "he went again to walk upon the
veranda." Finally, the intrusions of the author into this story,
characteristic of oral storytellers and of Anderson's borrowing
of their technique, did not go unnoticed by him; they were
not merely the slips of an untrained fiction writer. Although
the intrusions appear in the first writing of the story and were
not added later, Anderson in several instances smoothed off his
entrance into the tale and made his intrusion seem less blunt.

For example, "We will look briefly into the story of the hands. It may be our talking of them will arouse the poet . . ." was softened to "Let us look briefly into the story of the hands. Perhaps our talking of them will arouse the poet . . ." as though the story-teller realized that he might offend his audience by directing their attentions too obviously.

The process of writing "Hands," then, was much as Anderson suggested; the story was "an idea grasped whole as one would pick an apple in the orchard." But, to continue his figure, the manuscript indicates that after Anderson had picked the apple he examined it carefully for bad spots and polished its minor imperfections.

When a number of the *Winesburg* stories had been written and revised, Anderson set about getting the individual tales into print. Because of their unconventional subject matter and treatment, they were not likely to be acceptable to the popular magazines; but Anderson was known to the editors of several "little magazines." Since Floyd Dell still had the manuscript of *Windy McPherson's Son* and was still convinced that Anderson was a writer who should be published, he was likely to accept some of the tales for the *Masses*, of which he and Max Eastman were co-editors. Anderson apparently sent the early tales to Dell in the order that he wrote them, since "The Book of the Grotesque" and "Hands," the first two of the tales to be written and published, appeared in that order in the February and March, 1916, issues of the *Masses*. Later in the year Dell published "The Strength of God," but soon a dissatisfaction with the stories arose in the editorial offices of the *Masses*, and the later tales were voted down by the editors.

In the meantime one of the stories, "Paper Pills," had appeared in Margaret Anderson's *Little Review*. Anderson had contributed articles to the first two issues of this magazine in 1914, and he continued to publish sketches there during 1915 and 1916. Since the magazine was at this time still being published in Chicago, and since Anderson was a frequent visitor to Margaret Anderson's North Shore gatherings, it was not surprising that one of the early *Winesburg* tales should have been published in the *Little Review*.

The beginning of plans in the winter of 1915–1916 for a new "little magazine," the *Seven Arts*, offered another outlet for the stories. Edna Kenton had met Anderson in Chicago in the early winter of 1916 and had read several of his stories. She sent Anderson's name to Waldo Frank, one of the men who was slated to become an editor of *Seven Arts* when it began publication. Anderson and Frank corresponded during the winter and spring of 1916, and Frank was enthusiastic about a number of the *Winesburg* stories which Anderson sent him. In the summer of 1916 Anderson invited Frank to come to Lake Chateaugay in upper New York for a vacation, and the two spent much time during June and July discussing Anderson's work. By that time, [as] Frank has recently remarked [in a letter to this writer [in] 1949,] Anderson had "already written at least a majority of the Winesburg tales." Frank's admiration for Anderson's work grew during this summer, so that for the first issue of *Seven Arts*, in November 1916, he wrote the commendatory article, "Emerging Greatness," concerning Anderson's first novel (which by this time had been published). The second issue of *Seven Arts* had as its leading story "Queer," by Sherwood Anderson; the third issue printed "The Untold Lie" and announced that other *Winesburg* tales would follow. Two other tales did follow—"Mother" and "The Thinker"— before *Seven Arts* lost its subsidy and ceased publication.

Except for "An Awakening" and "A Man of Ideas," which were printed in the *Little Review* some months later, these were all of the *Winesburg* tales which appeared in magazines before their publication in book form in 1919. For the ten stories, Anderson later remembered, he received only $85, since of the three magazines in which they had appeared, only *Seven Arts* paid for its material. But for a writer who had published only three short stories before, the reception of the *Wines-*

burg tales by Floyd Dell, Margaret Anderson, and Waldo Frank must have led Anderson to believe that in such tales as these he had found his medium of expression.

Certain changes in the stories were made before Anderson submitted them to the magazines. Most of these were minor changes—revisions of punctuation and occasional changes of wording—but two were extensive. One was the rearrangement of the story "Hands" in the version published in the *Masses* mentioned earlier, noteworthy only since this is the story of which Anderson said, "No word of it ever changed." But the second, involving the *Seven Arts* version of "The Untold Lie," is more striking. In *Seven Arts*, the story opens:

When I was a boy and lived in my home town of Winesburg, Ohio, Ray Pearson and Hal Winters were farm hands employed on a farm three miles north of us. I cannot for my life say how I know this story concerning them, but I vouch for its truth. I have known the story always just as I know many things concerning my own town that have never been told to me. As for Ray and Hal I can recall well enough how I used to see them on our Main Street with other country fellows of a Saturday afternoon.

The first-person narrator continues, telling the story exactly as it is told in the book version, except for frequent intrusions like "as I remember him" and "I myself remember." Since in the book version the only entrance into the tale of characters in earlier tales is a brief mention of "boys like young George Willard and Seth Richmond," which might easily have been added to tie this tale loosely to the others, one might think that the *Seven Arts* version was an earlier one which had been reworked to fit into the collection of tales. This possibility has been seized upon by a student of Anderson who suggested[1] that not only did Anderson revise the magazine version of "The Untold

---

[1] Jarvis A. Thurston in "Sherwood Anderson: A Critical Study" (unpublished doctoral dissertation, State University of Iowa, 1946). The unpublished material in the Newberry Library Collection was not available at the time of Mr. Thurston's study.

Lie" to make it conform to the focus of narration of the other tales, but that the frequent intrusions of the author into the other tales are the results of faulty revisions of *their* earlier "I" (first person) versions. This writer concludes:

It is quite likely, I should say, that some of these stories were originally written from a first-person observer focus and then revised to tone down the "I"; others were written from the omniscient author focus. . . . The impression that one gains of most of the *Winesburg* stories is that they were written with the author doing the telling as an "I," and that this "I" appeared wherever it was necessary for him to do so. Later the number of "I's" was cut down either by direct elimination (and making the necessary changes) or by substitution of "George Willard."

This ingenious theory is, however, disproved by the manuscripts of the stories which are now available for study. None of the manuscript versions is of the "I" variety; and the manuscript of "The Untold Lie," like the others an omniscient author version, contains frequent revisions the *results* of which appear in the magazine version. Thus, as he revised "Hands" before submitting it to the *Masses*, Anderson must have revised "The Untold Lie" immediately before sending it to Waldo Frank for publication in *Seven Arts*; the "I" version was not the first but a revised one, and the original omniscient author version stayed in the pile of manuscripts to be used in *Winesburg, Ohio*.

Most of the *Winesburg* stories must have been written, as Anderson said, in a short period of time with one providing the germ for another. But a few of the stories seem surely to have been written later. We have seen that eighteen of the twenty-five tales were written on the backs of the interlocking earlier manuscripts and thus must have been composed together. Of the seven stories on the yellow advertising copy paper (and therefore suspect of being later) two, "Queer" and "The Un-

told Lie," were published in the first two issues of *Seven Arts*
and thus must have been written before, or at the latest, during Anderson's correspondence with Waldo Frank in the spring
of 1916. A third, "A Man of Ideas," was published in the
Little Review soon after the *Seven Arts* ceased publication, and
before the publication in the *Little Review* of "An Awakening," one of the early tales. The remaining four—"The Philosopher," "Death," "Sophistication," and "Departure"—are
the only ones which seem to have been written later.

There are two indications that "The Philosopher" was a later
addition to the group of tales. The story written as "Paper
Pills" and published under that title in the 1919 volume was
first published in the *Little Review* as "The Philosopher" in
June 1916, when, according to Waldo Frank, a majority of
the tales had been written. It is not likely that Anderson would
take the title of a story which was waiting to be published and
put it on another story. Furthermore, it will be noticed that
as the tales were written more and more details of setting were
added, so that in contrast to "Hands" and "Paper Pills," which
have only modest references to Main Street or the New Willard House, the later stories are filled with names of streets,
business houses, and minor characters. "The Philosopher" is
such a story; here, although half of the comparatively short
story is taken up by Dr. Parcival's tale of his earlier life away
from Winesburg, the rest of the narrative is filled with allusions to the *Winesburg Eagle*, its editor Will Henderson, Tom
Willy's saloon, the baggage-man Albert Longworth, Main
Street, Biff Carter's lunch room, and the railroad station, all
of which had been mentioned in earlier stories.

"Death," "Sophistication," and "Departure," the remaining
tales of those written on the advertising copy paper, are the
last three tales in the *Winesburg* volume. None was published
in a magazine, and all are filled with allusions to names and
places which had been mentioned earlier. "Death" is actually
two stories, the account of the love affair of Dr. Reefy and
Elizabeth Willard and the story of George Willard's reaction

to the death of his mother. It is preceded in the *Winesburg* volume by "The Untold Lie" and "Drink," tales which have their chief interest in characters outside the Willard family. But in "Death" the interest shifts back abruptly to Elizabeth Willard and her struggle with her husband over George's future. Dr. Reefy had not been mentioned since the early story "Paper Pills," but here he becomes Elizabeth Willard's lover just before her death, as the two most sympathetically treated of the mature characters in the book are brought together in a brief moment of escape from isolation. It seems as if Anderson realized that his "Book of the Grotesque" had become filled, and that to keep the novelistic quality of the work he would have to bring his chief characters to some end. Just as in *Windy McPherson's Son* and *Marching Men* it is the deaths of the mothers of Sam McPherson and Beaut McGregor which stir them to leave their villages permanently, so Elizabeth Willard's long-awaited death is the event which sends George Willard out of Winesburg and which prepares for the short résumé of his career in "Departure."

"Sophistication" is the culmination of the George Willard–Helen White affair which had been touched upon in several earlier stories, but which had not been given a full treatment. In it Anderson was able to show not only the final stage of George Willard's feeling for Helen White but also the growing sophistication which had resulted from his listening to the stories of the grotesques of Winesburg. Thus in the last two tales George Willard's affairs in Winesburg are brought to a close with the death of his mother and the establishment of a more mature relation with Helen White; he is ready for "Departure."

Whether a publisher suggested that the last stories be written to round out the career of George Willard or whether Anderson felt that they were needed to make his "Book of the Grotesque" something more than a mere collection of short stories cannot be determined. It is probable that the latter was the case. Anderson later said that although he had secured publication in magazines for some of the tales he wanted them put together in a single volume. "The stories belonged together," he said. "I felt that, taken together, they made something like a novel, a complete story [which gave] . . . the feeling of the life of a boy growing into young manhood in a town" (*Memoirs*).

But getting the items in "The Book of the Grotesque," as Anderson then spoke of it to Floyd Dell, published in a volume was a difficult matter. Anderson submitted the stories to John Lane, the English publisher of his first two novels, but the Lane firm had lost confidence in Anderson after the weak sales of his early books, and they refused the *Winesburg* stories on the ground that they were "too gloomy."

Anderson's early work, however, had found admirers in people like Waldo Frank, Floyd Dell, Theodore Dreiser, Ben Hecht, Margaret Anderson, and Francis Hackett. And it was Francis Hackett, then literary editor of the *New Republic*, who showed the manuscript of "The Book of the Grotesque" to Ben Huebsch, owner and editor of a small publishing house in New York which had already published Joyce's *Dubliners* and *A Portrait of the Artist as a Young Man* and Lawrence's *The Prussian Officer* and *The Rainbow*. Huebsch became interested, obtained Anderson's release from John Lane, and suggested the title *Winesburg, Ohio* for the stories. Finally, in April 1919, fully three years after most of them had been written, the episodes which had begun with the conception of a "Book of the Grotesque," written (in the main) as a connected series, were published as *Winesburg, Ohio*.

❋❋❋❋❋❋❋❋❋❋❋❋❋❋❋❋❋❋❋❋❋❋❋❋❋❋❋❋❋❋❋❋❋❋

WALTER B. RIDEOUT

Walter B. Rideout, Chairman of the Department of English at the
University of Wisconsin, was co-editor of *The Letters of Sherwood
Anderson,* and is at work on a biography of Anderson. He is also
the author of *The Radical Novel in the United States, 1900–1954,*
and other books. His introduction to Anderson's *Poor White*
appears in the Compass Books edition (1965).

THE SIMPLICITY OF
WINESBURG, OHIO

It is probably impossible, except impressionistically, to isolate
the essential quality of any work of art, but Hart Crane may
have come close to isolating that of *Winesburg, Ohio* when
in another context he wrote of Anderson himself that, "He has
a humanity and simplicity that is quite baffling in depth and
suggestiveness." Leaving the matter of "humanity" aside, one
is indeed struck on first reading the book by its apparent simplicity of language and form. On second or subsequent readings, however, he sees that the hard, plain, concrete diction is
much mixed with the abstract, that the sentence cadences
come from George Moore and the King James Bible as well
as from ordinary speech rhythms, that the seemingly artless,
even careless, digressions are rarely artless, careless, or digressive. What had once seemed to have the clarity of water held

---

From *Shenandoah,* The Washington and Lee University Review, XIII
(Spring 1962). Copyright 1962 by *Shenandoah.* Reprinted by permission
of Walter B. Rideout and *Shenandoah.*

in the hand begins to take on instead its elusiveness. If this is simplicity, it is simplicity—paradox or not—of a complicated kind. Since *Winesburg* constantly challenges one to define the complications, I should like to examine a few that perhaps lie closest beneath the surface of the book and the life it describes.

It has been often pointed out that the fictitious Winesburg closely resembles Clyde, Ohio, where Anderson lived from the age of seven to the age of nineteen and which became the home town of his memories. Even now the visitor to the two communities can see that Winesburg and Clyde are both "eighteen miles" south of Lake Erie; in both, the central street of the town is named Main, and Buckeye and Duane branch off from it; both have a Heffner Block and a Waterworks Pond; both lie "in the midst of open fields, but beyond the fields are pleasant patches of woodland." As recently as the summer of 1960, the wooden Gothic railroad station, from which Sherwood Anderson and George Willard took the train for the city and the great world, was still standing; and on the hill above Waterworks Pond, where George walked with Helen White on the darkened fairgrounds, one can yet see, over-grown with turf, the banked-up west end turns of the race track. Modern Clyde is perhaps half again as large as the town that the future author of *Winesburg* left in 1896, but the growth has shown itself principally in housing development on the periphery. The central village is basically unchanged, and even now to walk through the quiet old residence streets with their white frame or brick houses and wide lawns shaded by big elms and maples is to walk uncannily through a fictitious scene made suddenly real.

The more one learns of the town as it was in the 1890s, the more he sees the actual Clyde under the imagined Winesburg.[1] Anderson was a story-teller, of course, not a historian, and the

----

[1] I am grateful to be able to acknowledge publicly my great debt to Mr. Herman Hurd, Anderson's "closest friend" in his Clyde years, and to his son, Mr. Thaddeus Hurd, who have generously shared with me their memories of Sherwood Anderson and of Clyde.—W.B.R.

correspondence of the two communities does not have a one-to-one exactness. Nevertheless the correspondences become striking, particularly as one sees that in many instances Clyde names of persons and places appear only faintly disguised in the pages of *Winesburg*. Anderson wrote about Win Pawsey's shoe store, Surbeck's Pool Room, and Hern's Grocery; in the Clyde of the early 1890s there were Alfred Pawsey's Shoe Store, Surbeck's Cigar Store, and Hurd's Grocery, the last still very much in business. Wine Creek flows through Winesburg instead of the real Raccoon of Clyde, but the former follows the latter's course; and beyond the Wine rises the fictitious Gospel Hill in the same place as the actual Piety Hill, where the Anderson family lived for a time. Sometimes the disguise is somewhat less casual, though it may turn out to be merely a transfer of names. The owner of one of the two livery stables in Clyde was Frank Harvey, but there were Moyers in town, from whom Anderson borrowed half the name of Wesley Moyer for the livery stableman in Winesburg. Clyde personal names, it must be noted, are used almost exclusively for the minor characters, and except for one or two debatable possibilities no character, either major or minor, seems to be recognizably based on an actual resident of the town. The important matter, however, is that the "grotesques" of the several tales exist within a physical and social matrix furnished Anderson by his memories of Clyde.

That he should have visualized the locale of his tales so closely in terms of his home town is not surprising, and the reader may dismiss the matter as merely a frequent practice of realistic writers. Yet Anderson is not a realistic writer in the ordinary sense. With him realism is a means to something else, not an end in itself. To see the difference between his presentation of "reality" and the more traditional kind that gives a detailed picture of appearances, one needs only to compare the drug store on the Main Street of Sinclair Lewis's Gopher Prairie with that on the Main Street of Winesburg. Twice over, once as Carol Kennicott, once as Bea Sorenson sees them, Lewis catalogues the parts of Dave Dyer's soda fountain. Anderson, like his own Enoch Robinson preferring "the essences of things" to the "realities," merely names Sylvester West's Drug Store, letting each reader's imagination do as much or as little with it as he wishes. As with the drug store, so with many other landmarks of Clyde-Winesburg. As he repeats from tale to tale the names of stores and their owners or refers to such elements of town life as the post office, the bank, or the cemetery, there emerges, not a photograph, but at most the barest sketch of the external world of the town. Perhaps even "sketch" implies too great a precision of detail. What Anderson is after is less a representation of conventional "reality" than, to keep the metaphor drawn from art, an abstraction of it.

Realism is for Anderson a means rather than an end, and the highly abstract kind of reality found in Winesburg has its valuable uses. The first of these is best understood in relation to George Willard's occupation on the *Winesburg Eagle*. (Clyde's weekly newspaper was, and still is, the *Clyde Enterprise*, but Sherwood Anderson was never its reporter.) It has been suggested that the author may have made his central figure a newspaper reporter in order that he could thus be put most readily in touch with the widest number of people in town and most logically become the recipient of many confidences; yet Anderson's point is that exactly insofar as George remains a newspaper reporter, he is committed to the surface of life, not to its depths. "Like an excited dog," Anderson says in "The Thinker," using a mildly contemptuous comparison, "George Willard ran here and there," writing down all day "little facts" about A. P. Wringlet's recent shipment of straw hats or Uncle Tom Sinnings' new barn on the Valley Road. As reporter, George is concerned with externals, with appearances, with the presumably solid, simple, everyday surface of life. For Anderson the surface is there, of course, as his recurring use of place and personal names indicates; yet conventional "reality" is for him relatively insignificant and is best presented in the form of sketch or abstraction. What is important is "to see beneath the surface of lives," to perceive the intricate mesh of impulses, desires, drives growing down in the dark, unrevealed parts of the personality like the complex mass of roots that, below the surface of the ground, feeds the common grass above in the light.

But if one function of Anderson's peculiar adaptation of realism is, as it were, to depreciate the values of surfaces, a corollary function is constantly to affirm that any surface has its depth. Were we, on the one hand, to observe such tormented people as Alice Hindman and Dr. Parcival and the Reverend Curtis Hartman as briefly and as much from the outside as we view Wesley Moyer or Biff Carter or Butch Wheeler, the lamplighter, they would appear as uncomplicated and commonplace as the latter. Conversely, were we to see the inwardness of Moyer and Carter and Wheeler, their essential lives would provide the basis for three more Winesburg tales. (The real lamplighter of Clyde in the early 1890s was a man named John Becker. It may well have given him the anguish of a "grotesque" that he had an epileptic son, who as a young man died during a seizure while assisting his father in his trade.)

Yet a third function of Anderson's abstract, or shorthand, kind of realism is to help him set the tone of various tales, often a tone of elegiac quietness. Just how this is done will be clearer if one realizes that the real Clyde which underlies Winesburg is the town, not as Anderson left it in 1896, but the town as it was a few years earlier when, as he asserts in "An Awakening," "the time of factories had not yet come." In actual fact the "industrialization" of the small town of Clyde—which, it can be demonstrated, was strongly to condition Anderson's whole attitude toward machine civilization—came in a rush with the installation of electric lights in 1893—"Clyde is now the best lighted town in the state," boasted the *Enterprise* in its September 4th issue—with the paving of Main Street later that year, and with the establishment of a bicycle factory in the late summer of 1894. Subsequently Anderson was to give imaginative embodiment to this development in *Poor White*, but the Winesburg tales he conceived of as for the most part occurring in a pre-industrial setting, recalling nostalgically a town already lost before he had left it, giving this vanished era the permanence of pastoral. Here, as always, he avoids the realism of extensive detail and makes only suggestive references, one of the most memorable being the description in "The Thinker" of the lamplighter hurrying along the street before Seth Richmond and Helen White, lighting the lamp on each wooden post "so that their way was half lighted, half darkened, by the lamps and by the deepening shadows cast by the low-branched trees." By a touch like this, drawn from his memory of pre-industrial Clyde, Anderson turns the evening walk of his quite ordinary boy and girl into a tiny processional and invests the couple with that delicate splendor which can come to people, "even in Winesburg."

If Anderson's treatment of locale in his tales turns out to be more complex than it seems at first, the same can be said of his methods of giving sufficient unity to his book so that, while maintaining the "looseness" of life as he actually sensed it, the tales would still form a coherent whole. Some of these methods, those that I shall be concerned with, have a point in common: they all involve the use of repeated elements. One such device is that of setting the crisis scenes of all but five of the tales in the evening. In a very large majority of the stories, too, some kind of light partly, but only partly, relieves the darkness. In "Hands," "Mother," and "Loneliness," for example, the light is that of a single lamp; in "The Untold Lie" the concluding scene is faintly lit by the last of twilight; in "Sophistication" George Willard and Helen White look at each other "in the dim light" afforded, apparently, by "the lights of the town reflected against the sky," though at the other end of the fairgrounds a few racetrack men have built a fire that provides a dot of illumination in the darkness. Finally, many of the tales end with the characters in total darkness. Such a device not only links the tales but in itself implies meaning. *Winesburg* is primarily a book about the "night world" of human personality. The dim light equates with, as well as literally illuminates, the limited glimpse into an individual soul that each crisis scene affords, and the briefness of the insight is emphasized by the shutting down of the dark.

Another kind of repeated element throughout the book is the recurrent word. Considering the sense of personal isolation one gets from the atomized lives of the "grotesques," one would expect a frequent use of some such word as "wall," standing for whatever it is that divides each person from all others. Surprisingly that particular word appears only a few times. The one that does occur frequently is "hand," either in the singular or the plural; and very often, as indeed would be expected, it suggests, even symbolizes, the potential or actual communication of one personality with another. The hands of Wing Biddlebaum and Dr. Reefy come immediately to mind; but, to name only a few other instances, George Willard takes hold of Louise Trunnion's "rough" but "delightfully small" hand in anticipation of his sexual initiation, Helen White keeps her hand in Seth Richmond's until Seth breaks the clasp through overconcern with self, in the field where they are working Hal Winters puts "his two hands" on Ray Pearson's shoulders and they "become all alive to each other," Kate Swift puts her hands on George Willard as though about to embrace him in her desire to make him understand what being a writer means. Obviously the physical contact may not produce mutual understanding. The hand may in fact express aggression. One of the men who run Wing Biddlebaum out of the Pennsylvania town at night "had a rope in his hands"; Elizabeth Willard, who as a girl had put her hand on the face of each lover after sexual release, imagines herself stealing toward her husband, "holding the long wicked scissors in her hand"; Elmer Cowley on the station platform strikes George Willard almost unconscious with his fists before leaping onto the departing train. Nevertheless, the possibility of physical

touch between two human beings always implies, even if by
negative counterpart, at least the possibility of a profounder
moment of understanding between them. The intuitive awareness by George Willard and Helen White of each other's
"sophistication" is expressed, not through their few kisses, but
by Helen's taking George's arm and walking "beside him in
dignified silence."

As for George himself, one can make too much of his role as
a character designed to link the tales, unify them, and structure them into a loose sort of *Bildungsroman;* on the other
hand, one can make too little of it. Granted that Anderson
tended to view his own life, and that of others, as a succession
of moments rather than as a "figure in a carpet," that his
imagination worked more successfully in terms of the flash of
insight than of the large design, that his gift was, in short, for
the story rather than the novel, still through his treatment of
George Willard's development he supplies a pattern for *Winesburg, Ohio* that is as definite as it is unobtrusive. This development has three closely related aspects, and each aspect
involves again the repetition of certain elements.

The first aspect is obvious. Whatever the outward difference
between created character and creator, George's inward life
clearly reflects the conflict Anderson himself had experienced
between the world of practical affairs, with its emphasis on the
activity of money-making and its definition of success in financial terms, and the world of dreams, with its emphasis on
imaginative creativity and its definition of success in terms of
the degree of penetration into the buried life of others. The
conflict is thematically stated in the first of the tales, "Hands."
Wing Biddlebaum's hands are famous in Winesburg for their
berry-picking (hence money-making) skill, but the true story
of the hands, as told by "a poet," is of course that they can
communicate a desire to dream. Wing declares the absolute
opposition of the two worlds by telling George that he is destroying himself because " 'you are afraid of dreams. You want
to be like others in town here.' " The declaration indicates

that George has not yet resolved the conflict, and his irresolu-
tion at this point is reinforced by his ambivalent attitude toward Wing's hands. Unlike the other townspeople he is
curious to know what lies beneath their outward skill; yet his
respect for Wing and his fear of the depths that might be revealed make him put curiosity aside. The conflict between
practical affairs and dreams is again made explicit in the third
story of the book, "Mother," where it is objectified in the hostility between Tom and Elizabeth Willard and the clash of
their influences on their son. Winesburg is not a book of suspense, and thus early in the tales the conflict is in effect resolved when George implicitly accepts his mother's, and
Wing's, way, the way of dreams. From this point on both the
conflict and George's resolution of it are maintained in a formal sense by the opposition between the "daylight world" of
the minor characters and the "night world" of the major ones,
the grotesques. George continues to run about writing down
surface facts for the newspaper, but his essential life consists
in his efforts, some successful, some not, to understand the
essential lives of others. From these efforts, from the death of
his mother, from his achievement of "sophistication" with
Helen White, he gains the will to leave Winesburg, committed, as the final paragraph of "Departure" asserts, to the world
of dreams.

The second of these closely related aspects of George's development is his growing desire to be a creative writer and his
increasing awareness of the meaning of that vocation. George's
interest in writing is not mentioned until the book is half over,
when, in "The Thinker," it appears to have been an interest
that he had had for some time. He talks "continually of the
matter" to Seth Richmond, and the "idea that George Willard
would some day become a writer had given him a place of
distinction in Winesburg. . . ." At this point his conception
of writing centers on externals, on the opportunities the writer's life offers for personal freedom and for public acclaim. In
a remark that suggests a reading of Jack London, George ex-

plains to Seth that as a writer he will be his own boss: "Though you are in India or in the South Seas in a boat, you have but to write and there you are." Since writing for George is at this stage mainly a matter of fame and fun, it is not surprising to find him in "The Thinker" deliberately, and naïvely, planning to fall in love with Helen White in order to write a love story. The absurdity, Anderson suggests, is twofold: falling in love is not something one rationally plans to do, and one does not write thus directly and literally out of experience anyway.

Actually Kate Swift, in "The Teacher," has tried to tell George that the writer's is not "the easiest of all lives to live," but rather one of the most difficult. In one of those scenes where physical touch symbolizes an attempt to create the moment of awareness between two personalities, Kate has tried to explain the demanding principles by which the true writer must live. He must "know life," must "stop fooling with words," must "know what people are thinking about, not what they say"—all three being principles Anderson was to insist on himself as the code of the artist. That George is still immature both as person and as writer is signified at the end of "The Teacher" when he gropes drowsily about in the darkness with a hand and mutters that he has missed something Kate Swift was trying to tell him. This needed maturity comes to him only at the end of *Winesburg*. When, sitting beside the body of his dead mother, he decides to go to "some city" and perhaps "get a job on some newspaper," he is really marked already for the profession of writer, whatever job he may take to support himself, just as Anderson supported himself by composing advertising copy while experimenting with the Winesburg stories. In "Departure" the commitment of George Willard to writing unites with his final commitment to the world of dreams. For both George and his creator the two are indeed identical.

The third aspect of George's development provides another

way of charting his inward voyage from innocence to experience, from ignorance to understanding, from apparent reality of the face of things to true reality behind or below. Three stories—"Nobody Knows," "An Awakening," and "Sophistication"—have a special relationship. They all center on George's dealings with a woman, a different one in each case; they contain very similar motifs; they are arranged in an ascending order of progression. The fact that one comes near the beginning of the book, one about two-thirds of the way through, and one at the end suggests that Anderson was not without his own subtle sense of design.

The first story, "Nobody Knows," is in all ways the simplest. In it George Willard enters traditional manhood by having with Louise Trunnion his first sex experience. In relation to the other two tales in the sequence, the most significant elements of the story, besides the fact of actual sexual conquest, are George's lack of self-assurance at the outset of the affair, his bursting forth with a "flood of words," his consequent aggressiveness and failure to sympathize with his partner, and his action at the end of the story when he stands "perfectly still in the darkness, attentive, listening as though for a voice calling his name." The sexual encounter with Louise has been simply that. It has brought him physical satisfaction and a feeling of entirely self-centered masculine pride. His expectation of hearing a voice, however, would seem to be a projection of guilt feeling at having violated the overt moral code of the community even though "nobody knows."

In the second and third stories these elements, or their opposites, appear in a more complex fashion. In both "An Awakening" and "Sophistication," George's relation with a woman is complicated by the involvement of another man, though, significantly, Ed Handby in the former story is laconic, direct, and highly physical, while the college instructor in the latter is voluble, devious, and pompously intellectual. In both, too, the final scene takes place on the hill leading up to the fairgrounds, close, incidentally, to the place where Kate Swift tried to explain to George the difficulties that beset the dedicated writer. Yet the two stories have quite different, if supplementary, conclusions.

As George and Belle Carpenter walk up the hill in the final scene of "An Awakening," he feels no more sympathy for her, has no more understanding of her needs, than he had for Louise Trunnion; but before this last walk he has experienced an exaltation that keeps him from any fear of masculine incompetence. Earlier that January night a kind of mystical revelation has come to him when it seems as though "some voice outside of himself" announced the thoughts in his mind: "'I must get myself into touch with something orderly and big that swings through the night like a star.'" Unlike the situation at the end of "Nobody Knows," George actually "hears" the external voice, and the voice is now the positive one of inspiration, which has replaced the negative one of conscience. Thereafter he talks volubly to Belle, as he had to Louise; but when in "An Awakening" his "mind runs off into words," he believes that Belle will recognize the new force in him and will at once surrender herself to his masculine power. Now, in actual fact an insistence on the necessity of universal order—"'There is a law for armies and for men too,'" George asserts—is a characteristic of Anderson's own thinking particularly as expressed in the novel, *Marching Men*, which preceded the Winesburg tales in composition, and in the poems, *Mid-American Chants*, which followed; yet George makes this concept ridiculous at the moment because of his intense self-centeredness about his inspiration. As Kate Swift would have said, he is still playing with words, a destructive procedure for the artistic personality as well as for the non-artistic one. Holding the quite uninterested Belle in his arms, he whispers large words into the darkness, until the passionate, non-verbalizing Ed Handby throws him aside, takes Belle by the arm, and marches off. George is left angered, humiliated, and disgustedly disillusioned with his moment of mystic insight when "the voice outside himself . . . had . . . put new courage into his heart."

Where "An Awakening" records a defeat, "Sophistication" records in all ways a triumph. Though Anderson presents the moment in essay rather than dramatic form, there comes to George, as to "every boy," a flash of insight when "he stops under a tree and waits as for a voice calling his name." But this time "the voices outside himself" do not speak of the possibilities of universal order, nor do they speak of guilt. Instead they "whisper a message concerning the limitations of life," the brief light of human existence between two darks. The insight emphasizes the unity of all human beings in their necessary submission to death and their need for communication one with another. It is an insight that produces self-awareness but not self-centeredness, that produces, in short, the mature, "sophisticated" person.

The mind of such a person does not "run off into words." Hence Helen White, who has had an intuition similar to George's, runs away from the empty talk of her college instructor and her mother, and finds George, whose first and last words to her in the story, pronounced as they first meet, are "Come on." Together in the dimly lit fairgrounds on the hill overlooking the town of Winesburg, George and Helen share a brief hour of absolute awareness. Whereas his relationship with Belle Carpenter had produced in George self-centeredness, misunderstanding, hate, frustration, humiliation, that with Helen produces quite the opposite feelings. The feeling of oneness spreads outward, furthermore. Through his communication with Helen he begins "to think of the people in the town where he had lived with something like reverence." When he has come to this point, when he loves and respects the inhabitants of Winesburg, the "daylight" people as well as the "night" ones, the way of the artist lies clear before him. George Willard is ready for his "Departure."

Like Hart Crane, other readers will find the simplicity of
Winesburg, Ohio "baffling"; but it is very probably this paradoxical quality which has attracted and will continue to attract
admirers to a book that Anderson himself, with a mixture of
amusement, deprecation, defensiveness, and satisfaction, quite
accurately termed "a kind of American classic."

✿◈

HORACE GREGORY

Horace Gregory was a lecturer in poetry and critical theory from
1934 to 1960 at Sarah Lawrence College, Bronxville, New York.
His *Collected Poems* appeared in 1964. He is co-author with his
wife, Marya Zaturenska, of *A History of American Poetry: 1900–
1940*, and author of, among other books, *D. H. Lawrence: Pilgrim
of the Apocalypse*.

[AN AMERICAN HERITAGE]

. . . European readers who come to Anderson's *Winesburg,
Ohio* for the first time feel the proximity of a new speech, a
"new country," a fresh view of the Main Street that Sinclair
Lewis had opened for them. The interrelated stories of *Winesburg, Ohio* offer something that is less foreign to them than
the restless, half-satirical observant eye that guides the reader
so faithfully through the pages of Lewis's realistic novel. What
is felt in *Winesburg, Ohio*, felt rather than read, overheard
rather than stressed, is a memory of youth, of early "joys and
sorrows," and this is conveyed with the simplicity of a folk tale,
a style known in all languages. To the American reader another level of almost subterranean feeling is contained in Sherwood Anderson's novels and stories. The streets and landscapes
here depicted are close to the roots of an American heritage
which takes its definition from the writings of Emerson, Whit-

From the Introduction to *The Portable Sherwood Anderson*, edited by
Horace Gregory (New York: The Viking Press, 1949). Copyright 1949
by The Viking Press, Inc., and reprinted by permission of the publishers.

man, Thoreau, Melville, and Mark Twain. Critics with as diverse opinions of Anderson as those expressed by Lionel Trilling on one hand and Van Wyck Brooks on the other have agreed in recognizing these particular features of Anderson's "Americanism," his almost instinctive and acknowledged debt to writers who represent the Emersonian aspect of the Great Tradition in American literature. It is clear enough that Anderson's writings are of that heritage and not in the Great Tradition of Hawthorne and Henry James. But why were they "instinctively" so, why were they ranged so conclusively on the side of Thoreau and Whitman? As one reads Anderson's autobiographies and memoirs, it is absurd to think of him reading Thoreau, Emerson, and Whitman in the spirit of one determined to follow a "party line" in choosing the sources of his inspiration; it is absurd to think of him surrounded by books in order to draw "ideas" and intellectual convictions from them. His sources were the air he breathed, childhood memories of talk, of the few books loaned to him by schoolmasters, by older men in small Middle Western towns who took a fancy to the brilliant, sensitive, imaginative son of a Southern drifter and tall-tale-teller. These were the essentials of Sherwood Anderson's early impressions; they are the actual sources of whatever Anderson thought and saw and felt, and all other experiences, whether of reading or of sensitively overhearing conversation which flowed around him, were superimposed upon them.

The impact on Anderson's imagination of Thoreau and Whitman came in later life, but the important impressions of his boyhood were the associations of what is now called a "democratic" heritage: the diluted forms of oratory at Fourth of July celebrations, the speeches made at county fairs, the talk overheard at race tracks, and through the swinging doors of the nineteenth-century, Middle Western, small-town saloon. In these surroundings, legends of Abraham Lincoln flourished, floating upward into Ohio from Illinois and Kentucky—stories pertinent to Anderson's own half-Southern, log-cabin origins.

He, too, came from a "shiftless, drifting" family, and so he was particularly sympathetic to the picture of Lincoln reading books by the flickering, red glare thrown from a log-cabin hearth, to the figure of "the man of sorrows" and unrequited love, the shrewd country lawyer who told tall stories in the back rooms of general stores, the gaunt, distracted figure, clad in a nightshirt, pacing the floor of his bedroom in the White House, reading jokes aloud from an open book or periodical, and finally, the martyred President, who loved the North and South alike, the author of the Gettysburg Address—these pictures hung as icons in the mind of the impressionable boy.

Beneath the seeming contradictions of Anderson's discussions in his memoirs, novels, and topical essays of socialism, democracy, and the twentieth century "machine age," there lies a singular loyalty to the heritage of a Middle Western boyhood. It is in this connection that the year of his birth, 1876, and the place where he was born, Camden, Ohio, are of relevant meaning. Anderson grew up in a place that was permeated by that "religion of humanity" of which Emerson was the transcendental fountainhead, showering forth his concepts of the "oversoul" like rain from the clouds; across the prairies of the Middle West his name and Thoreau's represented New England "culture," and when their writings were read at all, which was only in small circles, they were tolerated with more respect than understanding. Those who lived through the postbellum years of the Civil War in the Middle West demanded both more and less of their own priests of "humanity" than they did of the memory of Emerson.

The new priests of the "religion of humanity" were champions of reason and of Herbert Spencer's *First Principles*, of Henry George's *Progress and Poverty* and Edward Bellamy's *Looking Backward*, of Robert Ingersoll's lectures on The Gods ("An Honest God Is the Noblest Work of Man") and on Individuality ("Every human being should take a road of his own. . . . Every mind . . . should think, investigate and conclude for itself"). These new priests spoke in the names of "democracy," "science," "progress," and "liberty"; most of them were in revolt against the older Protestant sects and denominations of New England, against Puritan restraints and moralities, and yet the shadows of older taboos were among their obsessions. Sherwood Anderson's generation in Ohio and Illinois felt in boyhood the presence of Ingersoll's "individuality" and his faith in "science" with greater intimacy, and, perhaps, greater clarity, than Thoreau's "Civil Disobedience."

Compared with Ingersoll's rhetoric, a flamboyant language of evangelical threats and promises ("Science took a tear from the cheek of unpaid labor, converted into steam, created a giant that turns with tireless arm, the countless wheels of toil."), Thoreau's writings seem austere, and his serene appreciation of solitude at Walden almost classic in feeling and puritanical. But to Anderson's generation the voice of Ingersoll was the voice of "progress"; it promised the arrival of a "new day" for those who had been attracted to The Noble Order of the Knights of Labor, and yet it shouted down with equal vehemence the totalitarian Utopia of Bellamy's *Looking Backward*. "We are believers in individual independence," said Ingersoll. "We invent . . . we enslave the winds and waves." It was through the invention of machines, and the tools to control, improve, and mend them, that the "religion of humanity" offered its rewards on earth to members of its congregation; and to Sherwood Anderson the delight of invention for its own sake never lost its spell. To invent became part of his pleasure in telling a story, and the very inventions of the machine age, an age whose virtues he came to distrust and to criticize, never lost their fascination.

It is clear that Ingersoll, whose attacks upon Christianity defeated his political ambitions (and left him, scarcely content, with the office of Attorney-General for the State of Illinois) had assumed heroic proportions in the Middle West during the early 1890s. Even so, it may still seem strange to link Anderson's name so closely with his. Anderson had little concern for merely rational arguments in favor of science, and

no respect whatever for inflated rhetoric, yet the sentiments of
Ingersoll, overheard or half-heard from the lips of talkers in
small-town newspaper offices and saloons, are of the same
character as those that filled the young and speculative mind
of George Willard in *Winesburg, Ohio*. The sentiments of
Ingersoll prepared Willard for the story of the Reverend Curtis
Hartman in "The Strength of God," and the same source of
inspiration provides a logic of its own for the arrival of Hugh
McVey, the inventor, the central figure, if not the "hero," of
Anderson's *Poor White*.

As we speak of Anderson's heritage and his place in American letters, it is never appropriate to name too loudly other
writers who directly influenced his writings; like D. H. Lawrence, Anderson is a singularly unbookish figure, an "original,"
a "maker" in his own right. He is also the self-educated writer,
whose brief stay at college (The college was Wittenberg at
Springfield, Ohio. "Later they called me back. They gave me
a degree," he wrote in his *Memoirs*.) was the least memorable
of his experiences. Yet like many self-taught writers, what he
read for pleasure held a place more deeply rooted in his imagination than the place held by required reading in the minds
of those who are "educated" by the thousands in colleges and
universities. As one reads Anderson's stories and autobiographies, three older writers come to mind: one is Herman Melville, another Mark Twain, and the third George Borrow. . . .

Anderson's debt to Mark Twain is less veiled than that to
Borrow, for Mark Twain's *Huckleberry Finn* is literally close
to an American time and place that Anderson knew. In his
letters to Van Wyck Brooks, Anderson speaks authoritatively
on the subject of Mark Twain, whom he sees as a distinctly
American phenomenon, a figure who stands in the company
of and between the figures of Lincoln and Whitman: "Twain's
way lies somewhere between the roads taken by the other two
men"; and in respect to Twain and Borrow, Anderson wrote,
"In my own mind I have always coupled Mark Twain with
George Borrow. I get the same quality of honesty in them,

the same wholesome disregard of literary precedent." Of the "real" Twain, Anderson wrote to Brooks, "Should not one go to Huck Finn for the real man, working out of a real people?" The people of Anderson's boyhood in the Middle West were but a single generation beyond Tom Sawyer and Huckleberry Finn, and there was an unbroken continuity between the two generations. Huckleberry Finn's skepticism concerning the virtues of church-going was of a piece with the world that Anderson knew, a world whose enjoyment was of the earth. Anderson's affinity to Mark Twain was as "natural," as unstudied as Anderson's memories of growing up and coming of age. Equally natural was the example of perspective taken from Borrow, choosing the life of the out-of-doors as the true center of worldly experience.

With Melville, Anderson's affinities are of a far less conscious order; they belong to the inward-looking, darkened "nocturnal" aspects of Anderson's heritage. The affinities to Twain and Borrow are of daylight character; they are clear and specific, and are sharply outlined within the lively scenes that Anderson created, but his kinship with Melville belongs to that diffused and shadowy area of his imagination which Paul Rosenfeld named as mysticism. As they spoke of his mysticism, even Anderson's best friends became confused because Anderson, like Borrow before him, distrusted philosophic generalities; for himself, he would have little or none of them; he would plead ignorance of large thoughts and pretensions, though he would gladly speak of how he came to write a story, and in *A Story-Teller's Story*, tell something very like another story to illustrate his point. He thought in symbols, in metaphors, in images, in turns of phrasing, in terms of a situation, or a scene of action—and in this language whatever is meant by his "mysticism" is half-revealed. The friendship of Ishmael, in *Moby Dick*, with the dark-skinned savage Queequeg has a quality akin to the quality of the boy's contact with Negroes in "The Man Who Became a Woman" or the sound of Negro laughter in Anderson's *Dark Laughter*. It was once fashionable

to call such "mysticism" Freudian, because it touched upon
the emotions of adolescent sexual experience. In Anderson
those emotions are transcended in "Death in the Woods,"
and whatever "mysticism" may be found within them, including the expression of mystery and awe, is of an older heritage
than are the teachings of Freud in America. Ishmael's decision
to share a bed with Queequeg—"Better sleep with a sober can-
nibal than a drunken Christian"—and the horror of Queequeg's first impression upon him is closely, if broadly, allied to
the mysteries, the transcendental qualities, of sexual experience in Anderson's stories, and to find that kinship one need
go no further than the story "Hands" in *Winesburg, Ohio*.
The diffused affinity that Anderson has with Melville is not a
facile one, for Anderson made it one of his few rules to stand
aside from "literary precedent," to re-create scenes of action
in terms of his own experience rather than to lean upon experiences gained from reading the works of others. The kinship
of Anderson's writings with *Moby Dick* embraces that side of
Anderson's imagination which is "non-realistic," and which
converts what is outwardly the simple telling of a story into a
series of symbolic actions. The fluttering, "talking" quality of
Wing Biddlebaum's "slender expressive fingers, forever active,"
in "Hands," is endowed with the mystery that Anderson makes
his readers feel. And when the Reverend Curtis Hartman in
"The Strength of God" breaks a church window with his fist,
the action carries with it undertones of symbolic, almost transcendental, meaning; the impulse which drove Curtis Hartman to his action was a force greater than his will, and with
appropriate irony he assigned that impulse to "the strength of
God."

Throughout many of Anderson's stories and in his autobiography, *Tar: A Midwest Childhood*, the figure of the boy
who is created to tell the tale bears a strong family resemblance
to Melville's Ishmael, and behind this figure there is the other
Ishmael, son of the bondwoman Hagar in Genesis. The figure
is one who will inherit no fortune, is of nomadic character; a

figure whose association with the Biblical story, half-concealed behind his obvious relationship to Huckleberry Finn, gives him a faint aura of transcendental kinship with the Old Testament. Literally, of course, the boy's mother, as she appears in *Tar*, is no Hagar, but the roving character of the family milieu is close enough to Hagar's wanderings in the desert to make explicit Waldo Frank's observations on *Winesburg, Ohio*, that Tar, growing older, is George Willard, and that "a Testamental accent and vision modulate every page of Sherwood Anderson's great story." So they do. Despite the "naturalism," despite the skepticism concerning the conventional moralities of the orthodox church-goers and the Reverend Curtis Hartmans, an atmosphere of Biblical vision and of semidivine "animal faith" attends these movements and awakenings in the physical world of Middle Western America. . . .

FREDERICK J. HOFFMAN

Frederick J. Hoffman has been Professor of English at the University of Wisconsin and the University of California at Riverside, and is now Distinguished Professor of English at the University of Wisconsin at Milwaukee. He is also the author of *The Modern Novel in America*, *The Twenties: American Literature in the Post-War Decade*, and co-author of *The Little Magazine: A History and a Bibliography*.

[ANDERSON AND FREUD]

At the peak of his career, in the mid-twenties, critics hailed Sherwood Anderson as the "American Freudian," the one American writer who knew his psychology and possessed a rich fund of knowledge and experience to which it could best be applied. Anderson had spoken of the repressed villager, the frustrated American businessman; he appeared to be admirably equipped to portray both, for he himself had had personal knowledge of both types. To the critic of the twenties, the villager or townsman, suffering from the hindering conventionalities of his time and place, and the businessman, deliberately shutting out life so that he might importune the goddess of success, were ideal patients for a psychoanalyst; and a writer who dealt intimately with them must have noticed the re-

---

From the chapter entitled "Three American Versions of Psychoanalysis" in *Freudianism and The Literary Mind* by Frederick J. Hoffman (Baton Rouge: Louisiana State University Press, 1957). Reprinted by permission of the publishers.

markable opportunity for the literary use of the new psychology.

This was, at any rate, the nature of Anderson's critical reputation. For one thing, the critics, determined to find influences, were scarcely willing to grant him a native talent, which was founded on personal experience and nurtured by a native sympathy for his subject matter. Was Anderson his own psychoanalyst? Did he proceed utterly unmindful of this influence? In order to answer these questions, it is necessary to determine the antecedent, local influences which affected Anderson's style and attitude. There is no lack of autobiographical material—for, besides the two admittedly autobiographical stories, *A Story-Teller's Story* (1924) and *Sherwood Anderson's Memoirs* (1942), there are the two autobiographical novels, *Windy McPherson's Son* (1916) and *Tar* (1926). In these, and in other sources, there is a mass of contradictory material, which has for some time since [Anderson's] death made the biographer's task difficult. We can at best hope only to settle upon certain recurrent themes which, if they are not drawn from life, can at least be regarded as matters with which Anderson's mind was preoccupied.

One of these important themes is Anderson's relationship with his parents. He calls his father a "ruined dandy from the South . . ." who was "made for romance. For him there was no such thing as a fact" (*A Story-Teller's Story*). He describes his own initiation into the world of letters as a rebirth: "And if you have read Freud you will find it of additional interest that, in my fanciful rebirth, I have retained the very form and substance of my earthly mother while getting an entirely new father, whom I set up—making anything but a hero of him—only to sling mud at him . . ." (*A Story-Teller's Story*).

This father is portrayed in Anderson's first published novel as "a confirmed liar and braggart" (*Windy McPherson's Son*). He describes a pathetic scene in which Windy McPherson offered to blow the bugle for a Fourth of July celebration, then, in a critical moment, revealed his utter incompetence with the instrument. And there are many other references to his father. In Anderson's image, the father possessed the same quality of vivid imagination that Sherwood was to exploit in himself, and there is a closer tie between the two men than one would gather from the citations made. In *Memoirs* Anderson devotes a chapter to explaining this ambiguous relationship. His father was "always showing off"; yet Anderson admits that there was a hidden bond of sympathy and common interest. Among the incidents which reveal this bond to him is a common adventure at a nearby lake: "For the first time I knew that I was the son of my father. He was a story-teller as I was to be. It may be that I even laughed a little softly there in the darkness. If I did, I laughed knowing that I would never again be wanting another father" (*Memoirs*). This is a last, considered view, a recognition of the fact that, in the field of literary art, Anderson was himself to demonstrate his father's skill in story-telling.

For his mother Anderson felt great sympathy and love. His desire to romanticize her, to show her a heroine who struggled boldly and patiently with poverty and loved silently but sincerely, results in several idealized portraits in his early works.

It is so wonderfully comforting to think of one's mother as a dark, beautiful and somewhat mysterious woman. . . . When she spoke her words were filled with strange wisdom . . . but often she commanded all of us by the strength of her silences [A *Story-Teller's Story*].

In his imagination he is always championing her cause against an irresponsible villain, usually some imaginative replica of his father. This devotion to his mother, though it has ample justification in fact, is part of Anderson's rationalization of his life —the "mother image" pursues him through his later years, and the fear that he may be like his father in his treatment of women colors much of his self-criticism.

These are obviously native influences, and he needed no textbook psychology to appreciate their weight or value. Aside from that, Anderson lived his own theory of the imagination, altogether separate from the world of fact. From the childhood which he describes in *Tar*, Anderson is forever shifting from the world of fact to the "larger world of fancy"; standards of honesty and intellectual integrity are presumably rigid in this latter world, though they cannot be evaluated by direct reference to the facts of the real world. The artist's deliberate entrance into the life of the fancy serves to free him of the restrictions of "Philistia," and secures his work against any tendencies he may have had toward prostituting his talents.

There are no Puritans in that life. The dry sisters of Philistia do not come in at the door. They cannot breathe in the life of fancy. The Puritan, the reformer who scolds at the Puritans, the dry intellectuals, all who desire to uplift, to remake life on some definite plan conceived within the human brain die of a disease of the lungs. They would do better to stay in the world of fact . . . (*A Story-Teller's Story*).

The world of fancy was often the real world—Anderson entertained the idea that the people of his dreams and visions might have more reality than his own physical self and the men and women who populated the ostensible world. His constant reading served apparently to feed his dream mind, or to give him "a background upon which I can construct new dreams" (*A Story-Teller's Story*). This world of fancy is the half-conscious state of daydream, supplemented by dreams and visions, for the most part elaborated upon by the dreamer. Dreams are for Anderson the most coherent expression of his other world. Dream fragments are the facts of the world of fancy. They are the means by which Anderson flees reality; most often, they are simply wish-fulfillments, with the artist playing a heroic role and gaining in fancy what he has failed to get in actual life. Yet they are not always this; he sometimes reports a dream which one may, with some misgiving, accredit as having actually been experienced:

Thoughts flitting, an effort to awaken out of dreams, voices heard, voices talking somewhere in the distance, the figures of men and women I have known flashing in and out of darkness. . . . Again the great empty place. I cannot breathe. There is a great black bell without a tongue, swinging silently in darkness. It swings and swings, making a great arch and I await silent and frightened. Now it stops and descends slowly. I am terrified. Can nothing stop the great descending iron bell? It stops and hangs for a moment and now it drops suddenly and I am a prisoner under the great bell.

With a frantic effort I am awake [A *Story-Teller's Story*]. . . .

This follows the pattern of an anxiety dream, with all its distortion and complicated symbolism. Yet Anderson regards the dream as the artist's birthright, an image of the fancy which he may treat as he pleases. He will retreat into it as a means of indirect expression of social criticism; in many respects his trances appear to be deliberately made, though their eventual effect may be genuine enough.

So, in Elyria, as he has pictured the incident in *A Story-Teller's Story* and elsewhere, he walks out of his place of business and his home, bound for the adventurous nowhere. To his astonished stenographer he says: " 'My feet are cold and wet and heavy from long wading in a river. Now I shall go walk on dry land . . .' " (*A Story-Teller's Story*). This dramatic renunciation of the business world, while it demonstrates a lively imagination, scarcely accords with the facts. According to newspaper dispatches of the time, Anderson was discovered on December 2, 1912, wandering about the streets of Cleveland, and was taken to a nearby hospital, to which his wife came immediately. The case was described as a "nervous breakdown," caused evidently by overwork. While he was still in the hospital, Anderson contemplated writing a book "of the sensations he experienced while he wandered over the country as a nomad. 'It is dangerous, but it will be a good story, and the money will always be welcome,' he said."[1] Upon his return from Cleveland, he spent two more months in Elyria and there made plans for his life in Chicago. The drama of the episode subsides considerably, in the light of these facts. These quotations suggest at best a tenuous relationship between two kinds of experience. He is not willing that these statements be criticized for inaccuracy; often they are imaginative reconstructions of the past, only major themes running through them, the details derived from the moment of composition. "When I had been working well," he says in his *Notebook*, "there was a kind of insanity of consciousness. There may be little nerves in the body that, if we could bear having them sensitive enough, would tell us everything about every person we meet." The hidden thoughts are dangerous and had best be glossed over by the fancy. As for the dreams which he is always reporting, "One feels sensuality, wonder, interest, quite naturally—is unashamed, does not try to be logical. . . . As for myself, I leave the fact that I have such dreams to the psychoanalysts" (*Notebook*).

With the help of Floyd Dell, whom he first met in 1913, Anderson was soon associating with the Chicago intellectuals in their "Greenwich Village." Anderson rarely participated in discussions of ideas, but was always ready to tell a story. Nevertheless, he was present when his friends discussed Freud eagerly as a new thing, and he agreed to an amateur analysis:

Freud had been discovered at the time and all the young intellectuals were busy analyzing each other and everyone they met. Floyd Dell was hot at it. We had gathered in the evening in somebody's rooms. Well, I hadn't read Freud (in fact, I never did read him) and was rather ashamed of my ignorance. . . .

And now [Dell] had begun psyching us. Not Floyd alone but others in the group did it. They psyched me. They psyched men passing in the street. It was a time when it was well for a man to

---

[1] Elyria (Ohio) *Evening Telegram*, December 6, 1912.

be somewhat guarded in the remarks he made, what he did with his hands [*Memoirs*].

Anderson had come to Chicago with his mind as yet only vaguely made up about the life of the artist. He was very timid about admitting that he was interested in writing. Whether or not he had found a parallel in the psychoanalytic approach to human behavior, he denied having actually read Freud or exploiting him in his writing. He was in the habit of reading widely, with no more deliberate purpose than to add to his dreams; his reading was unsystematic and diffuse; and he was perhaps jealous of his own originality. It was his habit to search out a man's works, once they had been referred to him, or he had seen some similarity to his own way of thinking. When the critics pointed to a Russian influence, "I began to read the Russians, to find out if the statement, so often made concerning me and my work, could be true" (*A Story-Tellers Story*). Sometimes he and his brother would get a copy of a book and read aloud from it; about the work of Gertrude Stein he reports [in his Preface to her *Geography and Plays*]: "My brother had been at some sort of a gathering of literary people on the evening before and someone had read aloud from Miss Stein's new book . . . he bought *Tender Buttons* and he brought it to me, and we sat for a time reading the strange sentences."

Whatever Anderson's reactions were to psychoanalysis, they were scarcely professional. With Dr. Trigant Burrow, the New York psychologist whose work had been approved by both Lawrence and Frank, Anderson held a long discussion of the matter. The argument concerned the ability of any one man successfully to enter into other lives. Burrow ended it by saying: "You think you understand but you don't understand. What you say can't be done can be done." The conversation demonstrates the conflict of two opposing minds concerning a central problem. [Burrow states in *Psychoanalytic Review* XIII (1926) that,]

As with the psychiatrist who has kept himself out of the mess and the psychoanalyst who has got himself into it, the result of our differing inquiries seems to me merely to have left us both on conflicting sides of the dilemma. We are both the unconscious instruments of private improvisation. In both, the theme we used owed itself, though unacknowledged, to the personal equation that secretly actuated our separate positions.

Anderson's opposition to psychoanalysis appears here to be founded upon a personal conviction that the "universal illness" of which he speaks in "Seeds" cannot be remedied by science, though it can be described by the artist. It is another assertion of his independence of the psychologists, and is this time supported by an accurate reference to it by the psychologist in question. In a letter [to this writer] Trigant Burrow has reaffirmed his opinion regarding Anderson's intellectual independence:

My feeling is that Sherwood Anderson was, like Freud, a genius in his own right. Anderson was a man of amazing intuitive flashes but again, like Freud, the chief source of his material was his own uncanny insight.

I can say very definitely that Anderson did not read Freud, nor did he draw any material from what he knew of Freud through others. Don't you think that all schools like to lay claim to an apt scholar? I think this largely accounts for the psychoanalysts' quite unwarranted adoption of Anderson. Of Anderson I would say that socially he was one of the healthiest men I have ever known. His counter-offensive in "Seeds" amply testifies to this. Indeed on this score many orthodox psychoanalysts might very profitably take a leaf from his book.

There is internal evidence, however slight, that leads us to suspect that Anderson was aware of the intellectual version of Freud and that he did not altogether dismiss it from his mind. The classic reference to Freud in Anderson's writings is the line given to Bruce Dudley: "If there is anything you do not understand in human life, consult the works of Doctor Freud" (*Dark Laughter*). Nothing further seems to have been done with this reference; it appears to be casual and of little consequence.

Elsewhere, when he deals with such matters as dreams, Anderson submits them to the psychoanalysts for further consideration, but he refuses to label his experience with any of their terms. Occasionally the language appears in his novels. In *Poor White* he refers to Clara Butterworth's vision on the train: "So strong was it that it affected her deeply buried unconscious self and made her terribly afraid." When he describes the dreams of Ben Peeler, Bidwell carpenter, he uses language similar to that of an analyst—though there is nothing in this description which Anderson could not have written without the aid of psychoanalysis. Ben's night is taken up with two dreams. In the first, he kills a man, or thinks that he has killed him. Then, "With the inconsistency common to the physical aspect of dreams, the darkness passed away and it was daylight" (*Poor White*). This is not without some significance, for it indicates a knowledge of the phenomenon of distortion in dreams (as the second dream itself does) and may imply either a deep personal interest in dreams, or a study of Freud's dream-interpretation, or even both. . . .

Those who were closest to Anderson during his life in Chicago and New York either do not refer to Freud at all or suggest moderately that Anderson and Freud are working along parallel lines. There seems little hesitancy, however, in associating the two men; and the temptation to ascribe an actual influence is easily indulged. The reasons for this easy ascription are not obscure. Most important, of course, was the recognition that Freud had contributed to American criticism the term *repression*, which acquired new significance, almost immediately, for the fields of sociology, history, biography, and literary criticism. Anderson was hailed as the leader in the American fight against conventional repression; his novels appeared coincidentally with the beginning of the interest in the new psychology. He dealt with frustration, in many cases with the frustration of normal sex expression. His dedication of *Winesburg, Ohio* to his mother is explained on the grounds that she first awoke in him "the hunger to see beneath the surface of lives." Had not the "new wisdom" been here clearly applied to the field of fiction? Anderson's use of dream symbolism and of the vision appeared also to play a role in influencing his critics. Not the least important, however, was the fact that Anderson hesitated himself to acknowledge any influence; that is, he never committed himself fully, in answer to his critics. Though in many other cases, such as the influence of Gertrude Stein, George Borrow, and James Joyce, he was ready enough to admit influences, and in some cases to embrace his "mentors" enthusiastically, he was oddly silent about Freud and psychoanalysis. The exaggeration of the critics was, therefore, pardonably easy to make.

(1) Anderson's early life in Ohio towns had much to do with his fundamental attitude toward his writing. Certainly he needed no handbook of psychoanalysis as a guide to using his eyes, his ears, or his imagination.

(2) When he came to Chicago for the first time in 1913, anxious to begin a writer's life, he had not as yet heard of psychoanalysis. The ideas in two of his earliest books, *Windy McPherson's Son* (1916) and *Winesburg, Ohio* (1919), so far as we can determine from internal evidence or from a consideration of the facts of Anderson's early "Chicago period," may safely be said to be his own.

(3) In Chicago, with Floyd Dell, the Lucian Carys, and Margaret Anderson, he participated in literary discussions, and it was here that he first became acquainted with the ideas and terms comprehended under the phrase "the new psychology." He noted the similarity in subject matter, remarked upon the popular habit of "psyching," but claims not to have gone any further than that.

(4) Beginning with *Poor White* (1920), though he did not alter radically his point of view, he noted that his field was

also being explored by psychoanalysis, whose researches bore many of the same marks which characterized his fictional approach. *Many Marriages* (1923) and *Dark Laughter* (1925), together with several shorter stories in *The Triumph of the Egg* (1921) and *Horses and Men* (1923), reflect this interest in frustrations and repressions, as they affect families, or unmarried women.

(5) Anderson developed his themes quite independently of Freudian influence, but with such a startling likeness of approach that critics fell into the most excusable error of their times; it seemed an absolute certainty that Anderson should have been influenced directly by Freud.

Throughout all of this Anderson maintains a skeptical attitude toward the new psychology; sometimes the reaction is simply humorous; at other times, as in the case of Trigant Burrow, he becomes actively insistent upon his independent position. That psychoanalysis encouraged hostility to the social sources of repression, especially in America, cannot be denied; but the Freudian deals only with the *individual problem* of neurosis, and has always hesitated to suggest changes in the social system which is in part responsible either for a neurosis or for its imperfect cure. Many writers of the twenties thought otherwise, however; to them psychoanalysis suggested a weapon for fighting the sources of repression, or an excuse for fleeing from them. Further, Anderson's frequent reference to the sex problems of his characters was likely to convince the critics more readily. They hesitated to distinguish between the clinical study of neurosis and the literary study of frustration. . . .

Were the critics altogether wrong in calling Anderson the "American Freudian"? There is no evidence that he wrote with Freud's works, or a psychoanalytic dictionary, at his elbow. The critics labeled Anderson as they did for this reason: almost any one of his characters could, at a certain stage of his career, have walked into an analyst's office and been justified in asking for treatment. May Edgley, Jesse Bentley, Fred Grey, Bruce Dudley, Hugh McVey, Mrs. Willard—each in his or her own way suffered, not physical, but psychic pain. For each the accepted way of life did not accord well with the inner, psychically motivated wish. In all cases the clinical report and Anderson's narrative report would have had a different conclusion. There is some justification in noting the parallel courses of psychoanalysis and Anderson's fiction, but there seems little evidence to prove that those two courses intersected at any vital points. It is as though Anderson were thrusting upon Freud the burden of clarifying the artist's analysis: "Men who have passed the age of thirty and who have intelligence understand such things. A German scientist can explain perfectly. If there is anything you do not understand in human life consult the works of Dr. Freud" (*Dark Laughter*). If you have been unable to follow with me into the lives of these characters, Anderson seems to be saying; if they still seem queer to you—if their acts are merely violent and inexplicably so—Dr. Freud has studied these matters calmly and scientifically, and he will aid you. But if you do go to him, you will have failed to understand much of what I wish to say to you. . . .

ALFRED KAZIN

Alfred Kazin taught at Black Mountain College, Smith College, and Amherst College, and is now Distinguished Professor of English at the State University of New York at Stony Brook. Among books he has published are the autobiographical volumes *A Walker in the City* and *Starting Out in the Thirties*, and two collections of essays: *The Inmost Leaf* and *Contemporaries*.

[THE NEW REALISM:
SHERWOOD ANDERSON]

. . . Even a classic of postwar emotion like Masters's *Spoon River Anthology*, which was perhaps not so much a portrait of a representative town as an image of Masters's own bitterness and frustration, posited a new freedom. To know the truth of American life was to rise in some fashion above its prohibitions; to recognize the tragedy so often ignored in commonplace lives was to lead to a healthy self-knowledge. Reveling in the commonplace, the new realists felt that with them the modern novel in America had at last come to grips with the essentials, and the vigor with which they described the sterility of their world had in it a kind of exuberance.

It was this personal quest in realism, particularly marked at a time when so many young writers seemed to have endured

From the chapter entitled "The New Realism: Sherwood Anderson and Sinclair Lewis" in *On Native Grounds: An Interpretation of Modern American Prose Literature* by Alfred Kazin (New York: Harcourt, Brace, 1942). Copyright 1942 by Alfred Kazin. Reprinted by permission of Harcourt, Brace and World, Inc.

life in a hundred different Spoon Rivers for the sole purpose of declaring their liberation in their novels, that so clearly distinguished these books from the night world of naturalism. And it was this same insistence on personal liberation that made Sherwood Anderson the evangel of the postwar deliveration. For Anderson, so often described as a "naturalist" at a time when any effort at realism was still associated with Dreiser's dour massive objectivity, even appeared to be inadequately conscious of objective reality. His great subject always was personal freedom; out of it he made a kind of left-handed mysticism, a groping for the unnamed ecstasy immanent in human relations, that seemed the sudden revelation of the lives Americans led in secret. If Sinclair Lewis dramatized the new realism by making the novel an exact and mimetic transcription of American life, Anderson was fascinated by the undersurface of that life and became the voice of its terrors and exultations. Lewis turned the novel into a kind of higher journalism; Anderson turned fiction into a substitute for poetry and religion, and never ceased to wonder at what he had wrought. He had more intensity than a revival meeting and more tenderness than God; he wept, he chanted, he loved indescribably. There was freedom in the air, and he would summon all Americans to share in it; there was confusion and mystery on the earth, and he would summon all Americans to wonder at it. He was clumsy and sentimental; he could even write at times as if he were finger-painting; but at the moment it seemed as if he had sounded the depths of common American experience as no one else could.

There was always an image in Anderson's books—an image of life as a house of doors, of human beings knocking at them and stealing through one door only to be stopped short before another as if in a dream. Life was a dream to him, and he and his characters seemed always to be walking along its corridors. Who owned the house of life? How did one escape after all? No one in his books ever knew, Anderson least of all. Yet slowly he tried to make others believe, as he thought he had learned for himself, that it was possible to escape if only one laughed at necessity. That was his own story, as everything he wrote—the confession in his *Memoirs* was certainly superfluous —was a variation upon it; and it explained why, for all his fumbling and notorious lack of contemporary sophistication, he had so great an appeal for the restive postwar generation. For Anderson, growing up in small Ohio villages during the eighties and nineties at a time when men could still watch and wait for the new industrial world to come in, enjoyed from the first—at least in his own mind—the luxury of dreaming away on the last margin of the old pre-factory freedom, of being suspended between two worlds. Unlike most modern American realists even of his own generation, in fact, Anderson always evoked in his books the world of the old handicraft artisans, the harness makers and Civil War veterans like his father, the small-town tailors and shoemakers, the buggy and wagon craftsmen of the old school. It was almost a forgotten America which he brought back out of the memory— the America of the old slumbering village towns, of religious stirrings, of the village workmen and saloonkeepers and stablemen; an America that could still remember John D. Rockefeller as a bookkeeper in Cleveland and watch a future titan of industry like Edward S. Harkness still running his little "variety" store on Main Street in Anderson's own Camden; and it was an America for whom Anderson, though he helped to lead "the revolt from the village," always, if sometimes unconsciously, spoke.

It was certainly on the basis of his experiences in this world that Anderson was able ever after to move through the world that Chicago now symbolized as if he, and all his characters with him, were moving in puzzled bliss through the interstices of the great new cities and factories. No other novelist of the time gave so vividly the sense of *not* having been brought up to the constraints, the easy fictions, the veritable rhythm, of modern commercial and industrial life. It was as if he had been brought up in a backwater, grown quaint and self-willed, a little "queer," a drowsing village mystic, amidst stagnant scenes; and the taste of that stagnance was always in his work. A certain sleepy inarticulation, a habit of staring at faces in wondering silence, a way of groping for words and people indistinguishably, also crept into his work; what one felt in it was not only the haunting tenderness with which he came to his characters, but also the measureless distances that lay between these characters themselves. They spoke out of the depths, but in a sense they did not speak at all; they addressed themselves, they addressed the world around them, and the echoes of their perpetual confession were like sound-waves visible in air.

"I would like to write a book of the life of the mind and of the imagination," Anderson wrote in his *Memoirs*. "Facts elude me. I cannot remember dates. When I deal in facts, at once I begin to lie. I can't help it." The conventional world for him was a snare that fearful little men had agreed among themselves to perpetuate; the reality lay underground, in men and women themselves. It was as if the ageless dilemma of men caught by society found in him the first prophet naïve enough, and therefore bold enough, to deny that men need be caught at all. His heroes were forever rebelling against the material, yet they were all, like Anderson himself, sublimely unconscious of it. The proud sons who rebel against their drunkard fathers, like Windy McPherson's son, sicken of the riches they have gained, but they never convince one that they have lived with riches. The rebels against working-class squalor and poverty, like Beaut McGregor in *Marching Men*, finally do rise to wealth and greatness, but only to lead men—as Anderson, though a Socialist in those early years, hoped to lead them—out of the factory world itself into a vague solidarity of men marching forever together. The businessmen who have revolted against their families, like John Webster in *Many Marriages*, make an altar in their bedrooms to worship; the sophisticated artists, like Bruce Dudley in *Dark Laughter*, run away from home to hear the laughter of the triumphantly unrepressed Negroes; the ambitious entrepreneurs, like Hugh McVey in *Poor White*, weep in despair over the machines they have built. And when they do escape, they all walk out of the prison house of modern life, saying with inexpressible simplicity, as Anderson did on the day he suddenly walked out of his paint factory in Ohio: "What am I going to do? Well, now, that I don't know. I am going to wander about. I am going to sit with people, listen to words, tell tales of people, what they are thinking, what they are feeling. The devil! It may even be that I am going forth in search of myself."

"I have come to think," he wrote in *A Story-Teller's Story*, "that the true history of life is but a history of moments. It is only at rare moments that we live." In those early days it was as if a whole subterranean world of the spirit were speaking in and through Anderson, a spirit imploring men to live frankly and fully by their own need of liberation, and pointing the way to a tender and surpassing comradeship. He had left his own business and family to go to Chicago—"there was a queer kind of stoppage of something at the center of myself"—and he would dream, in the tenement-house rooms where he wrote *Winesburg* after working as a laborer or an advertising writer, of the life that went on in those houses, a life that could be heard through thin partitions. "I had thought, then, on such evenings," he wrote twenty-five years later in nostalgia, "that I could tell all of the stories of all the people of America. I would get them all, understand them, get their stories told." Out of his wandering experiences at soldiering and laboring jobs, at following the race horses he loved and the business career he hated, he had become "at last a writer, a writer whose sympathy went out most to the little frame houses, on often mean enough streets in American towns, to defeated people, often with thwarted lives." Were there not people everywhere, just people and their stories to tell? Were there not questions about them always to be asked—the endless wonderment, the groping out toward them, the special "moments" to be remembered?

Living in the heart of the "Robin's-Egg Renaissance" in Chicago, as he called it later, it even seemed to Anderson that hardly anyone had ever before him in America asked the questions he needed to ask about people. The novels he knew did not tell their story; their creators were afraid, as the New England writers who had written too many of the first American stories before Dreiser were afraid. Between the people he saw and the books he read, Anderson saw the chasm of fear in America—the fear of sex, the fear of telling the truth about the hypocrisy of those businessmen with whom he too had reached for "the bitch-goddess of success"; the fear, even, of making stories the exact tonal equivalent of their lives; the fear of restoring to books the slackness and the disturbed rhythms of life. For Anderson was not only reaching for the truth about people and "the terrible importance of the flesh in human relations"; he was reaching at the same time for a new kind of medium in fiction. As he confessed explicitly later on, he even felt that "the novel form does not fit an American writer, that it is a form which had been brought in. What is wanted is a new looseness; and in *Winesburg* I had made my own form." Significantly enough, even such warm friends of the new realism as Floyd Dell and H. L. Mencken did not think the *Winesburg* stories stories at all; but Anderson, who had revolted against what he now saw as the false heroic note in his first work, knew better, and he was to make the new readers see it his way.

For if "the true history of life was but a history of moments," it followed that the dream of life could be captured only in a fiction that broke with rules of structure literally to embody moments, to suggest the endless halts and starts, the dreamlike passiveness and groping of life. What Gertrude Stein had for fifteen years, working alone in Paris, learned out of her devotion to the independent vision of modern French painting, Anderson now realized by the simple stratagem of following the very instincts of his character, by groping through to the slow realization of his characters on the strength of his conviction that all life itself was only a process of groping. The difference between them (it was a difference that Gertrude Stein's pupil, Ernest Hemingway, felt so deeply that he had to write a parody of Anderson's style, *The Torrents of Spring*, to express his revulsion and contempt) was that where Miss Stein and Hemingway both had resolved their break with the "rules" into a conscious principle of design, Anderson had no sense of design at all save as life afforded him one. Although he later listened humbly enough to Gertrude Stein in Paris— she had proclaimed him one of the few Americans who could write acceptable sentences—he could never make one principle of craft, least of all those "perfect sentences" that she tried so hard to write, the foundation of his work. Anderson was, in fact, rather like an older kind of artisan in the American tradition—such as Whitman and Albert Pinkham Ryder—artisans who worked by sudden visions rather than by any sense of style, artisans whose work was the living grammar of their own visions. Hemingway's bitterness against Anderson, it may be, was as much a recognition of the older man's advantage in his awkwardness as it was a revulsion against his self-indulgence and groping; but it is significant that it was just Hemingway's need of style and a deliberate esthetic in the novel that separated them.

Anderson did not merely live for the special "moments" in experience; he wrote, by his own testimony, by sudden realizations, by the apprehension of a mood, a place, a character, that brought everything to a moment's illumination and stopped there, content with the fumbling ecstasy it brought. It was this that gave him his interest in the "sex drive" as a force in human life (it had so long been left out), yet always touched that interest with a bold, awkward innocence. He was among the first American writers to bring the unconscious into the novel, yet when one thinks of how writers like Dorothy Richardson, Virginia Woolf, and James Joyce pursued the unconscious and tried to trace some pattern in the fathomless psychic history of men and women, it is clear that Anderson was not

interested in contributing to the postwar epic of the unconscious at all. What did interest him was sex as a disturbance in
consciousness, the kind of disturbance that drove so many of
his heroes out of the world of constraint; but once he had got
them out of their houses, freed them from convention, their
liberation was on a plane with their simultaneous liberation
from the world of business. It was their loneliness that gave
them significance in Anderson's mind, the lies that they told
themselves and each other to keep the desperate fictions of
conventionality; and it was inevitably the shattering of that
loneliness, the emergence out of that uneasy twilit darkness in
which his characters always lived, that made their triumph
and, in his best moments, Anderson's own.

   Yet it is a terrible thing for a visionary to remain a minor
figure. Where other minor figures can at least work out a
minor success, the visionary who has not the means equal to
his vision crumbles into fragments. Anderson was a minor figure, as he himself knew so well; and that was his tragedy. For
the significance of his whole career is that though he could
catch, as no one else could, the inexpressible grandeur of those
special moments in experience, he was himself caught between
them. Life was a succession of moments on which everything
else was strung; but the moments never came together, and
the world itself never came together for him. It was not his
"mysticism" that was at fault, for without it he would have
been nothing; nor was it his special way of groping for people,
of reaching for the grotesques in life, the homely truths that
seemed to him so beautiful, since that was what he had most
to give—and did give so imperishably in *Winesburg*, in stories
like "I'm a Fool," in parts of *Poor White* and *Dark Laughter*,
and in the autobiographical *Tar*. It was rather that Anderson
had nothing else in him that was equal to his revelations, his
tenderness, his groping. He was like a concentration of everything that had been missed before him in modern American
writing, and once his impact was felt, the stammering exulta-

tion he brought became all. That was Anderson's real humiliation, the humiliation that perhaps only those who see so much
more deeply than most men can feel; he knew it best of all.

I am a helpless man—my hands tremble.
I should be sitting on a bench like a tailor.
I should be weaving warm cloth out of the threads of thought.
The tales should be clothed.
They are freezing on the doorstep of the house of my mind.

"If you love in a loveless world," he wrote in *Many Marriages*, "you face others with the sin of not loving." He had
that knowledge; he brought it in, and looked at it as his characters looked at each other; but he could only point to it and
wonder. "There is something that separates people, curiously,
persistently, in America," he wrote in his last novel, *Kit
Brandon*. He ended on that note as he had begun on it twenty-
five years before, when Windy McPherson's son wondered why
he could never get what he wanted, and Beaut McGregor led
the marching men marching, marching nowhere. The brooding was there, the aimless perpetual reaching, that indefinable
note Anderson always struck; but though no writer had written so much of liberation, no writer seemed less free. He was
a Prospero who had charmed himself to sleep and lost his
wand; and as the years went on Anderson seemed more and
more bereft, a minor visionary whose perpetual air of wonder
became a trance and whose prose disintegrated helplessly from
book to book. Yet knowing himself so well, he could smile
over those who were so ready to tell him that it was his ignorance of "reality" and of "real people" that crippled his books.
What was it but the reality that was almost too oppressively
real, the reality beyond the visible surface world, the reality of
all those lives that so many did lead in secret, that he had
brought into American fiction? It was not his vision that was
at fault, it was that human situation embodied in him, that
story he told over and again because it was his only story—of
the groping that broke forth out of the prison house of life

and . . . went on groping; of the search for freedom that left
all the supplicators brooding and overwhelmed. Yet if he had
not sought so much, he could not have been humiliated so
deeply. It was always the measure of his reach that gave others
the measure of his failure. . . .

❀❂❀

JARVIS A. THURSTON

Jarvis A. Thurston, Professor of English, teaches creative writing and
contemporary literature at Washington University in St. Louis, and
is the editor of the magazine *Perspective*.

[TECHNIQUE IN *WINESBURG, OHIO*]

. . . Of the numerous relationships that can exist between
author and audience it is significant that Anderson rarely chose
the relationship involved in the dramatic method for which
Henry James was such a persistent spokesman. The authorial
self-effacement of the frequently anthologized "I'm a Fool"
and "I Want to Know Why" is distinctly uncharacteristic. Anderson's lack of interest in "what men think and say," his
view of the function of art, the kind of meanings he was usually working with, would almost preclude the use of objective
narrative methods. In *Winesburg* he found the relationship
between author and audience appropriately suited to an uneducated, intuitive man, who had come out of the wilderness
of the business world and had something to tell: it is essentially the role of the wise epic poet as it has come down into
modern times in a long line of English and American oral
story-tellers. The role permitted Anderson the close relationship of teller to audience, permitted the authorial "wisdom,"
the apparent artlessness of episodic structure, the moving back

---

From an essay originally entitled "Anderson and 'Winesburg': Mysticism
and Craft," published in *Accent*, Spring 1956. Copyright 1956 by Jarvis A.
Thurston. Reprinted by permission of the author.

and forth in time, and the moving in and out of the story as narrator and commentator. In the adaptation of the oral story to the written Anderson found for the first time in his literary career (*Windy McPherson's Son* and *Marching Men* had fumbled toward the "literary") a way of closing the gap between spiritual content and technique.

Though certain features of oral telling can be seen in more exaggerated form in some of the other *Winesburg* stories, "The Untold Lie" has most of the basic characteristics: the laying in at the beginning of blocks of background before the story proper is taken up; the apparent wandering away from the story because of some associational interest provoked by the mention of a name, object, or place; the frequent authorial intrusions in the form of "insights" and self-dramatizations; the shifts in time, and the occasional stopping of the story to lay in apparently overlooked materials necessary to the "point" of the tale.

In the opening page of "The Untold Lie" we are summarily told the names of the two characters—Ray Pearson and Hal Winters—where they live, their occupations, ages, marital status. Ray is characterized swiftly as "an altogether serious man . . . quiet, rather nervous . . . with a brown beard and shoulders rounded by too much and too hard labor." So much for Ray Pearson. Anderson then turns to Hal Winters. With the oral teller's fondness for the associational, he asks us—as if we might know him—not to confuse him with Ned Winters' family, a respectable family, for Hal is "one of the three sons of the old man called Windpeter Winters who had a sawmill near Unionville, six miles away, and who was looked upon by everyone in Winesburg as a confirmed reprobate." In oral telling the mention of any person, even though he may have little relation to the story, commonly results in a digression. And so it is here. One of the ten pages of the story is an account of Windpeter's death (as with most of Anderson's apparent digressions in these stories, this serves a purpose: Hal Winters comes from a spirited family that does not easily succumb to

the traps of life that have defeated the weaker and more respectable Ray Pearson). To get back from the digression the
teller has to address his listeners:

But this is not the story of Windpeter Winters nor yet of his son
Hal who worked on the Wills farm with Ray Pearson. It is Ray's
story. It will, however, be necessary to talk a little of young Hal
so that you will get into the spirit of it.

It is not until page four that the tale promised us begins with
"And so these two men, Ray and Hal, were at work . . . ,"
but the story is immediately interrupted by the teller's ad-
dressing us again to insist upon the reasons for Ray Pearson's
"distracted mood":

If you knew the Winesburg country in the fall and how the low
hills are all splashed with yellows and reds you would understand
his feeling.

From this point on the story is presented dramatically with
only two more brief interruptions; the latter of these—"Ray
Pearson lost his nerve and this is really the end of the story
of what happened to him"—is disarming, for the one page that
follows is really not the afterthought it appears to be; the
teller is enjoying his craftiness.

The *Winesburg* stories are "oral," but are not, of course,
merely oral stories written down. Since the meanings with
which he was working needed a subtlety of handling that had
little to do with the oral story as he knew it, Anderson solved
the problem of telling stories in which nothing much happens
externally by using a narrator-bard whose sympathetic vision
is never far away. His bard is like the writer in the prefatory
"Book of the Grotesque" (and not unlike Anderson's conception of himself as a "story-teller"):

. . . he had known people, many people, known them in a peculiarly
intimate way that was different from the way in which you and I

know people. At least that is what the writer thought and the thought pleased him.

He is a wise old man who has "entered into lives" and who has kept alive the "young thing" (imagination, fancy) within him that in that state between sleeping and waking (the daydreaming, creative state) brings a vision of truth (out of which the artist makes his art). For the old writer it is the truth that all the people he has known are grotesques: "Some were amusing [Joe Welling], some almost beautiful [Dr. Reefy], and one, a woman all drawn out of shape [Elizabeth Willard?], hurt the old man by her grotesqueness." Like Anderson he has written a book called "The Book of the Grotesque" (Anderson's title for Winesburg until his publisher persuaded him to change it) and has been saved from becoming a grotesque himself by the creative "young thing inside him."

Far from being the intrusive character that criticism has complained about, the narrator of Winesburg is central to the stories he tells. It is no accident that he occasionally appears as an "I" (for instance, in "Respectability": "I go too fast") or frequently appears as a commentator (in "Hands": "The story of Wing Biddlebaum's hands is worth a book in itself. Sympathetically set forth it would tap many strange, beautiful qualities in obscure men. It is a job for a poet."), for it is his presence, never very far away, that unites the stories through a consistent tone and perspective, and justifies the characterization, structure, and style. It is his oblique vision and pervasive sympathy which persuades the reader to tolerate what on the surface seems to be little more than character sketch or anecdote.

If Anderson's narrator seems to share his creator's traits, he is, nevertheless, a *persona* that makes possible Anderson's use in story of a frame of reference that might more appropriately have been used in poetry. That Anderson's poetry (his letters show a continuing fondness for *Mid-American Chants* and *New Testament* in spite of unanimous critical rejection) is a

formless mélange of Whitman, Sandburg, and the Old Testament does not disprove the rightness of Rebecca West's view
that Anderson was a poet who was trying to write prose.
Writers of the private life, as she observes, used to write verse.

In *Winesburg* Anderson used his narrator's mixture of inarticulate wisdom and naïveté in a controlled way that constantly suggests more than is said. Even risky passages like
those in "Hands" ("it needs the poet there") carry, in the
context of the book, an air of rightness. The inarticulateness
seems appropriate to his spiritually confused characters and
to a narrator whose wisdom is more of the heart than the
head. But by the time Anderson had got to *Tar* he had begun
to overwork exaggeratedly and too self-consciously the approach
he had discovered. In *A Story-Teller's Story* and in *Tar* the
narrator's naïveté frequently seems sham and the wisdom an
unconvincing sly smile, but the successful portions—and this
is true of not a few of Anderson's casual pieces in such books
as *Hello Towns!* and *Puzzled America*—depend upon that principle discovered for *Winesburg*: the exploitation for art of his
own quaint and quirkily religious personality. How much of
the narrator's personality is Anderson's and how much a *persona* we cannot determine; but as Howard Mumford Jones and
Walter Rideout have observed in their introduction to the
selected *Letters*, there are few writers whose letters so completely reaffirm what we have sensed about the personality
through acquaintance with the art.

It is also the pervasive presence of the quirkily religious
author-narrator that determines the essential characteristics of
Anderson's prose style, which, much criticism to the contrary,
is not adequately defined by Edmund Wilson as "a series of
simple declarative sentences of almost primer-like baldness" or
by Oscar Cargill as a "conscious simplicity of style." Such a
language would be obviously inadequate for a writer who has
a prophet's insight into modern spiritual desolation and who

feels that art is salvational. The role demanded a heightened language that is expressive of "wisdom," sympathy, and humility; and this language Anderson created out of a mixture of elements that he had natively at hand:

(1) the "literary" (a kind of belated village Johnsonese learned in the advertising experience and through his attempts to reproduce the educated language of the nineteenth- and early twentieth-century novelists he read—Cooper, Borrow, Austen, Wells):

Hidden, shadowy doubts that had been in men's minds concerning Adolph Myers were galvanized into beliefs ["Hands"].

The fruition of the year had come . . . ["Loneliness"].

(2) the biblical poetic (in the use of incremental repetition; expanded, rounded cadences; and diction—Anderson carried about with him pages torn from the Gideon Bibles that he found in the hotels in which he spent so much of his time both before and after he became a professional writer):

Youthful sadness, young man's sadness, the sadness of a growing boy in a village at the year's end, opened the lips of the old man. The sadness was in the heart of George Willard and was without meaning, but it appealed to Enoch Robinson ["Loneliness"].

Wing Biddlebaum became wholly inspired. For once he forgot the hands. Slowly they stole forth and lay upon George Willard's shoulders. Something new and bold came into the voice that talked . . . ["Hands"].

(3) the American colloquial (the kind of language commonly used by the American oral story-teller—Anderson was a great admirer of *Huckleberry Finn*; before his *Winesburg* was written he had a considerable reputation among his Chicago acquaintances as a story-teller, and by the testimony of both Anderson and the people in Clyde, Ohio, who knew him, Anderson's father was a memorable story-teller; interestingly An-

derson, who hated his father and loved his mother, came to remember his father with affection in A *Story-Teller's Story*, for he recognized in him one of the sources of his own craft):

Hal was a bad one. Everyone said that. There were three of the Winters boys in that family, John, Hal, and Edward, all broad-shouldered big fellows like old Windpeter himself and all fighters and woman-chasers and generally all-around bad ones.

Hal was the worst of the lot and always up to some devilment . . . ["The Untold Lie"].

(4) the English and American informal (the "middle" world of diction and syntax that is used wherever the English language is spoken):

Hop Higgins sat down by the stove and took off his shoes. When the boy had gone to sleep he began to think of his own affairs. He intended to paint his house in the spring and sat by the stove calculating the cost of paint and labor. ["The Teacher"].

Though it is the fourth of these ingredients that provides the basic stock of Anderson's narrative style, it is given an air of quaintness by being constantly flavored with the other ingredients, and particularly by the biblical poetic when Anderson is seeking to express the inarticulate intensity of feeling that seizes his characters. No one of the ingredients is used unmixed for more than a few sentences. Shifts from the language of the oral teller to a more formal diction and sentence structure, or to a mixture of the two, occur frequently in *Winesburg*. "A Man of Ideas" opens with the baldness of "He lived with his mother . . . His name was Joe Welling" and continues:

He was like a tiny little volcano that lies silent for days and then suddenly spouts fire. No, he wasn't like that—he was like a man who is subject to fits, one who walks among his fellow men inspiring fear because a fit may come upon him suddenly and blow him away into a strange uncanny physical state in which his eyes roll and his legs and arms jerk. He was like that, only that the visitation that descended upon Joe Welling was a mental and not a physical thing.

The colloquial element in *Winesburg* has been overstressed by critics, chiefly because of their looking backward from such stories as "I'm a Fool" and "I Want to Know Why," in which Anderson temporarily abandoned his author-narrator role for the objectivity of the uneducated main character telling his own story; these are the pieces that most closely link Anderson to Mark Twain and Gertrude Stein. Anderson commonly uses the colloquial in *Winesburg* as an indirect means of characterization, speaking about Hal, for instance, in the language that Winters himself might have used. We can observe, also, that the colloquial appears less frequently in the story about the philosophic Dr. Reefy (one of Anderson's self-portraits).

That the mixed language of *Winesburg* does not represent merely a stage toward a more colloquial language—even though there is a decrease of the "literary" that so mars the early novels —is indicated by the revisions of the stories for magazine publication (curiously, as William L. Phillips has proved, the magazine versions, though published before *Winesburg*, are revisions of the *Winesburg* manuscript). At the same time that he is increasing the role of the narrator by changing some of the commentary into the first person, he is also changing *that's* to *that is, couldn't* to *could not*, and seeking the economies of written language by eliding, for instance, the italicized clause in such a passage as this: "the puzzled look he had already noticed in the eyes of others *when he looked at them.*"

As I have already said, practically everything about Anderson—the mystical cast of his mind, his working habits, his views of the human personality and the function of art, to mention only a few items—precluded success as a novelist. All the novels, from *Windy McPherson's Son* to *Kit Brandon*,

leave one with the impression that they are, in spite of occasional good scenes, planless mixtures of narrative summary,
hortatory exposition, and weakly rendered drama. Clearly Anderson had no interest in how a character moves from A to D
in time. He had the lyric poet's interest in D. If A is mentioned at all it is as a contrast to D; there is no concern for
intermediate points or process. But the very cast of mind that
made the novel an uncongenial genre for Anderson permitted
him his kind of story, the "feel into things" (and the kind of
sensitive, Lawrencean reportage in *Hello Towns!* and *Home
Town*). Only in *Winesburg* did Anderson manage with some
success a structure larger than the single story. The nature of
that success needs to be defined and explained.

Anderson's earliest comment about *Winesburg* is in a November 14, 1916, letter to Waldo Frank:

I made last year a series of intensive studies of people of my home
town, Clyde, Ohio. . . . Some of the studies you may think pretty
raw, and there is a sad note running through them. One or two of
them get pretty closely down to ugly things of life. . . .

This thought occurs to me. There are or will be seventeen of
these studies [there were finally twenty-four]. Fifteen are, I believe,
completed. If you have the time and the inclination, I might send
the lot to you to be looked over.

It is my own idea that when these studies are published in book
form, they will suggest the real environment out of which present-
day American youth is coming.

Though the passage hints at George Willard's role, we cannot
know at what time, before or rather late during the composition, Anderson saw *Winesburg* as both a collection of tales and
a novel about Willard. Since Anderson had not formed any
close literary acquaintances outside Chicago before the fall of
1916, most of the literary comments in the letters are post-
Winesburg. (The majority of the stories seem to have been
written in late 1915 and early 1916—the earliest of the pieces,
"The Book of the Grotesque," was in the February 1916

Masses, and was followed in March by "Hands." A few of the pieces—certainly parts of the "Godliness" sequence and, possibly, the three closing stories—were written in 1917, or later.)

After the publication of *Winesburg* (1919) Anderson wrote to Van Wyck Brooks that "the novel form does not fit an American writer . . . it is a form which has been brought in. What is wanted is a new looseness; and in *Winesburg* I made my own form." And in December 1919 he wrote to Waldo Frank:

> Out of necessity I am throwing the Mary Cochran book [another of the unfinished novels] into the *Winesburg form, half individual tales, half long novel form.* It enables me to go at each tale separately, perhaps when I am ready to do it *at one long sitting.* My life now is too broken up for the long sustained thing. Every few days I must go wade in mud, in the filth of money making. [One of the most tortured periods of Anderson's life followed upon his being given by Horace Liveright a five-year guarantee of $100 a week for writing a novel a year.]

These statements and the interlockings of characters and places in the opening stories of *Winesburg* would seem to be evidence for Anderson's having begun with George Willard's dual role as confidant and protagonist in mind, but this does not necessarily indicate a unifying conception much more complicated than that he had observed in his reading in 1915 of Masters's *Spoon River Anthology.* Whatever the original conception may have been, a reading of *Winesburg* suggests that the novel was superimposed upon the tales at a rather late date and that the earlier pieces were not reworked to fit as well as they might into a new structure. (Anderson's revisions were usually minor; as we might expect, he rewrote rather than revised, since he depended upon a mood to carry him through to form.)

In sixteen of the twenty-four stories George appears as either protagonist or secondary character; in three other stories he is mentioned in some such passing remark as that in "The Untold Lie": "Boys like young George Willard and Seth Richmond will remember the incident . . ." Of the five stories in which George is not mentioned, one, "Paper Pills," is placed so early in the volume and is so definitely linked by its manner to the other tales that George's absence is not noticeable. The other four are the parts of the "Godliness" series, a self-contained unit which rests uneasily among the other stories. The heavy-handed preaching about industrialism there, the overt spiritual seeking, and the almost burlesque use of Biblical symbols and allusions in the Jesse Bentley parts are the more mystical Anderson of *Many Marriages* and *Marching Men.* Some years ago I wrote that "Godliness" was probably the matrix of a novel which Anderson intended to write about several generations of the Bentley family but recast, probably because he could not finish it, to form part of *Winesburg.* This supposition is now supported by an August 27, 1917, letter to Waldo Frank, written during the summer Anderson spent in the Chateaugay Lake country in New York:

. . . My mind has run back and back to the time when men tended sheep and lived a nomadic life on hillsides and by little talking streams. I have become less and less the thinker and more the thing of earth and the winds. When I awake at night and the wind is howling, my first thought is that the gods are at play in the hills here. My new book, starting with life on a big farm in Ohio, will have something of that flavor in its earlier chapters. There is a delightful old man, Joseph Bentley by name, who is full of old Bible thoughts and impulses.

The Jesse (as he was renamed) Bentley stories are the only ones not set in Winesburg, and even though the story of George Willard is being told, as Anderson said in 1931, "by telling the stories of other people whose lives touched his life," the story of Jesse Bentley seems to be no part of Willard's environment.

In casting George Willard in the role of village reporter Anderson generally makes credible his being the recipient of so many intimate stories, but the aesthetic effect of the individual stories is occasionally weakened by Willard's unnecessary appearance as listener or secondary participant. He interferes, for instance, with the role of the "wise" author-narrator in "Loneliness" in being introduced near the end of the story in explanation of how "we know about him [Enoch Robinson]." In stories like "Queer" and "Departure" the author-narrator makes no explanations as to the source of his knowledge of his character's private acts and thoughts.

The writing of both a book of stories and a novel in the same volume results in some inconsistencies, but it also explains certain matters. It explains the unnecessary endings, if one thinks of them as independent stories, of "Teacher" and "Death." It also explains why some of the stories like "Nobody Knows" and "Death" have a limited or ambiguous meaning if looked upon independently. "Nobody Knows" takes on an added significance when seen from the perspective of the George Willard-Helen White story in "Sophistication." "Death," broken into four sections, begins with Dr. Reefy, turns to his relationship with Elizabeth Willard (which involves much retrospective material about her early life and her marriage with Tom Willard), shifts to George's reactions upon the death of his mother, and ends on a footnote about the $800 that Elizabeth had hidden away. As part of the George Willard novel "Death" is not confusing; in it and the closing two pieces—"Sophistication" and "Departure"—Anderson is preparing for a conclusion that the George Willard story makes possible. The three final pieces pull together the fragments of George's experience. The sense of the past which has hung over the stories is brought into the present, and George leaves Winesburg carrying with him the sadness of a world that makes us lovers but does not give us our thing to love.

Though less successful as a novel than as a collection of tales, Winesburg is a kind of portrait of the Midwestern artist as a young man. Between the opening story in which Willard is fascinated by the love and fear expressed in Biddlebaum's hands and the closing story in which he leaves a Winesburg which is to "become but a background on which to paint the dreams of his manhood," much has happened to him: he has had his first sexual relation in an atmosphere of secrecy and guilt, been humiliatingly used as bait by a woman in securing a husband, experienced the communion of adolescent love, suffered at the death of his mother, and observed, as reporter for the village newspaper and as confidant of Winesburg's grotesques, the sadness and ugliness of life—and a little of its happiness and beauty.

In spite of Willard's unifying function, it is not, really, as a novel that *Winesburg* has its success as a totality. Structurally, like all of Anderson's longer work, it has serious flaws. The book's unity rests ultimately in its being, in effect, a series of mutually supporting prose poems on a theme, held together by the consistency of the author-narrator's attitude—a blend of the oracular and the sympathetic—toward subject and audience. This Anderson seems to have never clearly understood. Ironically it was *Winesburg*, his only long success, that confirmed for Anderson notions dangerous for a novelist. In 1930, in the wake of numerous novels rapturously begun and never finished, and after the bitterly unproductive years following *Dark Laughter* (1925), Anderson could still write to friends:

I have put away the machine thing for the time and am at work on a long story. The machine thing must, it seems to me, be let to come as it will. It must have poetic content. It can't be reasoned out or buttressed with facts. [As if he had ever reasoned his works out or buttressed them with fact.] It is all in a field where there are no facts.

As you know, poetry—the carrying of conviction to others through feeling through the medium of words—is a complex, difficult thing.

The very color of the words themselves, the feeling in the artist trying to release itself is a part of what must get over to the reader.

He never fully realized that it was his "vision" of life, the consequent views of art and artist, and his working habits that blocked his doing "the long sustained thing"—and gave to his short stories their quaint strength.

ROGER ASSELINEAU

Roger Asselineau, a leading French authority on Anderson, is Professor of English at the Sorbonne in Paris. He edited *The Literary Reputation of Hemingway in Europe* and is currently preparing a critical edition of Hemingway's work for publication in France.

LANGUAGE AND STYLE IN
SHERWOOD ANDERSON'S
WINESBURG, OHIO

There is truth, as well as wit, in Philip Rahv's theory that American writers can be divided into two groups: on the one hand there are the Palefaces who, like Henry James, are pale from book learning, and on the other the Redskins who, like Walt Whitman, sound their barbaric yawp from the rooftops of the world, unconcerned with questions of sophistication or refinement. Obviously Anderson is a Redskin, but a Redskin with Paleface blood in his veins, nevertheless; for his art is much less brutal and much more subtle than one might think. Scott Fitzgerald, who was himself the best and finest of story-tellers, was not mistaken. He confided one day to Maxwell Perkins: "He is one of the very best and finest writers in the English language today. God, he can write! . . . Simple! The word on the lips of critics makes me hilarious. An-

---

"Langue et Style de Sherwood Anderson dans *Winesburg, Ohio*," from *Configuration Critique de Sherwood Anderson (Configuration Critique No. 6), La Revue des Lettres Modernes*, 1963. Reprinted by permission of *La Revue des Lettres Modernes*, Paris. Translated by John H. Ferres.

derson's style is about as simple as an engine-room full of dynamos."

Fitzgerald was quite right. However, like all Redskins in American literature, Anderson was very fond of resonant and colorful words. In one of his first tales, an advertising man (himself, actually) is filled with admiration for a railroad employee who really knows how to swear (the sort of gift Mark Twain also appreciated):

"Well, I'll tell you," said the advertising man. "I was just thinking what a good man he would be in the advertising business. He knows the value of words, that fellow does. Did you hear the way he made that conductor and that engineer look faded out like a scorched shirt-front? He knows how to use words and that's why I think he'd make an advertising man. How to use words . . . that's what advertising is, just using words, just picking them out like that fellow picked out his swear words, and then dropping them down just in the right place so they seem to mean something . . . words are the greatest thing ever invented" ["The Undeveloped Man," *Chicago Agricultural Advertising*, 1904].

Whitman would have said the same thing. Anderson knew this and felt very close to the author of *Leaves of Grass*, whom he imitated whenever he wrote verse. In the following quotations, for example, the voice is definitely that of Whitman: "In the daytime my city is the son of a dreamer. He has become the companion of thieves and prostitutes," or "O my beloved—men and women—I come into your presence. It is night and I am alone and I come to you. I open the window so that you may come in. I am a lover and I would touch you with the fingers of my hands," or again in the same poem, "Do you not see, O my beloved, that I am become strong to caress the woman! I caress all men and all women. I make myself naked. I am unafraid. I am a pure thing."

Like Whitman in "Song of Myself," Anderson proclaimed at the beginning of *Tar*: "I, Sherwood Anderson, an American man, in my youth did so and so." And, speaking of Tar, who is essentially one of his "avatars," to borrow a term from the *Bhagavad-Gita* which the Transcendentalists were fond of, Anderson confides: "He loved to say over horses' names, racing words, horse words." And shortly after Tar adds: " 'If you put words together in just a certain way, they sound nice even though you don't know what they mean.' "

Despite this love of words, their music and their mysteriously evocative power, Anderson mistrusted them where Whitman did not. He resisted their fascination as glittering playthings: "I have had a great fear of phrase-making. Words . . . are very tricky things. Look, for example, how that man Mencken can rattle words like dice in a box. . . . Being . . . slow in my nature, I do have to come to words slowly. I do not want to make them rattle." It is not surprising, therefore, that the language of *Winesburg, Ohio*, contrary to what one might expect from an advertising man given to hyperbole and gratuitous grandiloquence, should be colorless and rather flat. The style is quite unaffected, for the most part containing little that is striking or arresting. There is, in fact, a certain poverty of style, which is surprising considering the richness of the subject. But the language is really more emotional than sensuous. Anderson is interested primarily in the interior reality rather than in material appearances, and thus he emphasizes emotions, sentiments, and subjective impressions rather than sensory experience. Lionel Trilling has put this quite well: "In Anderson's world there are many emotions, or rather many instances of a few emotions, but, there are very few sights, sounds and smells, very little of the stuff of actuality. . . . His praise of the racehorses he said he loved gives us no sense of a horse; his Mississippi does not flow; his tall corn grows out of the soil of his dominating subjectivity. . . . There are many similarities of theme between Anderson and D. H. Lawrence, but . . . Lawrence had eyes for the substantial and even at his most doctrinaire he knew the world of appearance."

Despite its exaggeration and some oversimplification, this

description is substantially correct. Sufficient verification can be had by applying it, for example, to the beginning of "Nobody Knows":

The night was warm and cloudy and although it was not yet eight o'clock, the alleyway back of the *Eagle* office was pitch dark. A team of horses tied to a post somewhere in the darkness stamped on the hard-baked ground. A cat sprang from under George Willard's feet and ran away into the night. The young man was nervous. All day he had gone about his work like one dazed by a blow. In the alleyway he trembled as though with fright.

To be sure, one finds in this passage a certain number of visual and auditory (though no olfactory) impressions. But there are really very few. Imagine what D. H. Lawrence would have done with a similar subject. Here the emphasis is on the nervousness of George Willard. The rest of the description is simply a backdrop that is rather sparse and lifeless in its detail. This is especially true of his description of the corn, as Trilling has noted. Two pages later, one reads: "The corn was shoulder high and had been planted right down to the sidewalk." This is no real cornfield, but rather painted scenery. Not one adjective in the sentence evokes feeling. It is true we have just been told that the corn is green, but less to specify the color than to indicate the season when the story takes place.

At least in this work, then, Anderson employs a vocabulary that is limited and sometimes flat or banal. The same words are used over and over. A word as inexpressive as "thing" may turn up several times on a page. It is used no less than five times in the fourth paragraph of the introduction. Other words that reappear quite frequently are "feel" and "think"; these accord with the subjective element in *Winesburg, Ohio,* of course. Anderson uses them constantly to introduce the ideas and opinions of his characters. Another vague but favorite word is "fix." It is found throughout the book. In American usage it can mean almost anything. Dickens joked about it in his *American Notes*. But the joke was apparently lost on Anderson, assuming he even knew of it.

Here and there, it is true, a few terms borrowed from the language of the engineers and scientists spring up; technical words of fairly recent origin, such as "piston-rods of his machinery of expression" ("Hands"), "galvanized" ("Hands"), "neurotic" ("Surrender"). The truth is, however, that Anderson detested industrialism too much to seek enrichment of his vocabulary in its neologisms, as Whitman had done.

His taste for the idyllic country life led him toward archaisms of a non-literary and rustic flavor such as still survive in certain rural areas of the United States, words like "afoot" ("Hands"), "unto" ("Hands"), "to set afire" ("Terror"), "abloom" ("The Thinker"), etc. In short, he was looking for a certain familiar tone found, for instance, in expressions like "she got nowhere" ("Mother"), "back of" instead of "behind," etc.

Sometimes Anderson draws upon a biblical vocabulary, but in *Winesburg, Ohio* this is virtually confined to the four-part tale, "Godliness," about an old farmer who imagines himself to be an Old Testament patriarch, and "The Strength of God," the hero of which is a minister. In the former, one finds passages such as the following:

"Jehovah of Hosts," he cried, "send to me this night out of the womb of Katherine, a son. Let thy grace alight upon me. Send me a son to be called David who shall help me to pluck at last all of these lands out of the hands of the Philistines and turn them to Thy service and to the building of Thy kingdom on earth."

And the Reverend Curtis Hartman uses expressions like "the woman of my bosom," or declares: "I will grope my way out of darkness into the light of righteousness." Such passages remind us that despite the efforts of Anderson and his characters to break free from it, they are products of a frontier culture where men and women read the Bible daily and children learned it by heart. Biblical language thus came quite naturally to Anderson. When he uses a phrase like "burnt offer-

350 WINESBURG, OHIO: CRITICISM

ing," it is not an allusion but simply an everyday expression.

What was important to him, though, was not words in themselves, but the communication through their medium of intuitions that lay close to his heart: "If you are to become a writer," he has Kate Swift tell George Willard, "you'll have to stop fooling with words. . . . You must not become a mere peddler of words. The thing to learn is to know what people are thinking about, not what they say" ("The Teacher"). Words were not enough, then. One must have something to say and know how to communicate effectively with the reader. It is therefore important to master the art of using words in such a way that they produce precisely the effect one is seeking. Everything depends on style, not on words.

The most striking trait of Anderson's style is the extreme simplicity of its snytax. Most of his sentences are built according to the same rudimentary model: subject, verb, object, complement, or a variant of this scheme: complement, subject, verb, object. Such adverbial clauses as there are are mostly temporal and widely separated. It is the exact opposite of a periodic style. Anderson proceeds by accumulation and juxtaposition and almost never relies on subordination. His stories are a series of independent affirmations placed end to end and strung together by innumerable "ands." This is probably an equally accurate description of the style of Mark Twain, who came before him, and that of Ernest Hemingway, who came after. To quote Joseph Warren Beach, we are dealing here with the "great leveling democracy of the 'and.'"

The result of this is that the reader often has the impression of a story told by word of mouth. Anderson has his roots in the great American tradition of story-tellers which flourished in the Middle West in the frontier period at a time when the village grocery store was the center of social life in the rural community. At the store men would gather, on the porch in summer, around the red-hot stove in winter, to swap stories. Like these anonymous tellers of tales, each with his inexhaustible supply, like his own father in fact, Anderson was a born story-teller.

However, despite the monotonous and very simple structure of the sentences, despite the oral character of the tales and the frequent colloquialisms, his style is not really familiar, and only rarely does it have the spontaneity and naturalness of the folk tale. In fact there is always a kind of stiffness or dignity about it. It is as if the writer were refusing to let himself go, determined to retain mastery over himself and his expression, or constantly supplying evidence of restraint. This prose is never the prose of speech; it is really stylized speech. This is especially obvious in Anderson's strong aversion to both relative and personal pronouns. He prefers to repeat nouns, a device which confers both independence and dignity on each sentence. As a result these stories are like nothing heard now or then in a small-town grocery store. They bear quite undeniably the mark of the special genius of their author.

Strangely enough, there is no difference in tone or manner between passages of pure narration and dialogue; nor is there any between the utterances of the various characters. Everything is in the same tone. They all speak in the same way, that of Anderson himself. And this was precisely Anderson's intention. He was not trying to present a photographic image of life, nor a faithful record of conversation. He wanted to re-create life so that his stories would be the fruit of imagination rather than exact observation.

My own belief is that the writer with a notebook in his hand is always a bad workman, a man who distrusts his own imagination. Such a man describes actual scenes accurately, he puts down actual conversation.

But people do not converse in the book world as they do in life. Scenes of the imaginative world are not real scenes ["A Writer's Conception of Realism," from *The Sherwood Anderson Reader*].

The style which results from such a conception of fiction is not without its faults. Undoubtedly it is fairly well suited to his material. It permits unpretentious description of incidents occurring in the everyday life of apparently colorless people, as well as calm revelation of the drama of their interior lives. But in addition to its occasional monotony, it is often more heavy, awkward, and prolix than one would like. This is frequently a result of pointless repetition or carelessness. In the last six lines of "Adventure," for example, the word "face" appears three times. This lack of polish and conciseness is characteristic. Elsewhere the expression remains confused, probably because the ideas the author is trying to express have not been completely formulated or lifted clear of their inchoate confusion. This is true, for example, of the passage on the different kinds of "truths" near the end of the introduction. In short, it is a style that lacks style. Although Anderson admired Gertrude Stein, he never tried to write "perfect sentences" as she did. And this is why Hemingway, who at first had taken him for a master, quickly turned away from him. He was susceptible to the awkward charm of Anderson's rambling tales, but he was convinced of the need for tighter form and stricter aesthetics.

Anderson had a different conception. His aim was not to sculpture stories which would then take on a life of their own quite independent of their author, but rather to make his readers share certain emotions which he regarded as important. In this he was a genuine Redskin. He once wrote, one recalls, an "Apology for Crudity." Like Whitman, he wanted to sing his "Song of Myself," but in the form of stories instead of poems. Despite appearances, Anderson is fundamentally a lyric poet rather than a story-teller. This can be seen by a close look at the images he was obsessed by, images that keep recurring in his stories just when one least expects them.

On the most elementary level the images used by Anderson in *Winesburg, Ohio* serve merely to color a sentence, and usually they are no more than clichés: Wing Biddlebaum "was submerged in a sea of doubts" ("Hands") or "he was like a fish returned to the brook by the fisherman" ("Hands"). None of these images is woven into the texture of the story. In the final analysis, they are quite extraneous.

At the other extreme there are images with which Anderson tries to express the inexpressible, the secret soul of his characters, as in the passage where the hands of Wing Biddlebaum undergo a whole series of strange metamorphoses from piston rods to "the wings of an imprisoned bird" ("Hands"), and later "fluttering pennants of promise" that bring to mind Whitman's "pennants of joy." The surface resemblance is of no consequence, however. The real significance lies in the deep awareness Anderson evokes of the hidden life of people and things. These images have no plastic value. The author is not interested in painting the outside but in suggesting what is inside, "the infinitude within," as Henry Michaux calls it.

Hands, in fact, seem to fascinate Anderson. In *Winesburg, Ohio* there are the hands of Dr. Reefy, wise and still but gnarled and strong like his thought, and gentle, too, beneath their rough appearance, like the doctor himself. There is a peculiar significance in hands for Anderson. They are symbols whose meaning is revealed near the end of the book when, speaking of George Willard's hands, he explains: "With all his heart he wants to come close to some other human, touch someone with his hands, be touched by the hand of another" ("Sophistication"). They signify communication between human beings. Love passes through them from one human being to another, as the story of Wing Biddlebaum shows.

Quite the opposite of the stereotyped images which are part of everyone's language, these metaphors constitute the personal language of Anderson and serve to express what he feels at the deepest level of his being about people and things. He uses this language most effectively to suggest the absolute isolation of those inhabitants of Winesburg who are walled in by life and shut off from love. Some episodes, some relationships remain a mystery. It is left to the reader to divine the true meaning of the woman in "Loneliness" who lies hidden in the clump of elders. The stories that make up *Winesburg, Ohio* are meditations on life in the form of images. They express at once Anderson's conviction that life is absurd and the love he was unable to keep from feeling for everything that exists. He made this very clear in the second-last story: "One shudders at the thought of the meaninglessness of life while at the same instant . . . one loves life so intensely that tears come into the eyes" ("Sophistication"). And all his characters symbolize the impenetrable mystery of life which both fascinated and amazed him.

Sherwood Anderson's art is thus, in the final analysis, that of a poet. For this reason he sometimes expresses himself in a prose that is rhythmical, full of assonance and musical repetition, and very close to free verse. An example is this passage from "Hands":

The voice that had been low and trembling became shrill and loud. The bent figure straightened. With a kind of wriggle, like a fish returned to the brook by the fisherman, Biddlebaum the silent began to talk, striving to put into words the ideas that had been accumulated by his mind during long years of silence.

Wing Biddlebaum talked much with his hands. The slender expressive fingers, forever active, forever striving to conceal themselves in his pockets or behind his back, came forth and became the piston rods of his machinery of expression.

This is the style of a poet obeying his inspiration. Anderson once described to a friend the first burst of inspiration he ever had:

Suddenly I began to write as I had never written. It did not seem to be me sitting there holding the pen. There was no me. It was as though some mysterious force outside myself had taken possession of me.

There were people everywhere, thousands, millions of people wanting their stories told. . . .

It was as though one of these began to speak through me. The pen began to run over the paper. I did not seek for words. They were there. They seemed to leap out from my hand to the paper [*Letters*].

He wrote his stories in one go, never revising, and this doubtless explains the lack of polish in his style. He preferred to rewrite a story completely rather than correct it. "I have never been one who can correct, fill in, rework his stories. I must try and, when I fail, throw away. Some of my best stories have been written ten or twelve times" (*Memoirs*). Elsewhere he recognized: "I am a professional writer with, I admit, a good many marks of the eternal amateur on me" ("A Writer's Conception of Realism").

Does this mean he was an anarchist as far as aesthetics were concerned? Not at all. He denied that rules have any real usefulness, as he denied the validity of laws which self-conscious artists impose on their work, but he knew that his inspiration obeyed secret laws which gave form and meaning to everything he wrote. That is to say, he believed like the Transcendentalists and all romantics generally, in the possibility of an "organic" form, a living form growing naturally with the material that forms its substance. He elaborated on this one day for Dwight Macdonald:

Why, indeed there are laws. There are laws all such men as Babbitt will never in their life comprehend. There are laws within the laws, laws that ride over the laws. . . . This thing called form in art. It exists, of course. It is the force that holds the thing of loveliness together [*Letters*].

Anderson was essentially an inspired amateur, a romantic poet who expressed the insights of sensibility in tales that have more or less the appearance of realism. Like all the Redskins, he was convinced that art is synonymous with artifice and he preferred life. But life for him was not synonymous with disorder and anarchy; he tried to remain detached from it and to express its essential beauty and hidden form. He was, moreover, prepared to make the necessary concessions to art so that this form might reveal itself more clearly. In this way he was able to create the spontaneous, though carefully wrought prose of *Winesburg, Ohio*, at whose secrets the preceding analysis has merely hinted.

◆❀◆❀◆❀◆❀◆❀◆❀◆❀◆❀◆❀◆❀◆❀◆❀◆❀◆❀◆❀◆❀◆❀◆❀◆

MALCOLM COWLEY

Malcolm Cowley, critic, poet, and literary historian, is the author of *Exile's Return*, *The Literary Situation*, and *The Faulkner-Cowley File*, and has edited *The Portable Faulkner*, *The Portable Hemingway*, *The Portable Hawthorne*, and other books.

INTRODUCTION TO
WINESBURG, OHIO

Rereading Sherwood Anderson after many years, one feels again that his work is desperately uneven, but one is gratified to find that the best of it is as new and springlike as ever. There are many authors younger in years—he was born in 1876 —who made a great noise in their time, but whose books already belong among the horseless carriages in Henry Ford's museum at Greenfield Village. Anderson made a great noise too, when he published *Winesburg, Ohio* in 1919. The older critics scolded him, the younger ones praised him, as a man of the changing hour, yet he managed in that early work and others to be relatively timeless. There are moments in American life to which he gave not only the first but the final expression.

He soon became a writer's writer, the only story-teller of his generation who left his mark on the style and vision of the generation that followed. Hemingway, Faulkner, Wolfe, Stein-

beck, Caldwell, Saroyan, Henry Miller . . . each of these owes
an unmistakable debt to Anderson, and their names might
stand for dozens of others. Hemingway was regarded as his
disciple in 1920, when both men were living on the Near
North Side of Chicago, Faulkner says that he had written
very little, "poems and just amateur things," before meeting
Anderson in 1925 and becoming, for a time, his inseparable
companion. Looking at Anderson he thought to himself,
"Being a writer must be a wonderful life." He set to work on
his first novel, *Soldier's Pay*, for which Anderson found a publisher after the two men had ceased to be friends. Thomas
Wolfe proclaimed in 1936 that Anderson was "the only man
in America who ever taught me anything"; but they quar-
reled a year later, and Wolfe shouted that Anderson had shot
his bolt, that he was done as a writer. All the disciples left him
sooner or later, so that his influence was chiefly on their early
work; but still it was decisive. He opened doors for all of
them and gave them faith in themselves. With Whitman he
might have said:

I am the teacher of athletes,
He that by me spreads a wider breast than my own proves the width
   of my own,
He most honors my style who learns under it to destroy the teacher.

As the disciples were doing, most of Anderson's readers deserted him during the 1930s. He had been a fairly popular
writer for a few years after *Dark Laughter* (1925), but his last
stories and sketches, including some of his very best, had to
appear in a strange collection of second-line magazines, pam-
phlets, and Sunday supplements. One marvelous story called
"Daughters" remained in manuscript until six years after his
death in 1941. I suspect that the public would have liked him
better if he had been primarily a novelist, like Dreiser and
Lewis. He did publish seven novels, from *Windy McPherson's
Son* in 1916 to *Kit Brandon* in 1936, not to mention the others
he started and laid aside. Among the seven *Dark Laughter*

was his only best-seller, and *Poor White* (1920), the best of the lot, is studied in colleges as a picture of the industrial revolution in a small Midwestern town. There is, however, not one of the seven that is truly effective as a novel; not one that has balance and sustained force; not one that doesn't break apart into episodes or nebulize into a vague emotion.

His three personal narratives—*A Story-Teller's Story* (1924), *Tar: A Midwest Childhood* (1926), and *Sherwood Anderson's Memoirs* (1942)—are entertainingly inaccurate; indeed, they are almost as fictional as the novels, and quite as deficient in structure. They reveal that an element was missing in his mature life, rich as this was in other respects. It does not give us, and I doubt that Anderson himself possessed, the sense of moving ahead in a definite direction. All the drama of growth was confined to his early years. After finding his proper voice at the age of forty, Anderson didn't change as much as other serious writers; perhaps his steadfastness should make us thankful, considering that most American writers change for the worse. He had achieved a quality of emotional rather than factual truth and he preserved it to the end of his career, while doing little to refine, transform, or even understand it. Some of his last stories—by no means all of them—are richer and subtler than the early ones, but they are otherwise not much different or much better.

He was a writer who depended on inspiration, which is to say that he depended on feelings so deeply embedded in his personality that he was unable to direct them. He couldn't say to himself, "I shall produce such and such an effect in a book of such and such a length"; the book had to write or rather speak itself while Anderson listened as if to an inner voice. In his business life he showed a surprising talent for planning and manipulation. "One thing I've known always, instinctively," he told Floyd Dell, "—that's how to handle people, make them do as I please, be what I wanted them to be. I was in business for a long time and the truth is I was a smooth son of a bitch." He never learned to handle words in that smooth fashion. Writing was an activity he assigned to a different level of himself, the one on which he was emotional and unpractical. To reach that level sometimes required a sustained effort of the will. He might start a story like a man running hard to catch a train, but once it was caught he could settle back and let himself be carried—often to the wrong destination.

He knew instinctively whether one of his stories was right or wrong, but he didn't always know why. He could do what writers call "pencil work" on his manuscript, changing a word here and there, but he couldn't tighten the plot, delete weak passages, sharpen the dialogue, give a twist to the ending; if he wanted to improve the story, he had to wait for a return of the mood that had produced it, then write it over from beginning to end. There were stories like "Death in the Woods" that he rewrote a dozen times, at intervals of years, before he found what he thought was the right way of telling them. Sometimes, in different books, he published two or three versions of the same story, so that we can see how it grew in his subconscious mind. One characteristic of the subconscious is a defective sense of time: in dreams the old man sees himself as a boy, and the events of thirty or forty years may be jumbled together. Time as a logical succession of events was Anderson's greatest difficulty in writing novels or even long stories. He got his tenses confused and carried his heroes ten years forward or back in a single paragraph. His instinct was to present everything together, as in a dream.

When giving a lecture on "A Writer's Conception of Realism," he spoke of a half-dream that he had "over and over." "If I have been working intensely," he said, "I find myself unable to relax when I go to bed. Often I fall into a half-dream state and when I do, the faces of people begin to appear before me. They seem to snap into place before my eyes, stay there, sometimes for a short period, sometimes longer. There are smiling faces, leering ugly faces, tired faces, hopeful faces. . . . I have a kind of illusion about this matter," he continued. "It is, no doubt, due to a story-teller's point of view. I have the feeling that the faces that appear before me thus at night are those of people who want their stories told and whom I have neglected."

He would have liked to tell the stories of all the faces he had ever seen. He was essentially a story-teller, as he kept insisting, but his art was of a special type, belonging to an oral rather than a written tradition. It used to be the fashion to compare him with Chekhov and say that he had learned his art from the Russians. Anderson insisted that, except for Turgenev, he hadn't read any Russians when the comparisons were being made. Most of his literary masters were English or American: George Borrow, Walt Whitman, Mark Twain (more than he admitted), and Gertrude Stein. D. H. Lawrence was a less fortunate influence, but only on his later work. His earliest and perhaps his principal teacher was his father, "Irve" Anderson, who used to entertain whole barrooms with tales of his impossible adventures in the Civil War. A great many of the son's best stories, too, were told first in saloons. Later he would become what he called "an almighty scribbler" and would travel about the country with dozens of pencils and reams of paper, the tools of his trade. "I am one," he said, "who loves, like a drunkard his drink, the smell of ink, and the sight of a great pile of white paper that may be scrawled upon always gladdens me"; but his earlier impulse had been to speak, not write, his stories. The best of them retain the language, the pace, and one might even say the gestures of a man talking unhurriedly to his friends.

Within the oral tradition, Anderson had his own picture of what a story should be. He was not interested in telling conventional folk tales, those in which events are more important than emotions. American folk tales usually end with a "snap-

per"—that is, after starting with the plausible, they progress
through the barely possible to the flatly incredible, then wait
for a laugh. Magazine fiction used to follow—and much of it
still does—a pattern leading to a different sort of snapper, one
that calls for a gasp of surprise or relief instead of a guffaw.
Anderson broke the pattern by writing stories that not only
lacked snappers, in most cases, but even had no plots in the
usual sense. The tales he told in his Midwestern drawl were
not incidents or episodes, they were *moments*, each complete
in itself.

The best of the moments in *Winesburg, Ohio* is called "The
Untold Lie." The story, which I have to summarize at the
risk of spoiling it, is about two farm hands husking corn in a
field at dusk. Ray Pearson is small, serious, and middle-aged,
the father of half a dozen thin-legged children; Hal Winters
is big and young, with the reputation of being a bad one. Suddenly he says to the older man, "I've got Nell Gunther in
trouble. I'm telling you, but keep your mouth shut." He puts
his two hands on Ray's shoulders and looks down into his
eyes. "Well, old daddy," he says, "come on, advise me. Perhaps you've been in the same fix yourself. I know what everyone would say is the right thing to do, but what do you say?"
Then the author steps back to look at his characters. "There
they stood," he tells us, "in the big empty field with the quiet
corn shocks standing in rows behind them and the red and
yellow hills in the distance, and from being just two indifferent workmen they had become all alive to each other."

That single moment of aliveness—that epiphany, as Joyce
would have called it, that sudden reaching out of two characters through walls of inarticulateness and misunderstanding
—is the effect that Anderson is trying to create for his readers
or listeners. There is more to the story, of course, but it is
chiefly designed to bring the moment into relief. Ray Pearson
thinks of his own marriage, to a girl he got into trouble, and
turns away from Hal without being able to say the expected

words about duty. Later that evening he is seized by a sudden impulse to warn the younger man against being tricked into bondage. He runs awkwardly across the fields, crying out that children are only the accidents of life. Then he meets Hal and stops, unable to repeat the words that he had shouted into the wind. It is Hal who breaks the silence. "I've already made up my mind," he says, taking Ray by the coat and shaking him. "Nell ain't no fool. . . . I want to marry her. I want to settle down and have kids." Both men laugh, as if they had forgotten what happened in the cornfield. Ray walks away into the darkness, thinking pleasantly now of his children and muttering to himself, "It's just as well. Whatever I told him would have been a lie." There has been a moment in the lives of two men. The moment has passed and the briefly established communion has been broken, yet we feel that each man has revealed his essential being. It is as if a gulf had opened in the level Ohio cornfield and as if, for one moment, a light had shone from the depths, illuminating everything that happened or would ever happen to both of them.

That moment of revelation was the story Anderson told over and over, but without exhausting its freshness, for the story had as many variations as there were faces in his dreams. Behind one face was a moment of defiance; behind another, a moment of resignation (as when Alice Hindman forces herself "to face bravely the fact that many people must live and die alone, even in Winesburg"); behind a third face was a moment of self-discovery; behind a fourth was a moment of deliberate self-delusion. This fourth might have been the face of the author's sister, as he describes her in a chapter of *Sherwood Anderson's Memoirs*. Unlike the other girls she had no beau, and so she went walking with her brother Sherwood, pretending that he was someone else. "It's beautiful, isn't it, James?" she said, looking at the wind ripples that passed in the moonlight over a field of ripening wheat. Then she kissed him and whispered, "Do you love me, James?"—and all her loneliness and flight from reality were summed up in those words. Anderson had that gift for summing up, for pouring a lifetime into a moment.

There must have been many such moments of truth in his own life, and there was one in particular that has become an American legend. After serving as a volunteer in the Spanish-American War; after supplementing his one year in high school with a much later year at Wittenberg Academy; and after becoming a locally famous copywriter in a Chicago advertising agency, Anderson had launched into business for himself; by the age of thirty-six he had been for some years the chief owner and general manager of a paint factory in Elyria, Ohio. The factory had prospered for a time, chiefly because of Anderson's talent for writing persuasive circulars, and he sometimes had visions of becoming a paint baron or a duke of industry. He had other visions too, of being sentenced to serve out his life as a businessman. At the time he was already writing novels—in fact he had four of them under way—and he began to feel that his advertising circulars were insulting to the dignity of words. "The impression got abroad—I perhaps encouraged it," Anderson says, "—that I was overworking, was on the point of a nervous breakdown. . . . The thought occurred to me that if men thought me a little insane they would forgive me if I lit out, left the business in which they invested their money on their hands." Then came the moment to which he would always return in his memoirs and in his fiction. He was dictating a letter: "The goods about which you have inquired are the best of their kind made in the—" when suddenly he stopped without completing the phrase. He looked at his secretary for a long time, and she looked at him until they both grew pale. Then he said with the American laugh that covers all sorts of meanings, "I have been wading in a long river and my feet are wet." He went out of the office for the last time and started walking eastward toward Cleveland along a railroad track. "There were," he says, "five or six dollars in my pocket."

So far I have been paraphrasing Anderson's account—or two of his many accounts, for he kept changing them—of an incident that his biographers have reconstructed from other sources. Those others give a different picture of what happened at the paint factory on November 27, 1912. Anderson had been struggling under an accumulation of marital, artistic, and business worries. Instead of pretending to be a little crazy so that investors would forgive him for losing their money, he was actually—so the medical records show—on the brink of nervous collapse. Instead of making a conscious decision to abandon his wife, his three children, and his business career, he acted as if in a trance. There was truly a decision, but it was made by something deeper than his conscious will; one feels that his whole being, psyche and soma together, was rejecting the life of a harried businessman. He had made no plans, however, for leading a different life. After four days of aimless wandering, he was recognized in Cleveland and taken to a hospital, where he was found to be suffering from exhaustion and aphasia.

Much later, in telling the story time after time, Anderson forgot or concealed the painful details of his flight and presented it as a pattern of conduct for others to follow. What we need in America, he liked to say, is a new class of individuals who, "at any physical cost to themselves and others"— Anderson must have been thinking of his first wife—will "agree to quit working, to loaf, to refuse to be hurried or try to get on in the world." In the next generation there would be hundreds of young men, readers of Anderson, who rejected the dream of financial success and tried to live as artists and individuals. For them Anderson's flight from the paint factory became a heroic exploit, as memorable as the choice made by Ibsen's Nora when she walked out of her doll's house and slammed the door. For Anderson himself when writing his memoirs, it was the central moment of his career.

Yet the real effect of the moment on his personal life was less drastic or immediate than one would guess from the compulsive fashion in which he kept writing about it. He didn't continue wandering from city to city, trading his tales for bread and preaching against success. After being released from the hospital, he went back to Elyria, wound up his business affairs, then took the train for Chicago, where he talked himself into a job with the same advertising agency that had employed him before he went into business for himself. As soon as he had the job, he sent for his wife and children. He continued to write persuasive circulars—corrupting the language, as he said—and worked on his novels and stories chiefly at night, as he had done while running a factory. It would be nearly two years before he separated from his first wife. It would be ten years before he left the advertising business to support himself entirely by writing, and then the change would result from a gradual process of getting published and finding readers, instead of being the sequel to a moment of truth.

Those moments at the center of Anderson's often marvelous stories were moments, in general, without a sequel; they existed separately and timelessly. That explains why he couldn't write novels and why, with a single exception, he never even wrote a book in the strict sense of the word. A book should have a structure and a development, whereas for Anderson there was chiefly the flash of lightning that revealed a life without changing it.

The single exception was of course *Winesburg, Ohio*. In structure the book lies midway between the novel proper and the mere collection of stories. Like several famous books by more recent authors, all early readers of Anderson—like Faulkner's *The Unvanquished* and *Go Down, Moses*, like Steinbeck's *Tortilla Flat* and *The Pastures of Heaven*, like

Caldwell's *Georgia Boy*—it is a cycle of stories with several unifying elements, including a single background, a prevailing tone, and a central character. These elements can be found in all the cycles, but the best of them also have an underlying plot that is advanced or enriched by each of the stories. In *Winesburg* the underlying plot or fable, though hard to recognize, is unmistakably present, and I think it might be summarized as follows:

George Willard is growing up in a friendly town full of solitary persons; the author calls them "grotesques." Their lives have been distorted not, as Anderson tells us in his prologue, by their each having seized upon a single truth, but rather by their inability to express themselves. Since they cannot truly communicate with others, they have all become emotional cripples. Most of the grotesques are attracted one by one to George Willard; they feel that he might be able to help them. In those moments of truth that Anderson loves to describe, they try to explain themselves to George, believing that he alone in Winesburg has an instinct for finding the right words and using them honestly. They urge him to preserve and develop his gift. "You must not become a mere peddler of words," Kate Swift the teacher insists, taking hold of his shoulders. "The thing to learn is to know what people are thinking about, not what they say." Dr. Parcival tells him, "If something happens perhaps you will be able to write the book I may never get written." All the grotesques hope that George Willard will some day speak what is in their hearts and thus re-establish their connection with mankind. George is too young to understand them at the time, but the book ends with what seems to be the promise that, after leaving Winesburg, he will become the voice of inarticulate men and women in all the forgotten towns.

If the promise is truly implied, and if Anderson felt he was keeping it when writing "Hands" and the stories that followed, then *Winesburg, Ohio* is far from the pessimistic or destructive or morbidly sexual work it was once attacked for being. Instead it is a work of love, an attempt to break down the walls that divide one person from another, and also, in its own fashion, a celebration of small-town life in the lost days of good will and innocence.

❀◈❀

WALDO FRANK

Waldo Frank has published more than thirty books, including novels, histories, and criticism, among them *Chart for Rough Waters* and *The Rediscovery of Man*. As managing editor of *The Seven Arts*, he published several chapters of *Winesburg, Ohio* in 1917.

WINESBURG, OHIO
AFTER TWENTY YEARS

Sherwood Anderson wrote his most famous book about a generation ago; and it reveals a Mid-American world that already then was a generation dead. A full half-century therefore divides the mind that reads the book today from the life it portrays. Since, from this adequate perspective, the work stands firm in its form, true in its livingness, strong in its light upon our present, it is clear that *Winesburg, Ohio* is a classic.

I had not reread the book since it was published. Many of its chapters were mailed to me in his own writing by Anderson himself, who then lived in Chicago and worked for an advertising house near Jackson Boulevard. I still see the long sprawling potent hand on the cheap paper, feel the luminous life that swelled miraculously from it. I recall sending him back one story which I wished to publish in *The Seven Arts*, because it was written down totally without commas; a few days later, it came back to me with commas sedulously spaced after

From "Homage to Sherwood Anderson" (*Story*, September–October, 1941). Copyright 1941 by Story Magazine, Inc. Reprinted by permission of Story Magazine, Inc.

each fourth or fifth word, irrespective of meaning. I had no doubt of the significance of this prose; otherwise, in 1916 I should not with such assurance have entitled my first essay on Anderson "Emerging Greatness"; but I know now that accidentals like the handwriting and the punctuation somewhat obscured for me, as the man's homespun did for many, the actual lineaments of this clear art. It is a dangerous hazard to reread, after twenty-five years, a book involved in the dreams and fervors of one's youth; it is a blessing when that book stands forth from the test a rediscovery . . . indeed a prophecy and an illumination.

The first impressive realization that came to me with my rereading was that *Winesburg* has form. The book as a whole has form; and most of the stories have form: the work is an integral creation. The form is lyrical. It is not related, even remotely, to the aesthetic of Chekhov; nor to that of Balzac, Flaubert, Maupassant, Tolstoi, Melville. These masters of the short story used the narrative or dramatic art: a linear progression rising to a peak or an immediate complex of character-forces impinging upon each other in a certain action that fulfilled them and rounded the story. For an analogy to the aesthetic of the Winesburg tales, one must go to music, perhaps to the songs that Schubert featly wove from old refrains; or to the lyric art of the Old Testament psalmists and prophets in whom the literary medium was so allied to music that their texts have always been sung in the synagogues. The *Winesburg* design is quite uniform: a theme-statement of a character with his mood, followed by a recounting of actions that are merely variations on the theme. These variations make incarnate what has already been revealed to the reader; they weave the theme into life by the always subordinate confrontation of other characters (usually one) and by an evocation of landscape and village. In some of the tales, there is a secondary theme-statement followed by other variations. In a few, straight narrative is attempted; and these are the least successful.

This lyric, musical form has significance, and the tales' contents make it clear. But it is important, first, to note that the cant judgment of Sherwood Anderson as a naïve, almost illiterate story-teller (a judgment which he himself encouraged with a good deal of nonsense about his literary innocence) is false. The substance of *Winesburg* is impressive, is alive, because it has been superbly *formed*. There are occasional superficial carelessnesses of language; on the whole, the prose is perfect in its selective economy and in its melodious flow; the choice of details is stript, strong, sure; the movement is an unswerving musical fulfillment of the already stated theme. Like Schubert, and like the Old Testament story-tellers, the author of *Winesburg* comes at the end of a psychological process; is a man with an inherited culture and a deeply assimilated skill. He is a type of the achieved artist.

The theme of the tales taken as a whole follows the same pattern as the individual "chapters"—although less precisely. "Hands," the first chapter, tells of Adolph Myers, alias Wing Biddlebaum, the unfortunate schoolteacher with sensitive, wandering, caressing hands, who gets into trouble because his loving touch upon his pupils is misinterpreted by a half-wit boy and the crude obscene men of the town. Because the tale is concretely, poetically realized, its symbolism is true; and because this symbolism is not intellectualized, not schematized, it would be false to tear it from its flesh-and-blood texture. Suffice it to say that the story suggests the tragic ambivalence of hands, which is the fate of all the characters of Winesburg. Hands, at the turn of the century, were making machines, making all sorts of things ("the thing is in the saddle"); making the world that was unmaking the tender, sensitive, intimate lives of the folk in their villages and farms. Hands are made for loving; but hands making mechanical things grow callous, preoccupied . . . fail at love. The second story is a straight variant of the theme; here, it is not the hand, the maker, that goes wrong; it is *thought*, which Doctor Reefy turns into written words—ineffectual scraps of wisdom jotted down, that become paper pills cluttering his pocket. The third chapter, "Mother," completes the theme-statement. Woman, the creator, the lover: the principle incarnate in Wing Biddle-baum's hands and in Doctor Reefy's thoughts, states the theme centrally. The form of the mother, frustrate, lonely, at last desperate, pervades the variations that make the rest of the book: a continuity of variation swelling, swirling into the cor-ners and crannies of the village life; and at length closing in the mother's death, in the loss forever of the $800 which Eliza-beth Willard had kept for twenty years to give her son his start away from Winesburg, and in the son's wistful departure. "He thought of little things—" as the train pulled out; they have become motes and beams carrying a distant sun to the reader.

I have spoken of suggested symbols. Suggestion, if you will *indirection*, is the quality of this lyric form; and no more *di-rect* expression could have been devised for a book which so precisely portrays a world avid for the expression of eternal truths and forced, by the decay of its old cultural foundation, to seek truth anarchically, hopelessly, indirectly.

It has become a critical commonplace that Winesburg faith-fully portrays the midwest village of two thousand souls dur-ing the post-civil war pre-motor age. Let us look. . . . No even bearably married couple is to be found in Winesburg; there are few marriages in the book, and these without ex-ception are described as the harnessing together of strangers by the bondage of sex or a morality hostile to the spirit. There is no communion with children. There is no fulfilled sex life, sex being an obsession, a frustration and a trap. There is no normal sociability between men and women: souls lonely as carnivorae for once in their lives burst into melodic plaint to one another, and lapse into solipsistic silence. There is indeed more muttering than talk. There is no congregated worship, and no strength to organized religion except in the sense of a strong barrier; as in the piteous tales of the Reverend Hart-man who sins by knocking a piece from his stained-glass church window (part of the figure of Christ) in order to gaze at the body of [Kate Swift] in bed. There is almost no joy, beyond the momentary joy of contemplating nature. And the most mature of the characters, Doctor Reefy, Seth Richmond, Elizabeth Willard, the Rev. Hartman, et al., do not evolve beyond a sharp negation of the things that *are*, in favor of a nebulous dream of "life."

Now, these omissions are purposive; and as aesthetically true as they are factually false. The author's art, perhaps unconsciously to himself, traces the frontier of emotional and spiritual action which, in that deliquescence of an agrarian culture which was rotten long ere it was ripe, was a line of *decay*, a domain of deprivation. In those very institutions and traditions which had been the base of the world's health, Winesburg was found wanting.

The positive substance of the book is the solitariness and struggle of the soul which has lost its ancestral props: the energy of the book is the release from these old forms into a subliminal search for new ones. The farms of Robert Frost's *North of Boston* are also peopled by broken, lonely lives; but their despair is hard, heroic. The folk of Winesburg are soft in a tenderness, in a nebulous searchfulness, that have gone farther in decay than the still standing families and churches of Frost's New England. In all the book, only irony—the author's irony—is hard.

This trait of Sherwood Anderson has been too little recognized. Consider the acrid irony in "Nobody Knows," where sex fulfillment ends in the boy's cowardly sigh of relief that "she hasn't got anything on me. Nobody knows"; in "The Awakening," that turns a moment of mystical insight into a brutal, humiliating sexual frustration; in "The Untold Lie" (one of the great stories of the world); in the chapters of Jesse Bentley, "the man of God" who is transformed by the sling of his grandchild, David, into a clumsy, puny, ineffectual Goliath. This hardness of irony in the author points to his spiritual transcendence over his subjects. Anderson has inherited intact a strength long since vaporized in Winesburg—and yet the heritage of Winesburg. His sureness of vision and of grasp enable him to incarnate in a form very precise the inchoate emotions of his people. To portray the deliquescence of America's agrarian culture beneath the impact of the untamed machine age required a man spiritually advanced beyond that culture's death. This is a law of art (and of ethic) ignored by the hardboiled Hemingway school, who depict their gangsters *on the level of the gangsters.*

Sherwood Anderson liked to think of himself as a primitive or neo-primitive artist; as a naïve unlettered story-teller. The truth is, that he belonged at the end of a cultural process, and shares the technical perfection which, within the limits of the culture's forms, only the terminal man achieves. One book was the pabulum of these people: the Bible. And a Testamental accent and vision modulate every page of Sherwood Anderson's great story. Moreover, the nebulosity of these poor souls' search is an end, a chaos *after* a world. That world was already drooping when it crossed the ocean; it had been, in England, a world of revealed religion and sacramental marriage, of the May dance and the sense of each man's life as mystery and mission. It lives in the past of Winesburg; it has become a beat and a refrain in the blood. In the actual experience of these men and women, it is a recidivism, a lapse away into organic echoes. Thus, of revealed religion and sacramental marriage, of the structures of social and personal responsibilities, nothing remains on the record but the memory and the dynamic yearning. Life has become a Prompter with the text of the dialogue and even the stage missing.

In sum, Sherwood Anderson is a mature voice singing a culture at its close; singing it with the technical skill of, literally, the *past master.* What in Winesburg, Ohio, of the year 1900 was authentic? The old strong concept of marriage? No: only the inherited knowledge that the embrace of man and woman must create a sacrament again. The old dogmas of the churches? No: only the inherited knowledge that there is God —even in sin, there is God; and that for want of a living Body formed of this new world, God is revealed in animistic gods of the corn, and even in the phallus. Thus the artist, distilling the eternal from the old doomed ways, becomes the prophet.

Sherwood Anderson's place at the end of a cultural cycle finds eloquent corroboration in the quality of his immediate imitators and disciples. Ernest Hemingway turned the nebulous seeking softness of the master's characters into a hardshell bravado. Winesburg's men and women are old souls, inheritors of a great Christian culture who have been abandoned and doomed to a progressive emptiness by the invasion of the unmastered Machine. (This is a process now at its nadir in the world.) In Anderson, however, these lives are transfigured by a mature and virile artist who is able to crystallize what is eternal in them as an aesthetic value. In Hemingway, an adolescent rationalizes the emptiness (which flatters his own) into a rhetorical terseness which flatters the emptiness of the reader; and the essential formlessness of the story is slicked up into plots borrowed from the thrillers. In Thomas Wolfe, the same formlessness becomes grandiose, the nebulosity becomes an elephantiasis, the yearning and lostness discreetly lyricized in Winesburg becomes a flatulent, auto-erotic *Ding an Sich*. What is vital since Anderson in American letters (a great deal, varying from such men as Faulkner and Caldwell through Hart Crane to such young poets as Kenneth Patchen and Muriel Rukeyser) is independent of the *Winesburg* tradition. But that is another story. . . .

The perfect readability of this book within our agonizing world proves the potential that lived—needing only to be transfigured—within a world already gone when *Winesburg* was written. Here are intrinsically great stories: as great as any in our language. The author, intellectually bound to the decadence of the agrarian age that he revealed, proves in himself a vital spirit, a creative promise that are ours. The village of these queer men beating the innocent bystander to prove they are not queer, of these sex-starved women running naked through the summer rain, was after all pregnant of the Great Tradition. The tender and humbly precise artist who painted these portraits bespoke the Tradition's still unimagined future.

MAXWELL GEISMAR

Maxwell Geismar is the author of a number of books on the twentieth-century American novel, among them *American Moderns: From Rebellion to Conformity, Rebels and Ancestors: The American Novel, 1890–1915,* and *Writers in Crisis: The American Novel, 1925–1940.*

SHERWOOD ANDERSON:
LAST OF THE TOWNSMEN

. . . Does *Winesburg, Ohio* belong to the "literature of revolt," as Ernest Boyd says—a revolt against "the great illusions of American civilization"? Is it a chronicle of those "cramped spirits," as Carl Van Doren says, who have been "repressed by village life"? On another level, does *Winesburg* deserve the charges of sexual perversion hurled at its author when the book appeared—was Anderson really the "Phallic Chekhov"? ("Was I a goner?" Anderson kept asking himself.) There were other charges, too, almost as horrific, which accused him of dealing with "commonplace people"—and certainly, for the conservatives of 1919, *Winesburg* may have appeared to be tunneling under all the established values of American life. And for some of the radicals of the day, *Winesburg was* exposing the sewers, and opening for public inspec-

---

From *The Last of The Provincials* by Maxwell Geismar (Boston: Houghton Mifflin, 1948). Copyright 1943, 1947, 1948 by Maxwell Geismar. Reprinted by permission of the publishers.

tion the inadequate drainage system of the luxurious American psyche.

Contemporary judgments of an important book usually reveal more of the contemporary than of judgment. Perhaps there was something "revolutionary" in these brief sketches of some Ohio townspeople: dentists, telegraph operators, rundown hotel-keepers, misunderstood grocers, and mournful mechanics. In the past our writers had often turned in dismay from such average figures of an average American order: inconsequential lives which Anderson set up against the Shakespearean nobles and the "super-subtle fry" of Henry James. To make matters worse, these obscure personages had even more obscure maladies, which, once recognized, were to persist and infect all future chronicles of small-town life from a sentimental *Our Town* to a sensational *Kings Row*. The hero of "Hands," for example, is a champion strawberry-picker—but Wing Biddlebaum is an inhibited champion, a homosexual strawberry-picker. His profession and his repressions may have seemed equally curious to some readers in the early twenties; and this array of ailing ordinary souls in *Winesburg* culminates with Anderson's tormented preacher who gazes out from his church upon an almost naked female schoolteacher—a teacher, moreover, who is *smoking*. In these respects, *Winesburg* does help to inaugurate a decade of revolt. It foreshadows the imminent crusade against bourgeois, Victorian, and puritanical taboos: it sets the stage for O'Neill's entrance.

Yet, preoccupied as Anderson may seem to be with sexual maladjustment, very early in the book you realize that his concern is not with human copulation, as it were, but with human isolation: and sex, which is a prelude to love as well as an ending, is the method used by Anderson, like D. H. Lawrence, to convey this isolation.

In "Surrender," Louise Bentley gives herself to her lover—because she is afraid that "there was no way to break through the wall that had shut her off from the joy of life"—

That was not what she wanted, but it was so the young man had interpreted her approach to him, and so anxious was she to achieve something else that she made no resistance.

Louise Bentley's story, to be sure, is "a story of human misunderstanding." But aren't all these stories about an inarticulate human misunderstanding? This "vague and intangible hunger" of Louise Bentley's for love and understanding in *Winesburg*, a hunger which, misunderstood, leads only to hatred of her husband, her son, and love itself, is symptomatic. In another of the stories, "Adventure," Alice Hindman, deserted by her lover, growing "old and queer," wants to ask the middle-aged drug clerk, Will Hurley, to sit with her, but again she is afraid he will not understand. "It is not him [that] I want. . . . I want to avoid being so much alone." Nor is this sentiment confined merely to women in Winesburg. The hero of "The Thinker," stumbles forward through the half-darkness feeling himself "an outcast in his own town." And in "Tandy" a visitor to Winesburg voices the underlying if always obscurely felt emotion of the town. "I am a lover and have not found my thing to love. That is a big point, if you know enough to realize what I mean. It makes my destruction inevitable, you see."

In a casual phrase uttered by the "stranger" of the story (as many of Anderson's finest intuitions are likely to appear in these "unnecessary" characters and oblique references) Anderson gives the crux of his message. The point of *Winesburg* is precisely that, while human understanding is so often disfigured and disjointed here—it is still possible. These people *are* lovers, and if their object of love hasn't been found, it *can* be found. "Many people must live and die alone even in Winesburg," Anderson says, and the "even," which invites a comparison, embodies the theme. This is surely the central meaning of the volume: the psychological factor that holds these apparently scattered and "plotless" sketches together and gives them an inner unity, just as the village scene gives them an outward unity.

For is it merely the later decades of chance and change which give *Winesburg* its haunting and tender quality today— its fragrance of fruit orchards, and its particular affectionate feeling for all the forms and habits of a disappearing rural society? "In those days," Anderson is fond of saying when he introduces his village customs and oddities, and how the phrase grows on us as we read the book! In those days when an older agrarian order bodied forth its enthusiasts and visionaries: when "servants" were unheard of in Winesburg, but hired help sat at table with the rest of the family; when "ideas in regard to social classes had hardly begun to exist" and all young women were simply "nice" or not nice. (And who could guess what orgies were held in Sandusky of a Saturday night? although Tom Little knows the people in the towns along his railroad "better than a city man knows the people who live in his apartment building.") There were trotting races in Medina in those days, when Whitney didn't own the horses, and ball games in which Ruppert didn't own the ballplayers, and the farmer by his stove was not yet talking "as glibly and sense-lessly as the best city man of us all." The figure of God was big in the hearts of men in those days, when the Bible was the only best-seller, and in the spring, after the rains, when the country around Winesburg was so fresh and delightful, the wagons of berry-pickers would be going by the Fair Grounds. Only a few, Anderson says, know the sweetness of "the twisted apples" which are left in the orchards of Winesburg after the best of the apples have been shipped off to the cities—and often the personages of the town, like its fruit, seem all the more tender for their crabbed appearance.

No, *Winesburg* is not a radical but a nostalgic document. This opening gun for a decade of revolt is not an indictment but an evocation of a society. As you follow Anderson's course to this point—the increasing fear of a standardized American social arrangement and the distaste for contemporary life which pervades his early novels as against the return, in *Mid-American Chants*, to the belief of his fathers in village streets and to those rich Midwestern cornfields through which you approach his group of Ohio tales—you see, certainly, that *Winesburg* answers his early conflicts. Like the stranger of his story, Anderson has found his "thing to love," the thing for which he has been searching, and without which, so he believes, his own destruction would be inevitable.

There are unpleasant events even in Winesburg. Always defending the part of imagination in his work, and proclaiming the "fact" to be subordinated to his fancy, Anderson is also firmly rooted in reality. "Into their lives," he remarks about one of his families here, "came little that was not coarse and brutal, and they were themselves coarse and brutal." Still, these older forms of cruelty sometimes had "a kind of beautiful childlike innocence"—and in the village life of Winesburg is Anderson's memory of a kind of innocence that marked American society before its descent into sin: with the industrial mistress as the new Eve, and the dynamo installed in the serpent's lair.

All the same—it *is* a memory. However real this village scene in Anderson's thoughts, it is nevertheless remote in fact; and can one live in a state of imaginary innocence? The print of the machine is on Winesburg itself. In "Godliness," Jesse Bentley realizes that the atmosphere of old times and places which he had always cultivated in his thoughts "was strange and foreign to the thing that was growing up in the minds of others":

The beginning of the most materialistic age in the history of the world . . . when the will to power would replace the will to serve and beauty would be well-nigh forgotten in the terrible headlong rush of mankind toward the acquiring of possessions, was telling its story to Jesse the man of God as it was to the men about him.

And the pressure of the new materialism grows stronger as *Winesburg* draws to a close, as the earlier compassion goes out of the tales and the stress on human inversion and social disorganization increases. While the neurotics "whom industrialism was to bring in such numbers" play out their role, the advent of the factories brings to a halting climax this account of an earlier rural existence.

In the final sections of the book, moreover, Anderson falls back upon a sort of literary sensationalism, and this pattern of a weak ending will recur in his work. It is a technical error, but is it a purely personal failing? Anderson is an advocate of the "plotless story," but is the story of American life, thus far, a little too plotless? Sherwood Anderson's history, as I say, is to be one of perpetual change, and already, in barely three years of a full twenty-five-year span of literary work, we have watched his transformation from a rebellious and power-seeking individualist to the lover of his communal Ohio tales: what he started out by condemning, he has already come to cherish. Yet the central issue remains: when Anderson turns from this rural scene, what is there in his own age that he can equally give himself to and belong with in order to avoid the threat of spiritual destruction?

We shall watch his next attempt to solve this problem while he traces the history of his native heritage under the pressure of social change, and leaves these tender and disappearing memories of Winesburg, Ohio. "Let peace brood over this carcass," says the young preacher of the tales in a testament to his dead father, and Sherwood Anderson might echo the sentiment as he mourns the passing of provincial life. . . .

EDWIN FUSSELL

Edwin Fussell has taught at the University of California at Berkeley and at Pomona College, and is Professor of English at the Claremont Graduate School and University Center, Claremont, California. He is the author of *Edwin Arlington Robinson* and *Frontier: American Literature and the American West,* and co-editor of *The Major Critics: The Development of English Literary Criticism.*
*

WINESBURG, OHIO:
ART AND ISOLATION

In 1915–16, when the sketches collected in *Winesburg, Ohio* were written, American culture was in the process of making its way from muck-raking to depth psychology; they have in common the discovery of hidden truth behind false appearances, and no one is going to be much surprised at the fact that such a deeply representative work of the time is likewise organized around the prevailing idea of "revelation" ("The people of the town thought of her as a confirmed old maid. . . . In reality she was the most eagerly passionate soul among them" ("The Teacher").). Anderson called attention to this aspect of the book's method when he dedicated it to the memory of his mother, "whose keen observations on the life about her first awoke in me the hunger to see beneath the surface of lives." All observation of the book is more or less constrained to begin from this primary motivation—"to see

From *Modern Fiction Studies* VI (Summer 1960). Reprinted by permisson of Purdue Research Foundation and Edwin Fussell.

beneath the surface of lives"—and to proceed to admit the improbability of there arising from this motivation fiction of the kind that we call realistic or naturalistic (those kinds being much less in a hurry to leave the surfaces behind). Recent readings are thus rightly concerned with revision of the 1920s' picture of a "realistic" Anderson—in the 1920s anyone who tried to tell the truth was a "realist"—and with the elucidation of Anderson's more lyric achievement: they are properly concerned with defining the emotions that sustain *Winesburg, Ohio*, for example, and with observing the means by which Anderson was occasionally able to render these emotions with such sweetness and clarity.

It goes without saying that the emotions are loneliness and incompletion, particularly as these emotions take their source from some failure of affection or of creative expression. There is no disagreement on this score: the new criticism takes up where the old criticism left off. Whether viewed as a writer of "exposé" or as a minor poet in prose, Anderson is indisputably the man who writes about discontinuity among persons and about the behaviors and feelings that spring from that discontinuity. Stated so baldly, it does not perhaps at once strike us as a theme capable of supporting a very ambitious fictional *oeuvre* (though it is not quite fair to imply that Anderson has nothing else to say); and we may even feel that without some act of judgment entered by the participating intelligence, or alternatively some connections made with other and more general truths, this vision of isolation may not be capable of supporting more than a static description of a pathetic situation. Yet it is particularly the possibility of such an act of judgment on Anderson's part, or of such a general extension of meaning, with respect to the pathos of his materials, that is most persistently ignored (perhaps because the pathos is in its own way so good); so that readers who come to *Winesburg*, or who come back, fresh from the criticism of it—and who reads even the minor classics these days entirely apart from the of-

fices of criticism?—are likely to see in it mainly a reflection of
the passivity of its critics and their easy satisfaction with its
pathos. Meanwhile its original impact becomes every year more
difficult to recapture or explain.

But upon the possibility of there really being in *Winesburg*
such a contribution of intelligent judgment consonant with
truths of broad applicability and thus qualifying and refining
the vision of grotesque isolation, would seem to depend the
book's chances of survival as more than a landmark in literary
history. It is this question that the present essay seeks to engage, if not definitively to answer. Obviously the answer can
be neither unassailable nor triumphant: *Winesburg* has been
repeatedly read, and if its acts of judgment were conspicuous
they would have been found out. We must be prepared to
accept a modest result and to content ourselves with remembering that the addition of a single note can change the character of a chord.

We may make a beginning by noticing how ambivalent, if
not confused, Anderson's feelings were toward the usual substance of his fiction. The ambivalence could doubtless be doc-
umented from a variety of fictional and biographical records;
but a single passage from *Poor White* (the novel immediately
following *Winesburg*) is entirely adequate to the outline and
dimensions of Anderson's dilemmas.

All men lead their lives behind a wall of misunderstanding they
themselves have built, and most men die in silence and unnoticed
behind the walls. Now and then a man, cut off from his fellows by
the peculiarities of his nature, becomes absorbed in doing something
that is impersonal, useful, and beautiful. Word of his activities is
carried over the walls.

Perhaps the most obviously glaring anomaly in this passage is
the way it envisages the artist, like all other men, living in
isolation and working out of it, yet sees in his case the isola-

tion mysteriously leading to creation instead of destruction.
The distinction is not explored, nor even, apparently, recognized. Moreover, there is curious uncertainty in the phrase
"cut off from his fellows by the peculiarities of his nature,"
which seems to imply that the "fellows" (whom Anderson has
been describing in *Winesburg* as almost universally "grotesque") are somehow less "peculiar," more "normal" perhaps,
than this artist who devotes himself to the "impersonal, useful, and beautiful." Finally, there is a contradiction which if
we notice it at all must strike us as even more bewildering than
the creation-destruction confusion, and which is equally un-
resolved: in the second sentence the artist is described as one
"cut off from his fellows," as if the "fellows" were in happy
communion with each other and therefore to be regarded as a
homogeneous group from which *his* peculiarities have alienated
him; yet in the first sentence Anderson tells us, sounding a
little like Thoreau and at the same time echoing both doctrine and metaphor from *Winesburg,* that "all men lead their
lives behind a wall of misunderstanding they themselves have
built."

It will be said that of course Anderson is not skillful in expository prose and that it is therefore quite beside the point
to submit to rational analysis a piece of writing so murky as
the passage from *Poor White.* That would be true if the criticism were undertaken for any other purpose than to locate a
center of tension in Anderson's feelings about this theme.
That center of tension may now be broadly defined as the
polarity of artist and society (and from Anderson's biography
we should expect no less), particularly as both terms are illuminated (or muddied) by the shifting values that it is possible to attach to the words "normal" and "isolated." In order
to see *Winesburg* clearly and as a whole, it is essential to bear
in mind both ends of the polarity and not allow ourselves to
be tempted, either by Anderson's ability to "see beneath the
surface of lives" or by the fantastic pathos of the *Winesburg*
victims, to focus all our attention on the grotesques. To do

so is at a stroke to give up half the book; worse than that, to give up the half which furnishes perspective and therefore significance to the other.

If we approach the novel from the direction of George Willard, the young reporter presumably on the threshold of his career as a writer, instead of from that of the *subjects* of the sketches, *Winesburg* composes as a *Bildungsroman* of a rather familiar type the "portrait of the artist as a young man" in the period immediately preceding his final discovery of *métier*. In order to arrive at the rare excellence of *Winesburg*, we must first see that it is a book of this kind; and then we must go on to see in what ways it is not typical of the *genre*, for it is in the differences that Anderson's merits are revealed. An initial formulation of this difference would mainly call attention to Anderson's almost faultless holding of the balances between his two terms, artist and society, a delicacy that was perhaps made easier for him by the genuine uncertainty of his feelings. To put it bluntly, there are few works of modern fiction in which the artist's relations with ordinary men are seen with such a happy blend of acuity and charity, few works of any age in which the artist and ordinary men are seen so well *as fitting together* in a complementary union that permits us to make distinctions of relative value while at the same time retaining a universally diffused sense of equal dignity. We need look no further for the cause of the remarkable serenity of tone of *Winesburg*.

This balancing of forces is the thing to hang onto; and it thus seems to me a mistake for Irving Howe, in his beautifully written description of *Winesburg* [in his book, *Sherwood Anderson*], to call so much attention to the grotesques' pathetically eager need to draw sustenance from George Willard without equally emphasizing how many of them come to him convinced that it is *they* who have something to give. It is only a superficial irony that so few of the gifts (like the mother's $800) can possibly have for the young writer the same values that have been assigned to them by the givers.

Their understanding is inevitably not the same as his, which is one of the general truths *Winesburg* readily enforces; but another is that without their gifts there would be no writer at all.

Everyone is ready to give George Willard good advice. Doctor Parcival urges him to write a book saying that all men are Christ and that all are crucified. Wash Williams is anxious to save him needless pain and trouble by putting him on his guard against "bitches." Joe Welling is pleased to confide in him a few secrets about the art of writing. Kate Swift, his former English teacher, tries to tell him to "know life" and "stop fooling with words." Perhaps none of this advice, in the form in which it is offered, is wholly sound. But it is well-intentioned, and one of the most engaging things in *Winesburg* is the way George Willard, on his part, is always ready to credit the local talkers with more wisdom than they may strike us as having. " 'I have missed something,' " he says [in "The Teacher"]. " 'I have missed something Kate Swift was trying to tell me' "; and he might as well be saying it of them all.

His mother has a more intimate and more comprehensive understanding of his needs and is thus appropriately the one who is able to articulate the representative prayer of all the grotesques: that " 'this my boy be allowed to express something for us both' " ("Mother"). For finally what the characters want of George Willard is to have their stories told (they are quite literally characters in search of an author); at the same time, they wish to have a stake in the way the stories are going to be told. Or say that they insist on having some share in the making of the artist whose task will be to expose them as they really are. Each in turn comes forward to offer his secret (the material of art) and to give up whatever fragmentary wisdom he may possess toward the development of the artist who will be the spokesman for everyone. Each one implicitly expects a reward for his contribution: the "release" into expressiveness which each needs but which only the artist may in real life encompass. Seen this way, the book begins to take on some of the formal quality of a procession, imbued like a ritual pageant with silent and stately dignity.

It has other kinds of motion, too; the relationship between writer and subject may, for instance, also be put in terms of an antithesis between development and fixity, an antithesis which we may not notice at first because George Willard's progress is so easygoing compared with the more explosive gestures of the grotesques. But throughout *Winesburg* runs the slow and often hidden current of George Willard's growth toward maturity; often the stream is subterranean and we are surprised to see where it comes out; sometimes it appears to lose itself in backwaters of irrelevance or naïveté. But all the time the book's current is steadily setting toward the ultimate "Departure." The torpidity of that stream is best taken as an expression of Anderson's humility, his refusal to sentimentalize the figure of the writer.

But we must not ignore the drift, for Anderson is equally clear (novelistically speaking) that the artist's essential quality must be defined as a capacity for the growth which he refuses to attribute to any of the grotesques. It is indeed the very description of their grotesqueness that each of them is forever frozen somewhere below the level of a full and proper development. Sometimes this incompletion is "their fault," sometimes not (unless it be more true to say that such a question of ultimate responsibility is meaningless); but there can be no doubt about Anderson's clear perception of the *fact*.

It is not enough, however, to see these figures as incomplete and to sense the pathos of their plight. It is not enough even to see that it is the glimmering awareness of their inadequacy that drives them to their futile efforts at revelation and communion. Ultimately it is only a sentimental reading of *Winesburg, Ohio* that fails to recognize that the grotesques' anxiety to escape their isolation is in itself excessive and truly symptomatic of their grotesquerie. It is of the utmost importance that their counterweight, George Willard, is almost alone among the inhabitants of *Winesburg* in being able to accept the fact of human isolation and to live with it. His willingness to do so is at once the sign of his maturity and the pledge of his incipient artistic ability.

The view of the artist presented in *Winesburg* is that of a man who joins sympathy and understanding to detachment and imperturbability. Anderson obviously sees the relation of art and life as from one point of view illuminated by an opposition between the freedom and flexibility which are necessary to the creative role and, on the other hand, the extremes of static and rigid over-commitment instanced by the grotesques. This is undoubtedly the distinction—flexibility versus rigidity—which Anderson rather unsatisfactorily tries to explain with a modern "humours" theory in the introductory "Book of the Grotesque." This book is clearly not unrelated to *Winesburg, Ohio* and is like it built on the "notion that the moment one of the people took one of the truths to himself, called it his truth, and tried to live his life by it, he became a grotesque and the truth he embraced became a falsehood." Anderson rather implies that what saved the old writer from becoming a grotesque himself (he is endangered by his obsession with his notion) is that he didn't publish the book. The clarity of Anderson's argument here is scarcely helped by his views about non-publication nor by his eccentric use of the word "truth"; but his general intention, a contrast between obsession and freedom, is plain enough. For the distinctions made in this introductory sketch are entirely continuous with the distinction made throughout *Winesburg* between George Willard and his fellow citizens, and are referable finally to one of those broad general truths or paradoxes about art and life that pervade the book, and in which Anderson's charity most winningly shows itself: namely, that the artist, in order to express the common passion, must remain free from entanglements with it, while those who actually *live* the common passion are by the very fact of their involvement prevented from coming to the threshold of complete self-realization and are thereby deprived of the release inherent in expression.

To remember that the "grotesques" are thus distorted and misshapen by their insistent involvement with life itself is to share Anderson's realistic perception of "normal" or "ordinary" people (as distinguished from the artist, who is "normal" in a different way); it is to participate imaginatively in Anderson's remarkable vision of humanity, a vision tender without sentimentality, tough without rancor. The grotesques must not be thought of as necessarily unattractive, for the truths that distend them include "the truth of virginity and the truth of passion, the truth of wealth and of poverty," properties or conditions either good or neutral, and not wholly unlovely even when carried to the excess that lays the grotesques open to the charge of "abnormality." Actually it is almost useless to attempt to retain any usual conception of "normality"— except in the sense of more or less "developed"—when dealing with Anderson (we have seen how he confused himself trying to use the word), for at the heart of his feeling is his uncommon ability to like people for what they are instead of for what they might be (a common failing among minor writers) while in the very act of seeing them as they are. And even if the grotesques are not, by virtue of their inability to develop into full and various normality, quite like other people, there still remains a question whether their lopsidedness does not especially endear them; and I think we must finally say that it does, that they are like Doctor Reefy's "twisted apples": "into a little round place at the side of the apple has been gathered all of its sweetness." What Anderson could never articulate in expository prose he manages so easily with the most commonplace image.

And so easy is it to allow one's attention to be monopolized by the grotesques! Their problem is presented first and their bizarre revelations continually keep it at the forefront of our perception. Meanwhile, as I have said, the current of the book is setting away from them toward the final story, "Departure," and, before that, the climactic tale, "Sophistication," wherein George Willard's maturity is to be realized and the final opposition between artist and society drawn. The placing of this climactic story is important: it immediately precedes "Departure," which is pointedly *anti*-climactic, and immediately follows "Death" (Elizabeth Willard). And it is in significant contrast with an earlier story, "Loneliness," about the artist *manqué* Enoch Robinson who "never grew up."

In "Sophistication" we may find—or infer—an attitude about art and loneliness sufficiently complex and sufficiently clear to enable us to read *Winesburg* without those distortions of meaning that follow upon the loss of any important part of an organic entity. It is one of the few stories in the book which has a happy ending and it concludes with what is for *Winesburg* a startling statement: "For some reason they [George Willard and Helen White] could not have explained they had both got from their silent evening together the thing needed. Man or boy, woman or girl, they had for a moment taken hold of the thing that makes the mature life of men and women in the modern world possible." It would be difficult to imagine a passage more explicitly pointing to the presence of the book's overarching meaning; but this is not to say that that meaning is very easy to grasp or to conceptualize without offering violence to a story of incomparable tact and delicacy (stylistic qualities happily matching the virtues it recommends).

George Willard's maturity has of course been coming on for a long time. In "An Awakening" (his), for instance, he has been shown (1) trying to get " 'into touch with something orderly and big that swings through the night like a star,' " (2) "muttering words" into the darkness, and (3) feeling himself "oddly detached and apart from all life." But these inchoate impulses, although more or less in the right direction, are quickly brought to an end by his foolish involvement with the milliner Belle Carpenter. By the time of "Sophistication" he is older and wiser. His mother's death has intervened. It is this death, no doubt, that enables him now "for the first time [to] take the backward view of life," to realize with the "sadness of sophistication" that "in spite of all the stout talk of his fellows he must live and die in uncertainty." The point of passage from adolescence to maturity is thus defined as the moment one "hears death calling"; and the universal response to an awareness of this moment is to "want to come close to some other human." But not too close; wherein lies the moral of the story.

"Sophistication" is nocturnal, but not that nightmare climate common to so many of the *Winesburg* stories, and as pleasantly informal as the evening stroll that provides its slight framework. First we see George Willard alone, "taking the backward view of life," and anxiously waiting for the hour when he can share his new sense of maturity with Helen White and perhaps compel her admiration of it. Helen White is undergoing a rather parallel transformation into womanhood, a transformation only vaguely felt by George Willard, and comparatively unfocused for us, since her imputed maturity—real or not, significant or not—is presented less for its own interest than as a complementary background for George Willard's achievement of tranquillity. ("The feeling of loneliness and isolation that had come to the young man . . . was both broken and intensified by the presence of Helen. What he felt was reflected in her.") Finally the two young people come together (each one from an atmosphere of "noise," meaningless superficial talk), and walk silently through the streets of Winesburg to the deserted grandstand at the fair grounds. So far as the story informs us, they never say anything to each other.

In the grandstand they are confronted by "ghosts, not of the dead, but of living people." One paradox leads to another: "The place has been filled to overflowing with life . . . and now it is night and the life has all gone away. . . . One shudders at the thought of the meaninglessness of life while at the same instant, and if the people of the town are his people, one loves

life so intensely that tears come into the eyes." This is perhaps
the climax of the story—and thus of Winesburg, Ohio—for at
this point Anderson's own ambivalent attitude toward experience, and toward the art that arises from it to proclaim its
ineradicable dignity, is fully embodied, not in terms of ideas
(which Anderson never learned to manipulate) but in terms
of their corresponding emotions encompassed in images.

Now that the summit of George Willard's emotional and
aesthetic development has been attained, we have a final look
at the artist's social role. It is all comprehended in a single
sentence, again paradoxical: "He wanted to love and to be
loved by her, but he did not want at the moment to be confused by her womanhood." (Presumably she feels the same.)
The point is that they recognize and respect the essential pri-
vacy (or integrity) of human personality: "In that high place
in the darkness the two oddly sensitive human atoms held
each other tightly and waited. In the mind of each was the
same thought. 'I have come to this lonely place and here is
this other,' was the substance of the thing felt." The loneliness is assuaged—there is no other way—by the realization that
loneliness is a universal condition and not a uniquely personal
catastrophe; love is essentially the shared acceptance by two
people of the irremediable fact, in the nature of things, of
their final separateness. But these are truths beyond the com-
prehension of the grotesques, and one reason why they, who
will not accept their isolation, are so uniformly without love;
like Enoch Robinson, they never grew up.

The artist, then, is not necessarily different from other
people, after all. Primarily, he is defined in terms of maturity
and in terms of the practical mastery of his craft (throughout
Winesburg, George Willard has been busy as a reporter, learning to fit words to life felt and observed). The craft is his
special secret, and it is not required that "normal" or "ordinary" people have it. They will have other skills, other secrets.
But what they might all share, ideally, is that mixture of par-
ticipation and detachment, love and respect, passion and criti-

cism, which is, Anderson tells us, the best privilege offered by the modern world to those who wish to grow up, and toward the attainment of which the writer's case—at first glance special, but ultimately very general—may serve as an eminently practicable pattern of virtue.

HERBERT GOLD

Herbert Gold has taught English at Western Reserve University in Cleveland, Wayne State University in Detroit, Cornell University, and the University of California at Berkeley. He is author of, among other novels, *Birth of a Hero*, co-editor of *Stories of Modern America*, and editor of *Fiction of the Fifties*.

WINESBURG, OHIO:
THE PURITY AND CUNNING OF
SHERWOOD ANDERSON

. . . He loved to create, he loved his fantasy as the lonely boy does. In his best work, as in some of the stories of *Winesburg, Ohio*, the fantasy is most controlled, or if not exactly controlled, simplified, given a single lyrical line. The novels had trouble passing the test of the adult imagination, being wild proliferations of daydream. The simple stories of Kate Swift ("The Teacher") or Wing Biddlebaum ("Hands") join Sherwood Anderson with the reader's sense of wonder and despair at the pathetic in his own past—childish hope of love, failed ambition, weakness, and loneliness. As music can do, such stories liberate the fantasies of our secret lives. However, musicians will agree that music is for listening, not to be used as a stimulus for fantasy. We must attend to the song itself, not take advantage of it and make it the passive instrument of our dreaming. In the same way, the great writer hopes to arouse and lead the reader's imagination toward a strong individual perspective on experience. Sherwood Anderson, however, was not of that vividly individualistic company, despite his personal hobby of eccentric Bohemianism. Rather, he was the dreamy, sad, romantic idler within each of us, evoking with nostalgia and grief the bitter moments of recognition which have formed him—formed all of us in our lonely America.

James Joyce used the word "epiphany," which he took from Catholic ritual, to name that moment of revelation when words and acts come together to manifest something new, familiar, timeless, the deep summation of meaning. The experience of epiphany is characteristic of great literature, and the lyric tales of Anderson give this wonderful rapt coming-forth time and time again.

In "The Untold Lie," for example, two men tenderly meet in order to talk about whether one, the younger, should marry the girl he has made pregnant. The older man, unhappy in his own marriage, wants to see the young man's life free and charged with powerful action as his own has never been. But it is revealed to him—revelation is almost always the climax of Anderson's stories—that life without wife and children is impossible and that one man's sorrows cannot be used by him to prevent another man from choosing the same sorrows. It would be a lie to say that the life of conjugal sorrows is merely a life of conjugal sorrows. The story finally breathes the sadness, the beauty, the necessary risks of grown-up desire. "Whatever I told him would have been a lie," he decides. Each man has to make his own decisions and live out his chosen failures of ideal freedom.

Many of Anderson's stories take for their realization objective circumstances which have a grandiose folkish quality, and many of both the most impressive and the most mawkish are concerned with an archetypical experience of civilization: the test which, successfully passed, commands manhood. Such a story as "The Man Who Became a Woman" objectifies even in its title the boy's wondering and fearful dreams. The end sought is manliness, that new clean and free life; failure is seen as a process of being made effeminate, or falling into old patterns of feeling and action. At his best in these stories, there is a physical joy in triumph which is fresh, clean, genial —we think of Mark Twain, although a Twain without the robust humor; at his weak moments, we may also think of the sentimental sick Twain, and we find also the maundering moping of a prettified Thomas Wolfe.

The line between the subjects of Anderson's stories and Sherwood Anderson himself is barely drawn. His relation as artist to his material, as shaper of his material, is as intense and personal as that of any modern writer. Unlike most writers dealing with unhappy and frustrated people, Anderson's work is absolutely authentic in the double sense—not merely in communicating the feeling of these people as people but also in giving us the conviction that the author shares both their bitter frustration and their evanescent occasional triumphs. By comparison with Sherwood Anderson, Dostoevski is a monument of cool detachment. His identification is perfect, sometimes verging on the morbid: "Everyone in the world is Christ and they are all crucified." He has a primitive idealism, a spoiled romanticism like that of Rousseau: we could be all innocent and pure in our crafts if the machines of America and the fates that bring machines did not cripple us.

This romantic idealism can be illustrated again by his treatment of another theme, marriage, in the story "Loneliness," in which he writes of Enoch Robinson: "Two children were born to the woman he married"—just as if they did not happen to Robinson at all, which is indeed the truth about the self-isolated personality he describes. "He dismissed the essence of things," Anderson can write, "and played with realities." Again the romantic Platonist sees a conflict between the deepest meaning and the facts of our lives, between what we do and what we "really" are. With a kind of purity and cunning, Anderson seems to thrive on this curiously boyish notion, the limitations of which most of us quickly learn. We work and love because we know that there is no other way to be ourselves than in relation to the rest of the world. The kind man is the man who performs kind acts; the generous man is a man who behaves generously; we distrust the "essential" generosity which is sometimes claimed for the soul of a man who watches out only for himself. And yet we can be reminded with a strange force by Anderson's conviction in his boyish dream of isolated personality that there is something totally private, untouchable, beyond appearance and action, in all of us. The observation is a familiar one, but the experience can be emotionally crucial. Cunningly Anderson makes us turn to ourselves again with some of his own purity.

The last sentence of "Departure" says of George Willard: "Winesburg had disappeared and his life there had become but a background on which to paint the dreams of his manhood." Abstracted people, playing out their time in the fragmentary society of Winesburg, these "heroes" are isolated, as Anderson himself was isolated, by art or unfulfilled love or religion—by the unsurmounted challenge of finding the self within relationship with others. It was the deep trouble of Anderson's own life that he saw his self, which could be realized only by that monstrous thing, the Life of Art, as flourishing in opposition to decent connections with others in society. Marriage, work, friendship were beautiful things; but the gray series of furnished slum rooms, in which he wrote, enough rooms to fill a city, were his real home. Writing letters and brooding behind his locked door, he idealized love, he idealized friendship. He withdrew to the company of phantom creatures. He hoped to guard his integrity. He kept himself the sort of child-man he described with such comprehending sympathy in the character of Enoch Robinson.

In many writers dealing with the grim facts of our lives, the personal sense of triumph at encompassing the material adds a note of confidence which is at variance with the story itself. Hemingway is a good example; his heroes go down to defeat, but Papa Hemingway the chronicler springs eternal. In Anderson this external note of confidence and pride in craft is lacking, except in some of the specious, overwilled novels which he wrote under political influences. Generally he does not import his poetry into the work—he allows only the poetry that is *there*—nor does his independent life as a creator come to change the tone of these sad tales. The stories of Winesburg are unselfconsciously committed to him as he is sworn true to them; the identification—a variety of loyalty—is torturingly complete; he is related to his material with a love that lacks aesthetic detachment and often lacks the control which comes with that detachment. They are practically unique in this among modern story-telling, and it is partially this that gives them their sometimes embarrassing, often tormenting, and unforgettable folk quality. Still they are not folktales, but, rather, pseudo-folktales. The romantic longing and grieving is not characteristic of the folktale, despite the other elements, a direct matter-of-fact story-telling, colloquial American language (complicated by chivalry and the Bible, but at its best not "literary"), and the authority of Anderson's pious devotion to his lives and people. Later, of course, the romantic judgment culminated in rebellion, sometimes in a kind of aesthetic rant against the way things are.

In "The Strength of God," the Reverend Curtis Hartman (as in a parable, Heart-man)

wondered if the flame of the spirit really burned in him and dreamed of a day when a strong sweet new current of power would come like a great wind into his voice and his soul and the people would tremble before the spirit of God made manifest in him. "I am a poor stick and that will never really happen to me," he mused dejectedly, and then a patient smile lit up his features. "Oh well, I suppose I'm doing well enough," he added philosophically.

These, as *The New Yorker* would put it, are musings that never got mused and philosophic additions that never got philosophically added. They have a curious archaic directness that amounts to a kind of stylization. The unanalytic simplicity itself is a sophisticated manner. As the officers of the Pharisees said, "Never man spake like this man." It recalls to us the day of the story-teller who suggested the broad line of an action, and allowed us to give our imaginations to it. Nowadays we demand detail upon detail, and the phrase "I am a poor stick" would require a whole book of exposition in the hands of most contemporary novelists.

The pathos of the pious man's temptation by the flesh has a flavor beautifully evocative of adolescence. We no longer think of "carnal temptation" as Anderson did. But we remember our fears and guilts, and are reminded of ourselves as great literature always reminds us. Hartman's silent, secret battle with himself over Kate Swift is given part of its bite by her own story—this pimply, passionate young schoolteacher who strikes beauty without knowing it and can find no one to speak to her. Her story is told with a brilliant delicacy that reflects Anderson's own strange reticence about women. Enoch Robinson, he says, "tried to have an affair with a woman of the town met on the sidewalk before his lodging house." To have an affair is his strange idiom for a pickup! (The boy got frightened and ran away; the woman roared with laughter and picked up someone else.)

Except for the poetic schoolteacher and a very few others, women are not women in Anderson's stories. There are the girls who suffer under the kind of sensitivity, passion, and lonely burning which was Anderson's own lot; and then there are the Women. For Anderson women have a strange holy power; they are earth-mothers, ectoplasmic spirits, sometimes succubi, rarely individual living creatures. In "Hands" they are not girls but "maidens," where the word gives a quaint archaic charm to the creature who taunts poor, damned, lonely Wing Biddlebaum. The berry-picking "maidens" gambol while the boys are "boisterous" and the hero flutters in his tormented realm between the sexes.

In somewhere like Wing Biddlebaum's tormented realm, Sherwood Anderson also abode. American cities, as he wrote, are "noisy and terrible," and they fascinated him. He got much of the noise and terror into his writing about big cities, and the quiet noise and gentle terror of little towns into his stories about them. And among the fright of materialistic life, he continually rediscovered the minor beauties which made life possible for him—the moment of love, of friendship, of self-realization. That they were but moments is not entirely the fault of Anderson's own character.

Anderson is shrewd, sometimes just, and has earned the right to even the unjust judgments he makes of other writers. How earned them? He was constantly fighting through both the questions of craft and the deeper risks of imagination. He has won the right to make sweeping pronouncements on his peers. Of Sinclair Lewis, for example, he offers the most damning, most apt criticism: "Wanting to see beauty descend upon our lives like a rainstorm, he has become blind to the minor beauties our lives hold." Sherwood Anderson wants the same thing, but holds to the good sense which a poet can still have in a difficult time: he clings to the minor beauties which give tenderness to his longing, a hope of something else to his despair. For this reason Anderson's critique of America finally bites more deeply than the novels of the ferocious sentimental satirist who was his contemporary.

Of Henry James, Anderson wrote that he is a man who "never found anyone to love, who did not dare love. . . . Can it be that he is the novelist of the haters? Oh, the thing infinitely refined and carried far into the field of intellectuality, as skillful haters find out how to do." The Jamesian flight from direct fleshly feeling offended Anderson. James objectified, stipulated, laid bare, and then suffused his entire yearning

personality over all his work, so that Isabel Archer and Hya-
cinth Robinson are, really are, Henry James, in all his hopeless
longing, and yet spiritualized, that is, without body, epicene
as James seems to have made himself in real life. George
Santayana believed that by withholding love from a specific
object it could be given "in general" to the whole world. This
is a curiously commercial, economical notion—the idea that
there is a limited amount of love and that we have the choice
of spending it on a few selfishly chosen objects or distributing
it generally. "In general" we know that this is nonsense; our
attachments to individuals are the models for our attachments
to humanity as an ideal; but like many sorts of nonsense, it
worked for Henry James to the extent that he really loved
some spirit of Art which his "puppets," his "fables," as he
called them, served.

Is Anderson, with all his mid-American distrust of intellectualized love, really so far from Henry James? He is strikingly
the perpetual adolescent in love with love rather than with a
specific girl with changing flesh. One can see him dreaming
after his dream girl even as he approached old age. His romantic chivalry, his lust for the proletariat, his fantastic correspondence in which the letters seem to be written to
himself, no matter how touching their apparent candor and
earnest reaching out—is he perhaps the other side of the coin
of his accusation against Henry James? To be the novelist of
lovers who did not dare to hate—this, too, is a limitation. He
seems obliged to love others as a function of his own faulty
self-love, and therefore his love of others seems *voulu*, incomplete, and his moments of hatred a guilty self-indulgence. He
presents an extreme case of the imperfections of an artist just
because of the disparity between his intentions and his per-
formance. He wanted to love, he wanted to sing of love. His
failures help to make still more brilliant his achievements in
certain of the stories of Winesburg, in "The Egg," and in
scattered paragraphs, stories, and sections of novels.

For the fault of bookish derivations for his feelings, Ander-

son substituted at his worst the fault of self-indulgent deriva-
tion from gratifications and dreads never altered after boyhood.
He carried his childhood like a hurt warm bird held to his
middle-aged breast as he walked out of his factory into the
life of art. The primitive emotions of childhood are the raw
material of all poetry. Sometimes the indulgence of them to
the exclusion of the mature perspectives of adult life prevents
Anderson from equaling his aspiration and own best work.

But this is a vain quibble. Who can do his best work always? What counts is the achievement, not the failures, however exemplary they may seem to a critic. "I have a lot I want
to tell you if I can," he wrote in a letter. "I am writing short
stories." The faults of unevenness, egotism, lazy acceptance of
ideals, and romantic self-glorification are as nothing against
the realized works of art which force their way through. Sherwood Anderson "added to the confusion of men," as he said
of the great financiers and industrialists, the Morgans, Goulds,
Carnegies, Vanderbilts, "by taking on the air of a creator." He
has helped to create the image we have of ourselves as Americans. Curtis Hartman, George Willard, Enoch Robinson, all
of the people of Winesburg, haunt us as do our neighbors,
our friends, our own secret selves which we first met one
springtime in childhood.

IRVING HOWE

Irving Howe, author of *Politics and The Novel*, critical biographies of Anderson and Faulkner, the recent books of essays, *A World More Attractive*, and other books, is Professor of English at Hunter College, New York, and the editor of *Dissent*.

THE BOOK OF THE GROTESQUE

Between Sherwood Anderson's apprentice novels and *Winesburg, Ohio* there stands no intermediary work indicating a gradual growth of talent. *Mid-American Chants* testifies to both an increasing interest in the possibilities of language and a conscious submission to literary influence, but it is hardly a qualitative advance over its predecessors. From Anderson's Elyria work to the achievement that is *Winesburg* there is so abrupt a creative ascent that one wonders what elements in his Chicago experience, whether in reading or personal relations, might have served to release his talents.

The list of writers to whom Anderson acknowledged a serious debt was small: George Borrow, Mark Twain, Ivan Turgenev. In the early 1920s D. H. Lawrence was added to the small group of masters who had decisively impinged on him, but in 1915 and 1916, the years when he wrote *Winesburg*, Anderson had, of course, not yet read Lawrence.

While his attachment to Borrow antedates his public career

From *Sherwood Anderson* by Irving Howe (New York: William Sloane Associates, 1957). Copyright 1951 by William Sloane Associates, Inc. Reprinted by permission of the publishers.

as a writer, it also testifies to a wish, once that career had begun, to fondle a certain image of himself as a literary personality. To Anderson, the artist always seemed a peculiarly fortunate being who could evade much of the drabness of daily life. By ordering his experience through the canny artifice available only to himself, the artist could establish a margin for the half-forgotten life of flair and largesse, could find a way of surmounting the barren passage of the routine. (Unlike those American writers who take great pains to insist that their occupation is as "normal" as any other, Anderson liked to proclaim the uniqueness of the artist's life.)

To a writer enamored of such a notion, the figure of George Borrow would naturally seem attractive. Borrow's picturesque narratives of gypsy life, virtually unclassifiable among the traditional genres, seemed significant to Anderson because they flowed from a conscious rejection of conventionality and charming because they did not flinch from the romantic, the garrulous, and the merely odd. Borrow provided Anderson with an image of a potential self: the sympathetic auditor of his people's inner history; and for the Borrovian hero who wanders among "backward peoples" he had a considerable admiration, particularly during those burdened years in Elyria when he thought the literary career an avenue to a liberated and adventurous life. Yet there are no significant traces of Borrow in any of Anderson's books; neither in subject matter nor in structure is there an observable line of descent from, say, *Lavengro* to *Winesburg*. The relation is one of personal identification rather than literary influence. Borrow, it seemed to Anderson, was above all a guide to how a writer might live.

If Borrow suggested an attractive style of life, Turgenev's *Memoirs of a Sportsman*, "like low fine music," set the very tone Anderson wished to strike in his prose. In Turgenev's masterpiece he admired most that purity of feeling which comes from creative tact, from the author's strict refusal to violate or impose himself on his characters. Between *Memoirs of a Sportsman*, which Anderson called "the sweetest thing in all literature," and *Winesburg* there are obvious similarities: both are episodic novels containing loosely bound but closely related sketches, both depend for impact less on dramatic action than on a climactic lyrical insight, and in both the individual sketches frequently end with bland understatements that form an ironic coda to the body of the writing. These similarities could certainly be taken as tokens of influence—if only we were certain that Anderson had actually read Turgenev before writing *Winesburg*.

When critics in the 1920s discovered that Anderson was indebted to Chekhov and Dostoevski (which he was not), he gleefully denied having known the Russian novelists until after the publication of *Winesburg*. This denial, however, is controverted by two statements in his correspondence, a remark in his *Memoirs*, and a recollection in an autobiographical fragment. His credibility as a witness of his own past is further damaged by the fact that in the early 1920s his publisher, probably at his instigation and certainly with his consent, issued a public statement denying that Anderson had read *Spoon River* before writing *Winesburg* and insisting that Masters's book appeared after the *Winesburg* sketches came out in magazines. Though the publisher was wrong on both counts, Anderson did not trouble to correct him. Like many untrained writers, he may have feared that an acknowledgment of a literary debt would cast doubt on the value or at least the originality of his work.

But if Turgenev's influence on Winesburg is not quite certain, there can be no doubt about Mark Twain's. Between the America of Anderson's boyhood, which is the setting of his best work, and the America of Huck Finn there are only a few intervening decades, and the nostalgia for a lost moment of American pastoral which saturates *Huckleberry Finn* is also present in *Winesburg*. Twain's influence on Anderson is most obvious in the early portions of *Poor White* and some of the stories in *The Triumph of the Egg* but it can also be seen in *Winesburg*, particularly in Anderson's attempt to use American speech as the base of a tensed rhythmic style. His identification with Borrow was to some extent a romantic whimsy, but his identification with Twain had a strong basis in reality. As he wrote to Van Wyck Brooks, Twain had also been an untrained man of natural talent "caught up by the dreadful cheap smartness, the shrillness that was a part of the life of the country"; Twain had also been bedeviled by the problem of success and the need to conciliate the pressures of East and West.

These were pervasive influences; none of them could have provided the immediate shock, the specific impetus that turned Anderson to the style and matter of *Winesburg.* Such an impetus, if one can be singled out at all, came not from any individual writer but from Anderson's dramatic exposure in 1913–15 to the Chicago literary world. When Max Wald, one of "the little children of the arts," lent him a copy of *Spoon River,* Anderson raced through it in a night. This, he excitedly told his friends, is the real thing—by which he meant that Masters, in his imaginary Midwestern village, had bared the hidden lesions of the American psyche. Had Anderson stopped to notice the appalling frustration that motivated Masters's book he might have been somewhat less enthusiastic, but for the moment *Spoon River* suggested that in a prose equivalent Anderson might find a form allowing more freedom than the conventional novel and yet resulting in greater complexity of meaning than could be had in any individual sketch. Masters hardly influenced the vision behind *Winesburg,* but he did provide intimations of how it might be organized.

At about the same time Anderson was introduced by his brother Karl to the early writings of Gertrude Stein. Anderson has recalled that he "had come to Gertrude Stein's book about which everyone laughed but about which I did not laugh. It excited me as one might grow excited in going into a new and wonderful country where everything is strange. . . ." The truth, however, was somewhat more complex than Anderson's memory. His first reactions to Stein were antagonistic:

at a Chicago party in 1915 he told Edna Kenton that he thought it merely funny that anyone should take *Tender Buttons* seriously, and shortly afterwards he even composed a parody of Stein for his advertising cronies.

But his inaccurate recollection had, as usual, a point of genuine relevance. For though he laughed at Stein when he first read her, she seems to have stimulated him in a way few other writers could. Nearly always one parodies, for good or bad, those writers who deeply matter. To Anderson Stein suggested that, at least in the actual process of composition, words could have an independent value: they could be fresh or stale, firm or gruelly, colored or drab. After reading the fanatically monosyllabic *Three Lives* Anderson would hardly try again, as he had in his first two novels, to write "literary" English. But despite such surface similarities as repetitions of key words and an insistently simple syntax, their styles had little in common. Stein's language was opaque, leading back into itself and thereby tending to replace the matter of fiction, while the language of *Winesburg* was translucent, leading quickly to the center of the book's action. Stein was the best kind of influence: she did not bend Anderson to her style, she liberated him for his own.

And that, essentially, was what the Chicago literary milieu did. It persuaded Anderson that American writers needed an indigenous style which, if only they were bold enough, they could then and there construct; it taught him that before language could be used creatively it might have to be crumbled into particles; and it made him conscious of the need for literary consciousness. For the time being that was enough.

Anderson has recalled that during the years immediately preceding *Winesburg* he would often take with him on advertising trips pages torn from Gideon Bibles, which he read over and over again. This recollection tells us most of what needs to be known about the making of *Winesburg*. Its author had not the slightest interest in religion, but his first involvement in a literary environment had made him aware of writing as writing and had taught him where to find its greatest English source. He had begun to work as a conscious craftsman: the resulting ferment was *Mid-American Chants*, the substance *Winesburg*.

The history of *Winesburg* is a curious instance of the way criticism, with its passion for "placing," can reduce a writer to harmless irrelevance. At various times the book has been banished to such categories as the revolt against the village, the rejection of middle-class morality, the proclamation of sexual freedom, and the rise of cultural primitivism. Whatever the justification for such tags may once have been, it is now quite obvious that Anderson's revolt was directed against something far more fundamental than the restrictions of the American village and was, for that matter, equally relevant to the American city; that *Winesburg* is not primarily concerned with morality, middle-class or otherwise, if only because most of its characters are not in a position to engage in moral choice; that while its subject is frequently tangential to sex it expresses no opinions about and offers no proposals for sexual conduct, free or restricted; and that its style is only dimly related to anything that might be called primitive. If read as social fiction *Winesburg* is somewhat absurd, for no such town could possibly exist. If read as a venture into abnormal psychology the book seems almost lurid, for within its total structure the behavior of its hysterics and paranoids is quite purposeless and, in the absence of any norms to which their deviations might be compared, even incomprehensible. In fact, if read according to the usual expectations of twentieth-century naturalistic or conventionally realistic fiction, *Winesburg* seems incoherent and the charge of emotion it can still raise inexplicable.

In its fundamental quality *Winesburg* is nonrealistic; it does not seek to gratify the eye with a verisimilitude to social forms in the way a Dreiser or a Lewis novel does. In rather shy lyrical outbursts the book conveys a vision of American life as a depressed landscape cluttered with dead stumps, twisted oddities, grotesque and pitiful wrecks; a landscape in which ghosts fumble erratically and romance is reduced to mere fugitive brushings at night; a landscape eerie with the cracked echoes of village queers rambling in their lonely eccentricity. Again and again *Winesburg* suggests that beneath the exteriors of our life the deformed exert dominion, that the seeming health of our state derives from a deep malignancy. And *Winesburg* echoes with American loneliness, that loneliness which could once evoke Nigger Jim's chant of praise to the Mississippi pastoral but which has here become fearful and sour.

Winesburg is a book largely set in twilight and darkness, its backgrounds heavily shaded with gloomy blacks and marshy grays—as is proper for a world of withered men who, sheltered by night, reach out for that sentient life they dimly recall as the racial inheritance that has been squandered away. Like most fiction, *Winesburg* is a variation on the theme of reality and appearance, in which the deformations caused by day (public life) are intensified at night and, in their very extremity, become an entry to reality. From Anderson's instinctively right placement of the book's central actions at twilight and night comes some of its frequently noticed aura of "lostness" —as if the most sustaining and fruitful human activities can no longer be performed in public communion but must be grasped in secret.

The two dozen central figures in *Winesburg* are hardly characters in the usual novelistic sense. They are not shown in depth or breadth, complexity or ambiguity; they are allowed no variations of action or opinion; they do not, with the exception of George Willard, the book's "hero," grow or decline. For Anderson is not trying to represent through sensuous images the immediate surface of human experience; he is rather drawing the abstract and deliberately distorted paradigm of an extreme situation, and for that purpose fully rounded characterizations could only be a complicating blemish.

The figures of *Winesburg* usually personify to fantastic excess a condition of psychic deformity which is the consequence of some crucial failure in their lives, some aborted effort to extend their personalities or proffer their love. Misogyny, inarticulateness, frigidity, God-infatuation, homosexuality, drunkenness—these are symptoms of their recoil from the regularities of human intercourse and sometimes of their substitute gratifications in inanimate objects, as with the unloved Alice Hindman who "because it was her own, could not bear to have anyone touch the furniture of her room." In their compulsive traits these figures find a kind of dulling peace, but as a consequence they are subject to rigid monomanias and are deprived of one of the great blessings of human health: the capacity for a variety of experience. That is why, in a sense, "nothing happens" in Winesburg. For most of its figures it is too late for anything to happen, they can only muse over the traumas which have so harshly limited their spontaneity. Stripped of their animate wholeness and twisted into frozen postures of defense, they are indeed what Anderson has called them: grotesques.

The world of Winesburg, populated largely by these backstreet grotesques, soon begins to seem like a buried ruin of a once vigorous society, an atrophied remnant of the egalitarian moment of 19th-century America. Though many of the book's sketches are placed in the out-of-doors, its atmosphere is as stifling as a tomb. And the reiteration of the term "grotesque" is felicitous in a way Anderson could hardly have been aware of; for it was first used by Renaissance artists to describe arabesques painted in the underground ruins, grotte, of Nero's "Golden House."

The conception of the grotesque, as actually developed in the stories, is not merely that it is an unwilled affliction but also that it is a mark of a once sentient striving. In his introductory fantasy, "The Book of the Grotesque," Anderson writes: "It was the truths that made the people grotesques. . . . The moment one of the people took one of the truths to himself, called it his truth, and tried to live his life by it, he became a grotesque and the truth he embraced a falsehood." There is a sense, as will be seen later, in which these sentences are at variance with the book's meaning, but they do suggest the significant notion that the grotesques are those who *have* sought "the truths" that disfigure them. By contrast the banal creatures who dominate the town's official life, such as Will Henderson, publisher of the paper for which George Willard works, are not even grotesques: they are simply clods. The grotesques are those whose humanity has been outraged and who to survive in Winesburg have had to suppress their wish to love. Wash Williams becomes a misogynist because his mother-in-law, hoping to reconcile him to his faithless wife, thrusts her into his presence naked; Wing Biddlebaum becomes a recluse because his wish to blend learning with affection is fatally misunderstood. Grotesqueness, then, is not merely the shield of deformity; it is also a remnant of mis-shapen feeling, what Dr. Reefy in "Paper Pills" calls "the sweetness of the twisted apples."

Winesburg may thus be read as a fable of American estrangement, its theme the loss of love. The book's major characters are alienated from the basic sources of emotional sustenance— from the nature in which they live but to which they can no longer have an active relationship; from the fertility of the farms that flank them but no longer fulfill their need for creativity; from the community which, at least by the claim of the American mythos, once bound men together in fraternity but is now merely an institution external to their lives; from the work which once evoked and fulfilled their sense of craft but is now a mere burden; and, most catastrophic of all, from each other, the very extremity of their need for love having itself become a barrier to its realization.

The grotesques rot because they are unused, their energies deprived of outlet, and their instincts curdled in isolation. As Waldo Frank has noticed in his fine study of *Winesburg*, the first three stories in the book suggest this view in a complete theme-statement. The story, "Hands," through several symbolic referents, depicts the loss of creativity in the use of the human body. The second story, "Paper Pills," directly pictures the progressive ineffectuality of human thought, pocketed in paper pellets that no one reads. And the third story, "Mother," relates these two themes to a larger variant: the inability of Elizabeth Willard, *Winesburg*'s mother-figure, to communicate her love to her son. "The form of the mother, frustrate, lonely, at last desperate," Frank writes, "pervades the variations that make the rest of the book: a continuity of variation swelling, swirling into the corners and crannies of the village life; and at last closing in the mother's death, in the loss forever of the $800 which Elizabeth Willard had kept for twenty years to give her son his start away from Winesburg, and in the son's wistful departure." In the rupture of family love and the consequent loss of George Willard's heritage, the theme-statement of the book is completed.

The book's central strand of action, discernible in about half the stories, is the effort of the grotesques to establish intimate relations with George Willard, the young reporter. At night, when they need not fear the mockery of public detection, they hesitantly approach him, almost in supplication, to tell him of their afflictions and perhaps find health in his voice. Instinctively, they sense his moral freshness, finding hope in the fact that he has not yet been callused by knowledge and time. To some of the grotesques, such as Dr. Reefy and Dr. Parcival, George Willard is the lost son returned, the Daedalus whose apparent innocence and capacity for feeling will redeem Winesburg. To others among the grotesques, such as Tom Foster and Elmer Cowley, he is a reporter-messenger, a small-town Hermes, bringing news of a dispensation which will allow them to re-enter the world of men. But perhaps most fundamentally and subsuming these two visions, he seems to the grotesques a young priest who will renew the forgotten communal rites by which they may again be bound together. To Louise Trunnion he will bring a love that is more than a filching of flesh; to Dr. Parcival the promise to "write the book that I may never get written" in which he will tell all men that "everyone in the world is Christ and they are all crucified"; to the Reverend Curtis Hartman the willingness to understand a vision of God as revealed in the flesh of a naked woman; to Wash Williams the peace that will ease his sense of violation; and to Enoch Robinson the "youthful sadness, young man's sadness, the sadness of a growing boy in a village at the year's end [which can open] the lips of the old man."

As they approach George Willard, the grotesques seek not merely the individual release of a sudden expressive outburst, but also a relation with each other that may restore them to collective harmony. They are distraught communicants in search of a ceremony, a social value, a manner of living, a lost ritual that may, by some means, re-establish a flow and exchange of emotion. Their estrangement is so extreme that they cannot turn to each other though it is each other they really need and secretly want; they turn instead to George Willard who will soon be out of the orbit of their life. The miracle that the Reverend Curtis Hartman sees and the message over which Kate Swift broods could bind one to the other, yet they both turn to George Willard who, receptive though he may wish to be, cannot understand them.

In only one story, "Death," do the grotesques seem to meet. Elizabeth Willard and Dr. Reefy embrace in a moment of confession, but their approach to love is interrupted by a stray noise. Elizabeth leaves: "The thing that had come to life in her as she talked to her one friend died suddenly." A few months later, at her deathbed, Dr. Reefy meets George Willard and puts out "his hand as though to greet the young man and then awkwardly [draws] it back again." Bloom does not find his Daedalus; the hoped-for epiphany comes at the verge of death and, as in all the stories, is aborted; the ritual of communal love remains unrealized.

The burden which the grotesques would impose on George Willard is beyond his strength. He is not yet himself a grotesque mainly because he has not yet experienced very deeply, but for the role to which they would assign him he is too ab-

sorbed in his own ambition and restlessness. The grotesques
see in his difference from them the possibility of saving themselves, but actually it is the barrier to an ultimate companionship. George Willard's adolescent receptivity to the grotesques
can only give him the momentary emotional illumination described in that lovely story, "Sophistication." On the eve of
his departure from Winesburg, George Willard reaches the
point "when he for the first time takes the backward view of
life. . . . With a little gasp he sees himself as merely a leaf
blown by the wind through the streets of his village. He
knows that in spite of all the stout talk of his fellows he must
live and die in uncertainty, a thing blown by the winds, a
thing destined like corn to wilt in the sun. . . . Already he
hears death calling. With all his heart he wants to come
close to some other human, touch someone with his hands.
. . ." For George this illumination is enough, but it is not for
the grotesques. They are a moment in his education, he a
confirmation of their doom. "I have missed something. I have
missed something Kate Swift was trying to tell me," he says
to himself one night as he falls asleep. He has missed the
meaning of Kate Swift's life: it is not his fault: her salvation,
like the salvation of the other grotesques, is beyond his capaci-
ties.

In the story "Queer" these meanings receive their most gen-
eralized expression, for its grotesque, Elmer Cowley, has no
specific deformity: he is the grotesque as such. "He was, he
felt, one condemned to go through life without friends and he
hated the thought." Wishing to talk to George Willard, he
loses courage and instead rants to a half-wit: "I had to tell
some one and you were the only one I could tell. I hunted
out another queer one, you see. I ran away, that's what I did."
When Elmer Cowley does call George Willard out of the
newspaper office, he again becomes tongue-tied in his presence. Despairing over "his failure to declare his determination
not to be queer," Elmer Cowley decides to leave Winesburg,
but in a last effort at communication he asks George Willard

to meet him at the midnight local. Again he cannot speak. "Elmer Cowley danced with fury beside the groaning train in the darkness on the station platform. . . . Like one struggling for release from hands that held him he struck, hitting George Willard blow after blow on the breast, the neck, the mouth." Unable to give Elmer Cowley the love that might dissolve his queerness, George Willard suffers the fate of the rejected priest.

From the story "Queer," it is possible to abstract the choreography of *Winesburg*. Its typical action is a series of dance maneuvers by figures whose sole distinctive characteristic is an extreme deformity of movement or posture. Each of these grotesques dances, with angular indirection and muted pathos, toward a central figure who seems to them young, fresh, and radiant. For a moment they seem to draw close to him and thereby to abandon their stoops and limps, but this moment quickly dissolves in the play of the dance and perhaps it never even existed: the central figure cannot be reached. Slowly and painfully, the grotesques withdraw while the young man leaves the stage entirely. None of the grotesques is seen full-face for more than a moment, and none of them is individually important to the scheme of the dance. For this is a dance primarily of spatial relationships rather than solo virtuosity; the distances established between the dancers, rather than their personalities, form the essence of the dance. And in the end, its meaning is revealed in the fact that all but the one untouched youth return to precisely their original places and postures.

When Anderson first sent his *Winesburg* stories to the *Masses, Seven Arts,* and the *Little Review,* he intended each of them to be a self-contained unit, as in fact they may still be regarded. But there was clearly a unifying conception behind all the stories: they were set in the same locale, many of the characters appeared in several stories, and there was a remarkable consistency of mood that carried over from story to story. Consequently, when Anderson prepared them for book publication in 1919, he had only to make a few minor changes, mostly insertions of place and character names as connectives, in order to have a unified book.

Particularly if approached along the lines that have been suggested here, *Winesburg* seems remarkably of a piece. The only stories that do not fit into its pattern are the four-part narrative of Jesse Bentley, a failure in any case, and possibly "The Untold Lie," a beautiful story measuring the distance between middle-age and youth. Of the others only "Tandy" is so bad that its omission would help the book. On the other hand, few of the stories read as well in isolation as in the book's context. Except for "Hands," "The Strength of God," "Paper Pills," and "The Untold Lie," they individually lack the dramatic power which the book has as a whole.

Winesburg is an excellently formed piece of fiction, each of its stories following a parabola of movement which abstractly graphs the book's meaning. From a state of feeling rather than a dramatic conflict there develops in one of the grotesques a rising lyrical excitement, usually stimulated to intensity by the presence of George Willard. At the moment before reaching a climax, this excitement is frustrated by a fatal inability at communication and then it rapidly dissolves into its original diffuse base. This structural pattern is sometimes varied by an ironic turn, as in "Nobody Knows" and "A Man of Ideas," but in only one story, "Sophistication," is the emotional ascent allowed to move forward without interruption.

But the unity of the book depends on more than the congruous design of its parts. The first three stories of *Winesburg* develop its major theme, which, after several variations, reaches its most abstract version in "Queer." The stories following "Queer" seem somewhat of a thematic afterthought, though they are necessary for a full disposal of the characters. The one conspicuous disharmony in the book is that the introductory "Book of the Grotesque" suggests that the grotesques are victims of their wilful fanaticism, while in the stories themselves grotesqueness is the result of an essentially valid resistance to forces external to its victims.

Through a few simple but extremely effective symbols, the stories are both related to the book's larger meaning and defined in their uniqueness. For the former of these purposes, the most important symbol is that of the room, frequently used to suggest isolation and confinement. Kate Swift is alone in her bedroom, Dr. Reefy in his office, the Reverend Curtis Hartman in his church tower, Enoch Robinson in his fantasy-crowded room. Enoch Robinson's story "is in fact the story of a room almost more than it is the story of a man." The tactful use of this symbol lends *Winesburg* a claustrophobic aura appropriate to its theme.

Most of the stories are further defined by symbols related to their particular meanings. The story of the misogynist Wash Williams begins by rapidly thrusting before the reader an image of "a huge, grotesque kind of monkey, a creature with ugly sagging, hairless skin," which dominates its subsequent action. And more valid than any abstract statement of theme is the symbolic power of that moment in "The Strength of God" when the Reverend Curtis Hartman, in order to peek into Kate Swift's bedroom, breaks his church window at precisely the place where the figure of a boy stands "motionless and looking with rapt eyes into the face of Christ."

Though *Winesburg* is written in the bland accents of the American story-teller, it has an economy impossible to oral narration because Anderson varies the beat of its accents by occasionally whipping them into quite formal rhetorical patterns. In the book's best stretches there is a tension between its underlying loose oral cadences and the stiffened superimposed beat of a prose almost Biblical in its regularity. Anderson's prose is neither "natural" nor primitive; it is rather a hushed bardic chant, low-toned and elegiacally awkward, deeply related to native speech rhythms yet very much the result of literary cultivation.

But the final effectiveness of this prose is in its prevalent tone of tender inclusiveness. Between writer and materials there is an admirable equity of relationship. None of the characters is violated, none of the stories, even the failures, leaves the reader with the bitter sense of having been tricked by cleverness or cheapness or toughness. The ultimate unity of the book is a unity of feeling, a sureness of warmth, and a readiness to accept Winesburg's lost grotesques with the embrace of humility. Many American writers have taken as their theme the loss of love in the modern world, but few, if any at all, have so thoroughly realized it in the accents of love.

DAVID D. ANDERSON

David D. Anderson is Associate Professor of American Thought and
Language at Michigan State University and is currently Fulbright
lecturer at the University of Karachi. He has published a critical
biography, *Louis Bromfield*, and is at work on a study of Sherwood
Anderson.

[THE GROTESQUES
AND GEORGE WILLARD]

. . . In the first of the sketches, "The Book of the Grotesque," utilized as a statement of purpose, Anderson points
out his approach in symbolic terms. As the title indicates, he
shows that the individuals he is dealing with in the stories
have each been twisted into psychological shapes having, in
most cases, little to do with external appearance. This distortion results from both the narrowness of their own vision and
that of others; in some cases the first is primarily at fault,
while in others it is the latter. From this point the problem
inherent in human isolation takes on two aspects: the first is,
of course, the specific cause in individual cases; the second
and more important is determining with exactness and hence
understanding the nature of each grotesque. Thus, in the book

From the essay entitled "Sherwood Anderson's Moments of Insight," in
Critical Studies in American Literature: A Collection of Essays by David
D. Anderson (Karachi, Pakistan: University of Karachi, 1964). Reprinted
by permission of the author and the University of Karachi, Bureau of
Composition, Compilation, and Translation.

he is approaching the understanding that Sam McPherson sought in a way that demands empathy, compassion, and intuition rather than fierce desire.

In this sketch, which characterizes an old writer who has attained understanding of his fellow men and has retired from life to observe men and to teach them understanding, Anderson defines his problem symbolically because he has learned that there is no direct, obvious cause but that there are causes as diverse as the individuals who make up the world. In the sketch the old writer reveals his secret knowledge of the nature of mankind, noting

That in the beginning when the world was young there were a great many thoughts but no such thing as a truth. Man made the truths himself and each truth was a composite of a great many vague thoughts. All about in the world were the truths and they were all beautiful.

. . . There was the truth of virginity and the truth of passion, the truth of wealth and of poverty, of thrift and of profligacy, of carelessness and abandon. Hundreds and hundreds . . . were the truths and they were all beautiful.

And then the people came along. Each as he appeared snatched up one of the truths and some who were quite strong snatched up a dozen of them.

It was the truths that made the people grotesques. . . . The moment that one of the people took one of the truths to himself, called it his truth, and tried to live his life by it, he became a grotesque and the truth he embraced became a falsehood.

Using this symbolic interpretation as a basis, Anderson sets off to use intuitive perception to try to find in the lives of the people with whom he is dealing whatever it is in themselves that has prevented them from reaching their full potential as human beings and that has cut them off from their fellows. He shows, too, his realization that the cause is not something as easily perceived and denounced as modern industrialism but that it is as old as the human race. False ideas, false dreams, false hopes, and false goals have distorted man's vision almost from the beginning. Anderson is attempting in the stories to approach these people who have had such indignities inflicted upon them as to become spiritual grotesques, and most importantly, he is attempting to understand them as people rather than as curious specimens of spiritual deformity.

Anderson's use of the word "grotesque" is quite important in this context. In its usual sense in reference to human beings it connotes disgust or revulsion, but Anderson's use is quite different. To him a grotesque is, as he points out later, like the twisted apples that are left behind in the orchards because they are imperfect. These apples, he says, are the sweetest of all, perhaps even because of the imperfections that have caused them to be rejected. He approaches the people in his stories as he does the apples, secure in his knowledge that the sources or natures of their deformities are unimportant when compared to their intrinsic worth as human beings needing and deserving of understanding. This approach is based on intuition rather than objective knowledge, and it is the same sort of intuition with which one approaches the twisted apples; he believes that one dare not reject because of mere appearance, either physical or spiritual; that appearance may mask a significant experience made more intense and more worthwhile by the deformity itself.

In the body of the book proper, following this introductory sketch, Anderson has set up an organizational pattern that not only gives partial unity to the book but explores systematically the diverse origins of the isolation of his people, each of whom is in effect a social displaced person because he is cut off from human intercourse with his fellow human beings. In the first three stories Anderson deals with three aspects of the problem of human isolation. The first story, "Hands," deals with the inability to communicate feeling; the second, "Paper Pills," is devoted to the inability to communicate thought; and the third, "Mother," focuses on the inability to communicate love. This three-phased examination of the basic problem of human isolation sets the tone for the rest of the book because these three shortcomings, resulting partially from the narrowness of the vision of each central figure but primarily from the lack of sympathy with which the contemporaries of each regard him, are the real creators of the grotesques in human nature. Each of the three characters has encountered one aspect of the problem: he has something that he feels is vital and real within himself that he wants desperately to reveal to others, but in each case he is rebuffed, and, turning in upon himself, he becomes a bit more twisted and worn spiritually. But, like the apples left in the orchards, he is the sweeter, the more human for it. In each case the inner vision of the main character remains clear, and the thing that he wishes to communicate is in itself good, but his inability to break through the shell that prevents him from talking to others results in misunderstanding and spiritual tragedy.

The first of the stories, "Hands," immediately and symbolically approaches a problem that as a phase of the over-all problem of human isolation recurs in Anderson's later work. The story begins by describing the remarkably active and expressive hands of an old recluse in the town. George Willard, a young reporter on the Winesburg *Eagle* and the unifying figure in the stories, is fascinated by the old man's hands, and in time the old man tells Willard his story: once, as a schoolmaster, he had been accused of homosexuality because in moments of excitement or affection he would tousle the hair of his students or touch them. Instead of being a means of expression, the old man's hands had become a source of shame to him, and he tried to keep them hidden. In the town he is a pitiful and fearful creature, always expecting the spontaneous actions of his hands to be misinterpreted.

The concept of hands as the basic tools of expression of the craftsman is very important in this story as it passes beyond the immediate and takes on overtones of the universal. As Anderson points out with increasing frequency during both this and the next periods of his career, man's efforts to communicate with his fellows have traditionally depended upon his hands because for many things words either do not exist or have been rendered meaningless. Hence, the hands of a craftsman, a painter, a surgeon, a writer, a lover communicate indirectly something of the truth and beauty that each of them feels inside. Although Anderson is fascinated by the idea, nevertheless he knows that the language of hands is as subject to misinterpretation as any other. In this story he points out that this is not only possible, but it is probable, that the widely held truth in this case, the existence of homosexuality, has become a falsehood because appearance has been accepted in place of truth. Symbolically he shows how such widely held truths become falsehoods have inhibited the forces in man that allow him to express himself intimately and creatively. Fortunately, however, he shows that the forces still exist, making their possessor the more human and the more deserving of compassion, because he has been deprived of the power to express his creativity.

In "Paper Pills" Anderson again writes of the relationship between a man's hands and his inner being, this time in the person of Doctor Reefy, a conventionally wise and perceptive country practitioner. Doctor Reefy is as cut off from effective communication with others as Wing Biddlebaum, but his problem is his inability to communicate his thoughts without being misunderstood. Because he recognizes this shortcoming, he writes his thoughts on bits of paper and puts the bits into his pockets, where they become twisted into hard little balls, which he throws playfully at his friend the nurseryman as he laughs.

Here Anderson carries further his introductory comment that there is no such thing as a truth, that there are only thoughts, and that man has made truths out of them through his own short sight. On the bits of paper Doctor Reefy knows that he is writing mere thoughts, but he knows that they would be misinterpreted if communicated directly, so to prevent them being reduced to the grim joke of misinterpretation he prefers that they become the means of a lesser joke in the form of paper pills. Cut off from attempts at direct communication through his knowledge of its inevitable misinterpretation, Doctor Reefy prefers that his paper pills be considered as bits of paper and no more; in effect, the hard shells of the pills represent the barriers of isolation that surround human minds, and Doctor Reefy, voluntarily isolating himself rather than trying to overcome those barriers, deliberately avoids inevitable misunderstanding.

Waldo Frank sees this story as representing the ineffectuality of human thought as it is isolated and fragmented on the bits of paper, but Anderson indicates no such shortcoming in the thoughts themselves. The difficulty, he points out, lies in the process of communication, which, as Reefy indicates, is something that cannot be carried out directly with any assurance of success. Rather than risk misinterpretation, he lets the paper pills be considered products of his hands rather than his mind. Yet, even while he throws them playfully at his friend, he hopes that his friend will see them in the light in which every craftsman hopes his work will be regarded—as a product that has taken shape through the work of his hands but that is expressive of his soul. Reefy knows that this intuitive understanding is as unlikely as direct understanding, and so he lets himself become a grotesque because he is unable to find a satisfactory means of communication. The shortcoming lies not in the thought but in the process of communication, and he prefers to convey his thoughts ironically in the form of a joke, even while he knows that faulty communication of the intimacies of human life is life's inherent tragedy.

The third story, "Mother," deals with the relationship between George Willard and his mother, Elizabeth Willard. In effect the story is the exploration of a theme that Anderson had adapted from his own experience and used in both *Windy McPherson's Son* and *Marching Men*: the inability to communicate love or understanding between mother and son. The relationship between the two is completely inarticulate, just as it was between mother and son in each of the novels and, more importantly, as Anderson's autobiographies show, as was the case between him and his own mother. As a result, although this phase is part of the over-all problem of isolation, Anderson feels that understanding in this area is vital. As the theme unfolds in this story, Elizabeth has been forced, through the ineptness of her husband, to take over management of both the family hotel, a failing business, and the inner affairs of the family proper. She is resented by her husband as a usurper, and, unable to love or respect him, she focuses her interest and love on her son, in whom she sees the potential for the individual fulfillment that her role as woman and as head of the household had denied her. Inwardly she was a mass of determination that violently defied anything that threatened her son; outwardly she was perfunctory, almost apologetic in his presence.

Consequently Elizabeth is continually afraid that her life, spent in opposing both the forces of conventional success and her husband, with her son as the stake, is indecisive and meaningless. She can only hope that somehow the boy understands. Finally he announces that he is going away: "I just want to go away and look at people and think." She is unable to reply, but she knows that she has won; "she wanted to cry out with joy . . . but the expression of joy had become impossible to her," and the story ends in perfunctory formality, the barriers still solid between them.

In these three stories Anderson sets forth the theme of the problem of human isolation in the three aspects that recur in most of the other stories. These three aspects, the inability to communicate one's feeling, one's thought, and one's love, are at the heart of the problem, and in the following stories he shows these shortcomings at work in other situations with other central characters but essentially as restatements of the same theme. In each of the characters something deep within him demands expression. In each case it is part of him that he wants desperately to share with others directly, and he is unable to do it, either through his own inability to break through the shell that surrounds him or else because society forbids it or distorts it. This inability makes him turn in upon himself, becoming a grotesque, a person deserving of understanding and wanting it desperately, but completely unable to find it except in occasional flashes, as in the embrace between Elizabeth and Doctor Reefy in "Death" and in the attempts made by many of them to seek understanding in George Willard. However, such moments merely serve to emphasize the intensity of their isolation as they are startled by a noise or as George misunderstands or fails to understand and leaves them behind in frustration.

As George Willard appears and reappears in about half of the stories as leading character, as an audience, or as a casual observer he lends a unity to the collection that makes it approach the novel form. Much more important, however, is his role in permitting full development of Anderson's theme. In two of the first three stories, "Hands" and "Mother," he plays the part that has been ascribed to him in more than half of the following stories. To each of the grotesques he appears to be what that individual wants him to be. To his mother he is an extension of herself through which her dreams may be fulfilled; to Wing Biddlebaum he is the symbol of the innocent love that had been denied him; to others he becomes, in turn, a symbol of a long-lost son, of father-confessor, of masculine strength and fertility, of innocent, undemanding human understanding. Each interprets George as he wishes, but to each he primarily serves the function of an ear into which can be poured the inner stirrings of fear, hope, love, and dreams of which each is made. Because he is part of the apparently integrated community in his job as reporter on the Winesburg *Eagle*, he represents to each of them the opportunity to restore communication with the world from which each feels excluded. These grotesques see in George the key that will release them from their personal prisons and enable them to resume normal human forms, either vicariously, as in the case of his mother and others, or directly, through understanding, acceptance, and love. Because George is innocent, unspoiled by the world that has rejected and isolated them, they see in him their only chance to return to the fellowship of men.

As a result, Wing Biddlebaum feels confident in his presence and is willing to walk freely with him through the town; his mother feels a sudden surge of strength in his presence; Doctor Parcival feels confident enough to reveal the secret behind his mask of hate—the overwhelming compassion that makes him declare that ". . . everyone in the world is Christ and they are all crucified"; Louise Trunnion in "Nobody Knows" seeks him out for a moment of love that manifests itself in sex. In following stories the role of George Willard parallels these. He is sought out, he receives confidences, he is receptive and sympathetic, and the grotesques for the most part go away momentarily satisfied, unaware that while they have found temporary release, they have not found freedom from the confines of their spiritual prisons.

Only in "Queer," the story of Elmer Cowley, does the grotesque resent the person of George Willard. Just as the others have seen Willard as the symbol of whatever will free them from their isolation, Elmer sees George as the manifestation of the society that rejects him. In this story Elmer resents George and yet attempts to establish satisfactory relations with him. Failing this, he assaults George, leaving him behind bewildered and half-conscious. As he hops a freight, Elmer voices his frustration by crying, "I guess I showed him. I ain't so queer. I guess I showed him I ain't so queer."

In this story Elmer Cowley points out the difficulty that the other grotesques thus far have failed to perceive: George Willard does not understand. All of the others had seen him as an extension of self that could not fail to understand and that could ease their passage into the intimacies of human life, and each believed that he did somehow understand, even as he left in sympathy but baffled or, as in the case of Louise

Trunnion, completely misunderstanding. But Elmer sees him as society, as the symbol of rejection, and finding himself tongued-tied in George's presence, he can do nothing else but assault George and then run off, defiant but defeated. Elmer sees that George as society does not understand, while the others fail to see that as son, as lover, as mirrored self, he does not understand either.

As the grotesques reveal themselves to George, they do not arouse in him the conventional understanding that they seek, but without realizing it, each of them is contributing to the growth of a more important kind of understanding in him. This kind is based on compassion and on the sincere desire to understand what these people are trying to tell him, and it does not result from objective analysis but from intuitive perception of the nature and worth of the individual. As the stories unfold he is still too young and inexperienced to grasp much more than that, but his contacts with the grotesques are drawing him closer to eventual understanding through teaching him the compassion and the empathy that will permit him in time to know and understand others.

In the development of George Willard, Anderson indicates that one can learn to seek out moments of understanding, of acceptance, of communication without the use of words that can be twisted, distorted, or misunderstood. Early in the collection George had completely misinterpreted a lonely plea, mistaking it for an invitation to a sex adventure; later, with Kate Swift he almost makes the same mistake, finally realizing that "I must have missed something. I have missed something Kate Swift was trying to tell me"; and finally, in "Sophistication" his brief meeting with Helen White brought him to realize that sex and love are not synonymous but that they are often confused. This realization makes possible for him the eventual achievement of understanding. In the process he has learned something of the nature of the human heart, both of others and of his own, and he has learned to open his heart and to listen with it rather than with ears that have become too accustomed to the sound of the truths become falsehoods all around him.

The sketch "Departure" is for George anti-climax. In the microcosm of human nature that is Winesburg he had learned the fundamental secret of human society: that one must reach out and accept and love; he had ". . . for a moment taken hold of the thing that makes the mature life of men and women in the modern world possible"; and he is ready to take his place in that world, taking with him something of each of the grotesques who had sought him out. As long as he remembers that secret he can never become one of them; he knows that understanding comes only in moments of uncomplicated acceptance and love. . . .

❀◈

CHARLES CHILD WALCUTT

Charles Child Walcutt has taught at Washington and Jefferson
University, Washington, Pennsylvania, and is now Professor of
English at Queens College, New York. He is author of, among other
books, *Tomorrow's Illiterates* and *Man's Changing Masks*.

[NATURALISM IN
WINESBURG, OHIO]

. . . Anderson's naturalism may be considered on three
planes: 1) His exploration of character without reference to
the orthodox moral yardstick; 2) his questionings, and his
quiet, suppressed conclusions as to what orders our Cosmos
and what is man's place in it; 3) his social attitudes, which
are left-wing and increasingly critical, as the years pass, of
American business enterprise. After briefly discussing these aspects of Anderson's work, I shall try to show how his naturalism, while making possible his marvelous insights into
personality, confronts him with a later version of the problem
of structure that baffled Hamlin Garland. Anderson's medium
is the short story or sketch. In the novel he is baffled by the
problem of form.

Understanding naturalism as a result of the divided stream

From the chapter entitled "Sherwood Anderson: Impressionism and The
Buried Life," in *American Literary Naturalism: A Divided Stream* by
Charles Child Walcutt (Minneapolis: The University of Minnesota Press,
1956). Copyright 1956 by the University of Minnesota and reprinted by
permission of the publishers, and of *The Sewanee Review*, where the
chapter first appeared.

of American transcendentalism[1] enables us to account for many confusions and contradictions which appear in the tradition. Does the appeal to nature, for example, commit us to reason or unreason? Is truth to be found in the study of the scientist, the insight of the mystic, or the simple reactions of the folk? In short, is reason or impulse to be most respected? These are old questions, indeed, but they seem no less confusing now than they have ever been, for never have the poles of Order and Frenzy whirled more bewilderingly around an unknown center. Respect for reason seems to be a part of modern naturalistic thinking, but so does respect for instinct. How can it be that these two contrary notions exist in the same general pattern of ideas? The answer is that the dichotomy between order and frenzy, between reason and instinct, is not the important or major one. In a larger scheme, authority goes at one pole, and at the other stands Nature, whose two children are Order (or reason) and Instinct. Under the orthodox dispensation man was to be enlightened by Revelation and controlled by the rule of Authority. Under the new, he is to find the truth in himself. Since the emotions have been most severely distrusted under the aegis of orthodoxy, it is natural

---

[1] "My thesis is that naturalism is the offspring of transcendentalism. American transcendentalism asserts the unity of Spirit and Nature and affirms that intuition (by which the mind discovers its affiliation with Spirit) and scientific investigation (by which it masters Nature, the symbol of Spirit) are equally rewarding and valid approaches to reality. When this mainstream of transcendentalism divides, as it does toward the end of the nineteenth century, it produces two rivers of thought. One, the approach to Spirit through intuition, nourishes idealism, progressivism, and social radicalism. The other, the approach to Nature through science, plunges into the dark canyon of mechanistic determinism. The one is rebellious, the other pessimistic; the one ardent, the other fatal; the one acknowledges will, the other denies it. Thus 'naturalism,' flowing in both streams, is partly defying Nature and partly submitting to it; and it is in this area of tension that my investigation lies, its immediate subject being the forms which the novel assumes as one stream or the other, and sometimes both, flow through it. The problem . . . is an epitome of the central problem of twentieth-century thought." (From *American Literary Naturalism, A Divided Stream* by Charles Child Walcutt. University of Minnesota Press, Minneapolis.)

that in the revolt against it the rationalism of the eighteenth century should precede the emotionalism of the nineteenth, and that the scientific materialism of the late nineteenth century should precede the second return to emotion that we see in the psychology of Freud and the fiction of Sherwood Anderson. In each trend the return to reason comes as the first rebellion against orthodoxy, the return to emotion the second. Anderson, in almost everything he writes, searches out the emotional values involved in an experience. He seeks to render the feeling of life to people in small towns and on farms who are struggling with all their *natural* ardor against the confines of tradition or the inhibitions of puritanism.

Anderson explores two major themes. One is discovery, the other inhibition. These themes correspond with the demands of the two branches of the divided stream of transcendentalism. The theme of discovery is the recognition of Spirit, the unfolding of the world and its perception by the intuition, the secret insight by which man's life is suddenly revealed to him. It comes when George Willard sits in the dark over the fairground with Helen White; when the adolescent narrator of "The Man Who Became a Woman" (in *Horses and Men*, 1924) after a night of extraordinary adventures, culminating in the illusion that he has turned into a woman, breaks through the veil of ignorance and confusion and goes forth to a new life; when Rosalind Westcott of "Out of Nowhere into Nothing" (in *The Triumph of the Egg*, 1921), who has gone home from Chicago to ask her mother's advice and has found only a complete lack of sympathy, walking through the night comes into possession of a delicious confidence in her powers: "She found herself able to run, without stopping to rest and half-wished she might run on forever, through the land, through towns and cities, driving darkness away with her presence."

The theme of inhibition appears in almost every story of Anderson's, and it relates to three general areas of cause and experience. The first is the problem of growing up. Every youth finds himself baffled, inarticulate, frustrated because he does not know what he wants out of life. He wants to be loved, more than anything else, perhaps, but he also wants to express himself and to communicate with others, and these needs cannot be answered until they are clearly recognized. Childhood and youth are therefore characterized by bottled-up yearnings, unshaped desires, and wild resentment. Second is the frustration which comes from the absence of a tradition of manners, that could lend graciousness and ease instead of the rawness and harshness that grow when people express themselves through broad humor, scurrility, and cruel pranks. Third is the problem of social opportunity which becomes increasingly important in Anderson's later work. People without education, mill workers in *Beyond Desire*, all the countless Americans who have not even a meager share of the opportunities which constitute the democratic dream of a full life for all—these live in endless spiritual privation, and passages which appear with increasing frequency in the later books suggest that Anderson shared the hatred of the oppressed for the vapid plutocrats who deprive them. This theme of inhibition obviously reflects the materialistic branch of the transcendental stream when it identifies spiritual and material privation. If Anderson ever suggested that all we need in America is a tradition of manners and devout observances to control the wildness of the yokel, he would be returning to orthodoxy and dualism. This he never does.

Rather he evolves the concept of the *grotesque* to indicate what small-town life has done to its people. The grotesque is the person who has become obsessed by a mannerism, an idea, or an interest to the point where he ceases to be Man in the ideal sense. This condition is not the single defect referred to by Hamlet:

> these men—
> Carrying, I say, the stamp of one defect,
> Being Nature's livery, or Fortune's star—
> Their virtues else—be they as pure as grace,

> As infinite as man may undergo—
> Shall in the general censure take corruption
> From that particular fault.

It is in the state where the defect has become the man, while his potentialities have remained undeveloped. Anderson describes it thus:

That in the beginning when the world was young there were a great many thoughts but no such thing as a truth. Man made the truths himself and each truth was a composite of a great many vague thoughts. . . .

And then the people came along. Each as he appeared snatched up one of the truths and some who were quite strong snatched up a dozen of them.

It was the truths that made the people grotesques. The old man had quite an elaborate theory concerning the matter. It was his notion that the moment one of the people took one of the truths to himself, called it his truth, and tried to live his life by it, he became a grotesque and the truth he embraced became a falsehood ["The Book of the Grotesque"].

Again and again the stories of Anderson are marked by a union of surprise and insight. What was apt to be merely shocking or horrendous or sensational in the work of Zola and Norris acts in Anderson's stories as a key to a fuller grasp of the extraordinary range of "normal" reality. He has got into the heart of bizarre, even fantastic experiences which are nevertheless universal. "Godliness: A Tale in Four Parts," in *Winesburg, Ohio,* presents the effects on children and grandchildren of the zeal for possessions and godliness that dominates the simple heart of Jesse Bentley. Jesse has the simplicity and power of a prophet; with these go the blindness of a fanatic and the pitiful ignorance of a bigot. When his grandson, David, is twelve, he takes him into the forest and terrifies him by praying to God for a sign. The boy runs, falls, and is knocked unconscious by a root, while the old man, oblivious

to the boy's terror, thinks only that God has frowned upon
him. When David is fifteen, he is out with the old man recovering a strayed lamb when Jesse conceives the notion that,
like Abraham, he should sacrifice the lamb and daub the boy's
head with its blood. Terrified beyond measure, the boy re-
leases the lamb, hits Jesse on the head with a stone from his
sling, and, believing he has killed the old man, leaves that
part of the country for good. As for old Jesse, "It happened
because I was too greedy for glory," he declared, and would
have no more to say in the matter. Here Anderson is, on the
surface, studiously objective, presenting only the cold facts;
but the delicacy and sweetness of his style invest this harsh
tale with a rare quality of understanding and love. The hidden life has never been more effectively searched out. Here
there is no judgment either of the fanatical old man or of the
terrified boy whose life he nearly ruins. Pity, understanding,
and insight there are—made possible by the naturalistic impulse to seek into the heart of experience without reference
to the limits or prepossessions of convention.

Winesburg, Ohio is full of insights into the buried life, into
the thoughts of the repressed, the inarticulate, the misunderstood. Most frequently frustrated is the desire to establish
some degrees of intimacy with another person. A tradition of
manners would accomplish just this by providing a medium
through which acquaintance could ripen into intimacy. Small-
town America has wanted such a tradition. In place of it, it
has had joking, back-slapping, and buffoonery which irk the
sensitive spirit and make him draw ever more secretly into
himself. The concluding paragraph of "The Thinker" shows
these confused and constricted emotions working at a critical
moment in the life of a boy who wanted to get away. He has
told a girl whom he has long known rather at a distance, that
he plans to leave Winesburg, and she has offered to kiss him:

Seth hesitated and, as he stood waiting, the girl turned and ran
away through the hedge. A desire to run after her came to him,

but he only stood staring, perplexed and puzzled by her action as he had been perplexed and puzzled by all of the life of the town out of which she had come. Walking slowly toward the house, he stopped in the shadow of a large tree and looked at his mother sitting by a lighted window busily sewing. The feeling of loneliness that had visited him earlier in the evening returned and colored his thoughts of the adventure through which he had just passed. "Huh!" he exclaimed, turning and staring in the direction taken by Helen White. "That's how things'll turn out. She'll be like the rest. I suppose she'll begin now to look at me in a funny way." He looked at the ground and pondered this thought. "She'll be embarrassed and feel strange when I'm around," he whispered to himself. "That's how it'll be. That's how everything'll turn out. When it comes to loving someone, it won't never be me. It'll be someone else—some fool—someone who talks a lot—someone like that George Willard."

In another story he speaks of "the quality of being strong to be loved" as if it were the key to America's need.

These ideas are all in the naturalistic tradition in that they are motivated by the feeling of need for their expression of the "inner man." Anderson assumes that this inner man exists and is good and "should" be permitted to fulfill himself through love and experience. The need is alive and eager; it is the social order that prevents its satisfaction.

Patterns emerge in *Winesburg, Ohio* through the growth of George Willard, who may be considered the protagonist of what connected story there is. George appears frequently, sometimes in an experience and sometimes hearing about another's. An extraordinary pattern emerges when George receives, late at night in the newspaper office where he works, a visit from the minister, who enters brandishing a bloody fist and explaining that he has been "delivered." "God," he says, "has appeared to me in the person of Kate Swift, the school teacher, kneeling naked on a bed." The minister has been peeping at her through a small hole in the colored window of his study. This night as his lustful thoughts were running wild, Kate, naked, beat the pillow of her bed and wept, and then knelt to pray, and the minister was moved to smash the window with his fist so that the glass would be replaced and he would no longer be tempted.

The turmoil in the schoolteacher's bosom resulted from a mixture of interest, desire, enthusiasm, and love. She had been thinking of George Willard, whom she wanted to become a writer, and had got so excited that she had gone to see him in the newspaper office, early the next evening, and for a moment allowed him to take her in his arms. George was only a youth at this point, and the schoolteacher's interest in his talents was perfectly genuine and unselfish, but she was also a passionate and unsatisfied woman in whom interest and desire interacted. When George put his arms around her she struck his face with her fists and ran out into the night again. Some time later the minister burst in, and it seemed to George that all Winesburg had gone crazy. George goes to bed later thinking that he has missed something Kate Swift was trying to tell him.

All the gropings reveal the failure of communication in Winesburg. The mores impose a set of standards and taboos that are utterly incapable of serving the pent-up needs in the hearts of the people. They regard themselves with wonder and contempt while they study their neighbors with fear and suspicion. And the trouble, which begins with the gap between public morality and private reality, extends finally into the personality of a rich and good person like Kate Swift. Because her emotions are inhibited she acts confusedly toward George; is desperate, frightened, and ashamed; and fails to help him as she had wanted to do.

The climax (perhaps it should be called the high point in George's life until then) of the book occurs when George and Helen White reach a complete understanding one autumn evening, sitting up in the old grandstand on the fairgrounds, rapt and wordless. "With all his strength he tried to hold and to understand the mood that had come upon him. In that high place in the darkness the two oddly sensitive human atoms held each other tightly and waited. In the mind of each was the same thought. 'I have come to this lonely place and here is this other,' was the substance of the thing felt." ["Sophistication"]. It is most significant that this experience is almost entirely wordless. The shared feeling, indeed, is of seeking and wondering. It is inarticulate because it occurs in a world without meaning. Such incidents suggest that men's instincts are good but that conventional morality has warped and stifled them. Interpreted in terms of the divided stream of transcendentalism, they show that the spirit is misdirected because its physical house is mistreated. When Whitman wrote

> Logic and sermons never convince,
> The damp of the night drives deeper into my soul
> Only what proves itself to every man and woman is so.

he was making the same plea for the liberation of body and spirit together that we infer from *Winesburg, Ohio*. I say infer, because Anderson does not precisely say this; one might infer that he regards these repressions as inseparable from life—that he takes the tragic view of man—but I do not think entirely so. The pains of growth are probably inevitable, but the whole world is not as confining as Winesburg, and Anderson seems to say that people *should* be able to grow up less painfully to more abundant lives. His protagonist does, and gets away from Winesburg, though he endures torments and misunderstanding and unsatisfied love which cannot be laid to Winesburg so much as to the condition of youth in this world.

But George Willard, who will escape, is different from Elmer Cowley, who is literally inarticulate with frustration and the conviction that everyone in Winesburg considers him "queer"; and from old Ray Pearson, who runs sobbing across a rough field through the beauty of an autumn evening in order to catch Hal Winters and tell him not to marry the girl whom he has got in trouble—not marry like himself and be trapped

into having more children than he can support and living in
a tumbledown shack by the creek, working as a hired hand,
bent with labor, all his dreams come to naught. These buried
lives are disclosed with heartbreaking insight. And as we reflect upon them we sense the aptness of the "naturalistic" view
of life that the author puts into the mind of George Willard
and also presents as his own thought. "One shudders at the
thought of the meaninglessness of life while at the same instant . . . one loves life so intensely that tears come into the
eyes" ["Sophistication"].

If the universe here seems meaningless, the needs and emotions of men are intensely meaningful. Anderson feels love for
them and pity for their desperate and usually fruitless quest-
ing. It is not therefore surprising that he should turn increasingly in his later works toward emphasis on the social and
institutional causes of their frustration. Like Hamlin Garland,
however, Anderson does not master the structure of the novel.
His poignant sketches, which contain some of the best and
most memorable writing in our literature, do not "connect"
naturally into the sustained expression of the longer form.
Perhaps the scale is too narrow or the feeling too intense and
special. Perhaps Anderson could not achieve the necessary objectivity. Certainly the patterns of protest and socialism do not
provide the sort of frame upon which he could weave.

Impressionism involves two or three attitudes and literary
modes which can be related to naturalism only by careful definition. In the first place, impressionism attempts to render the
quality of experience more closely, more colorfully, more delicately than it has been rendered. To this end it presents the
mind of a character *receiving* impressions rather than judging,
classifying, or speculating; and because it attempts to catch
the experience as it is received, that experience will not have a
reasonable order but a chronological or associational one. The
order in Anderson's work is one of its most striking qualities,
for he shows people thinking of several things at once, combining incidents in the past with present experience which now

makes those incidents relevant, and having at the same time
emotions which they cannot understand while they entertain
thoughts which do not do any sort of justice to their emotional states. As a device of presentation he tells his stories
through the minds of ignorant, or certainly unstudied nar-
rators who have no sense of selection and arrangement and so
give a story that has the tone and flavor of free association.
Here in the mixture of impressionist rendering of experience
and the device of the story told by a disorderly narrator we
find the heart of Anderson's form. He makes a virtue of beginning a story at the end and ending it at the middle. He
gives away information which would create suspense of the
conventional sort and yet contrives to produce a surprise and
a satisfaction at the end of his story by a psychological revelation or a sharing of experience that suddenly becomes coherent
out of the chaos of the narrator's apparently objectless rambling. Often what begins as incoherence emerges as the disorder caused by emotion which the story discloses and which
indeed turns out to be the cause of its telling. Such a story is
"I'm a Fool" (in *Horses and Men,* 1922). Its indignant narrator, who is all mixed up about money, horses, and girls, tells
about a day at the races and his meeting with a truly nice girl
who is strongly attracted to him. He tells her a pack of fantastic lies in order to impress her and of course comes too late
to the realization that he loves her and can never go back to
her and endure the shame of admitting to all the lies he has
told. The rambling story represents the ignorant and disor-
ganized character of the narrator. It reveals his naïveté and
his ludicrous confusion of values. It also shows how the absence of "manners" makes it impossible for him to establish
an easy intimacy with the girl. And finally it represents the
universal in this provincial story—the tendency of all young
men to brag before girls and be ashamed of themselves afterwards. The "disorderly" arrangement of the details in the story
finally appears quite orderly, for it is perfectly suited to the
kind of experience that it renders.

In addition to identifying new flavors of experience and providing a new order for story-telling, Anderson's impressionism quite obviously questions the established social and moral orders. It asks, "What *is* reality?" and repeatedly shows that the telling experience, the thing at the heart of life, is not what is ordinarily represented. Things do not make the kind of sense they are "supposed" to make. They are more complicated and more subtle than the public moralists have heart to see or words to express. This is the theme of *Winesburg, Ohio* and *The Triumph of the Egg*: what appears on the surface, what is commonly described, is not the true and inward reality. But what the true reality is remains a mystery, and characters continually discover that the world is complex, that evil and good are inseparable, and that their simple ideals are inadequate. But this discovery is pathetic because its bewilderment does not pass. . . .

❀❁❀❁❀❁❀❁❀❁❀❁❀❁❀❁❀❁❀❁❀❁❀❁❀❁❀❁❀❁❀❁❀❁❀

SISTER M. JOSELYN, O.S.B.

Sister M. Joselyn, O.S.B., is Chairman of the Department of English at College of St. Scholastica, Duluth, Minnesota. She is currently at work on a book on "the lyric story."

SHERWOOD ANDERSON
AND THE LYRIC STORY

At this date, not much remains to be done by way of appointing Sherwood Anderson a place among American writers; in fact he himself succinctly indicated his own position when he remarked in the *Memoirs* that, "For all my egotism, I know I am but a minor figure." There is little disagreement, either, about the work on which Anderson's reputation rests—*Winesburg,* "Death in the Woods," a few stories from *The Triumph of the Egg.* When we come to estimate the accomplishment represented by *Winesburg,* however, things are not quite so clear. There are those who wish, still, to view the collection as a frame-story, but they then must reckon with the difficulty of seeming to reduce all the stories to the dead level of equivalent exhibits. Those on the other hand who want to read *Winesburg* as an initiation novel about George Willard have to face the problem of resting their case upon a character who in the end remains the thinnest figment. To choose to rele-

---

gate Anderson and *Winesburg* to the limbo of regionalism is
no longer acceptable.

Perhaps the sanest way is to view *Winesburg,* an uneven
collection, as a special kind of amalgam of naturalism and
lyricism. Every reader, whether approvingly or not, acknowledges the lyric intensity of the best Anderson stories. To
Herbert Gold, Anderson is "one of the purest, most intense
poets of loneliness," while Irving Howe (who has also called
Anderson a "pre-poet") holds that no other American writer
"has yet been able to realize that strain of lyrical and nostalgic
feeling which in Anderson's best work reminds one of another
and greater poet of tenderness, Turgenev." Robert Gorham
Davis ascribes the "great impression" made by *Winesburg* to
its "freshness and lyric intensity." It is Paul Rosenfeld, however, who has seen most clearly that Anderson's lyricism is a
method as much as an effect, for to this reader, Anderson's
narratives "really are lyrics with epic characteristics, lyrics narrative of event."

In analyzing the elements that go into Anderson's lyricism,
Rosenfeld notes the "legendary tone, the repetitions of slow
rhythms and the loose joints" of the American tale, as well as
the personal feeling that rises from the region between Anderson's "conscious and unconscious minds." But Rosenfeld
places greatest stress on the purely verbal aspects of Anderson's
poetic quality, for

Anderson's inclusion among the authors of the lyric story . . .
flows first of all from the fact that, using the language of actuality,
he nonetheless invariably wrings sonority and cadence from it;
unobtrusively indeed, without transcending the easy pitch of
familiar prose. . . . He sustains tones broadly with assonances and
with repeated or echoing words and phrases. He creates accent-
patterns and even stanza-like paragraphs with the periodic repetition
or alternation of features such as syllables, sounds, words, phrases,
entire periods. . . . [Introduction to *The Sherwood Anderson
Reader*].

Many readers of Anderson will see these assertions as a part of Rosenfeld's special pleading and will doubtless be more inclined to share Irving Howe's belief that amidst the "chaos of his creative life Anderson had to cast around for a device with which to establish some minimum of order in his work" and found it "in the undulations of his verbal rhythms. . . ." Indeed, it is precisely in those pieces where he was "most at sea imaginatively" that "the rhythm is most insistently established."

Rosenfeld, I think it can be shown, is on much stronger ground when contending that Anderson's stories are—in other ways—"lyrics with epic characteristics," and in holding that

As for his own specimens of the lyric story-kind, they have "inner form" like Gertrude Stein's, but their rhythms are livelier, longer, more self-completive than those of the somnolent lady-Buddha of the *rue de Fleurus*. While wanting the suavity of expression in Turgenev's lyric tales, Anderson's share the warmly singing tone of the Russian's, surpass them of course in point of tension, and have the Andersonian qualities of subtlety of attack and humorous and acute feeling, perceptions of the essential in the singular, glamour over the commonplace, boldness of image. . . . Wonderfully they "stay by us." [*Sherwood Anderson Reader*].

What, precisely, is the "inner form" of Anderson's stories and how can they be said to be "lyrics with epic characteristics"?

In the first place it must be noted that the best Anderson stories always contain and lead up to a *revelation*, epiphany, or state of realized experience. Robert Morss Lovett has said that Anderson's stories "reach outward into the unknown," while Granville Hicks asserts that "Surfaces, deeds, even words scarcely concern him; everything is bent to the task of revelation." To Herbert Gold, "The experience of epiphany is characteristic of great literature, and the lyric tales of Anderson give this wonderful rapt coming-forth, time and time again." Irving Howe—uncomplimentarily—notes that Anderson "wrote best when he had no need to develop situations or show change and interaction—" but Anderson's own ideal of art is expressed precisely in his idealization of "the tale of perfect balance," with all its "elements . . . understood, an infinite number of minute adjustments perfectly made. . . ."

Summaries of Anderson stories reveal even less than is usually the case about the significance of the narratives; obviously in Anderson what is at stake is not histories, biographies, gossip, or even tales. From Anderson's best work one does derive an unmistakable sense of authentic experience being worked out from within, in the manner of the great Russians—Turgenev and Chekhov—with their unparalleled suggestiveness and extreme economy of means. Like the Russians, Anderson does not "import his poetry into the work—he allows only the poetry that is *there*" (Herbert Gold). The significance of an Anderson story has very little to do with the "facts" that are related but it has something to do with the arrangement of those facts and with the relationship of these "epic" elements to other, more properly poetic strains.

Anderson's abandonment of pure naturalism involved him in a movement away from structures dependent upon sequential action or gradually increased intensity and toward an arrangement of events which would better dramatize the centrifugal, diffused, resonant effect his materials called for. The halting, tentative, digressive style, and the circular, hovering or "Chinese box" approach to "what happened" thus do not so much demonstrate Anderson's affectation of the manner of oral tale-telling as they illustrate his understanding that the "epic" base of the story must be manipulated in such a way that weight is thrown upon the significance of the happenings as it reveals itself to the central consciousness and to the reader, rather than upon the events themselves. This is, of course, essentially a "poetic" strategy.

Moreover, as Jon Lawry has demonstrated in his reading of "Death in the Woods," the narrative strategy, by which the story is not really "told" to any assumed audience, makes it possible that "its process of growth and contact is discovered by the audience, through the act itself rather than through the narrator's relation of the act," for "The audience is invited to enter as individuals into a process almost identical with that of the narrator and to reach with him for contact with another life." This narrative method makes it possible for the "unacknowledged audience" to "share directly not only the narrator's responses but his act of discovering and creating those responses"—and this is precisely the "method" of the post-symbolist lyric. It is also the technique by which in Anderson fantasy is most controlled, or, "if not exactly controlled, simplified, given a single lyrical line," and ambivalent —if not contradictory—emotions enfolded within one action.

Before turning to an analysis of stories by Anderson which illustrate the lyrical effects we have been describing, we may mention briefly other marks of the poetic character of his narration: non-realistic, ritualistic dialogue, the use of symbols to embody and dramatize themes, and the exploitation of suggestiveness, "the art of leaving out." In thinking of the whole of Anderson's achievement it is well to bear in mind that he began his writing career "under the influence and patronage of the realists at the time when realism was being modified by symbolism" (Robert Morss Lovett).

The first story of *Winesburg*, "Hands," affords a vivid illustration of one of the ways in which Anderson manipulates his story-line in such a way as to evoke a maximum resonance from the events narrated. Normal time sequence is almost obliterated as Anderson penetrates with the reader further and further into the mysterious recesses of Wing Biddlebaum's mind. The tragedy of Wing Biddlebaum is of course presented by means of the things that happened to him—not even the lyric story can totally dispense with the "epic" elements essential for the narrative genres—but the events of Biddlebaum's life are presented neither straightforwardly nor in a conventional flashback sequence. Rather, Anderson uses a kind of box-within-box structure as he takes us into the interior mystery of his character by means of a series of vignettes in which Biddlebaum is revealed first through the eyes of the townspeople and the casual berry-pickers who pass his house, then through the eyes of George Willard (whom Anderson cunningly utilizes as both the confidant the plot requires and as an objective correlative for all that Biddlebaum seeks), and finally through the protagonist's own sense of himself. But these sections flow so smoothly through the story-teller's hands, and are so completely suffused with Wing Biddlebaum's consciousness, that we are not aware of any awkward juncture between sections. In this structure, the first event in Biddlebaum's "chronological" life becomes the last in the record of his emotional life, because the beating of the schoolmaster was the one event which both precipitated and contained the entire mystery of the man. With the presentation of this event, also, Anderson has brought his story to its maximum level of universalization, for without resorting to allegory but by remaining wholly within the confines of realism Anderson has made us feel that we are all Wing Biddlebaum and that we are also the men who cast him out of the village half dead, and that Biddlebaum's situation enfolds within it the entire condition of man. The last section of the story is a beautifully falling cadence; coming after the event of the beating, it simply shows us Wing Biddlebaum as he now is, as we have made him, as we are:

When the rumble of the evening train that took away the express cars loaded with the day's harvest of berries had passed and restored the silence of the summer night, he went again to walk upon the veranda. In the darkness he could not see the hands . . . . Although he still hungered for the presence of the boy, who was the medium through which he expressed his love of man, the hunger became again a part of his loneliness and his waiting. Lighting a lamp,

Wing Biddlebaum . . . prepared to undress for the night. A few stray white bread crumbs lay on the cleanly washed floor by the table; putting the lamp upon a low stool he began to pick up the crumbs, carrying them to his mouth one by one with unbelievable rapidity.

Anderson's exploitation of the symbolic aspect of the eating of bread, and of the hands themselves, requires no commentary.

Other kinds of dislocation of the narrative line appear in "Adventure," in "The Thinker," and in "Sophistication." In the first story, a report of the exterior events of Alice Hindman's life is counterpointed by an account of the development of her inward, emotional life. The patterns move in opposite directions, for while Alice's outward existence appears to run steadily downhill into dull meaninglessness, her inward life climbs with increasing intensity toward a climax of desperation and hysteria. A review of only the story's outward events would seem to confirm the frequent accusation that Anderson is given to assembling large, undifferentiated narrative masses out of which he is unable to bring order or illumination, yet when he is at his best, Anderson's unfolding of inner life— even when it is not so strongly cross-grained as in "Adventure" —does provide a sufficient makeweight for outward event, and in fact the outcome toward which the narrative strives is precisely an evocation of the *quality* of the relationship between inner and outward event. In Anderson, this evocation is essentially poetic or musical. And while restraint is not a trait usually ascribed to Anderson, it is this virtue of tact which rules such sections of his narrative as the conclusion of "Adventure," in which Alice Hindman, recalling herself from the wild scene in the street, goes weeping to bed with the words,

"What is the matter with me? I will do something dreadful if I am not careful," she thought, and turning her face to the wall, began trying to force herself to face bravely the fact that many people must live and die alone, even in Winesburg.

In "Sophistication," the "epic" elements are arranged in such a way that George Willard's restlessness and puzzlement are dramatized—rather than merely reported—through the structure itself with its jerky, spasmodic focusing and refocusing. Anderson, moreover, demonstrates a high degree of cunning in not attempting any sort of philosophic resolution of George's dilemmas but by providing instead a rather quiet culminating scene in which all the contradictory aspects of George's and Helen's consciousness are caught up in a symbolic action (is it ludicrous to see a resemblance to Yeats' use of the great-rooted blossomer?):

It was so they went down the hill. . . . Once, running swiftly forward, Helen tripped George and he fell. He squirmed and shouted. Shaking with laughter, he rolled down the hill. Helen ran after him. For just a moment she stopped in the darkness. . . . When the bottom of the hill was reached and she came up to the boy, she took his arm and walked beside him in dignified silence.

Other symbol-like devices appearing in the story are the cornfields, the dry leaves and trees, the stallion, and the grandstand. Anderson's conducting of the narrative is too loose and diffuse for these objects to form a genuine symbolic pattern, but their presence does add power to the lyric suggestiveness of the narrative.

Structure in "The Thinker" is much more complex. As in "Hands," the problem here is to develop for the reader the sense of a particular personality, in this case one not nearly so unusual as Wing Biddlebaum, and that of a much younger man. Anderson begins the story by describing in his rambling, tentative manner Seth Richmond's house, the circumstances of his mother's widowhood, and her present feeling for the boy. A quarter of the story elapses before we hear any words from Seth himself, but with his return from the runaway trip we are moved directly into his consciousness and from then on the story is told from Seth's point of view. At the same time, the eerie disjointedness of experience is conveyed directly with (for Anderson) surprisingly little editorializing as we follow the young man through his brief visit with George Willard, his eavesdropping on the quarreling hotel men, his meeting with old Turk in the street, and his unsatisfactory encounter with Helen. At almost exactly midpoint in the story comes the devastating self-revelatory comment that Seth "was not what the men of the town, and even his mother, thought him to be," for "No great underlying purpose lay back of his habitual silence, and he had no definite plan for his life." Observing from afar the sullen, furious baker with the empty milk bottle in his hand, Seth "wished that he himself might become thoroughly stirred by something . . . ."

For the elucidation of Seth's identity, Anderson has ranged around the central silence and dumbness of the young man various "talkers," including Turk Smollett with his "absurdly boyish mind," the half-dangerous old wood chopper "who hurries along the middle of the road with his wheelbarrow and its nicely balanced dozen long boards." Seth knew that

When Turk got into Main Street he would become the center of a whirlwind of cries and comments, that in truth the old man was going far out of his way in order to pass through Main Street and exhibit his skill in wheeling the boards. "If George Willard were here, he'd have something to say," thought Seth.

Along with the windy political quarrelers briefly overheard in the hotel lobby is grouped the emptily ebullient George Willard who announces, "I know what I'm going to do. I'm going to fall in love. I've been sitting here and thinking it over and I'm going to do it." The climax comes as Seth, equally disgusted and bored with George's prattle and his own silence, seeks out Helen White, who utters almost no words during their walk together.

The central meaning of the boy's encounter with all these persons is conveyed in two interpolations. In the first, during the silent walk with Helen, Seth remembers the moment the day before in a field where he had heard "a soft humming noise" and looking down "had seen the bees everywhere all about him in the long grass":

He stood in a mass of weeds that grew waist-high in the field that ran away from the hillside. The weeds were abloom with tiny purple blossoms and gave forth an overpowering fragrance.

Now imagining himself with Helen in that field, Seth thought he would lie "perfectly still, looking at her and listening to the army of bees that sang . . . above his head." But a little later, as the distant thunder moves closer and the spot where they are sitting is momentarily illuminated by lightning, "The garden that had been so mysterious and vast, a place that . . . might have become the background for strange and wonderful adventures, now seemed no more than an ordinary Winesburg back yard, quite definite and limited in its outlines." Unable either to go forward into a meaningful existence or to preserve his integrity by a return to innocence, Seth Richmond can only stand, after Helen's departure, "staring, perplexed and puzzled . . . as he had been perplexed and puzzled by all the life of the town out of which she had come." Again, it is through the arrangement of actions and by a quiet exploitation of the symbolic aspects of objects and events that Anderson succeeds in bringing before us a full-dimensioned protagonist fraught with the burdens and fleeting joys resembling our own.

It is in the *Winesburg* stories such as "The Thinker," "Adventure," "Hands," "Sophistication," and "The Untold Lie" that Anderson manages to reinforce a certain surface fidelity with what Ernest Boyd has called the "deeper realism which sees beyond and beneath the exterior world to the hidden reality which is the essence of things." By combining in a special manner the story's "epic" elements with characteristic lyric devices, Anderson is able, at least on occasion, to reach the "something totally private, untouchable, beyond appearance and action, in all of us" and thus exemplifies his own belief that "To live is to create new forms: with the body in living children; in new and more beautiful forms carved out of materials; in the creation of a world of the fancy; in scholarship; in clear and lucid thought. . . ."

❖❖❖❖❖❖❖❖❖❖❖❖❖❖❖❖❖❖❖❖❖❖❖❖❖❖❖❖❖❖❖❖❖❖

LIONEL TRILLING

Lionel Trilling is George Edward Woodbury Professor of Literature
and Criticism at Columbia University, New York. His critical books
include *The Liberal Imagination, The Opposing Self*, and *Beyond
Culture*, and he is also the author of a novel.

SHERWOOD ANDERSON

I find it hard, and I think it would be false, to write about
Sherwood Anderson without speaking of him personally and
even emotionally. I did not know him; I was in his company
only twice and on neither occasion did I talk with him. The
first time I saw him was when he was at the height of his
fame; I had, I recall, just been reading *A Story-Teller's Story*
and *Tar,* and these autobiographical works had made me fully
aware of the change that had taken place in my feelings since
a few years before when almost anything that Anderson wrote
had seemed a sort of revelation. The second time was about
two years before his death; he had by then not figured in my
own thought about literature for many years, and I believe
that most people were no longer aware of him as an immediate force in their lives. His last two novels (*Beyond Desire* in
1932, and *Kit Brandon* in 1936) had not been good; they were
all too clearly an attempt to catch up with the world, but the

---

From *The Liberal Imagination* by Lionel Trilling (New York: The
Viking Press, 1947). Copyright 1941, 1947 by Lionel Trilling. Reprinted
by permission of The Viking Press, Inc., and Martin, Secker and Warburg,
Ltd.

world had moved too fast; it was not that Anderson was not aware of the state of things but rather that he had suffered the fate of the writer who at one short past moment has had a success with a simple idea which he allowed to remain simple and to become fixed. On both occasions—the first being a gathering, after one of Anderson's lectures, of eager Wisconsin graduate students and of young instructors who were a little worried that they would be thought stuffy and academic by this Odysseus, the first famous man of letters most of us had ever seen; the second being a crowded New York party—I was much taken by Anderson's human quality, by a certain serious interest he would have in the person he was shaking hands with or talking to for a brief, formal moment, by a certain graciousness or gracefulness which seemed to arise from an innocence of heart.

I mention this very tenuous personal impression because it must really have arisen not at all from my observation of the moment but rather have been projected from some unconscious residue of admiration I had for Anderson's books even after I had made all my adverse judgments upon them. It existed when I undertook this notice of Anderson on the occasion of his death, or else I should not have undertaken it. And now that I have gone back to his books again and have found that I like them even less than I remembered, I find too that the residue of admiration still remains; it is quite vague, yet it requires to be articulated with the clearer feelings of dissatisfaction; and it needs to be spoken of, as it has been, first.

There is a special poignancy in the failure of Anderson's later career. According to the artistic morality to which he and his friends subscribed—Robert Browning seems to have played a large if anonymous part in shaping it—Anderson should have been forever protected against artistic failure by the facts of his biography. At the age of forty-five, as everyone knows, he found himself the manager of a small paint factory in Elyria, Ohio; one day, in the very middle of a sentence he was dictating, he walked out of the factory and gave himself to literature and truth. From the wonder of that escape he seems never to have recovered, and his continued pleasure in it did him harm, for it seems to have made him feel that the problem of the artist was defined wholly by the struggle between sincerity on the one hand and commercialism and gentility on the other. He did indeed say that the artist needed not only courage but craft, yet it was surely the courage by which he set the most store. And we must sometimes feel that he had dared too much for his art and therefore expected too much merely from his boldness, believing that right opinion must necessarily result from it. Anderson was deeply concerned with the idea of justification; there was an odd, quirky, undisciplined religious strain in him that took this form; and he expected that although Philistia might condemn him, he would have an eventual justification in the way of art and truth. He was justified in some personal way, as I have tried to say, and no doubt his great escape had something to do with this, but it also had the effect of fatally fixing the character of his artistic life.

Anderson's greatest influence was probably upon those who read him in adolescence, the age when we find the books we give up but do not get over. And it now needs a little fortitude to pick up again, as many must have done upon the news of his death, the one book of his we are all sure to have read, for *Winesburg, Ohio* is not just a book, it is a personal souvenir. It is commonly owned in the Modern Library edition, very likely in the most primitive format of that series, even before it was tricked out with its vulgar little ballet-Prometheus; and the brown oilcloth binding, the coarse paper, the bold type crooked on the page, are dreadfully evocative. Even the introduction by Ernest Boyd is rank with the odor of the past, of the day when criticism existed in heroic practical simplicity, when it was all truth against hypocrisy, idealism against philistinism, and the opposite of "romanticism" was not "classicism" but "realism," which—it now seems odd—negated both. As for the Winesburg stories themselves, they are as dangerous to read again, as paining and as puzzling, as if they were old letters we had written or received.

It is not surprising that Anderson should have made his strongest appeal, although by no means his only one, to adolescents. For one thing, he wrote of young people with a special tenderness; one of his best-known stories is called "I Want To Know Why": it is the great adolescent question, and the world Anderson saw is essentially, and even when it is inhabited by adults, the world of the sensitive young person. It is a world that does not "understand," a world of solitude, of running away from home, of present dullness and far-off joy and eventual fulfillment; it is a world seen as suffused by one's own personality and yet—and therefore—felt as indifferent to one's own personality. And Anderson used what seems to a young person the very language to penetrate to the heart of the world's mystery, what with its rural or primeval willingness to say things thrice over, its reiterated "Well . . ." which suggests the groping of boyhood, its "Eh?" which implies the inward-turning wisdom of old age.

Most of us will feel now that this world of Anderson's is a pretty inadequate representation of reality and probably always was. But we cannot be sure that it was not a necessary event in our history, like adolescence itself; and no one has the adolescence he would have liked to have had. But an adolescence must not continue beyond its natural term, and as we read through Anderson's canon what exasperates us is his stubborn, satisfied continuance in his earliest attitudes. There is something undeniably impressive about the period of Anderson's work in which he was formulating his characteristic notions. We can take, especially if we have a modifying consciousness of its historical moment, *Windy MacPherson's Son*, despite its last part which is so curiously like a commercial magazine story of the time; *Marching Men* has power even though its political mysticism is repellent; *Winesburg, Ohio* has its touch of greatness; *Poor White* is heavy-handed but not without its force; and some of the stories in *The Triumph of the Egg* have the kind of grim quaintness which is, I think, Anderson's most successful mood, the mood that he occasionally achieves now and then in his later short pieces, such as "Death in the Woods." But after 1921, in *Dark Laughter* and *Many Marriages*, the books that made the greatest critical stir, there emerges in Anderson's work the compulsive, obsessive, repetitive quality which finally impresses itself on us as his characteristic quality.

Anderson is connected with the tradition of the men who maintain a standing quarrel with respectable society and have a perpetual bone to pick with the rational intellect. It is a very old tradition, for the Essenes, the early Franciscans, as well as the early Hasidim, may be said to belong to it. In modern times it has been continued by Blake and Whitman and D. H. Lawrence. Those who belong to the tradition usually do something more about the wrong way the world goes than merely to denounce it—they *act out* their denunciations and assume a role and a way of life. Typically they take up their packs and leave the doomed respectable city, just as Anderson did. But Anderson lacked what his spiritual colleagues have always notably had. We may call it *mind*, but *energy* and *spiritedness*, in their relation to mind, will serve just as well. Anderson never understood that the moment of enlightenment and conversion—the walking out—cannot be merely celebrated but must be developed, so that what begins as an act of will grows to be an act of intelligence. The men of the anti-rationalist tradition mock the mind's pretensions and denounce its restrictiveness; but they are themselves the agents of the most powerful thought. They do not of course really reject mind at all, but only mind as it is conceived by respectable society. "I learned the Torah from all the limbs of my teacher," said one of the Hasidim. They think with their sensations, their emotions, and, some of them, with their sex. While denouncing intellect, they shine forth in a mental blaze of energy which manifests itself in syntax, epigram, and true discovery.

Anderson is not like them in this regard. He did not become

a "wise" man. He did not have the gift of being able to throw
out a sentence or a metaphor which suddenly illuminates
some dark corner of life—his role implied that he should be
full of "sayings" and specific insights, yet he never was. But in
the preface to *Winesburg, Ohio* he utters one of the few
really "wise" things in his work, and, by a kind of irony, it
explains something of his own inadequacy. The preface consists of a little story about an old man who is writing what he
calls "The Book of the Grotesque." This is the old man's
ruling idea:

That in the beginning when the world was young there were a great
many thoughts but no such thing as a truth. Man made the truths
himself and each truth was a composite of a great many vague
thoughts. All about in the world were truths and they were all
beautiful.

The old man [had] listed hundreds of the truths in his book. I
will not try to tell you all of them. There was the truth of virginity
and the truth of passion, the truth of wealth and of poverty, of
thrift and of profligacy, of carelessness and abandon. Hundreds and
hundreds were the truths and they were all beautiful.

And then the people came along. Each as he appeared snatched
up one of the truths and some who were quite strong snatched up
a dozen of them.

It was the truths that made the people grotesque. The old man
had quite an elaborate theory concerning the matter. It was his
notion that the moment one of the people took one of the truths
to himself, called it his truth, and tried to live his life by it, he
became grotesque and the truth he embraced became a falsehood.

Anderson snatched but a single one of the truths and it
made him, in his own gentle and affectionate meaning of the
word, a "grotesque"; eventually the truth itself became a kind
of falsehood. It was the truth—or perhaps we must call it a
simple complex of truths—of love-passion-freedom, and it was
made up of these "vague thoughts": that each individual is a
precious secret essence, often discordant with all other es-

sences; that society, and more particularly the industrial society, threatens these essences; that the old good values of life
have been destroyed by the industrial dispensation; that people
have been cut off from each other and even from themselves.
That these thoughts make a truth is certain; and its importance is equally certain. In what way could it have become a
falsehood and its possessor a "grotesque"?

The nature of the falsehood seems to lie in this—that Anderson's affirmation of life by love, passion, and freedom had,
paradoxically enough, the effect of quite negating life, making it gray, empty, and devoid of meaning. We are quite used
to hearing that this is what excessive intellection can do; we
are not so often warned that emotion, if it is of a certain kind,
can be similarly destructive. Yet when feeling is understood as
an answer, a therapeutic, when it becomes a sort of critical
tool and is conceived of as excluding other activities of life, it
can indeed make the world abstract and empty. Love and passion, when considered as they are by Anderson as a means of
attack upon the order of the respectable world, can contrive a
world which is actually without love and passion and not
worth being "free" in.[1]

In Anderson's world there are many emotions, or rather
many instances of a few emotions, but there are very few

---

[1] In the preface of *The Sherwood Anderson Reader*, Paul Rosenfeld,
Anderson's friend and admirer, has summarized in a remarkable way the
vision of life which Anderson's work suggests: "Almost, it seems, we touch
an absolute existence, a curious semi-animal, semi-divine life. Its chronic
state is banality, prostration, dismemberment, unconsciousness; tensity with
indefinite yearning and infinitely stretching desire. Its manifestation: the
non-community of cranky or otherwise asocial solitaries, dispersed, impotent
and imprisoned. . . . Its wonders—the wonders of its chaos—are fugitive
heroes and heroines, mutilated like the dismembered Osiris, the dismembered Dionysius. . . . Painfully the absolute comes to itself in consciousness of universal feeling and helplessness. . . . It realizes itself as
feeling, sincerity, understanding, as connection and unity; sometimes at
the cost of the death of its creatures. It triumphs in anyone aware of its
existence even in its sullen state. The moment of realization is tragically
brief. Feeling, understanding, unity pass. The divine life sinks back again,
dismembered and unconscious."

sights, sounds, and smells, very little of the stuff of actuality. The very things to which he gives moral value because they are living and real and opposed in their organic nature to the insensate abstractness of an industrial culture become, as he writes about them, themselves abstract and without life. His praise of the racehorses he said he loved gives us no sense of a horse; his Mississippi does not flow; his tall corn grows out of the soil of his dominating subjectivity. The beautiful organic things of the world are made to be admirable not for themselves but only for their moral superiority to men and machines. There are many similarities of theme between Anderson and D. H. Lawrence, but Lawrence's far stronger and more sensitive mind kept his faculty of vision fresh and true; Lawrence had eyes for the substantial and even at his most doctrinaire he knew the world of appearance.

And just as there is no real sensory experience in Anderson's writing, there is also no real social experience. His people do not really go to church or vote or work for money, although it is often said of them that they do these things. In his desire for better social relationships Anderson could never quite see the social relationships that do in fact exist, however inadequate they may be. He often spoke, for example, of unhappy, desperate marriages and seemed to suggest that they ought to be quickly dissolved, but he never understood that marriages are often unsatisfactory for the very reasons that make it impossible to dissolve them.

His people have passion without body, and sexuality without gaiety and joy, although it is often through sex that they are supposed to find their salvation. John Jay Chapman said of Emerson that, great as he was, a visitor from Mars would learn less about life on earth from him than from Italian opera, for the opera at least suggested that there were two sexes. When Anderson was at the height of his reputation, it seemed that his report on the existence of two sexes was the great thing about him, the thing that made his work an advance over the literature of New England. But although the visitor from Mars might be instructed by Anderson in the mere fact of bisexuality, he would still be advised to go to the Italian opera if he seeks fuller information. For from the opera, as never from Anderson, he will acquire some of the knowledge which is normally in the possession of natives of the planet, such as that sex has certain manifestations which are socially quite complex, that it is involved with religion, politics, and the fate of nations, above all that it is frequently marked by the liveliest sort of energy.

In their speech his people have not only no wit, but no idiom. To say that they are not "real" would be to introduce all sorts of useless quibbles about the art of character creation; they are simply not *there*. This is not a failure of art; rather, it would seem to have been part of Anderson's intention that they should be not there. His narrative prose is contrived to that end; it is not really a colloquial idiom, although it has certain colloquial tricks; it approaches in effect the inadequate use of a foreign language; old slang persists in it and elegant archaisms are consciously used, so that people are constantly having the "fantods," girls are frequently referred to as "maidens," and things are "like unto" other things. These mannerisms, although they remind us of some of Dreiser's, are not the result, as Dreiser's are, of an effort to be literary and impressive. Anderson's prose has a purpose to which these mannerisms are essential—it has the intention of making us doubt our familiarity with our own world, and not, we must note, in order to make things fresher for us but only in order to make them seem puzzling to us and remote from us. When a man whose name we know is frequently referred to as "the plowmaker," when we hear again and again of "a kind of candy called Milky Way" long after we have learned, if we did not already know, that Milky Way is a candy, when we are told of someone that "He became a radical. He had radical thoughts," it becomes clear that we are being asked by this false naïveté to give up our usual and on the whole useful conceptual grasp of the world we get around in.

Anderson liked to catch people with their single human secret, their essence, but the more he looks for their essence the more his characters vanish into the vast limbo of meaningless life, the less they are human beings. His great American heroes were Mark Twain and Lincoln, but when he writes of these two shrewd, enduring men, he robs them of all their savor and masculinity, of all their bitter resisting mind; they become little more than a pair of sensitive, suffering happy-go-luckies. The more Anderson says about people, the less alive they become—and the less lovable. Is it strange that, with all Anderson's expressed affection for them, we ourselves can never love the people he writes about? But of course we do not love people for their essence or their souls, but for their having a certain body, or wit, or idiom, certain specific relationships with things and other people, and for a dependable continuity of existence: we love them for being there.

We can even for a moment entertain the thought that Anderson himself did not love his characters, else he would not have so thoroughly robbed them of substance and hustled them so quickly off the stage after their small essential moments of crisis. Anderson's love, however, was real enough; it is only that he loves under the aspect of his "truth"; it is love indeed but love become wholly abstract. Another way of putting it is that Anderson sees with the eyes of a religiosity of a very limited sort. No one, I think, has commented on the amount and quality of the mysticism that entered the thought of the writers of the twenties. We may leave Willa Cather aside, for her notion of Catholic order differentiates her; but in addition to Anderson himself, Dreiser, Waldo Frank, and Eugene O'Neill come to mind as men who had recourse to a strong but undeveloped sense of supernal powers.

It is easy enough to understand this crude mysticism as a protest against philosophical and moral materialism; easy enough, too, to forgive it, even when, as in Anderson, the second births and the large revelations seem often to point only to the bosom of a solemn bohemia, and almost always to a lowering rather than a heightening of energy. We forgive it because some part of the blame for its crudity must be borne by the culture of the time. In Europe a century before, Stendhal could execrate a bourgeois materialism and yet remain untempted by the dim religiosity which in America in the twenties seemed one of the likeliest of the few ways by which one might affirm the value of spirit; but then Stendhal could utter his denunciation of philistinism in the name of Mozart's music, the pictures of Cimabue, Masaccio, Giotto, Leonardo, and Michelangelo, the plays of Corneille, Racine, and Shakespeare. Of what is implied by these things Anderson seems never to have had a real intimation. His awareness of the past was limited, perhaps by his fighting faith in the "modern," and this, in a modern, is always a danger. His heroes in art and morality were few: Joyce, Lawrence, Dreiser, and Gertrude Stein, as fellow moderns; Cellini, Turgenev; there is a long piece in praise of George Borrow; he spoke of Hawthorne with contempt, for he could not understand Hawthorne except as genteel, and he said of Henry James that he was "the novelist of those who hate," for mind seemed to him always a sort of malice. And he saw but faintly even those colleagues in art whom he did admire. His real heroes were the simple and unassuming, a few anonymous Negroes, a few craftsmen, for he gave to the idea of craftsmanship a value beyond the value which it actually does have—it is this as much as anything else that reminds us of Hemingway's relation to Anderson—and a few racing drivers of whom Pop Geers was chief. It is a charming hero worship, but it does not make an adequate antagonism to the culture which Anderson opposed, and in order to make it compelling and effective Anderson reinforced it with what is in effect the high language of religion, speaking of salvation, of the voice that will not be denied, of dropping the heavy burden of this world.

The salvation that Anderson was talking about was no doubt

a real salvation, but it was small, and he used for it the language of the most strenuous religious experience. He spoke in visions and mysteries and raptures, but what he was speaking about after all was only the salvation of a small legitimate existence, of a quiet place in the sun and moments of leisurely peace, of not being nagged and shrew-ridden, nor deprived of one's due share of affection. What he wanted for himself and others was perhaps no more than what he got in his last years: a home, neighbors, a small daily work to do, and the right to say his say carelessly and loosely and without the sense of being strictly judged. But between this small, good life and the language which he used about it there is a discrepancy which may be thought of as a willful failure of taste, an intended lapse of the sense of how things fit. Wyndham Lewis, in his attack in *Paleface* on the early triumphant Anderson, speaks of Anderson's work as an assault on responsibility and thoughtful maturity, on the pleasures and uses of the mind, on decent human pride, on Socratic clarity and precision; and certainly when we think of the "marching men" of Anderson's second novel, their minds lost in their marching and singing, leaving to their leader the definitions of their aims, we have what might indeed be the political consequences of Anderson's attitudes if these were carried out to their ultimate implications. Certainly the precious essence of personality to which Anderson was so much committed could not be preserved by any of the people or any of the deeds his own books delight in.

But what hostile critics forget about Anderson is that the cultural situation from which his writing sprang was actually much as he described it. Anderson's truth may have become a falsehood in his hands by reason of limitations in himself or in the tradition of easy populism he chose as his own, but one has only to take it out of his hands to see again that it is indeed a truth. The small legitimate existence, so necessary for the majority of men to achieve, is in our age so very hard, so nearly impossible, for them to achieve. The language Anderson used was certainly not commensurate with the traditional value which literature gives to the things he wanted, but it is not incommensurate with the modern difficulty of attaining these things. And it is his unending consciousness of this difficulty that constitutes for me the residue of admiration for him that I find I still have.

EPIFANIO SAN JUAN, JR.

Epifanio San Juan, Jr., has taught at Harvard University, the University
of California at Davis, the University of the Philippines, and now
teaches English at the University of Connecticut. He is the author of
The Art of Oscar Wilde.

VISION AND REALITY:
A RECONSIDERATION OF
SHERWOOD ANDERSON'S
WINESBURG, OHIO

. . . Lionel Trilling persuasively contends that a marked
discrepancy between life as Anderson conceives it and the
language he uses to convey to us this conception vitiates the
exemplary integrity of his fiction. Consequently, the moments
of enlightenment and conversion, as Anderson celebrates them
in *Winesburg, Ohio,* fail as acts of will to crystallize into acts
of the intelligence. For Trilling, therefore, Anderson's stories,
though dealing with many emotions, have "few sights, sounds,
smells, very little of the stuff of actuality" that give moral
value to the organic act of living. Ultimately Anderson's predi-
lection for insensate abstractions is said to betray a distasteful
lack of real sensory, as well as social, experience in his work.

Is it verifiably true, one may legitimately inquire, that Anderson's fiction betrays an absence (to use Henry James's

From "Vision and Reality: A Reconsideration of Sherwood Anderson's
Winesburg, Ohio," *American Literature* XXXV (May 1963). Reprinted
by permission of Epifanio San Juan, Jr., and Duke University Press.

phrases) of the "quality of felt life" or "the solidity of specification" that is necessary for any piece of fiction to be "interesting," that is, a significant impression of one of the myriad
forms of reality? A more analytic approach seems to be called
for if we are to appreciate more intensively the personal vision
of life and experience that Anderson projected in his fiction. . . .

In the introductory chapter of *Winesburg, Ohio* entitled "The Book of the Grotesque," Anderson presents initially
the theoretical motivations that underlie his basic theme:
"That in the beginning when the world was young there were
a great many thoughts but no such thing as a truth. Man
made the truths himself and each truth was a composite of a
great many vague thoughts. All about in the world were the
truths and they were all beautiful." According to Anderson,
man makes his truths. But "the moment one of the people
took one of the truths to himself, called it his truth, and tried
to live his life by it," he became a grotesque and the truth he
embraced became a "falsehood." That is, anyone who identifies himself absolutely with fixed schematic ways of doing,
feeling, and thinking, and tries to direct his life according to
these "vague thoughts" will inevitably distort the inner self
and its potentialities, since the inner self has the unexercised
capacity to demonstrate a range of *virtù* greater than any experienced situation could afford, or demand of it. Consequently, his truths, falsifying his nature, should, if he does not
stick to any one formulation of them, ideally lead to an in-
tenser enlargement of life and not to a constricted compass
of response and possibilities for the qualification of motives;
he should ideally initiate a greater intensity of critical self-
awareness, cognizant of the fact that to any one point of view
there exist horizons and landscapes that are closed to it;
hence, he has imperative need for constant inquiry, perpetual
examination of principles, and endless pursuit of other modes,
more organic and integrative, of self-expression.

The consensus of critical opinion about Anderson's protagonists so far has been generally negative, owing perhaps to the notion that there is in them a marked absence of any positive force or direction in the way they conduct their revolt against the milieu. Among others, Trilling bewails Anderson's success with the simple idea of "instinct-versus-reason" conflict as applied to characterization. In allowing this idea to remain simple and fixed, Anderson (Trilling points out) is logically led to adopt a one-sided outlook manifest in the compulsive, repetitive quality of his characters' behavior. And yet, despite this anomalous confusion of the author and his characters in a single point of view, could we, for instance, call Doctor Parcival (in "The Philosopher") a flat, unrealized character?

The truth is, I submit, that Doctor Parcival incarnates the intensest energy and amplitude of imagination which Anderson prized above all other qualities that we find solidified in the static normative values of any given society, revealed here in the choric comments of such typical Winesburg conformists as Tom Willard and Will Henderson. No doubt Doctor Parcival's tales defy category and summary: "they begin nowhere and end nowhere." Apart from this inherently ironical temper, his varied suppositions of his past life testify to the triumph of possibility and free initiative against the doctrine-bound moralizing and deterministic orientation of the average Winesburg citizen:

"I was a reporter like you here," Doctor Parcival began. "It was in a town in Iowa—or was it in Illinois? I don't remember and anyway it makes no difference. Perhaps I am trying to conceal my identity and don't want to be very definite. . . . I may have stolen a great sum of money or been involved in a murder before I came here. There is food for thought in that, eh?"

The exploratory tenor of the Doctor's recollections, his susceptibility to enlarge on facts until they assume fabulous proportions, leads, in effect, to his transcending the limitations of the social environment, and its stultifying, because static, assumptions. When he refuses to examine the dead child, terror overwhelms him; nevertheless his imagination anticipates all possible futures, even the worst, dwelling tentatively and experimentally, so to speak, on [such] concrete details as rope and lamppost in this passage:

"What I have done will arouse the people of this town." he declared excitedly. "Do I not know human nature? Do I not know what will happen? Word of my refusal will be whispered about. Presently men will get together in groups and talk of it. They will come here. We will quarrel and there will be talk of hanging. Then they will come again bearing a rope in their hands. . . . It may be that what I am talking about will not occur this morning. It may be put off until tonight but I will be hanged. Everyone will get excited. I will be hanged to a lamp-post on Main Street."

On this wealth of suppositions, this inexhaustible fund of hypothetical plotting and spontaneous prophecies of the future, Doctor Parcival transcends any dogmatic judgment that Winesburg may for the moment decree and impose. Spiritually he transcends the realm of facts and contingencies of human finitude by positing as many alternatives of personal fate as he could, finally subsuming all of them under a ruling insight: "everyone in the world is Christ and they are all crucified." With Christ goes the possibility for resurrection, renewal, and affirmation. And by force of his emotional convictions, this idea ceases to be a cold abstraction and becomes in him a living dynamic truth. . . .

What predominates in *Winesburg, Ohio* is precisely the complex of pictorial representation that stems from the writer's concentrated attention and exploitation of the sensuous potentialities of his material. For Anderson, form is essentially an organic element which follows the contours of an image, of a symbolic cluster of sensory impressions aimed toward delivering an objective immediate presentation of a character's inner struggles, the specific quality of inwardness that constitutes the "roundness" of his personality. Writing in the

Notebook, Anderson implicitly defines form as rhythm: "The rhythm you are seeking in any of the arts lies just below the surface of things in nature. To get below the surface, to get the lower rhythms into your hands, your body, your mind, is what you seek." Thus, Kate Swift's impulsive eagerness (in "The Teacher") to "open the door of life" to George Willard takes possession of her to such a degree that "it became something physical." Anderson frequently tends to embody abstractions in some organic or physical act, thereby capturing just the exact rhythm and movement of body and speech on which drama in fiction depends.

The rhythmic movement of Anderson's sentences and the variations of sense in the repetitions of phrases in syntactically varying contexts may be illustrated in George Willard's endeavor to define his ultimate decision in "Sophistication." Here the process of groping toward a climactic resolution is imitated and dramatized in the tempo and cadence of each unit of his soliloquy:

"I'll go to Helen White's house, that's what I'll do. I'll walk right in. I'll say that I want to see her. I'll walk right in and sit down, that's what I'll do," he declared, climbing over a fence and beginning to run.

Walking along Main Street, George listens to the fiddlers tuning their instruments: "The broken sounds floated down through an open window and out across the murmur of voices and the loud blare of the horns of the band. . . . The sense of crowding, moving life closed in about him." Four pages later, after George has discovered the meaninglessness of life, "the fiddlers, their instruments tuned, sweated and worked to keep the feet of youth flying over a dance floor." Through qualified repetitions, the development and changes in the character's attitudes are thus immediately conveyed. Similarly, Gertrude Stein's prose functions on the premise, implicit in Anderson's aesthetic, that "repetition is an essential strategy in composition; it guarantees similarity and forces the consciousness upon the nature of the thing seen while at the same time it provides the avenue along which movement and change may occur."[1]

The effective repetition of figurative patterns functions also as a method for attaining unity in the story. As a particular instance, the focus on Dr. Reefy's hands (in "Paper Pills") becomes the integrating center of his poignantly pathetic crisis in life. His hands, resembling "unpainted wooden balls," have the habit of putting down his thoughts in scraps of paper which then become "little round hard balls" in his pockets. The story of his courtship is then compared to "twisted little apples" which in turn evoke the image of his gnarled knuckles, and therefore the hands that write down his thoughts. What is the implication of this circularity or continuity of images? Dr. Reefy refuses, in effect, to be a sentimentalist, for thoughts —do they not compose the truths Anderson spoke of in "The Book of the Grotesque"?—become to him literally transformed into useless paper pills.

It may be said that life in *Winesburg, Ohio* often tends to move in a circular pattern either by force of habit and custom or by force of sympathetic obedience to the cycle of the seasons, to the life of the instincts and impulses in man. When George Willard (in "Sophistication") takes the "backward view of life,"

a door is torn open and for the first time he looks out upon the world, seeing, as though they marched in procession before him, the countless figures of men who before his time have come out of nothingness into the world, lived their lives, and disappeared again into nothingness.

This mood of bitter nihilism and despair extends to the interpretation of the people's gaiety during Fair time: "In the street the people surged up and down like cattle confined in a

---

[1] Frederick J. Hoffman, *Gertrude Stein* (Minneapolis: University of Minnesota Press, 1961), p. 20.

pen." After retrospective meditations comes the introspective search for the existential dimension of life, arriving finally at an insight as potently illuminating in application as the spectacle of the tragic human condition offered us by Pascal, Kierkegaard, or Kafka. George then formulates with impressionistic clarity his need for understanding, invoking nature to furnish metaphoric equivalents for life:

With a little gasp he sees himself as merely a leaf blown by the wind through the streets of his village. He knows that in spite of all the stout talk of his fellows he must live and die in uncertainty, a thing blown by the winds, a thing destined like corn to wilt in the sun. He shivers and looks eagerly about.

The strain of "cornfed mysticism" often alluded to by Anderson's critics has its roots here in the cycle of the season to which George, on the April morning of his departure, responds in a ritual of walking again on Trunion Pike to complete the circle of his maturity in Winesburg, showing his appreciation of the vibrant chiaroscuro of light and shade, the trilling resonance of melody in nature which, preserved in memory, would serve as the nourishment for his "growing passion for dreams":

He had been in the midst of the great open place on winter nights when it was covered with snow and only the moon looked down at him; he had been there in the fall when bleak winds blew and on summer evenings when the air vibrated with the song of insects.

. . . In "A Note on Realism," Anderson enunciated part of the aesthetic implications of his prose style, his peculiar manipulation of language, his personal beliefs as to the selection of facts and details in fiction: "The life of reality is confused, disorderly, almost always without apparent purpose, whereas in the artist's imaginative life there is purpose. There is determination to give the tale, the song, the painting Form" (*Notebook*). In a letter to a friend, he confessed his aspira-

tion "to try to develop, to the top of my bent, my own capacity
to feel, see, taste, smell, hear. I wanted, as all men must want,
to be a free man, proud of my own manhood, always more
and more aware of earth, people, streets, houses, towns, cities.
I wanted to take all into myself, digest what I could." Trilling's accusation that Anderson's fiction lacks "the stuff of
actuality" seems to me a gross mistake not only in the light
of Anderson's lifelong preoccupation with sensory experience,
its qualities and values, but also in the face of the testimony
of *Winesburg, Ohio* and its "prose of reality." Of Anderson's
artistic end we may say that, like Hemingway, he has always
sought the real thing, the sequence of motion and fact which
make the real emotion so that, as a result, the act being described is "no sooner done than said," becoming "simultaneous with the word, no sooner said than felt."[2] But let us
consider the evidence itself, "the solidity of specification" in
Winesburg, Ohio.

Anderson's power of visualization contributes in a large measure to the full realization of his characters' personalities. We
see this in Tom Foster's grandmother (in "Drink") with her
hands twisted out of shape so that "when she took hold of a
mop or a broom handle the hands looked like the dried stems
of an old creeping vine clinging to a tree." Belle Carpenter's
sensuality (in "An Awakening") and her callous nature are
epitomized in a few bold strokes: dark skin, gray eyes, and
thick lips. Joe Welling's face (in "A Man of Ideas") inscribes
itself in memory for one striking particularity: "The edges of
his teeth that were tipped with gold glistened in the light"—
an impression which convincingly sums up his unfeeling nature, and his devotion to the pursuit of material wealth. Tom
Willard's hands (in "The Philosopher") appear as though
"dipped in blood that had dried and faded," a statement

---

[2] Harry Levin, "Observations on the Style of Ernest Hemingway,"
Hemingway and His Critics, ed. Carlos Baker (New York: Hill and Wang,
1961), p. 110.

which may be construed to connote the sufferings and pain
he has inflicted upon George and Mrs. Willard and of which
he is so pathetically unaware.

Thus, in order to render and organize the inarticulate sensi-
bilities of his characters, Anderson exploits natural scenery as
an objective fact whose emotive charge or connotativeness may
act as an index or correlative key to the affective or psychic
situation of the characters. In "Drink," for example, the stage
for Tom Foster's exuberant flights of imagination are set by
the spring season evoked through a graphic delineation of
setting: "The trees . . . were all newly clothed in soft green
leaves . . . and in the air there was a hush, a waiting kind of
silence very stirring to the blood." Scenery also functions as a
reconciling force among conflicting interests, thereby destroying the isolation of selves and liberating the hidden undis-
covered self. In "The Untold Lie," Ray Pearson and Hal
Winters become all alive to each other upon perceiving the
beauty of the country in the failing autumnal light. In a sad
distracted mood, Ray Pearson feels the spirit of revolt rising
within him against all crippling commitments that make life
ugly. The open spacious field stimulates in him a desire to
"shout or scream," to do something "unexpected and terrifying," resisting the claims of the identity that Winesburg society has forced upon him on account of his past, his habitual
failings, utterly ignoring the qualitative worth of his infinite
cravings, his endless dreams.

We see, then, that objective details and situations, particularly those with a density of texture and a load of emotional
suggestiveness, usually appear in strategic places as a focus for
all those qualities which the characters are supposed to represent or demonstrate in word and action. Generally, they may
be construed as preparations for any idiosyncratic display of
feeling or as tactfully placed amplifications of a given mood
or tone; in effect, their presence serves as a contributing element toward accomplishing a total unity of effect. . . .

In *Winesburg, Ohio*, irony as a device assumes in general

1) the form of an objective situation running counter to the subjective interpretation of it by the character concerned, and 2) the form of utterances whose implications run counter to the surface meaning and tone of the words themselves. Let us illustrate the first.

Like almost all the protagonists in the book, Seth Richmond (in "The Thinker") wants love and freedom, but his passion evaporates in endless efforts at rationalization. This dilemma Anderson skillfully objectifies in the contrast between Seth's mental vacillations and the spontaneous productive activity of the bees amid the sensuous, extravagant forms and colors of nature. With the bees everywhere about him, "he stood in a mass of weeds that grew waist-high in the field that ran away from the hillside. The weeds were abloom with tiny purple blossoms and gave forth an overpowering fragrance. Upon the weeds the bees were gathered in armies, singing as they worked. Seth imagined himself lying on a summer evening, buried deep among the weeds beneath the tree."

Without the aid of a strong will, Seth could never affirm through sustained action any serious purpose in life. The scene suggests just those positive qualities that, conveyed through the description of an external landscape, prove antithetical to the internal state of the character concerned. An ironical effect is produced when, earlier, Seth the indecisive "thinker" finally resolves to see Helen:

Seth raised the knocker and let it fall. Its heavy clatter sounded like a report from distant guns. "How awkward and foolish I am," he thought. "If Mrs. White comes to the door, I won't know what to say."

Obviously the determined or decisive quality of the guns' report (the bees were referred to as "armies" above) directly mocks the wavering or hesitant gestures that he displays here in the rhythmical movement and tone of his language.

In "Respectability," Wash Williams has a deeply sensitive and poetic nature despite the ugliness of his features. In the house of his wife's mother (his wife has been guilty of adultery before he visits her), he observes that everything looks "stylish" and respectable. But respectability, symbolized by "plush chairs and couch," pales into insignificance beside the fierce, trembling hatred of Wash, his raw and tender feelings: "I ached to forgive and forget." But the mother outrageously treats him as though he were a seducer. The distinctly human aspect of Wash Williams' personality is finally rendered in the humor and gentle irony of the ending: "I didn't get the mother killed. . . . I struck her once with a chair and then the neighbors came in and took it away. She screamed so loud, you see. I won't ever have a chance to kill her now. She died of a fever a month after that happened."

Now let us illustrate the second type of irony. In "A Man of Ideas," Joe Welling, despite his occupation as Standard Oil agent with a life of simple mechanical routine, is described as "a tiny little volcano that lies silent for days and then suddenly spouts fire." In the thick of baseball fights, he would be making "fierce animal cries," acting as though possessed by a malignant spirit. Posing to himself the question "What is decay?" he ruthlessly begins pursuing facts to their absurd limits, arriving at the conclusion that "The World Is On Fire!" Clearly, Joe Welling's routine existence becomes the object of critical parody conducted by his own creative self—his animal cries, his clever syllogisms and systematic deductions working toward the fantastic distortion of practical reality from which his public mask virtually derives substance.

Whereas Joe Welling is a victim of candid naïveté and lack of critical self-awareness, Dr. Parcival exhibits the utmost degree of critical awareness possible, using comic understatement in order to immunize himself from any propensity for mawkish sentimentality. At the outset, he explains his eccentricity by attributing to his character "many strange turns." Visiting his father's corpse in the asylum, he is delighted in being treated like a king; then he pronounces over his father's body this slightly cynical prayer: "Let peace brood over this carcass."

His comic spirit, detached and ironical, finally assumes a grim, intensely self-wounding edge when he speaks of his brother's attitude of superiority which is climaxed by the ridiculous manner of his death. One feels here how Dr. Parcival, to prevent any future caricature of his attitudes, adopts in anticipation an utterly conscious self-critical stance:

"I want to fill you with hatred and contempt so that you will be a superior being," he declared. "Look at my brother. . . . He despised everyone, you see. You have no idea with what contempt he looked upon mother and me. And was he not our superior? You know he was. . . . I have given you a sense of it. He is dead. Once when he was drunk he lay down on the tracks and the car in which he lived with the other painters ran over him" ["The Philosopher"].

(Contextually viewed, whenever Dr. Parcival lauds himself— as, for instance, "a man of distinction"—this is usually expressed with a muted tone of self-hatred, self-doubt.) This critical self-awareness is perhaps implied by the description of his "black irregular teeth" and his strange uncanny eyes: "The lid of the left eye twitched; it fell down and snapped up; it was exactly as though the lid of the eye were a window shade and someone stood inside the doctor's head playing with the cord."

It seems to me thus far that the fundamental dilemma of George Willard, the central hero of the book, involves chiefly a search for order—primarily, an order between intention and act, thought and deed, dream and reality. We may discern this problem dramatized in the relationship of the three characters in "An Awakening" whose intentions are never fulfilled through appropriate modes of action. For instance, Belle Carpenter submits to George Willard's demands when, in fact, she loves Ed Handby. Ed Handby himself suffers from a particular deficiency epitomized by his having large fists yet a soft and quiet voice—that is, great physical strength coupled with impotency at verbal expression. Since society does not afford the means or the manners for the communication of

passion, Ed Handby, like Elmer Cowley (in "Queer"), can express himself only through bodily force; thus, when he comes
to woo Belle, his actions prove menacingly brutal.

George Willard senses this malaise of dissociation when he
asserts that men are not responsible for what they do with
women, implying thereby a lack of order or governing law to
sanction any definite harmonious kind of relationship between
the sexes. Although the ardent exercise of his intellect delights him, it leads him nowhere. In his walk he comes to a
place resembling "old world towns of the middle ages" that
all at once excites his fancy, arousing thoughts of a former existence and perhaps of lost innocence and purity. A strong
impulse drives him to a dark alley where he smells the rank
odor of manure from cows and pigs. His senses aroused, he
now feels oddly detached from all life, feeling "unutterably
big" and heroic amid the putrid squalor of the Winesburg
slums. The density and massive "thickness" of life has thus
released him from all self-centered, limiting speculations, in-
fusing fervent vitality in him which only words like "death,
night, sea, fear, loveliness" can transmit. Now a "twice-born
soul" (in William James's sense), George acquires a sense of
increased masculine power in his passage through the dark
alleyway—possibly an initiation into the mysterious realm of
instinct and impulse. Anderson believes that in youth there
are always two forces in conflict: the warm, unthinking little
animal, and the thing that reflects and remembers, that is, the
sophisticated mind. The reflective force reduces one to stasis
in which the will is inert until the moment of liberation when
sensations regenerate the spirit. Just as the rank smell of animal refuse awakens him from mental stupor, the rubbish and
the nail lead into a crystallization of an act:

George went into a vacant lot and, as he hurried along, fell over a
pile of rubbish. A nail protruding from an empty barrel tore his
trousers. He sat down on the ground and swore. With a pin he

mended the torn place and then arose and went on. "I'll go to Helen White's house, that's what I'll do" ["Sophistication"].

In this connection, we may cite the kindred experience of Kate Swift (in "The Thinker") who, like many others, becomes transfigured in her nocturnal wanderings. Despite her face which "was covered with blotches," "alone in the night in the winter streets she was lovely." Night and winter exalt her to the rank of a goddess: "her features were as the feature of a tiny goddess on a pedestal in a garden in the dim light of a summer evening."

Just this transformation of fact in art into what William Faulkner calls "the exactitude of purity" seems to be Sherwood Anderson's significant achievement. It is Faulkner, too, who is the only one to elucidate with vigorous precision Anderson's basic artistic motivation when he describes him "fumbling for exactitude, the exact word and phrase within the limited scope of a vocabulary controlled and even repressed by what was in him almost a fetish of simplicity, to milk them both dry, to seek always to penetrate to thought's uttermost end." Style is then ultimately the primary end of Anderson's art, an art practiced by a man whose epitaph is: "Life not death is the great adventure." . . .

JOHN T. FLANAGAN

John T. Flanagan is Professor of English at the University of Illinois at Urbana, and has also taught at the University of North Dakota, University of Minnesota, and Southern Methodist University. He is the author of *James Hall, Literary Pioneer of the Ohio Valley*, co-author of *Folklore in American Literature*, and editor of *America Is West*.

HEMINGWAY'S DEBT TO
SHERWOOD ANDERSON

. . . Hemingway's literary debt to Sherwood Anderson is less tangible than his obligations to Mark Twain, yet it cannot be denied. Even a brief stylistic comparison can be revealing. In 1951 James Schevill printed two paragraphs from *In Our Time* side by side with two paragraphs from *Winesburg, Ohio*. He added no comment, leaving the reader to draw the necessary conclusions, but the juxtaposition is striking. We see Nick Adams starting out on a fishing trip in the fall and George Willard leaving Winesburg for the big city in the spring. In each passage the protagonist acts without speaking, and the weather and background are carefully indicated. The sentences are short and staccato. Two of Anderson's sentences begin with adverbial clauses, none of Hemingway's. Each writer has several sentences introduced by the definite article and a common noun, and in both passages "and" is

From *Journal of English and Germanic Philology* (October 1955). Reprinted by permission of the editors and the author.

by far the most common conjunction. Adjectives are sparse and seldom cumulative, though Anderson in the penultimate sentence does write, "the silent deserted main street." Each sentence is a simple record of concrete action.

The closest analysis of Hemingway's style so far published is that by Harry Levin [in his "Observations on the style of Ernest Hemingway"]. After some general comments on Hemingway's attitude toward writing and his reaction against the Wilsonian rhetoric of the First World War period, Professor Levin concentrates on Hemingway's language and syntax. The critic calls attention to Hemingway's fondness for short words and to his overuse of "nice" and "fine." Repetition is obvious, and a few familiar verbs replace more precise terms. Adjectives are eliminated as far as possible in favor of nouns, and on the whole literary diction is avoided. In general, as Professor Levin observes, in Hemingway's writing sequence supersedes structure. He scorns the complex sentence and normally writes simple sentences or simple sentences loosely compounded. Yet it is common knowledge that through concreteness, precision, and bluntness Hemingway achieves extraordinary effects.

At the beginning of his literary career, Ernest Hemingway obviously shared many of Anderson's literary principles and was encouraged by Anderson's successful advocacy of them. Both men revolted against what seemed to them a kind of conspiracy to avoid the facts of life. Sex is not such a predominant motive in Hemingway's fiction as in Anderson's but both men treated it honestly and directly. For the euphemisms and vagueness of a belated Victorianism they had only contempt. Both writers likewise objected to the elaborate descriptive passages of a more formal age, to the jeweled diction, the elaborate figures, the purple prose. Anderson strove to be suggestive and atmospheric; Hemingway preferred to be blunt and specific. But neither man relished formal exposition or elaborate stage setting. It should be remarked here that the prolixity and repetition of Anderson's later work are not quite the same thing as the redundancy of the genteel tradition.

In their handling of plot, too, there are resemblances. Hemingway is the better story-teller largely because his narratives contain more action and therefore more drama, but also because he is more conscious of suspense, accelerated movement, and climax. Anderson's stories, on the other hand, depend more on nuances, on the right relationship of scene and character, on indirect revelation of crucial circumstances, on sympathetic insight into maladjusted or frustrated people. Yet both men rebelled against the story which was essentially a maneuvering of plot. Both men shunned the surprise ending and the purely narrative appeal. The impact of "Big Two-Hearted River" or "A Clean, Well-Lighted Place" basically derives no more from the action than "Death in the Woods" or "A Meeting South."

The preference of both men for simple, rather primitive characters must also be observed. One of the common charges made against Hemingway is that he is anti-intellectual, or at least that his characters rarely analyze or speculate. Men primarily concerned with action or emotion have little time for or interest in abstract ideas. But the same comment has been made about *Winesburg, Ohio.* Anderson's people too, real and poignant as they undoubtedly are, feel rather than think. Their whole contact with life is an emotional one, and their mental processes are either abeyant or absent. Both Hemingway and Anderson chose to present naïve, immature people, "primitives" in Hemingway's fiction, "grotesques" according to Anderson's own label. Indeed, Robert Penn Warren saw a striking resemblance between the figures of Hemingway and the rustic characters with whom William Wordsworth chose to deal. Novelist and poet repudiated the intellectual world of their own day, Wordsworth because it seemed unreal and limited, Hemingway because it had produced the mire and blood of a catastrophic war. But whereas Wordsworth's people were simple and innocent (the farmer, the child, the leech gatherer), Hemingway's became violent (soldiers, pugilists, gangsters).

It is this very violence, indeed, which is not only deeply characteristic of Hemingway but which cuts him off from most of his contemporaries and predecessors. The battlefield, the bullfighting arena, the prize ring, the mountain valley or forest glade where big game lurk, the ocean—these scenes Anderson never touched and would not have known how to handle. Moreover, the foreign and exotic localities which the *aficionado* of Hemingway comes to expect, these are also antipodal to Anderson's Middle Western small towns and country fairs. Even the extreme masculinity of Hemingway's later work is far removed from the sensitive, almost feminine approach which marks Sherwood Anderson's most perceptive fiction.

But it is the similarities rather than the differences which linger. The honest revelation of the protagonist of the story is characteristic of the best work of Anderson and Hemingway. According to Maxwell Geismar, the calculated formlessness of Anderson became transformed into the plain flatness of Hemingway. The brevity of the sentences, terse if not always crisp, the frequency of sentence parts joined by the conjunction "and," the scorn of conventional diction, the preference for and intelligent use of colloquial language, the careful and extraordinarily effective repetitions, the often poetic use of the familiar and the routine—these are characteristic of *both* Anderson and Hemingway and of no one else of their generation. Moreover, these qualities appeared in Anderson's work *first*, and at a time when Hemingway was in the usual formative stage.

It is possible that Hemingway adopted some of these techniques subconsciously, that he accepted their value without realizing their provenience. It is possible that Hemingway observed their strong contribution to the success of Anderson's fiction and that he was so sympathetic with them from the start that Anderson's initial success was the compelling factor in his own use of them. It is not only possible but probable that Hemingway, once having adopted these techniques, proceeded to modify them or even improve them until in his best work they no longer suggest their source and have become Hemingway's own. But Anderson was the friend and the inspiration of much of Hemingway's early work, as he was of other young writers who later outdid their early mentor. Of this select group Hemingway alone has failed to acknowledge his debt publicly.

WILLIAM FAULKNER

William Faulkner (1897–1962), who in 1924 had written some poetry but no fiction, met Sherwood Anderson, then at the height of his success, in New Orleans. Anderson had a germinal effect on Faulkner, and it was the example he set as a dedicated artist that started Faulkner writing novels such as *Light in August* and *Absalom, Absalom*, which led to his being awarded the Nobel Prize for Literature in 1949.

SHERWOOD ANDERSON:
AN APPRECIATION

One day during the months while we walked and talked in New Orleans—or Anderson talked and I listened—I found him sitting on a bench in Jackson Square, laughing with himself. I got the impression that he had been there like that for some time, just sitting alone on the bench laughing with himself. This was not our usual meeting place. We had none. He lived above the square, and without any special prearrangement, after I had had something to eat at noon and knew that he had finished his lunch too, I would walk in that direction and if I did not meet him already strolling or sitting in the Square, I myself would simply sit down on the curb where I could see his doorway and wait until he came out of it in his bright, half-racetrack, half-Bohemian clothes.

This time he was already sitting on the bench, laughing. He told me what it was at once: a dream: he had dreamed the night before that he was walking for miles along country roads, leading a horse which he was trying to swap for a night's sleep—not for a simple bed for the night, but for the sleep itself; and with me to listen now, went on from there, elaborating it, building it into a work of art with the same tedious (it had the appearance of fumbling but actually it wasn't: it was seeking, hunting) almost excruciating patience and humility with which he did all his writing, me listening and believing no word of it: that is, that it had been any dream dreamed in sleep. Because I knew better. I knew that he had invented it, made it: he had made most of it or at least some of it while I was there watching and listening to him. He didn't know why he had been compelled, or anyway needed, to claim it had been a dream, why there had to be that connection between dream and sleep, but I did. It was because he had written his whole biography into an anecdote or perhaps a parable: the horse (it had been a racehorse at first, but now it was a working horse, plow carriage and saddle, sound and strong and valuable, but without recorded pedigree) representing the vast rich strong docile sweep of the Mississippi Valley, his own America, which he in his bright blue racetrack shirt and vermilion-mottled Bohemian Windsor tie, was offering with humor and patience and humility, but mostly with patience and humility, to swap for his own dream of purity and integrity and hard and unremitting work and accomplishment, of which *Winesburg, Ohio* and *The Triumph of the Egg* had been symptoms and symbols.

He would never have said this, put it into words, himself. He may never have been able to see it even, and he certainly would have denied it, probably pretty violently, if I had tried to point it out to him. But this would not have been for the reason that it might not have been true, nor for the reason that, true or not, he would not have believed it. In fact, it would have made little difference whether it was true or not or whether he believed it or not. He would have repudiated it for the reason which was the great tragedy of his character. He expected people to make fun of, ridicule him. He expected people nowhere near his equal in stature or accomplishment or wit or anything else, to be capable of making him appear ridiculous.

That was why he worked so laboriously and tediously and indefatigably at everything he wrote. It was as if he said to himself: "This anyway will, shall, must be invulnerable." It was as though he wrote not even out of the consuming unsleeping appeaseless thirst for glory for which any normal artist would destroy his aged mother, but for what to him was more important and urgent: not even for mere truth, but for purity, the exactitude of purity. His was not the power and rush of Melville, who was his grandfather, nor the lusty humor for living of Twain, who was his father; he had nothing of the heavy-handed disregard for nuances of his older brother, Dreiser. His was that fumbling for exactitude, the exact word and phrase within the limited scope of a vocabulary controlled and even repressed by what was in him almost a fetish of simplicity, to milk them both dry, to seek always to penetrate to thought's uttermost end. He worked so hard at this that it finally became just style: an end instead of a means: so that he presently came to believe that, provided he kept the style pure and intact and unchanged and inviolate, what the style contained would have to be first rate: it couldn't help but be first rate and therefore himself too.

At this time in his life, he had to believe this. His mother had been a bound girl, his father a day laborer; this background had taught him that the amount of security and material success which he had attained was, must be, the answer and end to life. Yet he gave this up, repudiated and discarded it at a later age, when older in years than most men and women who make that decision, to dedicate himself to art, writing. Yet, when he made the decision, he found himself to be only a one- or two-book man. He had to believe that, if only he kept that style pure, then what the style contained would be pure too, the best. That was why he had to defend the style. That was the reason for his hurt and anger at Hemingway about Hemingway's *The Torrents of Spring,* and at me in a lesser degree since my fault was not full book-length but instead was merely a privately-printed and -subscribed volume which few people outside our small New Orleans group would ever see or hear about, because of the book of Spratling's caricatures which we titled *Sherwood Anderson and Other Famous Creoles* and to which I wrote an introduction in Anderson's primer-like style. Neither of us—Hemingway or I—could have touched, ridiculed, his work itself. But we had made his style look ridiculous; and by that time, after *Dark Laughter,* when he had reached the point where he should have stopped writing, he had to defend that style at all costs because he too must have known by then in his heart that there was nothing else left.

The exactitude of purity, or the purity of exactitude: whichever you like. He was a sentimentalist in his attitude toward people, and quite often incorrect about them. He believed in people, but it was as though only in theory. He expected the worst from them, even while each time he was prepared again to be disappointed or even hurt, as if it had never happened before, as though the only people he could really trust, let himself go with, were the ones of his own invention, the figments and symbols of his own fumbling dream. And he was sometimes a sentimentalist in his writing (so was Shakespeare sometimes) but he was never impure in it. He never scanted it, cheapened it, took the easy way; never failed to approach writing except with humility and an almost religious, almost abject faith and patience and willingness to surrender, relinquish himself to and into it. He hated glibness; if it were quick, he believed it was false too. He told me once: "You've got too much talent. You can do it too easy, in too many different ways. If you're not careful, you'll never write anything."

During those afternoons when we would walk about the old quarter, I listening while he talked to me or to people—anyone, anywhere—whom we would meet on the streets or the docks, or the evenings while we sat somewhere over a bottle, he, with a little help from me, invented other fantastic characters like the sleepless man with the horse. One of them was supposed to be a descendant of Andrew Jackson, left in that Louisiana swamp after the Battle of Chalmette, no longer half-horse half-alligator but by now half-man half-sheep and presently half-shark, who—it, the whole fable—at last got so unwieldy and (so we thought) so funny, that we decided to get it onto paper by writing letters to one another such as two temporarily separated members of an exploring-zoological expedition might. I brought him my first reply to his first letter. He read it. He said:—

"Does it satisfy you?"

I said, "Sir?"

"Are you satisfied with it?"

"Why not?" I said. "I'll put whatever I left out into the next one." Then I realized that he was more than displeased: he was short, stern, almost angry. He said:—

"Either throw it away, and we'll quit, or take it back and do it over." I took the letter. I worked three days over it before I carried it back to him. He read it again, quite slowly, as he always did, and said, "Are you satisfied now?"

"No sir," I said. "But it's the best I know how to do."

"Then we'll pass it," he said, putting the letter into his pocket, his voice once more warm, rich, burly with laughter, ready to believe, ready to be hurt again.

I learned more than that from him, whether or not I always practised the rest of it any more than I have that. I learned that, to be a writer, one has first got to be what he is, what he was born; that to be an American and a writer, one does not necessarily have to pay lip-service to any conventional American image such as his and Dreiser's own aching Indiana or Ohio or Iowa corn or Sandburg's stockyards or Mark

Twain's frog. You had only to remember what you were. "You
have to have somewhere to start from: then you begin to
learn," he told me. "It dont matter where it was, just so you
remember it and aint ashamed of it. Because one place to
start from is just as important as any other. You're a country
boy; all you know is that little patch up there in Mississippi
where you started from. But that's all right too. It's America
too; pull it out, as little and unknown as it is, and the whole
thing will collapse, like when you prize a brick out of a wall."

"Not a cemented, plastered wall," I said.

"Yes, but America aint cemented and plastered yet. They're
still building it. That's why a man with ink in his veins not
only still can but sometimes has still got to keep on moving
around in it, keeping moving around and listening and looking
and learning. That's why ignorant unschooled fellows like you
and me not only have a chance to write, they must write. All
America asks is to look at it and listen to it and understand
it if you can. Only the understanding aint important either:
the important thing is to believe in it even if you dont understand it, and then try to tell it, put it down. It wont ever be
quite right, but there is always next time; there's always more
ink and paper, and something else to try to understand and tell.
And that one probably wont be exactly right either, but there is
a next time to that one, too. Because tomorrow America is going
to be something different, something more and new to watch
and listen to and try to understand; and, even if you cant understand, believe."

To believe, to believe in the value of purity, and to believe
more. To believe not in just the value, but the necessity for
fidelity and integrity; lucky is that man whom the vocation of
art elected and chose to be faithful to it, because the reward for
art does not wait on the postman. He carried this to extremes.
That of course is impossible on the face of it. I mean that, in
the later years when he finally probably admitted to himself
that only the style was left, he worked so hard and so labor-

iously and so self-sacrificingly at this, that at times he stood a little bigger, a little taller than it was. He was warm, generous, merry and fond of laughing, without pettiness and jealous only of the integrity which he believed to be absolutely necessary in anyone who approached his craft; he was ready to be generous to anyone, once he was convinced that that one approached his craft with his own humility and respect for it. During those New Orleans days and weeks, I gradually became aware that here was a man who would be in seclusion all forenoon—working. Then in the afternoon he would appear and we would walk about the city, talking. Then in the evening we would meet again, with a bottle now, and now he would really talk; the world in minuscule would be there in whatever shadowy courtyard where glass and bottle clinked and the palms hissed like dry sand in whatever moving air. Then tomorrow forenoon and he would be secluded again— working; whereupon I said to myself, "If this is what it takes to be a novelist, then that's the life for me."

So I began a novel, *Soldiers' Pay*. I had known Mrs. Anderson before I knew him. I had not seen them in some time when I met her on the street. She commented on my absence. I said I was writing a novel. She asked if I wanted Sherwood to see it. I answered, I don't remember exactly what, but to the effect that it would be all right with me if he wanted to. She told me to bring it to her when I finished it, which I did, in about two months. A few days later, she sent for me. She said, "Sherwood says he'll make a swap with you. He says that if he doesn't have to read it, he'll tell Liveright (Horace Liveright: his own publisher then) to take it."

"Done," I said, and that was all. Liveright published the book and I saw Anderson only once more, because the unhappy caricature affair had happened in the meantime and he declined to see me, for several years, until one afternoon at a cocktail party in New York; and again there was that moment when he appeared taller, bigger than anything he ever wrote.

Then I remembered *Winesburg, Ohio* and *The Triumph of the Egg* and some of the pieces in *Horses and Men,* and I knew that I had seen, was looking at, a giant in an earth populated to a great—too great—extent by pygmies, even if he did make but the two or perhaps three gestures commensurate with gianthood.

Topics

FOR DISCUSSION AND PAPERS

To use this critical edition to best advantage, the student must keep in mind that his chief concern is with the text of *Winesburg* and his own response to it. Hence he should not only read *Winesburg* before he reads the critics, but reread it in the light of whatever topic he chooses to work on before seeking help from the critical essays collected in Part II. The critics can help the student find his way around *Winesburg*; it is better if he does the driving himself.

The secondary source material for this volume has been selected with the aim of increasing the student's understanding of *Winesburg*, but also it is hoped it will add to his appreciation of various critical approaches to literature in general. The best way to increase one's understanding or appreciation of any subject is, of course, to ask questions about it and try to answer them. The questions about *Winesburg* that follow are divided into seven categories; six of these are intended to offer meaningful approaches to the book, and a seventh covers topics that cannot be categorized. In each category the simpler, more specific questions can be answered from the material in this volume, and will also serve as topics for discussion and themes. These lead into larger, more general questions, subjects for papers that often require library research as well. (A composition handbook should be consulted on the preparation of research papers.) While it is hoped the questions will stimulate a variety of provocative oral and written responses, they are by no means exhaustive. They scarcely hint, for example, at the biographical question of *Winesburg*, or the book's relation to Anderson's other works. Those questions you, the student, are prompted to ask yourself will, of course, constitute potentially the most valuable approach.

1. *The Critics*: Probably the most difficult task for the student-turned-critic is to learn how to make the best use of secondary sources. The most obvious pitfall lies in the temptation to accept the critic's opinion as the last word, then to wish a plague on him and his tribe when some other critic's last word on the subject turns out to be contradictory. The truth is that there are few indisputably right or wrong "answers" in literary criticism. Notwithstanding claims to the contrary, literary criticism is largely a matter of opinion, once it goes beyond the obvious. Opinions and judgments, however, are convincing or unconvincing depending on the evidence adduced to support them. Though the critical opinions and judgments in this book are probably based on better information than you have, you will notice that the critics are far from unanimity in their views of Anderson and *Winesburg*.

You might examine, in this connection, the contrasting views of Fussell and Gold on the meaning of the theme of isolation in *Winesburg*. Trilling, Asselineau, and San Juan are engaged in a debate about the kind of reality represented in *Winesburg*; you might summarize the opposing arguments and from your own reading of *Winesburg* support the critic you find most convincing. Again, attempt to justify from your own reading of the book Howe's conclusion that few American writers who have taken "as their theme the loss of love in the modern world . . . have so thoroughly dealt with it in the accents of love," or Trilling's negative corollary to this that "the affirmation of life by love has the effect of negating life." Another paper might summarize the case against Anderson as argued by Trilling and Gold, and then evaluate their objections.

The view of each critic is limited by his need to focus on only a few aspects of the book. To appreciate this, identify the particular focus in the interpretations of "The Untold Lie" by Phillips, Thurston, Gold, and Cowley; or of "Sophistication" by Walcutt, Thurston, Fussell, Rideout, and Sister M. Joselyn; then, taking theirs into consideration, write your own interpretation of either story.

Similarly, each view is conditioned to some degree by quite legitimate critical bias. It would make an illuminating study to compare and contrast the predominantly sociological approach of Geismar with the predominantly psychoanalytic approach of Gold, or the impressionistic approach of Gregory with the New Critical approach of Thurston or San Juan. Among others, Donald Heiney, *Recent American Literature* (New York: Barron's Educational Series, Inc., 1958), pp. 552–73, has defined and analyzed these various schools of criticism.

In the final analysis, the critics are doing the same thing you are being asked to do. They are answering questions to gain a better understanding of a literary work. Some critics gain this understanding by placing the work in the context of literary history or of a particular literary tradition. Horace Gregory, for example, says of *Winesburg* that "the streets and landscapes here depicted are close to the roots of the American heritage which takes its definition from the writings of Emerson, Whitman, Thoreau, Melville, and Mark Twain." He refers to Anderson's "instinctive and acknowledged debt to writers who represent the Emersonian aspect of the Great Tradition in American literature. It is clear enough that Anderson's writings are of that heritage and not in the Great Tradition of Hawthorne and Henry James." Transcendentalism, the movement which embodies "the Emersonian aspect" and with which Thoreau and Whitman are associated, offers an interesting commentary on the world of *Winesburg*. A topic might be suggested by reading Emerson's essay, "Self-Reliance," along with the discussion of transcendentalism in Rod

W. Horton and Herbert W. Edwards, *Backgrounds of American Literary Thought* (New York: Appleton-Century-Crofts, Inc., 1952), pp. 112–21.

Another paper, on the kinship of Anderson with Melville, might start with Gregory's observation that "the horror of Queequeg's first impression upon him [Ishmael] in *Moby Dick* is closely, if broadly, allied to the mysteries, the transcendental qualities of sexual experience in Anderson's stories, and to find that kinship one need go no further than the story 'Hands' in *Winesburg, Ohio*. . . . The kinship of Anderson's writings with *Moby Dick* embraces that side of Anderson's imagination which is 'non-realistic,' and which converts what is outwardly the simple telling of a story into a series of symbolic actions." After you have discussed the kinship of "Hands" with Ishmael's first impression of Queequeg, explore *Moby Dick* and *Winesburg* for other evidence of the kinship Gregory describes.

Anderson's attitude toward life in the small Midwestern town at the close of the last century is likened by some critics to that of Edgar Lee Masters in his *Spoon River Anthology*, a collection of American village epitaphs laying bare the frustrations and hypocrisies of American village life; Kazin finds similarities in Sinclair Lewis's novel *Main Street*, a bitter satire of American middle-class life. Read one of these books and discuss the relationship between its author's attitude and Anderson's.

2. *Theme and Meaning*: An author tries to embody in a work of fiction a theme, an idea, a meaning, that clothes the characters and action of his story with significance. While their specific formulations of its theme or meaning naturally vary, the critics are generally agreed on what *Winesburg* is about. Frank says it is about "the solitariness and struggle of the soul which has lost its ancestral props." Howe says it is "a fable of American estrangement, its theme the loss of love." Walcutt says the theme is that "what appears on the surface,

what is commonly described, is not the true and inward reality. But what the true reality is remains a mystery, and characters continually discover that the world is complex, that evil and good are inseparable, and that their simple ideals are inadequate." In *Poor White*, Anderson's next book, there is a sentence that might be taken as another statement of the theme of *Winesburg*: "All men lead their lives behind a wall of misunderstanding they themselves have built, and most men die in silence and unnoticed behind the walls." In your opinion, which of these statements of theme has the most validity, and why? Do you have one of your own which you prefer? Does Anderson offer any solution to the problem? Carl Van Doren, in *Contemporary American Novelists* (New York, 1922), pp. 153–57, views *Winesburg* as a revolt from the American village; Geismar sees the book as a nostalgic return to it. Which is it? Could it be both? If so, does nostalgia or rejection predominate? What does Anderson reject? What does he value?

It may surprise you to learn that *Winesburg* was at first considered morally offensive by many readers (cf. "Anderson on *Winesburg, Ohio*"). It wasn't banned in Boston, but it was burned publicly by the library board of a small New England town which may have been very similar to Winesburg. Why is the book no longer considered immoral? Is there a sense in which *Winesburg* is a profoundly moral rather than an immoral or amoral book? Many readers, perhaps the majority, hailed *Winesburg* as a long-overdue blast against puritanism in American life. Puritanism was thought of at the time as a worn-out collection of ingrained conventions and taboos, repressive and rigid in its dogma, devoid of any true Christian spirituality, and hypocritically subservient to a materialistic, bourgeois ethic. As Norman Holmes Pearson says: "Puritanism which originally had risen as a movement against conformity and deadening ritual had by now become itself conformity and ritual" ("Anderson and the New Puritanism," *Newberry Library Bulletin*, II [December 1948], p. 53). Waldo

Frank's *Our America* (New York, 1919) is another attack on neo-puritanism published in the same year as *Winesburg*. How do the stories of one or more of these characters reflect the new puritanism: Wing Biddlebaum, Jesse Bentley, Wash Williams, Curtis Hartman, Kate Swift, Enoch Robinson, Belle Carpenter, Tom Foster?

3. *The Grotesques*: Since "The Book of the Grotesque" is a kind of philosophical prologue to *Winesburg*, it may well be that Anderson intends it as an important part of the book. What specifically is its function and what does it contribute to *Winesburg*? What difference would its omission have made?

In this prologue, Anderson says that "the grotesques were not all horrible," and later he describes the story of one grotesque, Dr. Reefy, as "delicious, like the twisted little apples . . . that the pickers have rejected." These are the sweetest apples, but their sweetness is known "only to the few." Using the metaphor of the apples, elucidate Dr. Reefy's story or that of some other grotesque, at the same time asking yourself who or what in *Winesburg* is grotesque, if these people are not grotesques in the usual sense of the word?

There will always be debate over how typical or "real" Anderson's grotesques are. You might join the debate by supporting or refuting Gold's observation that "all of the people of Winesburg haunt us as do our neighbors, our friends, our own secret selves which we first met one springtime in childhood." It is possible, if you are clinically inclined, to identify the particular psychological maladjustments of some of the grotesques and do case-studies on them. Another paper might identify (with the help of Howe, Frank, Kazin, Fussell, and David Anderson) the origins or causes of their underlying spiritual sickness.

Since *Winesburg*, writers of fiction have continued to find significance in the figure of the grotesque. The grotesqueness of Flannery O'Connor's misfits, especially in *Wise Blood* and *A Good Man Is Hard to Find*, is akin in its origins to that found in *Winesburg*. Like Anderson's grotesques, these people have discovered "truths"; it was "the truths that made the people grotesques." And Milton J. Friedman, in "Flannery O'Connor: Another Legend in Southern Fiction," *English Journal* LI (April 1962), pp. 233–43, suggests that Dr. Parcival's strange notion about crucifixion may have served as a model for Hazel Motes' Church Without Christ in *Wise Blood*. You might read an O'Connor book in order to discuss her conception and use of the grotesque as compared to Anderson's. Instead of Flannery O'Connor, you could use Carson McCullers' *The Ballad of the Sad Café*, or James Purdy's *Malcolm*, or Bernard Malamud's *A New Life*. Ihab Hassan's "After the Grotesque," *Shenandoah* XIII (Spring 1962), pp. 62–65, might make a good springboard for the paper.

There are obvious similarities to be studied, too, between Anderson's queer, defeated, and sometimes tragic characters and those in Edwin Arlington Robinson's poems (for example, Cliff Klingenhagen, John Evereldown, Richard Cory, Miniver Cheevy, Eben Flood, Flammonde, Luke Havergal, and the victim of "Eros Turannos"). Are there any similarities between the quality of life in *Winesburg* and the cultural and spiritual sterility of life in T. S. Eliot's "The Waste Land" or "The Hollow Men"?

4. *George Willard*: The principal character of *Winesburg* is George Willard, the young newspaper reporter to whom the grotesques tell their stories. George's story is told, as Anderson says, "by telling the story of [these] other people whose lives touched his life." In what ways do his relationships with the grotesques help to mature him? What about the rest of his life in Winesburg, his relationships with women, for example? How typical an adolescent does George seem to you? How does Anderson regard him? You could deal with all these questions in the one paper: look for evidence in *Winesburg* first, then read the passages in Howe, Walcutt, Fussell, Rideout, and David Anderson on George.

After the death of his mother near the end of the book, George leaves his home town, the scene of his growing-up, for the city. Though "the serious and larger aspects of his life did not come into his mind," his departure does raise larger questions in the mind of the reader. In what way is his departure a kind of death also, an end as well as a beginning? Besides the city, does he know where he is headed, or what he is searching for?

George Willard has a kinship with other youthful innocents in fiction whose initiation into adulthood is analogous to his own. It would be profitable to write a paper comparing and contrasting George Willard with Twain's Huckleberry Finn, or with Melville's Billy Budd; or to take some more recent examples, with Stephen Dedalus (in Joyce's *Portrait of the Artist as a Young Man*), or Nick Adams (in Hemingway's *In Our Time*), or Ike McCaslin (in Faulkner's *The Bear*), or Eugene Gant (in Wolfe's *Look Homeward, Angel*), or Holden Caulfield (in Salinger's *Catcher in the Rye*), or Tarwater (in Flannery O'Connor's *The Violent Bear It Away*).

5. *Form and Technique*: One of the principal reasons for the excellent critical reputation *Winesburg* enjoys is to be found in the excellence of its form. It is perhaps the one book in which Anderson achieved a perfect union of form with content, a perfect way of saying what he wanted to say. *Winesburg* is usually regarded as a novel in form; actually it is a cycle of stories, a fictional form well established in many literatures, and perhaps especially in American literature—partly for economic reasons (magazines liked series of stories about the same character or background), but partly also through the influence of *Winesburg*. Hemingway's *In Our Time*, Steinbeck's *The Pastures of Heaven* and *Tortilla Flat*, Faulkner's *The Unvanquished* and *Go Down, Moses*, Caldwell's *Georgia Boy*, Mary McCarthy's *The Company She Keeps* are all cycles of stories by writers who knew *Winesburg*. (Anderson comments on his "own form"; see "Anderson on . . . ," p. 14.) As

Malcolm Cowley suggests, this form resembles the novel in its use of certain consistent and consecutive, i.e. novelistic, elements. How strong are these elements in *Winesburg* (unity, sequential development of character, over-all meaning, etc.)? Can we say that the book as a whole tells a unified story? What story?

Recurrent symbols and patterns of imagery are two more unifying elements found in the novel. Read the discussions by Howe, Asselineau, and Rideout of symbols such as rooms and hands in *Winesburg*; then examine other symbols such as doors ("Loneliness" and others), rain ("Adventure," "Loneliness"), cornfields ("Nobody Knows," "Sophistication," and others), snow and ferrets ("The Teacher"), paper pills, Wash Williams and seeds ("Respectability"), bees ("The Thinker"), "everyone in the world is Christ" ("The Philosopher"), Elizabeth Willard's unused hoard of money ("Death"). Symbolic acts might also serve as the subject of a paper: some examples would be Wing Biddlebaum's picking up of the crumbs; Jesse Bentley's attempted sacrifice of the lamb; Elmer Cowley's beating George Willard with his fists; Helen White's tumbling George down the hill; Ray Pearson's running to warn Hal Winters. A similar study could be made of the function of *Winesburg*'s imagery, considering such questions as its contribution to the over-all tone of the book, its sensory appeal, its repetition through motifs that contribute thematically to the book. In addition to the critics mentioned above, Thurston and San Juan will be of help in answering these questions.

Anderson once said he had "come to think that the true history of life is but a history of moments. It is only at rare moments that we live." And Cowley says that Anderson's stories are not incidents or episodes, but moments or epiphanies (as in Joyce's *Dubliners*), in which characters reveal their essential being, in which Anderson pours a lifetime into a moment of revelation. Using Cowley's discussion of "The Untold Lie" as a model, discuss the moments of revelation or epiphanies in "Hands," "Adventure," and "The Strength of

504 WINESBURG, OHIO: CRITICISM

God"; or choose other examples to discuss. A more ambitious paper would compare Anderson's use of the fictional epiphany with Joyce's in *Dubliners*.

Some readers feel the characters in *Winesburg* do not converse, but rather soliloquize or talk about themselves to themselves, just as they do when alone. If this is Anderson's intention, what are the implications for the characters and their world? What other characteristics does their speech have? Does Anderson differentiate their speech? How? Another charge is that these people are caricatures, not characters; that they are mere vehicles for an idea, not rounded, lifelike creations. Is it possible they are none of these, nor intended to be? With what principles did Anderson create them?

Richard Chase, in *The American Novel and Its Tradition* (New York, 1957), p. 139, says, "Wherever we find, in writers such as Stephen Crane, Sherwood Anderson, Sinclair Lewis, Faulkner or Hemingway himself, a style that flows with the easy grace of colloquial speech and gets its directness and simplicity by leaving out subordinate words and clauses, we will be right in thinking that this is the language of Mark Twain." After reading Anderson's own comments on his style (see pages 13–14), you might examine the detailed comparison of this style with Hemingway's in Flanagan, then make an analogous study of the style of Anderson and Twain in *Huckleberry Finn*, say. An essay by Seymour Gross, "Sherwood Anderson's Debt to *Huckleberry Finn*," *Mark Twain Journal* XI (Summer 1960), pp. 3–5, 24, while not concerned with *Winesburg*, could serve as a model of procedure here.

Winesburg has been regarded as an example of realism (Kazin), naturalism (Walcutt), cultural primitivism (Oscar Cargill, *Intellectual America* [New York, 1941]), myth (James Schevill, *Sherwood Anderson* [Denver, 1951]), impressionism (Walcutt), mysticism (Thurston), fantasy (Gold), and lyricism (Sister M. Joselyn). Consult a handbook of literary terms, such as *A Handbook to Literature*, by W. F. Thrall, Addison Hibbard, and C. Hugh Holman (New York, 1960), on the meaning of these terms, then find evidence pro and con for applying some or all of them to *Winesburg*. Finally, give your own ideas on how *Winesburg* should be classified.

6. *The Social Context*: Though Anderson is quite unconcerned with most of the social issues of the *Winesburg* period (the 1890s) there are three which pervade the book. These are industrialization (which has resulted in the decay of handicrafts and small stores), sex (actually the disastrous results of the suppression of sex), and interpersonal communication (the failure of which is a result of cultural decay). A paper might be done on Anderson's attitudes toward these issues and how he reveals them. A research topic on Anderson's attitude toward industrial change in *Winesburg* and other books might be suggested by the discussions of his proletarian sympathies in V. F. Calverton's *The Newer Spirit* (New York, 1925) and *The Liberation of American Literature* (New York, 1932). Robert S. and Helen M. Lynd's *Middletown* (New York, 1929) is a sociological history of the development of a Midwestern small town from a craft to an industrial community in the period 1890 to 1924. The Lynds' delineation of the pre-industrial community affords an interesting parallel to *Winesburg*, while the study as a whole gives an insight into the kind of town Winesburg might have become.

Winesburg was probably a rather typical American small town of its day. If you know a comparable small town of the present day (the population of Winesburg was about 1800), it would be interesting to examine some of the changes—in occupations, leisure, communications, community activities—that have taken place in small-town life.

7. *Additional questions*: There are a few more questions about *Winesburg* which do not belong to any particular category, but which are worth asking nevertheless. For example, there is the question of the reasons for the lasting popularity of *Winesburg*, and the related question of whether it can be

considered "a kind of American classic," as Anderson termed it.

Then there are papers to be done on (a) *Winesburg* and the idea of the artist, (b) *Winesburg* as a film, and (c) *Winesburg* and Freudianism. Both (b) and (c) involve outside research. Regarding (a), it is noteworthy that throughout his career Anderson was concerned with the role of the artist in America. At the end of *Winesburg* when George Willard, the Midwestern artist as a young man, looks back from the train, "the town of Winesburg had disappeared and his life there had become but a background on which to paint the dreams of his manhood." From your reading of the book and the critics (e.g., Fussell, Rideout), what is Anderson's conception of the qualities an artist must have and the role he must play? For (b), consult George Bluestone's *Novels into Film* (Baltimore, 1957), then discuss problems and possible solutions in a movie adaptation of *Winesburg*; or test your solutions by writing an adaptation of your own. For (c), read Hoffman's essay together with the discussion of Freudianism in *Backgrounds of American Literary Thought*, pp. 331–59, or with some other treatment of Freudianism's cultural and literary applications, then from the evidence in *Winesburg* give your analysis of the use Anderson makes of Freudian ideas.

Finally, write an original critical appraisal of *Winesburg*; use the essays in this book to illustrate and support your points, but make sure your thesis is derived from your own reading of the stories themselves.

Bibliography

BOOKS BY SHERWOOD ANDERSON

Windy McPherson's Son. New York: John Lane Company, 1916.

Marching Men. New York: John Lane Company, 1917.

Mid-American Chants. New York: John Lane Company, 1918.

Winesburg, Ohio. New York: B. W. Huebsch, Inc., 1919.

Poor White. New York: B. W. Huebsch, Inc., 1920. Also in the Viking *Portable Sherwood Anderson,* 1949. Edited and with an introduction by Walter B. Rideout, Viking Compass Edition, 1966.

Triumph of the Egg. New York: B. W. Huebsch, Inc., 1921.

Many Marriages. New York: B. W. Huebsch, Inc., 1923.

Horses and Men. New York: B. W. Huebsch, Inc., 1923.

A Story Teller's Story. New York: B. W. Huebsch, Inc., 1924.

Dark Laughter. New York: Boni and Liveright, 1925.

The Modern Writer. New York: Gelber, Lilienthal, Inc., 1925.

Sherwood Anderson's Notebook. New York: Boni and Liveright, 1926.

Tar: A Midwest Childhood. New York: Boni and Liveright, 1926.

A New Testament. New York: Boni and Liveright, 1927.

Hello Towns. New York: Horace Liveright, 1929.

Perhaps Women. New York: Horace Liveright, Inc., 1931.

Beyond Desire. New York: Liveright, Inc., 1932.

Death in the Woods. New York: Liveright, Inc., 1933.

No Swank. Philadelphia: The Centaur Press, 1934.

Puzzled America. New York: Charles Scribner's Sons, 1935.

Kit Brandon. New York: Charles Scribner's Sons, 1936.

Plays: Winesburg and Others. New York: Charles Scribner's Sons, 1937.

Home Town, ed. Edwin Rosskam. New York: Alliance Book Corporation, 1940.

Sherwood Anderson's Memoirs. New York: Harcourt, Brace and Company, 1942.

The Sherwood Anderson Reader, ed. Paul Rosenfeld. New York: Houghton Mifflin Company, 1948.

The Portable Sherwood Anderson, ed. Horace Gregory. New York: The Viking Press, 1949.

Letters of Sherwood Anderson, eds. Howard Mumford Jones and Walter B. Rideout. New York: Little, Brown and Company, 1953.

WINESBURG, OHIO:
SECONDARY SOURCES

The following is a list of *Winesburg* criticism, including the essays in this book, as well as periodical articles and chapters from books on wider subjects. I have briefly annotated the latter. Where the title of an essay has been altered for this book, the new title is given in brackets.—Ed.

Anderson, David D. *Critical Studies in American Literature: A Collection of Essays*. Karachi: Bureau of Composition, Compilation and Translation (University of Karachi), 1964. Pp. 108–31. ["The Grotesques and George Willard."]

Asselineau, Roger. "Langue et style de Sherwood Anderson dans *Winesburg, Ohio*," *La Revue des Lettres Modernes*, Nos. 78–80 (1963), 121–35.

———. "Réalisme, rêve et expressionisme dans *Winesburg, Ohio*," *Archives des Lettres Modernes*, II (April 1957), 1–32. Anderson's technique based on symbolism and expressionism rather than on realism.

Berland, Alwyn. "Sherwood Anderson and the Pathetic Grotesque," *Western Review*, XV (Winter 1951), 135–38. Explains the grotesques as crucified because real life prevents their escape to the dream life they desire. This is pathos without sentiment, but also without tragedy.

Bowden, Edwin T. *The Dungeon of the Heart: Human Isolation and the American Novel*. New York: The Macmillan Company, 1961. Pp. 114–24. Isolation as the unifying theme of the sketches.

Boyd, Ernest. Introduction to *Winesburg, Ohio*. New York: The Modern Library, 1919. *Winesburg* as part of the revolt against "the great illusions of American civilization."

Budd, Louis J. "The Grotesques of Anderson and Wolfe," *Modern Fiction Studies*, V (Winter 1959–60), 304–10. Traces the influence of Anderson on Wolfe; finds in "Sophistication" a detailed foreshadowing of *Look Homeward, Angel's* closing scene.

Burbank, Rex. *Sherwood Anderson*. New York: Twayne Publishers, Inc., 1964. Pp. 61–77. Discusses the influence of the post-Impressionists and Gertrude Stein on *Winesburg* before centering on George Willard as the symbolic counterpoint of the grotesques.

Chase, Cleveland B. *Sherwood Anderson*. New York: R. M. McBride, 1927. Pp. 31–40. A damning-with-faint-praise, typical of early (and some later) *Winesburg* criticism.

Clark, Edward. "*Winesburg, Ohio*: An Interpretation." *Die Neueren Sprachen*, VIII (December 1959), 547–52. Explains the essential human condition, for Anderson, as lying in "the inward burning of a desire for self-expression," and the salutary suffering that comes from realizing that desire in action.

Cowley, Malcolm. "Anderson's Lost Innocence," *New Republic*, CXLII (February 15, 1960), 16–18. An excellent reappraisal of *Winesburg*.

——. Introduction to *Winesburg, Ohio*. New York: The Viking Press, Inc., 1960.

——. "Sherwood Anderson's Epiphanies," *London Magazine*, VII (July 1960), 61–66. Anderson's mark on the writings of Hemingway, Faulkner, Wolfe, and others assessed in terms of the Joycean "moment of vision."

Faulkner, William. "Sherwood Anderson: An Appreciation," *Atlantic Monthly*, CXCI (June 1953), 27–29.

Flanagan, John T. "Hemingway's Debt to Sherwood Anderson," *Journal of English and Germanic Philology*, LIV (October 1955), 507–20.

Frank, Waldo. "*Winesburg, Ohio* after Twenty Years," *Story*, XIX (September–October 1941), 29–33.

Fussell, Edwin, "*Winesburg, Ohio*: Art and Isolation," *Modern Fiction Studies*, VI (Summer 1960), 106–14.

Geismar, Maxwell. *The Last of the Provincials*. Boston: Houghton Mifflin Company, 1943. Pp. 233–39. "Sherwood Anderson: Last of the Townsmen."

Gochberg, Donald. "Stagnation and Growth: The Emergence of George Willard," *Expression*, IV (Winter 1960), 29–35. Discusses the shaping and balancing of his growth toward maturity by the grotesques as making George "an influential and singular character in American literature."

Gold, Herbert. "*Winesburg, Ohio*: The Purity and Cunning of

Sherwood Anderson," *The Age of Happy Problems.* New York: The Dial Press, 1962. Pp. 196–209.

Gregory, Horace. Introduction to *The Portable Sherwood Anderson.* New York: The Viking Press, 1949. ["An American Heritage."]

Hoffman, Frederick J. *Freudianism and the Literary Mind.* Baton Rouge: Louisiana State University Press, 1945. Pp. 229–50. ["Anderson and Freud."]

———. "The Voices of Sherwood Anderson," *Shenandoah,* XIII (Spring 1962), 5–19. A summing up of Anderson's literary significance, part of which derives from his role as analyst of human loneliness in *Winesburg.*

Howe, Irving. *Sherwood Anderson.* New York: William Sloane Associates, 1951. Pp. 91–109.

Kazin, Alfred. *On Native Grounds: An Interpretation of Modern American Prose Literature.* New York: Harcourt, Brace and Company, 1942. Pp. 162–73. ["The New Realism: Sherwood Anderson."]

McAleer, John J. "Christ Symbolism in *Winesburg, Ohio,*" *Discourse,* IV (Summer 1961), 168–81. *Winesburg* as an allegory of passion, sacrifice, and redemption through love.

Mahoney, John. "An Analysis of *Winesburg, Ohio,*" *Journal of Aesthetics and Art Criticism,* XV (December 1956), 245–52. A technical analysis applying "voice and address theory" to the utterances of the characters to account for the book's peculiar emotional effect.

Phillips, William L. "How Sherwood Anderson Wrote *Winesburg, Ohio,*" *American Literature,* XXIII (March 1951), 7–30.

Rideout, Walter B. "The Simplicity of *Winesburg, Ohio,*" *Shenandoah,* XIII (Spring 1962), 20–31.

Rosenfeld, Paul. Introduction to *The Sherwood Anderson Reader.* Boston: Houghton Mifflin Company, 1947. Discusses how, like "the writers treasured by humanity," Anderson brought to his art "the unity and totality of man." His is a "miniature universal art made of music and picture, realism and lyricism, naturalism, the heroic, the idyllic, the mystical."

San Juan, Epifanio, Jr. "Vision and Reality: A Reconsideration of Sherwood Anderson's *Winesburg, Ohio,*" *American Literature,* XXXV (May 1963), 137–55.

Schevill, James. *Sherwood Anderson: His Life and Work.* Denver: The University of Denver Press, 1951. Pp. 93–108. Anderson as "replacing the myth of the small town virtues with the myth of the grotesques."

Sister M. Joselyn, O.S.B. "Sherwood Anderson and the Lyric Story,"

The Twenties: Poetry and Prose, ed. Richard E. Langford and William E. Taylor. DeLand, Florida: Edward Everett Press, Inc., 1966. Pp. 70–73.

Sullivan, John A. "Winesburg Revisited," *Antioch Review*, XX (Summer 1960), 213–21. Anderson's hometown as having deliberately forgotten him. " 'He made the town seem dirty.' "

Thurston, Jarvis. "Anderson and 'Winesburg': Mysticism and Craft," *Accent*, XVI (Spring 1956), 107, 128. ["Technique in *Winesburg, Ohio*."]

Trilling, Lionel. *The Liberal Imagination*. New York: The Viking Press, 1950. Pp. 33–43.

Walcutt, Charles Child. "Sherwood Anderson: Impressionism and the Buried Life," *Sewanee Review*, LX (Winter 1952), 28–47; reprinted in *American Literary Naturalism: A Divided Stream*. Minneapolis: University of Minnesota Press, 1956. ["Naturalism in Winesburg, Ohio."]